A REIGN OF STORM AND MADNESS

MORTAL GODS
BOOK TWO

LUCINDA DARK

MORTAL GODS 2

A
REIGN
OF
STORM
AND
MADNESS

USAT BESTSELLING AUTHOR LUCY SMOKE WRITING AS

LUCINDA DARK

You carry both lightning and thunder
in that space between your bones and soul.
Become the storm you are hiding from;
a hurricane does not run from the rain.

— Nikita Gill, *Your Soul is a River*

For my own little found family.
I wouldn't be here without y'all.

Developmental Edits by Heather Long

Line Edits by Your Editing Lounge

Proofreads by Alexa Books

Cover Design by Simply Defined Art

Format by Smoking Hot Covers

CONTENTS

Glossary/List of Gods   xiii

1. Ruen   1
2. Kiera   8
3. Kiera   21
4. Kiera   28
5. Kalix   37
6. Kiera   45
7. Kiera   59
8. Theos   68
9. Kiera   74
10. Ruen   82
11. Kiera   89
12. Kiera   104
13. Kiera   108
14. Kiera   116
15. Kalix   124
16. Kiera   129
17. Ruen   143
18. Kiera   150
19. Kiera   161
20. Theos   170
21. Kiera   177
22. Kiera   187
23. Kiera   198
24. Kiera   205
25. Kiera   215
26. Theos   233
27. Kiera   239
28. Kiera   246
29. Kiera   254

30.	Kiera	262
31.	Kalix	281
32.	Kiera	289
33.	Kiera	304
34.	Kiera	316
35.	Kiera	330
36.	Ruen	342
37.	Kiera	350
38.	Kiera	363
39.	Theos	372
40.	Kiera	379
41.	Kiera	388
42.	Kiera	395
43.	Kiera	404
44.	Kiera	416
45.	Kalix	425
46.	Kiera	439
47.	Kiera	446
	Thank you for reading!	453
	About the Author	455
	Also by Lucinda Dark	457

GLOSSARY/LIST OF GODS

Axlan: (Lower God) God of Victory

Azai: (Upper God) God of Strength

Caedmon: (Upper God) God of Prophecy

Day of Descendance: a national Anatol holiday to celebrate the day that the Gods descended upon the mortal realm.

Dea: (ancient language) endearment meaning either "goddess" or "fortune/treasure."

Demia: (Lower God) Goddess of Birds

Denza: money, currency

Divinity: magic or otherworldly abilities possessed only by those who are Gods or descended from Gods.

Dolos: (Lower God) God of Imprisonment

God City: a city chosen as tribute to the Gods, usually more opulent and wealthy than smaller cities that are ruled by God Lords.

God Lord: a God/Goddess that has been granted rights to rule over a specific town, city, or territory as its governing head.

Hatzi: (Lower God) God of Travel

Hinterlands: unsettled lands outside of mortal and immortal civilization inhabited by monsters and Nezeracians. The only piece of land upon the Anatol Continent that is not ruled or inhabited by Divine Beings.

Maladesia: (Lower God) Goddess of Praise

Mortal God: a mortal with God/Divine ancestry

Narelle: (Lower God) Goddess of Scribes

Nezeracians: nomadic mortal tribes or individuals that usually live in the hinterlands.

Pachis: (Lower God) God of Study

Sigyn: (Upper God) Goddess of Strife

Talmatia: (Lower God) Goddess of Vanity

Terra: term used for the human/mortal servants that dwell and serve the Gods and God children within the Mortal Gods Academies.

Tryphone: (Upper God) King of the Gods

CHAPTER 1
RUEN

Something vicious and wicked rips at my gut. It slices its cold, cruel talons through my insides and if I didn't know it was all in my head, the pain, the hurt, the—I cut that thought off with a shake of my head as I watch the sun rise over the frothy waves. To the east.

I often wonder what changes would my life have taken had my brothers and I been taken to Perditia instead of Riviere. What I know of the place is minor, but I do know that Azai—our sire—avoids it like the plague. Just that fact alone makes it a desirable home. A place far from his reach, far from the center of the cruelest Gods. A place that even Tryphone, himself, respectfully keeps his distance from.

Would anything have been different had I gone to the eastern mountains? I wonder silently. *Would I have avoided meeting the Terra now residing down within the lowest dungeons?*

I close my eyes and inhale slowly through my nose and exhale out of my mouth as I try to stifle that unerring

1

emotion that has wracked me since the night I visited my Terra—no, since I visited Kiera—down in the dungeons.

Quiet footsteps echo along the path leading to the overlook I'm currently standing before. Few people—Mortal Gods or not—brave the icy breath of the morning air to see the sunrise here. Those that have previously ... well, suffice it to say that this broken point is not for those who wish good lives for themselves.

Therefore, the sound of someone's approach has me turning back the way I came, angling my body in such a way as to not give away the fact that I'm curious, but instead to make it look like a natural shift on my feet.

The dark gleam of ebony skin and cool, misty eyes that are most certainly not of this world have me tensing further the second I recognize them. *Caedmon.* I face the sight before me once more and grind my teeth. Any other God, I'd be happy to contend with at this moment. Axlan, with all his bluster and aggression. Narelle, with her cold cutting eyes. Even Dolos would be preferable at this moment. All of them, I could shield against. I could draw the walls up and let the ice fall into place, hiding my truths. But not him.

Never him.

Caedmon doesn't say anything as he slows his gait and approaches where I stand against the jagged stone railing that looks out across the blackened sea and the cloudy mountains so far in the distance that they're mere specs in my imagination. Far below, the sound of the ocean crashes against the cliffside, angry and unforgiving. Much like my own damn mind.

I look down. Rocky pillars jut up and out of the black, blue, and gray swirling waters like knives. Sharp and unrelenting. One step off and I know it won't matter how

2

much Divine blood resides within me, my death would be slow and deserved. This place truly has earned a reputation, and therefore, it seemed like the perfect place to contemplate my current thoughts as the day arrives—just as impossible to stop as the inviting waters below. It would be so quick...

"Nasty way to go," Caedmon speaks, sounding half-amused. My brows shoot up and at the same time my body goes rigid with the silent threat in those words. I didn't know that the Prophecy God could peek into another's head like that.

Caedmon chuckles, low and musical in sound. "I can't read your mind," he says, guessing my thoughts if his words are to be believed, "but I think I've known you long enough and well enough to know what you're thinking about as you stand here at the edge of the world."

The muscles along my spine loosen but only slightly. Until he continues.

"But also, I saw you jumping off this ledge this morning in my dreams last night, so that might have helped to guess your thoughts." He doesn't sound disapproving as he reveals a piece of my potential future as if it's little more than talking about what he'll have for lunch.

I blink and gape at him. Shock courses through me. "I jump?"

Caedmon sets one long-fingered hand on the railing, golden rings glinting in the early morning rays, and turns to settle himself more firmly on the uneven stones. "*Jumped*," he clarifies in the past tense. "That moment has passed and unless my visions show me a different thread, I doubt you'll do it." He swipes his hand through the air with a casualness I don't feel, that I never feel around Gods such as him. No matter how long I've resided near or around them, it's as if my own body and mind can sense the danger they present. I can't ever relax around them, not really. Not even around Caedmon.

"I..." Words fail me. I don't know what to say to his confession, how to explain why I feel so Gods damned reprehensible. What I've done to feel this way.

Caedmon cants his head towards me, the earthen brown eyes of his deep and shallow all at once. If I didn't know personally how strong Tryphone's own abilities are, how vicious he can be when threatened, then I'd say that a man of Caedmon's power is more apt for King-hood. He *seems* all-knowing and yet, he never lets on whether he truly is or not.

Despite the icy chill in the air, the God of Prophecy is dressed relatively lightly. In another of his casual suits, a black darker even than his skin etched in gold and various matching ornaments. Pearl and gold clustered buttons vertically line the center of his chest and twin spike-like earrings dangle to just above his shoulders. His wide, full lips stretch into a soft smile before he speaks again.

"Today is the third day, isn't it?" he asks.

That enigmatic emotion that has plagued me for these last few days rises back to the surface. I grit my teeth against the pain that shreds my insides as if the damn thing has become a living and breathing monster in my stomach bent on punishing me for my sins.

"A hundred lashes is quite a lot." His words are another stab to my gut and then a wicked twist.

"Why are you here?" I snap the question at him, needing something—*anything*—to distract myself from what will happen in a few short hours. Rage darkens my mind, clouding through me, and only by sheer force of will—and the fact that I know I couldn't possibly kill Caedmon, not that I'd want to—do I hold it in check. Once the sun is fully risen and everyone's filed into the arena, Kiera will be brought forth and ... she will be punished. Because of me. Because of *my* mistake.

Shame. That is what the monster that clings to my soft underbelly is called. Vile and justified in its torment of me over the past few days, it clings to my bones and slides between my ribcage, leaving long jagged scratches as it goes. Scars that I will wear beneath my skin to match the ones that I wear over it.

"Because of my vision," Caedmon finally answers, "but also because I thought it pertinent to tell you that should you feel some way about your Terra"—my eyes cut to his and I feel them burn with power for a moment before it fades—"perhaps a meeting with Dolos will curb your guilt."

My jaw goes slack and my brow furrows. "Meet with Dolos?" I repeat. "What will that do? He's already announced to the entire Academy that she's to be punished today. There is no stopping it."

"No, there's not." Caedmon's expression twitches at his own statement, but before I can figure out why, he continues. "However, he only ever announced how many lashes she's to receive within his office, so if someone were to say ... offer to take half of those before she even reaches the arena, perhaps she will fare better."

Take half of the lashes. I shake my head. "Dolos would never agree to—"

Caedmon sighs and holds up a flat palm, facing me, to stop my words from reaching fruition. "Dolos is just like Axlan," he states. "It is perhaps a God's most powerful weakness to be so attached to the source of our abilities, but not all beings are as perfect as they like to believe." *That doesn't sound like a God talking.* He clicks his tongue. "Should you bow before Dolos and offer him that which he cannot live without, he will not refuse." Those cool soil rich eyes land on me once more and I swear that they're peering right through my very soul. My hands itch to close into fists, to fight that uncanny feeling he evokes. I suppress the urge. "All you need to know is that if you wish to make up for your error in some way, a bargain must be struck."

One hundred lashes. Enough to kill a mortal—no matter how mouthy or brave or damned intelligent they are. And yes, I know Kiera to be all of those things. It had been proven again and again from the moment she'd first arrived. How she'd looked each of us in the face without flinching. How she'd outsmarted Theos' little game with Malachi. How she'd figured out that it was I who'd turned her in and that I'd used my own abilities to sneak into Dolos' office to watch her sentence.

If a bargain must be struck then I will do it.

"I have to go." The words are out of my mouth before I even realize I'm moving, sliding past Caedmon.

"Be smart, Ruen," Caedmon calls over his shoulder as I start jogging down the pathway that led me here, the stones laid beneath my feet flattened over years of trekkers coming to this point. Some for silence and solitude and some ... for a different kind of silence and solitude. The latter half of those visitors the reason this spot now bears the name The Point of No Return.

The fresh wounds hidden beneath my tunic burn with pain, a bastard's way of repenting. My footsteps pick up speed and soon enough I'm full-on sprinting. Back towards the towering spires of the Academy's rooftops, like shards of gray and black eyes reaching for the quickly blossoming skies.

I'd blamed her. A miscalculation on my part. I blamed the starlight-haired beastly beauty of the Terra assigned to my brothers and me. The truth sits in the pit of my stomach.

I have to make it right.

The space between my brain and skull throbs with a dull, ever-present ache.

"*Fuck.*" The curse slips free as I sprint around the corner, clipping a massive boulder so fast that it rips a tear into the side of my jacket's arm. The leathery material splits and I feel blood ooze from the fresh cut. It doesn't matter.

Faster, I urge my legs. Faster. Before the sun fully rises, before the Academy wakes, before the arena fills. Before it's too late.

CHAPTER 2
KIERA

Three days stuck in the dark. Three days in absolute silence and isolation. If I hadn't done this exact thing as another one of Ophelia's training tests, I'd have gone insane by now. By the skies, I probably already am insane. After all, I'm sitting here thinking of what I'm going to do to the Darkhaven brothers when I get out of here and my punishment is finished. Specifically to Ruen Darkhaven.

One hundred lashes. I scratch out the final line on the wall with my fingernail, counting down my sentence just to give myself something to fucking do as I wait and wait and wait. I'll have to make it through one hundred lashes if I'm to get my revenge on him. Ruen was right, as much as I hate to admit it, that much for a human is ... impossible. Just surviving without giving my identity away will be a feat in itself.

My bones still feel achy and stiff from how little I've moved in the last seventy-two hours. My stomach rumbles with hunger, aching and empty. Just as I'd suspected, there'd been no mice or rats down here during my stay. No snakes. No ... *anything* to try and kill and eat. Even raw, anything in my belly would have been better than this void that threatens to turn its biting teeth on me. Cold puffs of transparent air waft in front of my face with each breath. I cup a hand over my stomach and sigh before using my other to withdraw the little leather band that I've kept hidden under my tunic and cloak and hold it up in front of my face.

The Belladonna swirls in dark purple droplets, clinging to the inside of the glass vial Regis had given me. I bet he didn't think I'd need to use it so soon. I'm so hungry that I'm almost ready to drink it right now, but I know I need to wait until just before the lashing begins. I drop the vial, letting the leather band clutch it, and swing it towards my chest right between my breasts.

With my back to the stone wall and the hard ground beneath my ass, I groan and stretch my sore and tired muscles. There's hardly enough room to stand up in this cell, much less try and move around it. I'm not used to being so stationary. I get to my shaking feet, using the wall as leverage.

I stagger over to the far wall, the corner where the scent of mist and salt is strongest. It's so dark down here, practically pitch black save for the cracked sconce of fire on the wall outside my cell. It took me several hours before I realized the liquid sluicing through the single fracture in that upper corner wasn't sewage or urine. It smelled clean, nothing like the stench permeating through the rest of these dungeons. When I'd finally given in and tried it, the taste on my tongue had been cold more than anything else and though sometimes there was a hint of salt that suggested ocean water, after the last three days of drinking it, I determine that it must be rain with a hint of the sea because the salt doesn't make me even more dehydrated than I already am from lack of other sustenance.

Pausing in front of the corner, with my back to the cell bars, I watch as a fresh stream of water comes pouring out of that crack and the one alongside it. One is rain and one is ocean water—someone who'd stayed here before must have cast some sort of Divinity magic over it to separate the liquids because it doesn't happen naturally. I don't know how they'd had any Divinity with the underlying buzz of brimstone reverberating in these walls or how they'd managed to use it, but I don't care. All I know is that one of those cracks has drinkable water and I fucking need it.

Salty sea water will do nothing but curdle in my stomach, dehydrating me and making me that much thirstier. Pressing my cupped hands flush to the cold stone, I watch with barely repressed longing as the water fills my palms. I wait until it's at least half full before I yank my hands away and set my lips to the liquid pooling there. I slurp it up, drinking it down in long gulps before repeating the process once, twice, three more times.

My stomach sloshes and rebels, not wanting more water, demanding something with more sustenance. *Food.* Gods, I'd kill for some food right now. Three days might seem like nothing, but when all you have to do is think down here in the dark, the constant hunger takes over the mind and it's all I can focus on.

Too damn bad, I think to myself. *This is all we've got.* The lone sconce outside my cell flutters like a pathetically weak little flame that might go out at any moment.

Once I've filled myself to the brim with as much water as I can stomach, I release my now freezing hands from the stone wall and collapse back into my own little corner, breathing heavily. Damn Dolos. The sick sadistic prick. I assumed he'd merely get his high from imprisoning me here, but with the lashings he's got planned after three days of starvation still to go, he must be a bastard that gets his rocks off by weakening an already trapped prey as well.

I hope it's him, I think to myself. If he's my target, I will *relish* in killing him. In making him suffer before I end it. That is ... if I can get close enough to his weirdly shrouded form without feeling like I'm being locked up and chained down all over again.

The sound of shrieking rusted hinges pours into the near silent darkness of the dungeons. I flinch as light pours from the staircase. Fuck, I hadn't realized how dark it was down here until fresh light was let in. Footsteps echo up the gray, cracked dungeon walls, rebounding throughout the mostly empty underground space, getting louder and louder as the person grows closer before stopping entirely just outside my cell.

I peer out from beneath the hood of my cloak, finding a guard standing there with a disinterested expression on his face and a ring of keys hanging from one finger. His face is unfamiliar, but I know for certain he's not one of the same two guards who brought me here the first time. He's a Mortal God though. That much I do know. I can sense the pale eeriness of his weak Divinity wafting off him. Were my own Divinity not hidden beneath the power of the brimstone embedded in the back of my neck, he would be able to sense mine too.

The guard is a male in what appears to be his mid to late forties, his age revealed by the streaks of gray through his otherwise dark hair. I can't be entirely sure since Mortal Gods age differently from humans, but we *do* age. His frame is large, bulky even, and covered in the form-fitting armor that all guards wear—black leather tunics and trousers, the fabric thick to ward off chill especially as winter grows ever closer. He bends and slides a key into the cell lock. The clang of the key turning and the mechanism opening rings throughout the otherwise quiet interior of the dungeons.

I scan down to the pair of iron cuffs that dangle from his belt. Those are for me. Wholly unnecessary, not that he would know. His Divinity is so feeble, barely resonating out of him at all that he must be of a much lower Tier than the Darkhavens. Third Tier maybe. I wonder if documented Mortal Gods ever manage to grow out of the system the Gods put them in when they're in the academies. If not, then perhaps that's why he has a job like this, guard and prisoner retriever.

I crawl to my feet, knowing what's about to happen now as I shore up my breath and strength. A bite of nervousness that I thought I'd long since repressed edges up my throat. Even if I can handle pain, that doesn't mean I like it. Self-preservation has me hesitating before I emerge from the cell.

It'll be fine, I tell myself. I've dealt with something similar in the past. Worse, probably—all for the sake of training, to ensure that even if I am, somehow, found out, I'll never give up all the lives in the Underworld. One sacrifice for the lives of many. I repeat it in my head. Over and over again until a rather helpful part of my mind reminds me that this isn't even like Ophelia's punishments. Those lasted for hours, days—I honestly can't remember. They blur together. This will just be one punishment with limited hits. A piece of cake.

Even as I try to convince myself of the ease with which I'll handle this, I still reach up and pluck the vial off my leather band and hold it in my palm as if it's some sort of sacred artifact of old meant to ward off bad spirits. The cell door hangs open, and I hold the poison in my grip as the guard motions me forward.

"Come on," he snaps. "Don't make me come in after you."

The urge to bite back at him rides me hard, especially as anticipatory nervousness clogs my throat. If I'm already considered an impertinent Terra ... but, no. I can't act any more rebellious than I already have. At least, not in front of those who would definitely run to Dolos at the first opportunity. For the sake of appearances, I will be cowed. I will be subservient. Just for today.

Still, the guard's annoyed tone makes me contemplate shoving the Belladonna down his throat and seeing what happens. I want to—badly—but I don't. Subservient Terra *don't* kill their guards, I remind myself.

I stride out of the cell and turn towards the man, gritting my teeth as he huffs a breath. It must be so damn hard to come down here and drag a girl who's been starving in the dark for three days to the arena. He takes my hands, not bothering to force me to open my fists as he clamps the iron cuffs around my wrists in front of my body. I roll my eyes.

He doesn't notice.

"Come," he grumbles, clearly not happy at having been the one given this task. He doesn't say anything more and doesn't wait to see what I'll do as he makes his way back to the stairs and ascends to the upper floors. His ego is stifling. It's as if it doesn't even occur to him that I *could* fight back much less that I would were I not

13

meant to stay here after this punishment and await my orders.

Freedom, I remind myself. True freedom. That's what I'm doing this for. That's what I'm staying for, suffering for. Once my contract has been paid back to Ophelia and the Underworld, the brimstone in my neck will be removed and I can go *home.* The word echoes in my head with a longing I've shoved down for so long that the fresh wave of nostalgia and loss hits me like a ton of bricks.

Once this is all over, I can actually *make* a home and I never have to answer to anyone else again, be tied down or ordered by anyone else. I can just exist—free from the Gods' prying eyes and safe in the Hinterlands. The force of that desire hits me like a storm, but I don't let it wash me away. No. I hold on as it rocks through me. I let it give me strength as I trail the guard up the stairs and into the morning sun.

It's not even that bright, but I've been in the darkness for so long that it blinds me. I duck my head, using the guard's broad back to block out most of its direct rays, and keep walking. My feet trudge across the stone floors and the farther we go, the more recognizable the Academy's surroundings get.

I spot the familiar buildings and stone archways that lead toward the Terra quarters for bathing or eating and the ones that lead to the forbidden gardens and courtyards. Another eye roll overtakes me, hidden from the guard since he hasn't paused once to look behind him. I'm cuffed, but there's not even a chain leading from the cuffs to his grip. He just walks along as if he expects that I'll do what's expected of me. And ... well, he has a point. I am following him after all.

Still, this is all so ridiculous. The lashings. The imprisonment. All of it, over pettiness and rules meant to show-case who's in charge. I resent the tightness that takes over my muscles, bunching my spine and spilling down my legs and arms as I keep walking.

The guard leads me out of the lower levels and the residential areas. Finally, we arrive back to the place where several Mortal Gods died not but a few days ago. I follow him down a long, darkened tunnel, sighing with relief at the muted light despite what I know waits for me at the open end on the far side.

We enter the arena and when I half expect there to be cries and cheers, I hear only stone-cold silence. I tilt my head up, confused, thinking perhaps they hadn't yet called the Academy to witness my punishment. They're there though. Students. Staff. Faculty. All of them sit in the stands in much the same way as they had several days ago for the Advancement Battles. There are a few icy smiles, cruel eyes glittering in amusement, and some that are straight-up passing coins back and forth—betting on how long I'll last or even if I'll die here today, no doubt.

Ahead, at the very end of the arena, in the curve on the farthest side, I spot three familiar faces. My muscles tighten all over again, this time for a different reason. Rage and resentment and something else I can't name swarm my insides, ripping into me like creatures from the darkest depths of the ocean—the kind that lure sailors and others into their waters before dragging them beneath the sea's surface to feast upon their flesh and bones.

The three of them are standing rather than sitting and watching me with a mixture of expressions. Theos looks distressed, his brows tight and his lips drawn down. When he catches my gaze, he leans forward as if on instinct. *Shit.* I look away immediately. Bad fucking idea—it'd been such a bad idea to give in to him that night.

The next face I spot is Kalix. Unlike Theos', his expression is wholly unreadable. His green eyes are like frozen moss. There's no warmth and no light within them. As he watches me, his pupils thin and lengthen like slits rather than the rounded pupil of a mortal. I blink and his pupils are back to normal.

Finally, there's Ruen. Ruen *fucking* Darkhaven. My academy master and my betrayer. His hands are cupped over the lip of the railing that separates the stands from the arena several feet lower. He looks ... pained. Sweat dots his brow and his face is slightly reddened. I scan him, wondering what the fuck ... blood. I spot it, just a few droplets of it on his throat, further back and almost unnoticeable. Had he fought with Theos? I swap my gaze back to the Darkhaven in question, but he's not even looking at his brother. No? What the—

I don't get a chance to finish that thought as the morning sun glints off something metal in the center of the arena as we approach. My attention snaps back to what's in front of me.

Twin chains embedded into the hard, half-frozen ground greet me. My heart begins thundering within my breast. Sweat beads pop up along my spine. So many eyes. *Too* many eyes. All watching me. Their twisted lips and poorly hidden bets slither under my skin, an awareness I wish I didn't have.

At least not *everyone* is out for my blood today. I have to contend with that. Ruen had seemed guilty when he'd seen me three days ago; hopefully he hurts watching me just as much as I'll hurt taking these lashes. Gods, I hope the knowledge that *he* did this rips him apart because I know that no matter how hard I'll try, I won't be able to act subservient to him after this. I'm an assassin, not a Gods-damned actress. I'd never been meant for long-term missions like this and it's a miracle I haven't outed myself yet.

If this is a test from Ophelia, then I'm sorely failing it.

The guard strides for the place marked with an X that looks to be carved with sticks or the blunt end of a sword between those two chains. I pause as I spot a dark-haired Terra dressed in a dirty cream-colored tunic and brown trousers quickly scraping away what looks like congealed blood in the dirt and sand mixture that covers the floor of the fighting arena.

The chains draw my eyes again. There is a solid length of several feet on either side, each ending with cuffs splattered with that same blood that the Terra is now hurrying to finish raking away with a long wooden handle that boasts several metal tongs on one end digging into the dirt.

Now is the time, I decide, cupping my hands together. The pads of my thumbs press against the little cork holding the vial closed and it slips free, sliding into the dirt and sand at my feet. I step over it and keep going before placing my fists to my lower face so that it looks like I'm praying. Maybe I am, but it's not to any God. I part my lips and tilt my head back. I swallow the vile purple liquid, the Belladonna tasting of the ground and sweet berries.

I press a purple-coated kiss to my knuckle and raise my hands toward the sky to hide what I've done. The guard in front of me pauses and looks back, and I lower my hands shakily to my front once more. Within seconds,

I can feel the Belladonna's effects. My Divine Blood tries to fight it. I know it does because I sway on my feet slightly as both collide within me.

Dizziness assails me as the guard reaches for my bound hands and uncuffs them. The iron circlets fall to my feet, lifting up a cloud of dust against my worn boots. His wide fingers encircle my wrists and drag me, and I stumble forward. Once we're in place between the lines of the chains set in the center of the arena, he doesn't wait, stripping my cloak from me and tossing it to … a new Terra that approaches, I realize as I turn my head and catch sight of a familiar face.

My cloak lands against Niall's chest with a thump. He's pale and trembling. His hair hangs in long shaggy brown strings around his soft cheeks and rounded forehead as if he's been running his fingers through the strands all morning. I try to muster up a smile but that only makes him catch his breath as tears fill his eyes. The guard sets about his task of clamping a new cuff on each of my wrists, separating my arms, and pulling them out at my sides tight until I can feel the burn in my ligaments.

My breathing quickens and I swallow against a suddenly dry mouth. Chains. Restrictions. I hate them. I breathe heavily through my teeth. In and out. *In and fucking out.* I can handle this. I *have* handled this, I tell myself. I've been through so much worse. This is nothing.

Even so, as the guard puts his hand on my shoulder and pushes me down onto my knees, I feel my head begin to swim with old memories that I try and fail not to dredge up. No, no, not now. I need to stay in the moment. I need to focus. Fighting those old memories though as the Belladonna's poison is working through my bloodstream is harder than ever.

I hear Niall's sharp intake of breath a moment before I feel the calloused pads of the guard's fingers at the back of my neck. He swipes my long silver braid out of the way, tossing it over my shoulder. The frayed strands flutter against my collarbone. Itchy. So damn itchy. I feel like little tiny bugs are crawling all over me. Not spiders. Spiders I could handle, but bugs with dozens, hundreds more legs. All of them sliding beneath the fabric of my skin to crawl over muscle and bone. I want to vomit, but there's nothing in my stomach save for water and bile.

The guard locks his fingers against the back of my tunic's collar and then he shreds it right down the middle. Cold morning air washes over my bare flesh. My eyes pop open and I hadn't realized I'd closed them. The tunic before me sags forward low, almost too fucking low. The bindings circling my middle, keeping my breasts contained sag a moment later as, instead of using his fingers this time, he sets the edge of a blade against my flesh—a dagger, I belatedly realize—and slices upward.

The bindings fall away, collapsing towards my lower back and stomach on either side of my body. That's it. There is to be no cushion, no barrier for these lashings. Just my skin and the whip of leather the man who steps into the arena behind me wields. The God, I remind myself as Axlan is not a man at all but a Divine Being.

I look back to see him as I hear several gasps throughout the crowd. Axlan, the God of Victory. The length of leather braided into a single long cord is held loosely in his hand. It cracks, the sound echoing throughout the arena as he sizes it up and gets a feel for it.

Fuck. Me.

I turn my head towards the crowd as the guard who'd brought me here barks an order at Niall. I can sense

Niall's hesitation, but he backs up a step and then another and another until they're both striding from the ring and leaving me, bound and half-naked in front of the entire Academy populace. The various Terra in attendance throughout the stands watch with their faces blanched of color and their eyes full of fear. As if seeing me is a reminder of what will happen to them should they rise up against the Gods.

That's what I am. A reminder. A warning. Damn Dolos.

Still, my eyes hunt through the crowd, seeking … I find them once again.

The Darkhavens.

I set my gaze on each of them once more.

Theos, Kalix, and Ruen stand across from me. Even if there's no hint of smugness or amusement in their expressions, I find resentment bubbling up in my gut. Some logical part of my brain acknowledges how out of place they look amongst the crowd of other Mortal Gods —all of whom have taken their seats and are casually watching. None of them bother with the cushioned benches at their backs. They remain standing.

The three of them standing like prisoners themselves, waiting for their turn at the gallows.

Good, I think as Axlan cracks that damn whip once more, testing the loudness and strength a second time.

Ruen's hands sink into the wooden barrier and railing between us as he leans forward. His brows are low over what I know to be midnight blue eyes. He mouths something to me, but I don't know what it is, not before Axlan's footsteps grow closer, not before the first lash burns across my flesh. Once it does, once blood begins to flow, I know nothing else but pain.

CHAPTER 3

KIERA

There is a roaring in my head so loud that it sounds as if the winds themselves have taken up residence in my ears. It's louder than anything I've ever heard before. It overwhelms my senses, even the raw, open bleeding ones.

How many lashes have I had now? Five? Ten? I lost count so quickly that it blurs in my mind. Perhaps that's the Belladonna working. Over and over again, the whip bites into my flesh and then drags downward, slicing through muscle and nerves.

Each mark burns through me, carving me open as warm blood oozes from my shoulders and leaks down towards the crack of my ass hidden by my trousers. The whip cuts so deep into me, I swear I can feel air on the bones of my spine.

I sag forward. Were it not for the cuffs and chains, I would be face first into the grit and dirt before me, uncaring of whether or not anyone can see my chest anymore. Nudity or modesty. None of it matters anymore.

The only thing I can focus on is the spasming pain in my body.

By the twentieth lash, at least I think that's the number we're at, the pain fades away entirely. If I'm crying, I don't feel the tears. If I'm awake, I don't know. They wouldn't continue if I passed out from the pain, would they? I can't imagine anyone getting their rocks off watching an unconscious Terra being shredded, face down in dirt and sand of the arena's pit, but then again— the Divine Beings are cruel creatures whose enjoyments I've never understood.

Dimly, I'm aware of my surroundings. The grit in my eyes and beneath my kneecaps, digging past the fabric of my trousers. Kneeling on sand is yet another pain that I must deal with. The quiet murmurs of the crowd are a low hum in the back of my mind. Their eyes, ever watchful and present, burn into my face. I feel all of them and none of them. My lashes flutter as something soft and gentle moves over my flesh. Water. I feel like water is being poured over me. As if my flesh isn't shredded, but instead being washed and cleaned. All the sweat and dirt and grime that's covered me fades away as if it was never there in the first place.

Every small scar and wound is soothed. The grotesque feeling of blood under my nails that I've carried with me for years disappears. It's not real. None of it, but it's nice nonetheless. What would it be like to be entirely clean again? To be blameless, sinless. It must be something like this, I realize.

The fluttering touch of someone's fingers moves over my face, tracing my features, starting at my brow and then moving down on the outside of my face to my jawline. I let my eyes close completely, blocking out the image of my surroundings, of the Gods and Mortal Gods and the arena, and suddenly, I find myself somewhere wholly different. Somewhere ... *soothing*.

When was the last time I'd ever felt soothed?

With my father? Perhaps. He'd been a strong man. Well taught and more intelligent than most others who lived in the Hinterlands. He'd been gruff and often stoic, and the rare gentleness from him had been short-lived. After he was gone, there was no one else left to be gentle. No one who cared enough to try for a bastard God-child who was more dangerous alive than dead.

The sun's heat on my aching spine is no longer as vicious as it once was but simply warm. Feather light, those gentle fingers trace over my body, offering comfort. Without intending to, I arch for it, leaning into that relieving embrace. There's a start from the invisible creature as if they didn't anticipate my reciprocation. Then, before I can pull back to reality, it covers me wholly.

Arms around me. A hot breath on my face, moving down. It pauses over my lips and then touches my throat. A silent groan works its way up my throat. Without the pain I know I should be feeling, these sensations are far more sensual than I'd expected. The unknown presence eases away slightly as if realizing my discomfort with feeling this way.

When I open my eyes again, it's not to find bloodied dirt and sand under my knees but soft grass that sways in an invisible breeze. I look up and up some more until I see distant mountains topped with snow. Flowers bloom all around me and for the first time in days, I finally feel warm again. All the ice that's filled my veins has fallen away and I sigh in relief as the sun's rays pour over me. My lips curve upward into a smile.

Nothing hurts. My back isn't sore from sleeping on cold hard stone. My skin isn't flayed to within an inch of my life. Even my head is clear of the Belladonna's poisonous effects. The dizziness. The swollen dryness on my tongue. It's all gone. How, I don't know.

Invisible ghostly hands trail down my face and into my hair once more. I suck in a quick breath. Those hands are familiar, but I can't place them. I turn my head and gasp when to the other side, the tie that holds my braid is gently pried free. The silver length of my hair unwinds, falling around me in long straight strands that flutter in that gentle wind.

It tickles my skin as those phantom hands lift the locks. Whoever he is, he's feeling me out. Testing whether I'm real or not. How I know it's a he, I can't say, but the entity, the energy that creeps closer to me, encloses me in this space feels masculine. Protective almost. Remorseful.

Have I died? I open my mouth to ask the question, but no words come out. I can't speak here, I realize. There's no real air. Everything around me, the ground, the grass, the wind. It's all an illusion. A carefully crafted spell woven around me to block out what's actually happening.

Realizing that, admitting the truth to the fake world created around me, breaks whatever hold the Divinity has on me and causes the false illusion to shatter, breaking apart entirely. Pain rushes back into my senses.

I gasp, scream, cry out. Tears burn out of my eyes unbidden and I cannot stop them this time. I sob as one final lash cuts across my back and then halts. All the grime that had been washed away before slams into me. Sand beneath my nails as I dig them into the dirt at my knees. Trembling, cold—so fucking cold—the warm blood raining over my back soaks into the seat of my pants, drenching my backside.

Distantly, I'm aware of Axlan stepping back. I can scent him—his sweat and power and energy. His Divinity ripples like a wave through the air, scenting of fire and citrus. He enjoyed what he did to me, is flying on some sort of Victory high destroying me has given him. I'm on my hands and knees, panting for breath that scrapes through my raw throat and before I can stop it, the muscles of my stomach bunch and contract. Bile and water spew out of my mouth, soaking the sand.

Coughing, I let it all out, not caring how weak it makes me appear. Perhaps it's a good thing to seem weak here. I don't have the energy to plan for it though. It just is.

Rough arms unlock me from the chains and I nearly plant myself face-first into the ground. If it weren't for the arms that lock onto my biceps and drag me upward. My head spins, faster and faster. I'm going to vomit again.

I try to open my eyes, but when I do, all I see is gray-blue skies and sunlight. It burns into my skull, making the pounding at the back of my head that much worse. Too much all at once. Everything is too fucking much.

My body is half-dragged, half-lifted as I'm turned towards the tunnel. Above it, in the awning where the Gods of the Academy sit and watch the proceedings, Dolos steps forward, his shrouded body cloaked in darkness, moving as if he's floating rather than walking. I try to focus on him, try and fail. I can't even stand upright, held aloft by the guards on either side of me. Cool air washes over my back and I nearly bow in agony as just that gentle breeze caresses the open and bared muscles that have been shredded through on my spine. Black dots dance in front of my vision. Dolos begins speaking.

"Let this be a reminder to all," he calls out over the crowd, "that we, your Gods, are merciful. Follow our command, our rule, and all you will know is safety. Fail to do so, and your punishment may be far worse than the Terra's known as Kiera Nezerac." I sense more than see his gesture in my direction. Only the burn of eyes on my body tells me he's directing them to look at me. The visual reminder of their fucking mercy. Ha. Mercy my ass.

"Breaking protocol may not seem like such a horrible offense," he continues, as if he knows keeping me here, dangling between his lackeys is a new torture all on its own. "One mistake can turn into many. One broken rule, one broken law, can sow the seed of anarchy. Our world is protected by the Gods, and as such, respect is due. Any Terra will meet the same fate if not worse than our friend here." Another gesture. I'd like to give a gesture of my own, a foul one. "Remember that you all have a place in this world of ours and keeping to the lines that maintain our society is what will separate Gods and humans and Mortal Gods alike from animals."

Fuck him. Fuck him. *Fuck. Him.* If he senses my thoughts, Dolos doesn't react. I lift my head, sinking it back on my shoulders as I force myself to peer up at him on his dais. Violence rings in my ears. Retaliation. Vengeance. I hunger for it even as I'm near collapse.

Belatedly, I recognize what I'd promised myself earlier. How I'd sworn that I'd act subservient today, just for today, but I find that I can't. I'm in so much pain, stripped bare by it that I can't stop the venom that fills my eyes as I glare at him.

Dolos doesn't so much as blink at whatever expression I must have on my face. He merely waves his hand to the guards on either side of me and I find myself being dragged forward a moment later. My boots drag in the dirt and sand, drawing twin parallel lines between as I'm hauled forward, towards the darkened tunnel.

Just before the darkness overtakes my form entirely and the warmth of the sun is stolen, I hear one of the guards mutter something under their breath. "Lucky Terra," he huffs. "If I were Dolos, I would've given her the full hundred lashes instead of a mere fifty."

Fifty? My thoughts catch on that statement. I'd only received half of the original lashes? Why? The question permeates my mind, circling around and around as the Belladonna's dizziness overtakes me again and just before we reach the end of the tunnel, I hunch over and curse silently as I upchuck once more, spilling nothing but saliva and bile this time. My lips twitch as the guards curse in disgust. I hope I puke at least once more before they drop me off wherever they're taking me. I hope I vomit all over both of them.

CHAPTER 4
KIERA

O nce released from the chains and dismissed from the arena, the elder Mortal God guards drag me along the corridors, my booted feet scraping the stones underneath. Blearily, I force my head up even as the movement pulls at the shredded skin along my upper back. We're not heading towards the dungeons, thank fuck, but instead to the more familiar sight of the north tower.

Reaching the stairs and gritting my teeth through their awkward and uncaring maneuvering is a testament to my training. Each step up is like yet another lash across my back. I breathe heavily as my head swarms with that dizziness. The insects I felt crawling all over me as I'd been forced to kneel before the entire Academy and accept my punishment have returned. They sidle up and down my open wounds and over my skin. I want to rip my own soul out of my body just to get the sensation to stop.

If anyone is concerned with the blood dripping all over the half-naked Terra as she's paraded through their hallways, no one dares speak a word of it. The door to my room is kicked open by one of the guards and without so much as a careful hand, they drop me. My knees buckle as their grip, which had held me up for the majority of the walk here, is suddenly gone. I hit the floor, sending up a cloud of dust around my legs, and the scream of pain that threatens to spill out lodges in my throat. Silent tears track down my cheeks. Blood slips down my shoulder blades and spine. I can feel my trousers sticking to the skin of my ass. Itchy and painful.

"You're relieved from duties for the week," one of the guards says behind me, his voice gruff and just as unforgiving as the ground beneath me. "Be grateful that the Gods showed you mercy."

With that, they're gone, slamming the door behind them on their way out. I stay like that for several long moments. I don't know if it's minutes or hours, but what I do know is that the sun has waned by the time I finally have the energy to move. With one hand pressed to the floor, I drag a leg out from under me and place my sole against the wooden planks. I stretch upward, meaning to stand.

All at once, though, the pain hits me with a fresh wave of fire. Black dots fill my vision, growing larger and larger until they completely encompass everything. My leg collapses once more and the ground rushes up to meet my face. Darkness falls before it actually hits, and for that, I am grateful.

My head feels foggy, as if wads of cotton have been shoved into my earholes far enough that they've taken up residence right alongside my brain when I wake. I'm still on the floor, I realize a moment later, lying prone and vulnerable. With a dry, panting mouth, I turn my head from the wall and stare, unseeing, at the light from the moon shining in through the slit of a window in my room.

Has it been a day? I wonder. *Or longer?* The tingles of pain embedded into my back are my answer. A day then.

Breath after breath invades my chest, filling up my lungs before wheezing back out. Exhaustion clings to my every pore. My limbs feel heavier than they ever have, but I fight off the desire for sleep. Every small noise—from the footsteps of people passing outside my door to the soft chirping of insects and the skittering of spiders within the walls—makes my muscles bunch and jump beneath my flesh.

It's been a long time since I felt quite this vulnerable. With the poison's effects slowing down my healing speed and the unwashed, unmedicated skin of my back open to the raw elements, I doubt I'd be much of a fight for anyone should they attempt to kill me now. So, I keep my eyes peeled. I breathe deeply, counting down invisible minutes as I work to quell my own focus on the pain.

Those minutes turn to hours and by the third one, I'm so achingly aware of my surroundings that the moment there's a change in the air, I'm on high alert. Footsteps have long since disappeared from the corridors as the night has grown older, but it's not footsteps I hear that disturb me. It's the rattle of metal and glass.

Jerking my head up to look at my window, I ignore the sharp stretch of skin that the movement produces and the following cramp of pain in my back. A shadowy figure from outside the tower window takes hold of the metal grate that crisscrosses over the glass and bends it outward before reaching inside and pulling the single pane open and away from the frame.

It's too small for him to fit through. Before that thought is finished echoing in my head, however, the figure disappears entirely and a giant black thing slithers into the opening it's made. Giant green eyes peer back at me as the snake hits the floor just inside the room and then it moves for me, slipping back and forth, its muscles bunching and releasing at such a rapid rate to keep it moving that it's hard for me to keep track.

My heart picks up speed. Even in my agony, I recognize that this creature's sudden appearance isn't right. The faster my pulse thrums in my breast, however, the more the pain in my back seems to swell.

The snake disappears from view and then there's no hint of the serpent that just entered my space, and in its place is the nearly silent sound of footsteps on the uneven wooden boards of my bedroom floor. I'm in too much agony to even lift my head though. If someone's here to kill me then they came at the perfect time. My body won't even move when I demand it.

My eyes crack open, but the room is spinning. Up is down and down is up. Over and over again, I'm flipping and the only thing that tells me I'm not falling through the sky itself is the grain of the wood pressed into my sore cheek.

The presence of the stranger in my room is quiet. He doesn't speak for the longest time, but I can feel the burn of his gaze on me, roving over my naked, shredded back. My mouth is dry, so dry that when my tongue peeks out to lick at my lips, it comes back tasting of blood. Just that small movement made the skin split. My stomach rolls.

A sigh escapes the intruder and then hard hands grip my shoulders. Fire, burning hot and violent, arches down my spine. My mouth is too arid, my tongue too swollen, for me to make any sort of sound but a hoarse squeak. The man doesn't stop what he's doing though as he lifts me into strong arms, against a massive chest. I close my eyes as tears threaten to spill over. He smells ... familiar somehow, like oakwood and sea salt. I breathe it in and the rapid pulse of my heart slows, slugging through my veins in soft, steady beats when it should be racing. Perhaps, it too has no energy left.

The one holding me in his arms strides the short distance to my bed and carefully lays me down, rolling me so that I'm not on my back. If there was anything in my stomach, it would threaten to expel. I don't know if I'm thankful now for Dolos' command to keep me starved for three days before my punishment or not.

With my face nearly pressed into the stone wall that my bed is shoved against, I try to force my hand up. My fingers twitch in response, but the limb refuses to move. *Shit.*

Hot hands grip the tattered remains of my tunic and finish rending it from my body. He rips the sleeves clean down instead of trying to force my arm up to remove it from my person. My flesh pebbles as cold air rushes over me. It soothes the heat in my back. Still, I can't turn over to see who it is that's helping me.

It's not Ruen, that much I know for sure. His smell is parchment and firewood. It's permanently marked in my mind from my time in Dolos' office and the secret way he'd hidden himself there, watching as my punishment was announced.

Definitely not Theos. I'd been close enough to the

golden-eyed, white-haired Darkhaven to know that his scent is marked by spice and rum even when he's not drinking. That's all I can think of when I smell the bitter-sweet amber liquid.

If this man is neither of them, then that only leaves one more that has the kind of strength to lift me and carry me and care for me the way he is now.

Kalix.

The fact that the most unstable of all the Darkhaven brothers is here right now *tending* to me is unnerving. If it weren't for the Belladonna coursing through my body, filling my veins with sluggishness, I'd likely already be up and healing. I try to work some saliva into my mouth, pushing it towards my lips to wet them as Kalix finishes pulling off my tunic.

Cool metal touches the top of my trousers at the back and I close my eyes, unable to tell him to stop as he slices through the seam and then begins to cut that, too, off my body. No words are exchanged. He's completely silent as he works, stripping me bare. A wash of air floats over my backside. The sound of something thumping on the floor behind me alerts me to the fact that he just used some sort of conjuring Divinity.

I'm learning more and more about him—all things I didn't want to know but will likely help me if he's one of my targets. That is, if there is even a fucking target in the first place. I close my eyes and repel the angry thoughts I have towards Ophelia, focusing only on the here and now.

So, Kalix can turn into a snake and he can conjure objects. Big deal. I can summon spiders to do my bidding, and the shadows ... well, they've always been somewhat attracted to my presence, but it's not like I can control them. All Mortal Gods have abilities like this. It's nothing new.

A wet cloth touches my back and for once, the saliva in my mouth does its job in giving me a voice. "Ahh!" I cry out and immediately arch away from the touch.

Kalix's hard hand grips my shoulder and he says nothing as he ignores my sharp sound of pain and continues to wash my back. Tears fill my eyes and overflow, streaking down my cheeks.

Fuck. It hurts. Huge gasping sobs wrack my chest, quiet but violent. I can feel where the pieces of my flesh are flayed open. Each pass of that wet cloth is another lick of pain. It goes on forever, or at least, it feels like it does. He pulls the cloth away, rewetting it every once in a while, or cleaning it perhaps. I don't know. I'm too focused on breathing through my teeth and trying not to gag so hard I vomit up my organs to concentrate on much else. My face is soaked by the time he finishes, my mouth filled with the taste of salt.

The second his hands leave me, I gasp in relief. I tremble beneath him, my whole body shivering against the cot. From pain or cold, I can't tell. I thought this would be similar to the training I went through in the Underworld, but it's not. The Belladonna keeps me from healing. The wounds are open and fresh and I am so utterly defenseless right now that the new tears that spring to my eyes are not of pain but fear.

No! A hiccup lodges in my throat. *You are not afraid. You do not feel fear.* I yell the words in my mind, but that doesn't make them any truer. The fear clings to me like an unwelcome monster, crept out from under my bed to hover over me. Its mere presence shrinks my own until I become a tiny speck I do not recognize. No longer am I the woman, the assassin, that bore Ophelia's torture, that has killed those much more powerful than me.

I am simply a girl. Frozen in terror. Clenching my teeth to keep from begging.

Old, sinister memories rise to the surface. Things I've long since buried. Burning ashes in my memory. Blood-covered snow. The brimstone in the back of my neck throbs. Oh, how it had mutilated the Divine piece of my soul to have this damned shard planted beneath my skin —a tether to my Master, to the life I was forced to live.

Kalix's hands are uncompromising as he pushes me onto my front. Soft fabric wraps around my legs, smoothing up my calves and then my thighs. No under-wear though. I don't think of it. How he manages to get the trousers on me and fasten them without lifting me is a testament to his Divinity. All the while, I lie there, shiv-ering, spent, and wholly not myself.

My lips part, cracked and bleeding, and finally, I manage to utter a single word. "Don't..."

I don't know what I'm asking for. Don't kill me? Don't hurt me anymore? Don't let this happen again? That one word is the only thing I manage to get out, though, as those black dots from before blink into view.

Kalix's voice is a low grumble, thunder filling my ears as I feel the bed dip beneath me. I'm floating, confusion pouring through my mind as the most disturbing of the Darkhavens hovers over me like the shadow of Death, himself.

Oakwood and sea salt invade my senses. It's not unwelcome. I inhale it, letting it fill my lungs, letting it be the strength that allows me to beat back the encroaching fear. My lashes flutter against my cheeks and though there's movement above me, movement that bends the mattress and dips in strange motions, I find that I can't keep myself awake any longer.

Fresh tingles wake up the damaged nerves in my back. A thick sort of liquid hits my spine and soaks into the open wounds. A gasp escapes me as I feel the bolting rush of Divinity—someone else's Divinity—race through me, attaching to the bloodied mess of my muscles. More darkness expands from the corners of my visions.

"What..." I croak out the word, unable to get a full question out as Kalix stops whatever he's doing. His groin is on top of my ass, I realize. A thick, hard length of what can only be an iron-hard cock presses against the curve of my ass. Why does he have an erection right now of all times?

A mixture of confusion and disgust rolls through me. What the fuck is he doing? How depraved is he? A fresh, different kind of fear bolts through me like an arrow. He wouldn't...

My body spasms as a blaze of pain wrecks my senses. Hot liquid, far less thick than before, splashes over my back. Kalix covers me with it, from the top of my shoulder blades down to the small of my back. I bow and arch, fighting the misery that consumes me.

My lips part again, a dry scream ripping free.

Then there's nothing.

CHAPTER 5
KALIX

There is only one way I know to heal. It's an old recollection from a long ago class I'd taken when we'd first arrived at the Academy. *Something of Divine origin can be offered in the essence of mending mortal flesh.* It's been written in one of our texts, though our Divine instructors had merely glossed over the fact as it'd been made clear that we were not to offer such a thing. Mortals, after all, are born to grow old, to inhale disease, to die. To take that away from them and offer them a piece of our flesh or fluid would be to damn them, though it was never explained why.

Still, if my fluid is what this little mortal needs, then it is what she will get. She has yet to completely show me every piece of her and I cannot see the fire burn in her eyes if she's dead. Sure, I could crack open her body and root around within her ribcage after her heart has stopped beating, but once gone, a living creature can never be brought back and she's the only thing that amuses me these days. There's something about her that has my serpents on edge, as if they sense another beast lying in wait within her, and I want to entice that creature out to play.

I've never done it before. Never had a reason or desire to. The Terra lies half-unconscious before me. Despite the moonlight color of her hair, her lashes are charcoal dark as they throw shadows over her cheek with her head turned towards the stone wall. Her back is a shredded mess, even after I cleaned the slices Axlan had made in her flesh.

Thin and thick lines crisscross over what once was a perfect smooth expanse of pale ivory flesh. I stare down at the red marks, her skin flayed open at the sides and curling up and outward, at the blood still leaking from them as I adjust her on the pathetic excuse for a bed in her quarters. That is, if a single closet-sized room with nothing more than a cot, a nightstand, and few other small pieces of furniture all shoved next to each other can be considered 'quarters.'

My lips twitch with disgust as I cast another look around the darkened space. The last time I'd been here, I'd been so focused on her that I hadn't given this dusty hovel a second thought.

I bite back the urge to trash the place, tear the door off its hinges, and wreck the walls. Anger curls through my limbs and I find my fingers digging into fists as I restrain myself lest I hurt the one beneath me in my outburst.

Gaze falling, I trace the soft curve of her cheek with my eyes. Then I get on top of her.

The springs of the cot contract, squeaking loudly with the noise as I throw one leg over both of hers and sit back on my haunches, keeping myself slightly above her so as not to give her too much of my weight. Not while she's hurt. My little mortal doesn't even flinch—as if she doesn't hear the bed, as if she hardly feels me rising above her.

Inhaling, I close my eyes and picture her as she had been in the arena. I unfist one hand and reach for my belt with my other. The leather slides from the loops of my trousers easily, and when I unlace the ties, my cock rips free.

Arousal slithers beneath my flesh. Oh, how she'd glared at the three of us. Eyes turned accusingly on Ruen. The arousal skitters as I fist my cock, freezing for a moment. *Ruen.* My thoughts darken in rage.

No. I shake my head and tighten my hold at the base of my shaft, switching back to her. How she'd looked. A furious queen. She'd practically glowed with the promise of retribution and she hadn't fought, but she hadn't been afraid either. There'd been no fear in her eyes as she'd been chained and shoved to her knees. As her tunic and bindings had been torn and cut.

I open my eyes, finding the figure beneath me. My eyes land on the fresh wounds on her back. I swallow a grunt as my fist strokes up and then back down. Up and down. Again and again. Hunger rolls in my gut. Desire. The war of right and wrong was never mine to wage. I'm always on the side of the dark and despicable. Pain and fire. It's far more interesting here—*she* is far more interesting to me than any that have come before her.

My hand flies over my cock, reaching the head and cupping over myself as I squeeze once and then begin the descent. I stare at the markings that I know will likely scar. On a body as fragile as hers...

I grit my teeth as the swell of release bubbles up within me. Too soon. Not soon enough. A haze descends over my vision—there and then gone in the blink of an eye. Control. I'm losing control.

The sounds of hissing voices echo in my head. Questions. Thoughts. Curiosity. They want to know about this one. They want to know why she entrances me. So would I. Still, I shove their thoughts back with a violent command.

Later, I order the voices of my familiars. Immediately they back off and once more, I'm able to focus on the woman under me.

Had I wielded that whip, her skin would not be torn so harshly. My free hand hovers over the side of her spine where a particularly brutal lash has opened her skin to the air, revealing muscle beneath. Axlan could have gone harder, could have sliced her down to the bone, but he hadn't. A small mercy.

I would not have given her any mercy, but I would have made her enjoy it. A groan lodges in my throat as once again, release barrels towards me. Lightning races up my spine. My cock kicks in my grip, the skin drawing tight. Still, she doesn't move. She is neither awake nor asleep, but somewhere in between.

The grip of my fingers becomes unforgiving. Yes, if I had been the one to punish her so, she would have left with her skin intact, but her mind wrecked. I would have made her question everything she's ever known of pain, made her crave my callous touch. Each strike would have had her arching to meet me, rising to gift her flesh to mine.

Instead, Ruen had allowed this—I bite down a curse as it threatens to spill from my lips. *Focus,* I tell myself. *Focus on the Terra.* If I cannot then I'll lose my own damned erection and then where will she be without a Mortal God's fluids to help aid her healing.

Bastard Gods—forbidding us from calling another of our kind with healing abilities.

Rage cuts through the stimulation of my own hand. I want more. I want to part her legs and slide into the waiting heat between. I want to watch her eyes widen as I call upon my familiars and let them slide over her naked flesh as I dive between her thighs and suck from her a release so great and terrible that she won't even notice the scales sliding over her, keeping her pinned in place for me.

So beautiful is she. With her silver hair and eyes like cutting moonstones and storm clouds. My release slices up my spine, and a sigh escapes my lips. Beneath me, her lashes twitch, barely noticeable. Does she even know I'm still here?

My mouth tingles with the urge to lean over and turn her head back further. To take her full rose-colored lips with my own and truly taste her. A mortal. A Goddess. Neither means much to me. But she—she is wholly different.

It is in my nature to lust over pretty things that amuse me. It is my folly that they all eventually lose their shine. Yet even coated in blood and grime, I find her fascinating still. No loss in her glow, only a temporary reprieve from the light.

With one final stroke, my shaft leaps against my palm and I release a long, low hiss as my cum jerks from my cockhead. Thick, pale ropes rain down over her back and only then does she blink, finally, as if she feels something.

Breath saws in and out of my chest as I wait for the fluid to take effect. A moment passes. Then two. I frown as my cum sits over her blood and wound-marked back. *Nothing.*

Another silent curse. *Damn it.* I tuck my now spent cock quickly back into my trousers and lace them up but leave the belt as I, instead, lift my forearm to my mouth. A concentrated flash of power and I channel some of my familiar's features. Twin spikes of fangs protrude from my gums, punching out as I sink them into my own flesh.

"What—" She doesn't finish her hoarse, half there, question.

I rip the flesh clean off my own muscle and blood pours down my arm, flowing over her back. A choked scream echoes from her lips, her body jerking and then collapsing in the next instant as unconsciousness pulls her under.

Yes, I suppose that's not a shock. Not after all that she's been through. It's more surprising that she's managed to remain conscious as long as she has. I shake my head and use my hands to smear my blood over her wounds and flesh, painting her in me. My cum. My blood. My fluids heating as they touch her. *Finally.*

Within seconds, my arm begins to tingle as I heal. The skin knitting back together. Something sour scents the air as I peer down the little mortal's spine.

Acidic. Floral. *Wrong.* I sniff again and then taste the air with my tongue before hissing and nearly leaping away from her and off the bed entirely.

I bound onto my feet, my upper lip peeled back over my fangs as I glare down at the mess of her back. Even as my blood and cum soaks into her open wounds, little droplets of purple rise. I know what the damn stuff is without touching it. There's another scent below that acrid one, something far more telling. I blink. It cannot be right. It must be *my* Divinity that I smell there. My head tilts to the side, though, as I stare down at her back for another long moment. Yes ... my Divinity.

My attention peels away from her back to glance towards her face. The Terra's dark brows are scrunched in discomfort, her lips parted as she pants even in sleep. My blood is already working. I can tell as the strain on her face eases slightly. Still, it will be a few days before she's fully ready to return to her duties, before she's well enough for me to interrogate her.

I shove a hand up my face and through my hair, gripping the strands and debating pulling them out altogether. In the next moment, I drop my fingers and instead peel off my tunic, the wash of cream the only color on me. I redress the unconscious Terra in it, my fingers skimming her sides—to the clear outline of her ribs—as I pull it down.

Cold fury fills me. Unanswered questions spin through my mind. I take a step back and then another and another.

The window beckons me as my method of entering and exiting if I am to keep my presence here a secret. No doubt, Ruen's little stunt this morning before the public lashing of our Terra has the Academy faculty watching us with far more hawkish eyes.

I turn away from the little mortal once more and buckle my belt as I stride toward the glass pane. My skin tingles as I prepare to shift. I pause once, though, and look back at her.

When she wakes, she'll have much to explain. She better pray to far kinder Gods than the ones in this world because there's only so long I'll be able to hold myself back from demanding to know why the fuck there's *poison* in her blood after such a harsh punishment.

And if Axlan is responsible—if he and Dolos conspired to lace that damned whip with it—well, I've been waiting for far too long to kill our wardens, and she is about to give me the perfect excuse.

CHAPTER 6
KIERA

My back still aches with a fierceness that only being whipped into unconsciousness can cause. After the night Kalix snuck into my room and did whatever it was he'd done—something I can hardly remember—the temporary alleviation of my pain is gone. Though I can feel my skin knitting back together, slower than usual thanks to the poison steeping in my blood, the reminder of my agony lingers, swollen and raw. The worst kind of pain I've ever encountered even more so than the torture that had been part of my training in the Underworld.

The Belladonna works. Too well, if I'm honest. Perhaps, a less potent poison would have at least had me up and out of bed by now, pretending as if I was weak and in pain, but not *actually* being weak and in pain. I silently curse myself for my own inadequacy because that's all I *can* do.

Now, I'm drowsing against my cot, my back to the wall rather than to the door or the open air above me, a habit of facing all manner of exits and entrances to the room. I hadn't so much as fallen asleep before Kalix had come and gone as I'd passed out, face down on the bed, too swept up in the scorching agony at my back to do much else.

I'd passed out after Kalix, too, before I could adjust my body, before the training beaten into me could take effect. The fact that it's been two days since and I'm *still* this way is more of a cause for concern than the actual whipping itself. If I can't heal quickly then I'm as good as a sitting duck. A *dead* sitting duck if someone finds out the truth about me or they decide that leaving a punished Terra alive is too much generosity on their stone-cold Divine hearts.

When I feel a rush of cool air against my cheeks, my eyes pop open. The door moves, gaping with such concentrated slowness and silence that can only mean someone with Divinity is entering my room. That—plus I was pretty sure I'd managed to crawl up from my bed at some point and lock the damn thing before falling into unconsciousness again. I can still recall the sharp stag-gering steps I'd taken towards it and the way my knees had nearly buckled when I'd finally made it back to my bed.

Lock or no lock, I know it makes no difference if someone truly wants to get in here and get to me. That one tiny barrier, though, does its job. It alerts me to a change in the atmosphere. That someone has infiltrated, and my body tenses all over as my heart begins to race in my chest, in my ears, pounding with such gusto that I swear to the Gods it'll beat up my throat and out of my mouth.

The golden halo of hair coated in moonlight pouring in from my tiny sliver of a window that appears through the cracked door doesn't ease the rapid thrum of my heartbeat. *Theos*. Reaching beneath my pillow, I wrap my hand around the hilt of my dagger. My back is on *fire*. Every muscle screams for relief that I can't provide, not if we might have to fight for our life.

My heart squeezes inside me. A pang of something I'm not sure I wish to dissect rippling through my calm exterior. Had Dolos ordered him to finish me off since their damned whipping hadn't done the job? It'd been made pretty clear to me from the Terra orientation that those who offended the Gods were not exactly asked to leave the grounds. No, they were more likely to be put *in* the ground ... permanently. What if this is just more torture before they actually come for me? Before they decide to silence my impertinent mouth forever?

Before I can ask myself 'why him?' though, 'why Theos?', he sets his eyes on me and jolts to a stop when he sees that I'm awake. *Shit*. I should've kept my eyes closed or shut them when I realized who it was. Now the edge of surprise is gone. My muscles tense in preparation for a battle, and I'm not entirely sure I can make it much of one. Not with the wounds on my back and the fact that any movement causes the shredded skin of my spine to stretch with renewed fire. Unfortunately, that one motion, my single act of stiffening my muscles does nothing but send sharp ripples of pain sliding down my spine and through the open and aching flesh of my wounds.

My hand eases against the dagger's hilt but doesn't release it completely. I hiss out a long breath as I blink rapidly, shoving the burning tears that threaten to break free back into oblivion from whence they came. Theos takes my distraction as an invitation, and he slides the rest of the way into the small room that sits below the Darkhavens' chambers. The door closes with a snick and another follows as he locks—or rather, re-locks—it. The rapid pace of my heart stutters. I hope he can't smell the fear in the sweat beads that pop up along the back of my neck.

"You're awake," he says quietly.

Unable to keep my discomfort and agony at bay, I flick him an annoyed glance. "Why are you here?" I demand, unable to force even a hint of subservience into my tone. The wolf that crawls beneath my flesh is a wounded animal, a raging monster. Angry. Hurt. Fearful. She doesn't wish to show vulnerability, and so she doesn't. If Theos wants to kill me for it, then so be it. At least it'll put me out of my Gods-damned misery.

Unfortunately, though, Theos doesn't end my unhappy and agonized existence. In fact, if he's at all bothered by my disrespectful tone, he doesn't show it. Instead, he strides towards me. His long legs eat up the distance between us as he narrows the small space between the door to my bedside in seconds. He doesn't stop until he's close enough that I can feel the heat of him. I unintentionally sway closer to it, images of tangled arms and sheets and hot, wet flesh slide over the back of my mind, caressing me like he had that night.

Mistake. The word pours through my mind once again. *It'd been a fucking mistake to sleep with Theos Darkhaven.*

Once again, I stiffen. And once again, my body punishes me for it. The stretching of my shredded flesh with the movements of my muscles brings tears to the corners of my eyes.

Don't cry, I tell myself. *Don't you dare cry. No one here cares if you're in pain and no one cares if you cry.*

Despite that cold reminder, I can still feel the prickle of awareness along my arms and the soft burning in the back of my eyes. As if the tears are resting there, just beyond my reach. I can neither wipe them away nor let them free so they just sit and they wait. If they're waiting for the day I'll unleash them, though, then they're going to be waiting a long Gods damned time.

Theos' puckered brow, as he stares down at me with an unreadable expression, forces me to try and sit up on my own. His hands are empty, hanging limply by his sides. Though I feel much better with the sensation of the cool hilt of my dagger against my palm, I unclamp my fingers from around it before I pull my hand out from beneath the thin pillow.

I pause.

Then, for some reason, I quickly push the dagger away from the edge closest to Theos, and carefully reach back, slipping it beneath my mattress as I hook my hands around the side of the bed to make it look like I'm using my hold as help to sit up further. I don't trust that Theos will take the hint that I'm most assuredly giving him via my angry expression, tense posture, and lack of dutiful respect to not come closer.

After all, everything I've learned about the Darkhaven brothers over the last few weeks is contrary to anything I would have expected from them. From the actual love and care they show their friends and the grief they hide from the world to the small bits of respect they show me —small bits of course, not including Ruen's spectacular attempt at getting rid of me—even though I'm a Terra.

Before I can open my mouth and demand to know

why Theos is here again, he looks at the nightstand and frowns. "Someone else was here." It's a statement, not a question. Yet, there's a light of confusion and curiosity and something else in his eyes when he glances from the nightstand to me again and then back. I don't want to pick apart that last emotion in those sunset-colored eyes of his. I don't have the energy to.

I follow Theos' gaze and frown at the pitcher full of water and the glass sitting there, taking up nearly the entire minuscule space of the small rickety table that masquerades as a nightstand. Beside the water is a small bag of crackers—something a sick person would be able to eat easily. *I* certainly hadn't been the one to put them there, neither the water nor the food. Had it been Kalix then? After I'd passed out? That doesn't seem like something he'd do, but it must have been. I was sure there'd been no one else since.

I turn my attention back to Theos to find that I was correct in my assessment of his intentions. He isn't taking the hint at all. Theos leans down, his face coming closer to mine, his lips and eyes mere inches from my own. It happens so quickly. The fact that I didn't even hear him shift causes my heart to leap once more within my chest. Is it because I'm wounded?

With a shaky hand, I lift my palm to my face and feel the sweat that has long since dried on my skin. Does it seem hotter than normal? Have I gotten a fever? An infection? I've seen a few common assassins lose their lives to the remnants of an old wound, infections, fevers, or illness in their blood, but I've never been one of them. The Divinity I possess should have kept it all at bay and yet … just how well did this fucking Belladonna work? My fingers itch to scratch at that place beneath my hair at the back of my neck, where the shard of Brimstone lies.

"Answer me, Kiera." My shoulders go rigid at the low, dangerous tone of his voice. It's like a silken-covered blade, that sound. "Was someone else here?"

"It didn't sound like a question," I throw back at him, biting down on the words to keep other ones—far more offensive and insulting ones—at bay.

"I'm making it one," he says. A moment later, a softer note of a musical quality is threaded through the two words he demands of me. That silk loses its sharpness and becomes as soothing as honey. "Tell me." *Persuasion*. Damn him.

"Kalix." I blurt his brother's name out before I can think better of it. In fact, I can't seem to think about it at all. My head is swimming with pain and exhaustion and thirst. My eyes revert to the water on the nightstand. If Kalix had left that water here, then there's no doubt that I shouldn't drink it. With his unusual nature, I wouldn't put it past him to slip something into it and see if I'll survive whatever else he wants to do to me than simply taunt me in my vulnerability.

This whole damned Academy is nothing but a pit of snakes. It'd been a fool's hope that brought me here, the hope that I'd ever manage to escape my contract with the Underworld, with Ophelia. Likely a trap or a trial entirely made up of her own desire to keep challenging me, to test me continuously. She would never be sure of me. She'd never be sure of anyone—not with the way she lived. In the shadows and dark, a queen sitting in madness needing those around her but unable to trust. I pity her as much as I'm grateful to and resentful of her.

Theos sighs, the soft whoosh of his breath blowing

out over my face. It smells of something spicy and deep. Rum? Had he been drinking before he came here? Because of Darius ... or because of me this time? The springs beneath my cot squeak as he sets a hand down on the edge and swivels to sit alongside me.

"What are you doing?" The question shoots out from me as he takes hold of my shoulder and pushes. Skin stretches and I cry out in shock at the red-hot fire as it zips up my back. I recoil from him, that movement too causing just as much pain as the first had. Those tears from earlier rise back to the surface. I stomp on them, squashing them into nothingness.

"Shit, sorry," Theos' apology comes a moment too late. He releases me at once but the pain still remains.

Fresh sweat beads pop up along my neck and forehead as I fight back the urge to gag. I'd already vomited up bile and water, all that resided within my stomach, not long after waking the first time, and the involuntary muscle spasms that take over upon the action do nothing to dampen the pain. I don't look to the floor where it'd happen, afraid to see it there. If Theos notices—and with his Divine abilities and heightened senses, he should—he doesn't comment. Clamping my fingers around the edge of the bed, digging into the metal, I breathe through my teeth in long hissing sounds.

"I was only trying to see the wounds," Theos murmurs, his tone far softer than I've ever heard it before —outside his bedroom that is. No longer cajoling, yet still silken and sweet. I hate that sweetness. In my current state, I struggle to know if he means it or if it's simply another manipulation. That little piece of my heart that I've tried to protect for the last decade craves something gentle, something kind.

I bite back an angry retort and pray that my next words come out with less venom than I'm currently feeling. "Any touch close to them ... pulls at the skin," I say, still panting in heaving breaths as the pain subsides.

Theos is quiet for a moment and then a long-suffering sigh slides from his lips. Him? What the hell does he have to sigh about? I'm the one with a back so shredded that it feels more like strings of ribbons cling to my muscles rather than actual flesh. I can feel his gaze on me, the cool rich warmth of his burning golden eyes, so like seeing the crest of a sunrise over the distant shores, and finally, I look at him. Really look at him. I meet his gaze and this time, I don't try to hide.

I let him see all the pain and agony in my expression, the resentment, the exhaustion that I'm sure darkens the skin beneath my eyes. Theos doesn't blanch from it. He doesn't shy away. Instead, he—far more carefully than before—lifts a palm to my face. He cups my cheek, his fingers like molten fire against my freezing skin. Cold? Wasn't I just hot? I feel ... *ugh,* groggy.

The swarm of darkness that had taken me into oblivious sleep before is creeping back in. I'm so damned tired. Not just in body, but in mind and soul too. Like all the energy I'd maintained, the effort I'd gone to in order to remain awake and aware as that whip had cut into my back over and over again, each lash slicing through flesh and muscle and leaving me bleeding out in front of the entire academy, has washed away. I've used it up. There's nothing left.

"You need more rest," Theos says quietly. "Lie down." His hand falls away from my face and my eyelids droop. I'm not even sure if he's using his persuasion on me or if it's just my own weakness that actually has me following his command. All I know is that I cannot resist it for much longer.

Theos shifts from the bed, standing and helping me as he reaches down, and instead of letting me just collapse back against the paper-thin pillow at the old, rusted iron headboard of the cot, he gently settles me down, holding my neck and head up with his palm when I can't anymore.

I don't trust him. I can't *trust him,* I remind myself. Yet, he treats me as if I'm fragile and he is terrified to break me. Fresh tears burn in the back of my eyes. When was the last time someone was this kind to me? He must be using his persuasion. I tell myself that, even when his voice, as he speaks, holds little to no actual Divine power.

"Close your eyes, Kiera." I fight it, fight against the urge to do as he says. Maybe it's because it's more natural to be ornery and bristly than it is to accept the truth of his words. I *do* need more rest. Sleep will heal me, it always does. I'm not sure if I can sleep with him in the room though. I don't want to find out if I'm just as truly broken deep down as I suspect. If even with this invisible truce between us I'm still so damned bitter and cold that I can't accept a modicum of tenderness because I just can't trust it or myself anymore.

"You should go," I say, even as I lie back down on the mattress that sags in most places. The outline of the dagger beneath practically digs into my side. "I doubt they want you to be here to take care of me after..." I let my words trail off. There's no sparkle or gleam in his eyes that belies whether or not he understands what I mean, but I know he does. As much as I hate to admit it—even in silence to myself—he and I are similar. Both trapped here with nowhere else to go and no idea how to fix the hollow aching damage we both hold in our chests.

I sigh again, breath misting in front of my face. Hot. Cold. Hot. Cold. I can't remember what I am anymore. "Just ... go," I finally tell him. "I'll be fine." Hopefully, I'm not lying.

But Theos doesn't go. He doesn't say a word as he shuffles me back, further against the wall without pushing me so far that my ripped-apart back touches it, until there's a sliver of space on the edge of the sodden mattress. Space for him, I realize a moment later as he toes off his shoes and then bends, reaching behind him to fist the fabric of his tunic in one hand and pull it up and over his head, dropping it to the dirty floor without seemingly a second thought.

I put my hand up against his naked chest as he climbs into the bed alongside me, pushing back as I gape up at him. All thoughts of sleep are driven back, not far, but just enough. "What are you doing?"

Those iridescent golden eyes of his land on me. Instead of answering, though, Theos' gaze travels down my face to my throat and then further. He pauses over the loose tunic I don't remember changing into, but I somehow must have because how else would it have appeared on me? I look down, following his gaze to find that my nipples are peaked against the fabric. Their outlines clearly visible without my bindings.

"I'm in no mood to—" I begin only to be cut off as he growls at me.

"I am not here to fuck you, *Dea*." The deep offended noise he makes in the back of his throat is anything but sarcastic. "You are hurt and we've been forbidden to request a healer for you. I am doing the only thing I know that will help."

"What?" I blurt out the question, stunned by his response. They were forbidden from requesting a healer? Had they already tried?

Theos shuffles down and doesn't say another word as he reaches for the scratchy woolen blanket that'd been discarded at the end of the bed. Gripping it with a disapproving scowl gracing his lips, he yanks it up and over the both of us. It's the only cover aside from our clothes to shield me from the new cold air that's swept into the room. Is that cold air, though, or my own body? At times I feel so damned hot and then shivering with cold. It's unnatural.

"I don't want you here," I try again, shoving lightly against his chest. As much as I can with my back throbbing in pain. My bones fucking ache. My head is pounding with an incessant low beat that won't go away. "*Leave*." The word escapes me, practically a plea for him to return to the warm comfort of his own chambers.

I cannot sleep with another near like this. I haven't slept like this in years, not since my dad—no I won't let myself think of him. Not here, not now that I've become this damaged thing that has to kill to survive. He'd be fucking ashamed of me. He'd be so fucking sad at what I've become.

Those tears again prick at my eyes and I slam them closed, blocking out Theos' unflinching face and the quiet thoughts that flit through my mind. I hope he can't see them, can't read how cracked open I am right now. Once my eyes are closed, I find I can't reopen them. My body won't let me. The exhaustion has finally won over. It has sunk its claws deep into me and it's dragging me down, down, down into the darkest of depths.

"Fine then," I hear myself whisper, the sound barely a crackle of noise in the deafening silence of the room. *His* silence. Because, even throughout my demands and pushes and begging for him to leave, he still hasn't. It's as if he's waiting for me to tire myself out.

Gods, how I wish I had some brimstone of my own if only to keep him and his selfishness at bay. One night, I'd told myself. I'd told *him*. It had only been one night. Yet, as I feel Theos' body inch ever closer in this pathetic excuse for a bed, the heat of him spilling over me, relegating the sharp, jarring shivers that overtake me into less violent trembles, I wonder if I'd suspected it would be more than that. If I'd secretly hoped that *someone*, even another Mortal God, could understand what it's like to live in a world that's constantly trying to rip you in half. Born of two wholly different entities and belonging, yet, to neither side.

The silence stretches on for so long that I swear I've fallen asleep to the hot and hard feel of his front against mine, of his muscles offering their warmth. But when he speaks, I know I haven't quite slipped beyond that cliff yet.

"I know Ruen did this," Theos says, his voice hoarse. It's barely a whisper in the deadened air above us, as if he doesn't want to admit this. "He was wrong, Kiera. He was wrong to do it and I'm sorry you had to go through that. I'm so fucking sorry."

He's not the one who should be sorry, I think, unable to voice the words as that oblivion clings to me, slowly but steadily tugging me further and further into the dark.

I want to open my mouth and tell him to shut up.

That if he's going to be here, then he might as well let me sleep in peace. I don't want him here. I've never wanted anyone here with me in these moments. When I'm battered and broken and beaten. Even Regis had been turned away time and time again when I'd come back from jobs bleeding and swollen and so damned soiled that I hadn't wanted anyone around me, not even myself. I'd wanted to rip my own body away, dump it in an ocean, and just fly. Let go and roar over the clouds, soaring higher and higher until no one and nothing could ever touch or taint me ever again. Not the piss and shit of the dead. Not the actions I'd done. Not even the blood in my own veins.

Theos doesn't leave though. In spite of my rigid posture and how I try to hold myself as far from him on the small bed as I can, he merely settles a wide palm on my thigh and shifts closer still. That hand on my thigh makes my mouth go dry. He cups and kneads the muscles there, softly, with far more care than he had when he'd tried to push me down on the bed before—as if he'd forgotten my actual wounds. His fingers move up and down in careful motions, working through the knots as best he can in our current position and I remember what it was like to have his hands on me for a different purpose altogether.

Close. He's so damned close. I hate it. Loathe it. Can't bear it, and yet … the prying motions of his fingers digging into my thigh over and over again are the last vestiges of the world that I feel before everything winks out of existence. Before that dark oblivion drives up one final time, wraps its talons around my still fighting body, and yanks me into that cool, dark night.

CHAPTER 7
KIERA

The sun rises on the seventh day following my punishment, marking the end of my reprieve from Terra duties. Dull muted light illuminates my otherwise dreary room in the north tower, but I'm almost relieved for it to be here.

By the fifth day of my incarceration, I'd felt well enough to stand and walk around my room. I'd taken to jogging in place and stretching the sore muscles of my back and arms and legs—all of which were not accustomed to being ill-used for so long.

Now that the week is up, I wake to find myself clearer headed than I have been since the moment I'd ingested the Belladonna. A poison I'll likely keep on the back burner for future missions even if I am grateful for Regis' foresight. More importantly, though, when I open my eyes on my final day, I find that I am blessedly and thankfully *alone*. There's no golden-eyed, white-haired Darkhaven in my bed to annoy the shit out of me with his mere presence. My eyes drift to the solid indent and outline of his shape in my thin mattress in memory.

I sit up as the sun's morning rays hit the barrier between the floor and wall across the room and stretch my tired and achy muscles. My back still twinges, but I'm definitely stronger than I had been throughout the week. Even if I'd been allowed to eat food dropped off outside my door by a quiet and nervous Niall, I look forward to actually leaving this tower. I make a mental note to thank Niall as I suspect he was the only one brave enough to deliver that much needed food.

Discomfort twinges through my spine and, using a small compact mirror that I'd stowed away in my bag when I'd first arrived at the Academy, I check the whip marks now staining my spine. They're red and still slightly swollen. Since the whip itself wasn't coated in a dusting of brimstone, there's a good chance these won't even scar, but I'll keep my back covered regardless as the markings finish mending.

I marvel at my own healing ability. The Belladonna had often made me dizzy or tired for most of the week, even after I'd started feeling better. I'd assumed that it would have worked even harder against closing the marks Axlan had left on me. Thankfully, not only are they closed and scabbed over—I'd taken the edge of a nail and pricked at the end of one lower on my back where I could actually reach—but the marks had seemed healed even beneath the scabs. Not that I'll be telling anyone that.

Wrapping an extra set of bindings I'd kept in my small pack around my chest and tucking the end of them between my breasts, I release a sigh of relief at feeling fully covered for the first time in days. I would have thought having them encircled around my back might cause the scarred flesh to ache further, but it's just the opposite. I feel as if I'm shedding a skin rather than putting a new one on, as if this horrible experience is behind me and I can simply move on—lingering pain or no.

Leaning over the bed, I lift the cream-colored tunic that I'd been wearing for the last few days and frown at it. I sniff the fabric, noting that it smells faintly of oakwood. It's definitely not mine. Unfortunately, however, as I scour the rest of the room, I can't find another tunic. I glance at the single dress that Regis had managed to stuff into my bag before I'd left. It's a dull, brown thing. Thick for the winter months with a bodice that laces up the front, easy for someone without help to do themselves. I contemplate it but decide against it. A tunic will be looser against my skin and far less painful.

"I should have brought more clothes," I mutter to myself as I slip back into the unfamiliar tunic and tuck it into the top of my trousers.

A knock sounds on my door just as I finish dressing, sans cloak since it had never been returned to me. My body goes stiff all over. I scan the thin wooden frame of the door for a moment before I dive towards the bed, ripping up the mattress and yanking one of the daggers from its hiding place. With careful, fast maneuvers, I slip it beneath my clothes at the small of my back, keeping the handle against my spine for quick reach if needed.

"Yes?" I call hesitantly, glancing at my pack and the various other hiding places where I've snuck my weapons in the room. I hate only having one blade on me, especially after my punishment and the threat of being found out, but it's not like I can just walk out of here covered in knives and expect no one to notice.

"Can I come in?" The muffled voice on the other side sounds light, almost breathy, and ... familiar, but not at all masculine.

I stride towards the door instead of answering and turn the knob in my fist, letting the wood swing inward to reveal the person standing in the short, darkened corridor. Surprise fills me. Maeryn stands there, her bright red hair pulled back impossibly tight and high, giving her features a sharper appearance. Little braids line the sides of her head as the rest of her mass of curly hair falls over her back.

She's dressed for the cold in a long-sleeved cream-colored dress with a brown, fur-lined cloak that only reaches halfway down her legs and cuts open to allow the sleeves of her dress to poke through where one arm is raised to knock again. Unlike Terra, Mortal Gods are not expected to wear uniforms, so it's no surprise to see her dressed as such. No, it's her presence that is the surprise.

My gaze roves over her in cautious interest and suspicion until I notice the figure standing behind her. Niall's cheeks are slightly flushed, his own hair brushed back and tucked behind his ears. There are slight dips beneath his eyes, shadows of purple, I realize. Despite that, he brightens when he sees me standing and offers me a smile.

Like his Mortal God, he is dressed for the cold. His dark gray uniform trousers and matching tunic peeking out from beneath the woolen cloak covering his shoulders. I spot my own cloak folded nice and pretty in his arms.

Maeryn steps forward and I immediately back up. "Your confinement is over," she says. "Niall informed me that you hadn't been allowed any visitors through the week or the attention of a healer, so I thought I'd stop by since he intended to bring your cloak back to you now that you're free to move around the grounds today."

No visitors? I think. Well, that explains why Niall had merely slipped the food next to my door before disappearing rather than try to talk to me as he normally would. It comes as no surprise that the Darkhavens had completely ignored that edict too.

My attention falls back to the Second Tier Mortal God before me. I vaguely recall Niall mentioning her parentage and the fact that her healing ability had stemmed from her God uncle. When her hand reaches out, obviously intent on touching me, I sidestep her, moving out of reach.

"Thank you for the offer," I say, "but I don't think that's a good idea."

Her lips dip. "What do you mean?" she asks, confusion clouding her pretty green eyes. "You're hurt. You can't be completely healed."

She reaches for me again, and again, I move away, holding up a hand. "I'm not," I say honestly, though I am faring better than would be natural for any human, and I don't want her finding that out. "But I wouldn't want either of you to get into trouble on my behalf."

"Kiera," Niall says, capturing my attention as I shift my head and look over Maeryn's shoulder at him. "Please, just let her check your wounds ... there's no way you're healed enough by—"

"What do we have here?"

Niall's face pales and he releases a startled noise as he jerks back and accidentally slams himself into the wall on the other side of the corridor. His eyes widen as he turns his head, slowly, to face the newcomer. Maeryn's open expression closes in an instant. She, too, pivots to face the man who steps into view.

"Kalix." Maeryn's once gentle tone is now completely hardened. *Interesting.*

With his slightly shaggy hair, normally hanging around his ears and chin, pulled up and held into a messy bundle on the back of his head with a leather band, Kalix steps into view and grins down at Maeryn. "Mary," he says in response to her greeting.

Her hands clench into fists at her side as she glares at him. "My. Name. Is. Maeryn," she growls.

I glance from her face to Kalix's. Whatever strange conversation is going on within the air between the two of them, it's clear that Maeryn does not like this Dark-haven brother. I can't blame her. He's not exactly the easiest person to like. I still remember the odd feeling of Kalix sitting on his haunches over me and my shredded back and the way he'd poured what felt like acid over my open flesh. I shudder at the memory and shove it down. That's something we will have to discuss later.

"I-I brought Kiera's cloak!" Niall rushes to explain, half stepping in front of Maeryn as if she isn't ten times more durable than he is. "I a-apologize for the rudeness, Master Kalix." He bows his head, prostrating himself before Kalix Darkhaven as if he half expects even speaking to the Mortal God to be the final nail in his coffin.

I roll my eyes and step around Maeryn into the hall. Ignoring Kalix, I reach for the cloak still held in Niall's grip. When he feels my hands on his, Niall's head jerks up, eyes widening in fear a moment before he realizes it's just me.

"Thank you," I say quietly, meaning the words. His grip on the fabric releases and I snap it out, regretting the way it makes him flinch back ever so slightly, before encircling it around myself and then tying it at my throat. "I appreciate you bringing this to me."

I turn back to Maeryn. "And I appreciate the offer for healing," I say to her, "but I wouldn't want you to earn the ire of Sir Dolos. I think it's best if your Terra avoids me for the time being." The sharp inhalation from Niall is the only sound he makes in protest. He knows I'm right, and if he doesn't, then I'll have to force the issue. Because with this latest stunt from the Darkhavens and the newfound attention the Academy faculty and staff will no doubt be eyeing me with, I don't have much of a choice but to curb any potential collateral. And if he sticks near me, Niall will be such collateral.

Maeryn's brow creases, but she doesn't say a word. I can see it in her eyes—she knows I'm right, even if she refuses to say as much. A moment passes, and then she finally nods to me before turning on her heel and stepping out of my room into the corridor of the north tower.

"Come, Niall, I wish to eat before classes begin." She doesn't look back as she starts walking. Niall, on the other hand, does. His eyes remain on me even as his feet carry him further away. I wait, half expecting him to bump into the wall or trip over his own two feet as he walks forward, but he turns back to give me the saddest puppy dog look I've ever seen on another being.

When the two of them are finally gone, I whirl to Kalix. My lips part and I stop myself. One whipping was enough for me. The next punishment I receive for breaking their asinine rules will likely be death.

I bite down on my tongue and grit my teeth. "Did you require something of me, Master Kalix?" No matter how hard I try to sound perfectly courteous, the words cut out of my lips as if they're verbal daggers.

Twin dark brows arch up and he blinks at my inquiry. A second passes. Then another and another. His head tilts to the side as he gazes at me, eyes slowly roving down from my face to the rest of my body. Heat pours into my veins as he pauses at the outline of my breasts, bound beneath my wrappings under the cream tunic. A smirk blossoms on his face.

"Yes," he says. "I require honesty, little mortal."

I honestly *would love to stab him in the throat,* I think.

Before I can respond verbally, however, Kalix continues on. "But I think that might be asking a bit much from you now as I expect you're still recovering from your punishment." He turns his back to me and releases his folded arms as he moves for the stairs leading up to the top floor of the north tower. "Follow me," he says. "The others wish to see how you're doing."

Tingles of power race through my limbs. All it would take is a single moment of weakness on his part. With his back turned, and his attention focused on the stairwell, I could do it, I realize. I could reach back, unsheathe my dagger, and have it planted in his skull in seconds. He wouldn't even see it coming.

Then I remember how he'd snuck into my room and washed my back. I remember now where the smell of the tunic I'm wearing comes from. *Him.* It's his tunic, not my own and he'd given it to me when I hadn't had one left.

I should *not* feel indebted.

Trudging after him, I level a dark glare on the expanse of his shoulders and then drop down to his ass as he walks higher, placing the rounded curves of his backside at eye level with me. A very nice, muscular backside.

I blink and shake my head. Fucking Gods. The Belladonna is still fucking with my head. Or so I tell myself.

CHAPTER 8
THEOS

R uen is deathly silent—so silent that I continuously forget he's in the room—as we wait for Kalix to arrive with the Terra. He hasn't spoken a word in the last seven days during her recovery. I suspect he knows that Kalix and I snuck away to care for her. Yet, he hasn't commented on that either.

Good, I think. Because I fear one word from him would send me into the final tailspin I just don't fucking need. One word from him and I'd be hard-pressed not to take a brimstone blade to his throat and give him yet another one of the scars that mar the rest of his body. Not that the Gods even deign to allow us to touch those. No. Brimstone blades and other weapons either made of or dusted with the stone are not for us to wield. They're too dangerous.

The floorboards outside the door creak and a moment later, I'm on my feet as it swings inward. Kalix appears first and then, as he steps to the side, I catch sight of the Terra. Her face is leaner than before this past week. The skin beneath her eyes is darker. But the storm cloud color surrounding her pupils is bright and ripe with emotion. Volatile emotion. My breath catches in my throat as she steps into the doorway and Kalix closes the door behind her.

"We need to talk," he says, flipping the lock before passing his hand over the handle. The ghosting shadow of a snake drops from his palm—the smallest of creatures. It slithers through the keyhole in a flash.

I sigh and for the first time in seven days, I feel my muscles relax. His familiar will keep a lookout in case any of the Academy's Divine ones have sent spies in any form —Terra or familiars themselves—to listen in on our conversation.

Now that the creature has ensured our privacy, I find myself striding towards our Terra in a flash. She jerks back slightly when one moment I'm across the room and the next I'm standing before her. I don't hesitate to take her shoulders in my hands and turn her around.

"Let me see your wounds—"

Before I can finish the command, the little mortal is gone. The movement so fast that I know she hadn't been the one to do it. I turn accusatory eyes on Kalix as he grins at me a few feet away with her arm in his grip.

"Now, now, brother," he says calmly. "Let's not get too intimate this soon. Oh, wait." He grins and cocks his head to the side. "Too late for that, isn't it?"

"Give her to me," I demand, reaching for her once more.

Kalix yanks her back out of my reach and clicks his tongue at me. "You do not command me, Theos," he says with a smile spreading to show teeth. "Leave the little mortal alone." His hand drops from her arm quickly and my attention shifts to her face.

There's no emotion there. Nothing. Just cool indifference. I hate it.

"*Dea*, you know we never intended for you to—" I begin, my chest aching at the cold look in her eyes only to halt as a gruff voice speaks behind us.

"I'm glad to see you up and about." At once, the three of us—Kalix, Kiera, and I—turn to face Ruen who's now standing several feet from us.

If ice was an emotion, then the look on the Terra's face would be layered in hoar frost. "As am I, Master Ruen." Voice like a glacial blade, Kiera bows her head slightly in his direction.

Shit fuck.

Kalix makes a sound in the back of his throat that is half amused and half rage. Considering his obvious interest in our Terra—and the fact that she's held out this long despite our long-forgotten bet—he's been none too happy with our eldest brother since her imprisonment.

Ruen looks at her, eyes spanning from her face to her throat and then her chest and hips and back again. A growl threatens to rip free from me and I step in front of her. "Well, now that we know you're alright," I say, turning back to face her. "We should inform you of a few new changes the Academy has requested." Demanded is more like it.

Kiera's attention shifts back to me. "As you say, Master Theos." She inclines her head again, the embodiment of a chastised servant. The dinner I ate last night curdles in my gut. I loathe this space between us— fucking abhor the fact that I cannot simply tell her to stop calling me 'Master.' Not now. This isn't my bedroom and we are not tangled in sheets and limbs, sweaty and soaked in pleasure.

I take a step back from her and another and another until I reach the lounge once more. I reach down and pick up the package that had been delivered to our chambers late last night by an elder Terra. Wrapped in parchment, I already know what lies within and it feels like something disgusting in my palm as I hand it to her.

She takes it and I note how careful she is to not touch her fingers to mine as the package passes between us. I swallow reflexively as she undoes the rough tie holding the paper closed, and when it opens, it reveals a new uniform. She stiffens at the sight of it. Bile dances in my stomach as the paper falls away, drifting to the floor.

A snort leaves Kalix, breaking the tension unveiled by the uniform. I glare at him as Kiera slowly turns and faces him. I can see it on her face—the desire to say something, to demand an answer from him, but she's careful. She keeps it locked inside.

That, more than anything else, eases the pain in my chest. She's not beaten down. She's angry. Fucking pissed. And she should be. Thankfully, though, she's careful too. She knows just how precarious her position is now.

Her punishment had been a warning to all other Terra, just as this new uniform is too. It's a way to mark her, to brand her for her insolence. Instead of the casual dark gray of the regular Terra's attire, this new uniform is darker. The fabric has no lightness to it. It's entirely made of black fabric, dipped and dyed by the elder Terra themselves, no doubt, to show her just how she's to be marked from here on.

In a place where uniformity is safer, she has been set apart for the disrespect of having broken a rule—one of the great rules of the Academy. I damn Dolos for it.

Would damn him physically if I didn't think he'd kill me without a second thought. If I didn't think my death would set off a chain reaction in Kalix and Ruen—as enraged by my eldest brother as I am right now.

"You are to wear this new uniform while you remain on Academy grounds," I say, biting out the words that had been relayed to us the previous night. "Should you require a new uniform, you will not be permitted to wear a regular one henceforth. Your disrespect will be known to all and you will continue to provide services as a Terra along with"—I breathe through my nose—"extra tasks to repay the Divine Ones for their mercy."

She continues to stare at the fabric in her hands. Knuckles white as she grips it so tight, I worry she might end up stomping past me and throwing it into the raging fire within the fireplace.

Instead, Kiera nods. "I understand." The words are a mere whisper, but even the quietness of her tone cannot hide the sheer fury in her voice.

I suck in a breath, but before I can speak, Kalix beats me to it. "If you're to survive here, little mortal," he says, swinging an arm over her shoulders, causing her to stiffen. I flinch, wondering if it brings any pain to her back, but she merely tips her head back to look at him, showcasing no evidence of the agony I remember on her features. "I suggest hiding your rage—if we can sense it, then there's no doubt that others will as well."

Gray eyes narrow on his face, but she doesn't deny her own emotions. Instead, she nods once. "I will take that into consideration, Master Kalix." Her attention returns to me, deftly avoiding Ruen's presence at my back. "May I return to my room to redress?" she asks.

"Yes, of course."

With that, she bows her head and twists herself out from under Kalix's grip. Behind her back, Kalix flicks his fingers and the door unlocks and swings open before she reaches it. She doesn't look back or even jump at the Divine ability. She simply steps through the doorway and disappears down the stairwell.

I scrub a hand down my face. "Fuck." The curse slips free.

Kalix chuckles and walks past me, clapping me on the shoulder as he goes. "And so dawns the age of our little mortal's vicious hatred," he murmurs, sounding more amused and excited than upset.

I close my eyes. There is nothing crueler than the hatred of a person you want to care for you.

CHAPTER 9
KIERA

I am marked and everyone knows it. If I thought the other Terra avoided me before, when all they knew of me was that I serve the Darkhaven brothers, now, days after I've been re-introduced to the routine of the Mortal Gods Academy, they outright ignore me.

No, that's not entirely correct. Some of the other Terra recognize and acknowledge me in the unique way of turning and sprinting, often stumbling or slamming themselves into walls, in an effort to get away the second they spot me. As if merely being in my presence would be enough to sentence them to the same punishment they all witnessed.

The only Terra not to run screaming in the opposite direction when faced with me is Niall. Though, he too, seems rather strained by my new status within the Academy. Whenever he lingers close to me, the other Terra either avoid looking at him as well or glare at him.

How I wish I could tear the Gods down from those pedestals they put themselves on. I bet if they were down in the muck and filth like the rest of us, they'd get just as bloody, just as dirty.

My hands clench into fists as Niall and I walk down the back hallway corridors of the Terra residence building. It's become all too clear that Niall and I have some sort of relationship to the Terra elders. Dauphine and Hael know that he's my friend and for that, I am increasingly regretful.

Had I known that befriending the slender boy who looks more innocent than worldly would put him in this precarious position, I would have turned away from him that first day at orientation. It's too late now.

As if reminding me of that fact, I peer at the small black spider that slides over the back of his dark gray uniform tunic and disappears into the back of his collar. Even if he doesn't know it, that spider is there for his protection. It, among many others, is keeping a careful lookout on Niall and his own Master as well as the rest of the Academy and keeping me informed should anything happen. There's a low level of buzzing heat that races along my flesh that warns me something very well might.

"Here." Niall swallows as he stops before a familiar door. It's the twin to Hael's office, made of dark scarred wood with a plaque that hosts Dauphine's name. I peer at him, waiting for him to reach for the door handle, but he surprises me.

Instead of performing the task he's been assigned— bringing me to the head Terra—he stares at the door as if it's about to turn into a mystical being of old with a thousand eyes and rows of terrifying teeth. Niall's pale face grows whiter by the second, so much so that the light smattering of freckles on his features—one on his forehead, another on his jaw, and a third just to the side of his cheek—stand out. I never noticed them before.

With a sigh, I reach up and touch his shoulder. He jumps as if I've branded him and those wide, doe-brown eyes of his that remind me of wild, innocent animals in the Hinterlands swing to me. "I'll be alright," I assure him, hoping I'm not lying. "Thank you for bringing me."

Niall's features tighten at my words and his eyes turn misty. "I-I—" He wants to apologize, but I can't let him. Not knowing who could be—*who most likely is*—listening.

So, I let my hand fall away from his shoulder and I reach for the door myself, lifting my other palm, fingers curled inward as I rap upon the wood three times and wait for a response. Niall's gulp is audible.

Dauphine answers quickly. "Come in," she commands from the other side.

I nudge Niall. "Go back to your duties," I whisper to him. "I'm sure Maeryn is waiting."

He looks back at me, lips thin and pale. "I'll ask her to see you again if you—"

I shake my head. "I appreciate it," I say, "but no, I'd rather not get either of you involved." That, added to the fact that I can't possibly understand why another Mortal God would pity a Terra like me—even if it's at the behest of her own. I still remember that night in the courtyard, the flower she'd handed me. It had been the nail in my coffin, so to speak. The proof—as if Dolos or any other God needed any—that I'd disregarded the rules of the Academy and therefore needed reprimanding. I'm as confused by her unnerving friendliness as I am by the Academy walls that feel as if they're slowly inching towards me, closing me in and keeping me trapped.

She's curious and I can't have anyone being any

more curious about me than they already are. I've already fucked up far more than enough for this mission.

With a careful breath, I release the tension in my shoulders, forcing them down, and nudge Niall again. "Go on, I'll see you later," I assure him.

Finally, he takes a step back and I move forward, turning the handle and letting myself into Dauphine's office. Without looking back at Niall, I close the door behind me and lift my gaze to the woman sitting behind the spindly desk shoved towards the back wall.

Just like Hael's office, this room feels like a more opulent version of the Terra bedrooms. Smooth, clean floors that hardly creak as I walk across them towards the slit of a fireplace on the side of the room. Flames crackle in the hearth, fluttering against the blackened and charred brick insides.

It's warmer than the corridor for sure. Almost too warm, as the heat has little other place to go but up the skinny chimney and the cold that leaches in from the tiny vertical window at Dauphine's back is hardly enough to balance the temperature in the room. Too hot in the winter, and I'll bet it's too fucking cold in the summer as well.

I say nothing as Dauphine stares at me over the half-rimmed glasses perched on her long nose. I've never seen her wear them before. They make her look far older than I originally thought her to be. A woman far closer to her sixties than her forties or fifties.

Her eyes, shrouded in masked emotion, dip to the black uniform I'm currently wearing. I'm thankful at the very least for the trousers that I'd been given rather than the skirts other female Terra wear. Still, though, the black is a sign of the Gods' displeasure with me. Dauphine's lips curl downward at the sight.

My lips twitch. She doesn't approve of the new uniform either. Interesting.

Dropping her quill to the desk, Dauphine sits back and removes her glasses, letting them fall to her breasts, held around her neck by the thin beaded ties that hang from either side of the frames.

"Though your original punishment has been meted out by our gracious Dean," she begins with a wiry twist of her lips, "your insolence and disrespect to our institution will continue to remain an infraction upon all Terra. Therefore, you will also be receiving added tasks to better serve the Academy and its needs."

I remain quiet. Waiting. That's what I do best. Watch and wait. If she's impressed by my lack of distress at her words, she doesn't comment.

Ripping a page up from her desk she waves it at me. "You will continue to serve the Darkhavens during the day," she states. "Your duties with them will conclude after dinner and you will be required to visit the library three days a week to help the Terra there by any means they request of you. There are a few … others"—I tilt my head to the side as she pauses there—"that have also requested your assistance. This"—she holds out the parchment in her hand—"is your new schedule."

I step forward to take it, unsurprised by the added responsibilities even if I am frustrated by the new leash it feels like. There will be little extra time for me to do much more than eat and sleep with these new restrictions. Certainly no time for me to hunt down my target once I get word—*if* I ever do get word, that is. I'm starting to feel as if this mission is little more than another of Ophelia's tests.

Dauphine jerks the paper back as I reach for it, her dull brown eyes meeting mine. "You are a symbol to the rest of this Academy, Kiera Nezerac," she states. "You are a symbol of the Gods' mercy." Her eyes narrow on me with meaning. "The Gods do not often show such mercy."

I am well aware. The words linger on the tip of my tongue, but I bite down, keeping them back.

"Should you fail to live up to their expectations this time," Dauphine continues. "You will not be the only one to suffer."

Cold ice etches into my heart, creeping around the organ I thought died long ago, but somehow forgot to stop beating. *Is she saying what I think she's saying?*

As if she senses my thoughts—or perhaps the shock I feel has surfaced against my will—Dauphine inhales sharply and nods. "There are plenty of mortals willing to take any and all of our positions here at this Academy," she says. "It would take nothing for the Gods to wipe us all out and begin anew."

No no no. I grit my teeth. I cannot have more lives on my conscience. Yet, Dauphine continues to stare at me, and I finally recognize what that enigmatic emotion was when I first came in. The shadow hovering behind the anger and irritation at having to deal with me. I'm surprised it's taken me this long to realize it. I know it all too well.

She's fucking terrified. Because as much as she dislikes me, as angry as she is at having been put in this situation alongside me, she knows that one more wrong move from me will likely have the rest of the Terra completely wiped out.

"Do the others know?" The question squeezes out of my lungs.

Slowly, Dauphine shakes her head. Her stiffened, sharply pulled back hair is tied in a bun at the back of her head, the grays glinting with the firelight and sunlight pouring in through the window at her back. "It would cause mass hysteria," she confesses. "Which is why you shall not reveal this truth to anyone else." The fear recedes, and in its place is pure determination as she glares up at me once more. "Your life is no longer your own, Kiera Nezerac."

I want to laugh at her statement. My life hasn't been my own for a long damn time. It's nothing I'm not used to. However, this new burden feels far heavier than before. Unlike those of the Underworld, the Terra here at the Academy are innocents. They are not trained assassins or thieves. They are not killers. By comparison, these mortals are all as innocent as babes. And now their lives are resting on me appeasing the Gods.

My stomach sinks lower. Bile touches the back of my throat. I swallow it down.

"Understood," I say in response. My fingers close over the paper in her hand and Dauphine releases it after a moment more of staring me down—as if doing so can further punctuate the severity of this situation.

I wish for nothing more than to cut my losses, send a messenger to Ophelia, and retract my agreement to perform this mission. Now, however, as the invisible shackles of Dauphine's words wrap around my wrists and throat, I know that I won't.

I can't run. I can't leave. If I disappear without warning, they all die. I have no doubt this threat includes Niall's life. I close my eyes as the parchment in my hand falls against my side. I don't even bother to look at it. I already know that I'll do whatever it says, regardless of the tasks assigned to me.

Enough blood stains my hands; adding more would be gluttonous of me.

Damn fucking Dolos.

CHAPTER 10

RUEN

The strain of hunger and interest permeates the classroom. It sets my teeth on edge as the feeling of it crawls over my limbs and down my spine. My own power rises from a core of steel that resides within me. Despite the pangs of my ravaged back, the skin covering my spine tightening with each shift in my seat, I clench my hands into fists and a waft of darkness spreads out from beneath my palm. It drops to the desk, sliding over the grain of the flat polished wooden slats, squirming and wiggling like live worms. I close my eyes, briefly trying to call the power back to me, but it denies my internal request.

Theos' eyes shoot down as he spots its release. I turn my head and glare down at one of the Second Tiers a few seats lower than my own at the back of Narelle's class. His dark head of hair is turned as he eyes the Terra where she stands against the wall along with the others. He's not at all the normal type of Mortal God to go after claimed Terra. I only dimly recognize him from a battle two years prior when he'd advanced from Third Tier to

Second. His name, however, escapes me. He must not have been memorable even if he'd made it out of the battles alive.

Try as I might, I cannot deny the urge to follow his gaze to where it's focused solely on my Terra. Her face still maintains the lines of sharpness that have yet to fill out after her days of starvation and then minimalistic eating during the healing process. Her shoulders are proud and thrown back, as if she's aware of the eyes on her and doesn't care. The only other servant who even bothers to stand nearby is the skinny brunette boy that Maeryn is so protective of.

A fist squeezes around my heart before lances of remembered pain from my own lashing skitter down my back. I reach back, my fingers gripping my shoulder as I casually try to work out some of the stiffness in the muscles there. It doesn't work. My hands fall back to the desk and more darkness wafts from my grip.

They're looking at her like she's a feast for their eyes, all of them. The students. The other Terra. Even Narelle, I notice, is decidedly working *not* to look her way. The black clothes she wears are a stark contrast to the gray stone behind her. The gray uniforms of the other Terra do their job, making them blend into the background, but unfortunately for Kiera, she's like a wickedly dark beacon now. Drawing everyone's attention far more than before.

I can't tell if it's bravery that keeps her chin lifted or if it's pure stubbornness. Probably a bit of both.

I inhale sharply through my nostrils, trying to convince myself not to react. As if my ability has a mind of its own, though, and it no longer accepts my control, the tendrils of darkness flow over the desk in front of me and slip along the floor. Curling around the chair legs, it reaches for the Second Tier—whose name I won't even bother learning—and zaps up his back.

Despite knowing I shouldn't, my lips spread into a smile as he stiffens. The illusion I send him is violent. Disgusting. He turns away from the sight, his face paling as sweat dots his forehead. Theos' steady golden gaze remains on my face. I don't look back at him as I unclench my fists and twist my fingers through the air, commanding the illusion now that it's slipped free. It's too late now.

The Second Tier immediately doubles over, his head slamming into his desk as he gags and then turns away from the friend at his side to retch into the aisle. Narelle, our instructor for this class and the Lower Goddess of Scribes, from where she stands at the front of the classroom, grimaces in disgust. The nosy asshole's body heaves with effort as he dispels his breakfast over the steps. It smells of eggs and putrid sourness.

Flicking her bony fingers at the boy, she grumbles. "Someone get him out of here," she snaps, revulsion clear on her face and in her voice as she curls her upper lip back at the sight of him heaving once more, a fresh wave of bile and puke spewing from his lips. "*Now!*" she barks with more intensity.

One of the Terra against the wall—the one furthest from Kiera, I note—jumps away from the stone and hurries towards the Second Tier. Hooking an arm beneath the Second Tier's arm and helping him up, the Terra, a pinch-lipped boy with a scar lining the side of his neck, hefts his Master against his side and hurriedly leads him from the room.

Narelle flicks her own fingers and the vomit that had decorated the steps ceases to exist, evaporating into nothingness as if it had never been. I sit back in my seat, my shoulders sagging with a modicum of relief I haven't felt in days.

She quickly goes back to the map on the wall and begins talking once more. "The first of the Great Gods descended into this realm, born of the Brimstone Mountain off the coast of Ortus," she states. "Tryphone, our King, and then his wife, Danai, Goddess of Motherhood. Many others followed, blessing the land of Anatol with their powers and gifts."

"And spreading their seed far and wide," Kalix says.

Several heads turn, lips twitching as others laugh. Narelle pauses, narrowing her eyes on my brother. He merely shrugs at the heinous glare she sends his way. Unbothered. I'm thankful for the comment, though, as the few students who'd noticed my actions with the Second Tier have retracted their interest and chuckle at Kalix's coarseness.

"You are part of that seed, Kalix Darkhaven," Narelle sniffs primly. "Your gifts stem from one of our Greatest of Upper Gods, the God of Strength himself."

"If he's so fucking strong," Kalix replies, "then why can't he ever seem to hold himself back from impregnating as many mortal women as he lays his eyes on?" Kalix arches a brow and there's a distinctive wrinkle upon Narelle's beak-like nose at his words.

"As the God of Strength, Azai is also the God of Virility," she snaps. "Were it not for him, you would not exist, *boy*."

"Oh, Madam Narelle," Kalix replies, leaning back and kicking his legs out as he runs a hand down the length of his tunic, right towards his fucking crotch like the damned idiot he is, "I am no boy." I grit my teeth and resist the urge to slam his head into the table to get him to stop. What gratitude I'd had dries up.

Narelle lifts one brow, arching it at him even as her amusement gets the better of her. "Only boys consider themselves men before they truly are," she states, "but if you're so intent on disrupting my class, perhaps you can finish the lesson for me?"

Kalix groans and drops his hand away from his trousers. "What's the fucking point?" he grouses. "Everyone knows that the Gods came from the Brimstone Mountain in the South. We know that it's the site of the first Academy and that it's regarded as the holiest place on our continent. I have no interest in teaching such a subject. I'd prefer swordplay."

"Well then, I suggest you keep your mouth shut for the duration of the class period and let me be the one to teach this subject. Your swordplay will come soon enough."

Kalix gestures for her to continue, disinterest plain on his face. Narelle, however, doesn't say anything more to him as she turns back to the map and continues. The moment everyone's attention has been recaptured and my brother's outburst and distraction have come to an end, I lean over to him.

"If you ever do that again," I warn him, "I'll fucking slit your damn hamstrings before a mock battle."

On my right, Kalix snickers. I flick my gaze to him and he gives me a smirk. "Not going to thank me for covering for your ass?"

Tension digs into my muscles, solidifying them to stone. "I don't know what you mean," I say coolly. I do know, however, that too much insult to Narelle would have her caning not Kalix, but our fucking Terra. Another wound and round of healing that she likely can't bear.

Against my better judgment, my attention flashes to the side, over Kalix's shoulder where she stands, face unmoved by the scene before her as she stares stiffly at the wall opposite her over all of our heads.

Kalix doesn't miss my glance and gives me a solid nod of approval. "Any way we could get you to play like this more often, brother?" he asks quietly. "Because if so, I'm certainly willing to risk sliced hamstrings."

I arch a brow. "Is that so?"

On my left, Theos sighs. "I'm still pissed at you," he murmurs, low enough that no one outside of our small circle likely can hear. "You've yet to truly apologize to her."

"Mortal Gods do not apologize to humans." Even as the words leave me, though, they feel wrong. The urge to turn and look at the human in question slams into me with all the violence of a storm. It comes on so quickly that I'm already half-turned in my seat before I realize what's happening, and I have to pivot back to face forward before I finish the rotation. I cross my arms over my chest.

My attention settles on Narelle as she waves her hand over the board at the head of the classroom and a map begins to appear. Long lines stretch around the continent of Anatol and then stars appear over three individual places. One on the northern cliffs, one in the eastern mountains, and the final, an island in the south.

Kalix cracks his neck to the side and leans back in his seat, tipping the front two legs up off the floor as he teeters precariously as if on a knife's edge. "I do believe this little human of ours is the most interesting thing I've seen in a long damn time," he says absently.

My head whips towards him. "*No.*" The denial shoots from my lips.

One corner of my brother's lips twitches upward. "What? It's not like Theos hasn't already fucked her," he says.

"That won't happen again."

Theos goes stiff at my side. "Says who?" His words are cold, and when I look back at him, it's to find his jaw clenched and his eyes narrowed.

For fuck's sake. I grit my teeth. "She is nothing but fucking trouble," I hiss at the two of them. "She—"

"What I do with my Terra," Theos cuts me off, "is none of your fucking concern, *brother*." He bites out the last word with no small amount of venom. "Stay out of it."

Once more, my hands curl into fists. Only this time, instead of letting my illusions span outward to release the fire broiling inside, I tamp them down. "If you have something to say to me," I growl as Narelle chatters on about the great history of the Divine Beings and how they entered this world, "then you can say it in the ring."

Golden eyes flash with fire. "Consider it a fucking challenge," he snaps back.

Kalix chuckles again. "This is going to be fun."

CHAPTER II

KIERA

S parks fly off the ends of clashing blades, raining down in front of the two Darkhavens brandishing their swords at each other. My head is full of fog and exhaustion. Dauphine's words from the day before swirl in my mind, and today is my first day with the addition of my new tasks. Once this is over, I'll be reporting to the Academy's library for extra work. The 'others' Dauphine had mentioned weren't noted in my new schedule and that concern hovers over me like a dark cloud.

I need to get a message to Regis. He needs to know how things have changed. The lashing and now ... my new routine. Then there's Carcel's arrival to think of. It's hard to think of anything though as I'm forced to stand and watch the Darkhavens practice their swordplay.

As distracting as they are in their classes, they're doubly so here. Kalix laughs, the sound catching on the stone walls surrounding us and echoing up to the sky as Ruen dives for him. Kalix relaxes back on his heels as Ruen circles him, crouched low, his face dotted with sweat. Unlike Ruen, however, Kalix has divested himself of his shirt and stands atop the deadened grass ring of their personal practice courtyard covered in nothing more than his trousers, boots, and the gleam of his perspiration. The chill in the air does nothing to stifle his obvious exertion.

I'm only so strong.

As if the bastard suspects it, too, he turns, swinging his sword up and over his knuckles before capturing the hilt once more and flicking a look my way.

Avoid. Avoid. Avoid. I order myself, repeating the word in my head as I narrowly evade his gaze. Unfortunately, averting my eyes from Kalix leads me to Theos, who sits off to the side watching me.

With his back to the outer wall of the buildings surrounding this courtyard as he reclines on the stone bench beneath him, Theos tips his head down. A single lock of white-gold hair falls over the side of his forehead, but those liquid sunset eyes remain in place. Fixated. Too damn dangerous.

My heart thuds against the prison of my ribcage. *What the fuck am I doing?*

Metal shrieks against metal once more, jerking my attention away from him and back to the battle going on in front of me as I stand with my back to the wall and my hands clasped against my back, waiting for whatever they might need. Not a single one of them acknowledges the flutterings of snow as the sky overhead darkens. The temperature dropped hours ago and I swear I can feel ice creeping over my boots. I glance down, but there's nothing. Being cold will put strange feelings into your head.

Ruen releases a growl, and I lift my gaze just in time to see him bare his teeth at Kalix as his brother laughs once more and swipes his sword down, deflecting Ruen's next thrust.

I follow the movements of their bodies with rapt attention. My own muscles stiffen and relax as I correct some of their actions in my mind. Were it me between them, were I the one fighting Kalix, I wouldn't attempt any feints such as the ones Ruen does. Kalix isn't that type of fighter. He's the dangerous sort. The kind who sees so much without ever truly revealing it. I note it in the way he moves before Ruen has—avoiding thrusts and attacks before Ruen even begins them.

He's not fighting so much as he's predicting each of his brother's movements. Not that Ruen is a poor fighter, he's just not the proper counter to Kalix. It's obvious they know too much about each other because, despite Kalix's easy avoidance of Ruen's attacks, the psychotic Darkhaven still finds himself on the defensive as Ruen steers him around the pseudo-ring.

"Damn it, Kalix," Ruen curses, dodging and rolling sideways as he swings out his sword, catching his brother against the side.

A wound opens on the right of Kalix's abdomen, the skin splitting in a thin line, and he reaches down, idly fingering the cut there. The pads of his fingers coat red with his own blood and when he pulls them away, he lifts his head. His forest-green eyes look directly at me as he slips his crimson blood-stained thumb into his mouth and licks it clean. By the time he lowers his hand back to his side, the wound has healed and all that remains are the smudges of red above his trousers.

A bell rings in the distance, the sound calling an end to the day. Ruen stands back and yanks his hand up and over his flushed face, pushing the dark strands of his ink-black hair away from his eyes. The cold has long since leached away what little warmth I had. So, when I shift against the wall, dropping my hands away from my back, little tingles attack my limbs, reminding them that they exist.

"We should get changed and cleaned for dinner," Ruen states.

No one answers him. The heavy silence of the court-yard remains. I press my teeth together, refusing to feel guilty for the obvious tension that remains between him and his brothers. From Theos' apology to me when he'd snuck into my bedroom, it's clear that I'm the reason for that distance and tension.

I never asked for it though. None of it. Not Ruen's betrayal and certainly not his brothers' support.

I bow to the three of them. "I must take my leave," I state. "I'm to report to the Academy library for extra duties."

Theos frowns at me and stands from his seat. "Extra duties?" he parrots.

I nod. "I apologize for not informing you," I say. "I thought you were already aware, but because of my actions, I've been informed that my schedule will double and I'll be assisting the Terra of the Academy library." Perhaps not only Terra, but I won't know until those 'others' Dauphine mentioned make themselves known.

Kalix strides across the courtyard to the stand of weapons that had been brought out by the Terra in charge of these private courtyards and tosses his sword into the mix. It glances off the stand and knocks it over, causing the rest of the weapons to go crashing to the ground with loud, clanging noises.

"You're our Terra," he growls. "Your duties with us are more important."

I press my lips together. "The subject of my *ownership*," I seethe at that fucking word, hating it with every fiber of my being, "is at the discretion of the Academy."

Kalix's expression darkens and his jaw clenches tight. He takes a step towards me and to anyone else, it would be a threat. I don't flinch. Instead, I tip my chin up further. Waiting. Daring him to do something. Punish me? No, he won't.

Ruen catches his shoulder and halts him. "Of course," Ruen says, though he doesn't look at me.

What? I think at him. *Can't meet my gaze?*

Anger sizzles in my veins. I kind of wish I'd been the one to train with him in this courtyard. Wish I'd been the one with a blade in my hand. I'd love to show him just how I feel about still being under his command. He might be acting far more courteous due to his own guilt, he might be a poor, sad, broken little Mortal God, but I don't give a shit.

He played the game and we both lost. He's a fucking asshole.

"I'll be going then." I deadpan and without another word, I turn and exit the courtyard. As soon as I'm within the corridor, more warmth enters my veins.

The complicated mess of this mission has well and truly fucked me. More than Regis, I need to get in contact with Ophelia directly. I must know if this was simply another of her tests or if there truly is a client and target. As it stands, I've been here months—fucking months—and there's been no update, no progress.

Ophelia will know what to do about Dauphine's confession. My fingers curl into fists at my sides, my nails digging little half-moons into my palms as anxiety skitters through me. She has to. I can't think of another who would be better equipped to help me in this way.

Getting out of this debacle, out of the Mortal Gods Academy, without killing or being the cause of death for so many will surely indebt me to her further. That dream of disappearing into the Hinterlands, of giving up the life I live in the shadows, is quickly fading from the realm of possibility.

Fuck me, but sometimes I wish I was more like Ophelia. I wish I could be callous. I wish I could be as natural and talented at taking lives, at erasing my guilt as she was. Maybe then I could walk away without looking back, even if I know doing so will kill Niall and plenty of others. All of them innocent.

The Academy's library is not a place where I've spent much time or any time at all beyond my initial introduction to the grounds. The Darkhavens are high enough on the Mortal God Tier hierarchy that anything they could ever need or want is more often brought to them than they're forced to seek it out themselves. A pity, considering, as I step through the thick double doors into what is quite possibly the largest room I've ever seen in my life.

Rows and rows of large arching bookshelves line each wall. The scent of parchment and ink hangs in the air. Curving windows, each of them just as tall and wide as the others, line the dome ceiling. The rays of receding sunlight pour in through each of them, throwing a canopy of various colors through the stained glass over the books and down to the desks that linger between each row of shelves.

I've stopped at some point, staring up at the windows and into the crystalline eyes of one of the depictions etched into the glass. It reminds me of the woman from Caedmon's office. Her sorrowful face and the darkness that surrounded her pale body as if she was a ghost encased in dozens of ravens' wings.

This place. The windows. The quiet reverence I feel as I stand amidst the tomes and dust. *It's...*

"Beautiful, isn't it?" A familiar soft, masculine voice speaks up, both finishing my thought before I have a chance to and offering a question by way of greeting. It startles me from my reverie so abruptly that I rip my gaze away from the images above me and whirl to face the man who steps out from the stacks of books.

Caedmon is dressed impeccably as always in rich royal colors of blue and gold. His tunic is snow white against his dark skin where it peeks out from the opening of the indigo jacket. The stitches shine bright, glimmering like the sun matching the pads over his shoulders. A careful floral design lines the front of his lapels.

My eyes lift to meet his. They're lighter than I remember. Instead of graveyard brown, they appear almost honeyed—like bleeding sap from a maple tree. I blink and suck in a quick breath before I jerk my gaze down and bend, offering my bow as a sign of respect.

Of all the Gods I'd expected to be one of the 'others' Dauphine had mentioned, Caedmon had slipped my mind. It hadn't occurred to me that the lone God who had shown me sympathy and even kindness would want to see me again.

"You may lift your head, Kiera." Caedmon is quick to

command me, but I keep my eyes trained on the floor. Something unsettling grips my chest.

Why him? I have to wonder. *Why is he here?*

Silent footsteps move towards me, stopping a hair's breadth away as I see the tips of his polished boots beneath me. I swallow reflexively as the crackle of Divine energy spills over me, sliding over the back of my neck and down my spine. I want to reach up and slap a palm over the place where the brimstone still sits beneath my flesh, a mark not unlike the new uniform, a reminder of my place in the world.

Something tells me that Caedmon isn't here by coincidence but by design. "Kiera." I close my eyes at the gentleness in his tone. I dislike gentleness. I can't trust it. When fingers graze my shoulder, my eyes shoot open again, but still, I don't move. I don't look up. It takes all my strength not to pull away as Caedmon's hand moves along my shoulder and his fingers touch my chin, forcing my head up so that I have no other choice but to meet his softened gaze.

"You may relax," he says. "There's no one else here but you and I."

Lie? I can't tell. My heartbeat thunders in my ears. His posture is relaxed. Yet that only makes my muscles tighten impossibly further. Distrust sings in my blood and the still lingering effects of the wounds not yet completely healed on my back remind me that regardless of his seemingly kind eyes, Caedmon is a Divine Being. A powerful one, at that. He is the God of Prophecy. I am little more than an ant he's chosen not to step on.

His full lips twitch as if he can read my thoughts and when his hands move away from my chin, releasing me, I finally stand up.

"Did you know that your eyes flash a brighter silver when you're emotional?" he asks casually.

"What?" I gape at him.

His lips quirk, the corner of his mouth tipping upward. "Your eyes are like starlight and storm clouds all at once," he murmurs, and when he gazes at me I have the distinct feeling that he's not so much looking at me as he is looking through me. As if he's seeing someone else entirely. "Tell me something," he says, shaking his head as if ridding himself of untoward thoughts. "Do you get your eyes from your mother or father?"

I blink. "I'm not entirely sure," I answer him honestly.

He arches a brow, the action looking almost regal rather than curious. "You don't know?"

I bite down on my tongue wondering how much to tell him. Discerning which truths are harmful and which are innocent is not quite something I've ever been good at. Not like Ophelia. Not like Regis.

After what feels far too long, past the point of politeness, I answer him. "My father died when I was young," I say, choosing honesty. "I don't remember much of my mother, but I think my eyes are likely from her."

"Did she die as well?" The question, coming from Caedmon, doesn't sound like actual interest, but asked as if it's part of a dance he feels the need to complete. A step towards something I can't yet see.

"I don't know," I repeat.

He hums, the sound musical and soothing. My senses strain closer to him, relishing in the soft melodious note of his voice. I grind my jaw and grip the sides of my trousers, digging my hands into the fabric, threatening to rip it with the strength I extend in an effort to remain still.

Caedmon turns away and a breath I hadn't realized I was holding rushes out of my chest. "I'm sure you're still healing," he says as he takes a few steps away and moves towards a bookshelf. "So when it became clear that Dolos intended to punish you further, I volunteered to have you help me with my research."

"Your research?" I repeat.

I eye his back warily. My fingers stretch out at my sides, cramping from just how harshly I'd been gripping my trousers. The weight of the blade at the small of my back and in one of my boots is heavier than usual.

Caedmon lifts a hand and a light flares to life above our heads. My chin jerks upward as I realize that the last remains of sunlight have disappeared and the windows above are all dark now. More lights appear above the rows of bookshelves, lining the long corridor of parchment and ancient tomes before us.

The God of Prophecy looks back at me over his shoulder, the twist of his lips belying his amusement. "Yes," he says. "Being immortal is ridiculously boring, so many of my brethren—myself included—often find ourselves obsessed with the mysteries of the world."

I step after him. "What kind of mysteries?" The question feels pulled from somewhere deep within me, but once it's out there, I refuse to take it back.

Caedmon half-turns back to me but looks to the stack of books before him, his attention fixated on the volumes as he scans the shelf. "There are plenty of mysteries in this world, Kiera," he says. "Ones far older than even the Gods."

The history lesson from earlier that day resurfaces in my mind. I'd been distracted by Kalix as he'd antagonized the Goddess of Scribes in that reckless way of his. The memory of her words, though, hadn't disappeared. In fact, I'd latched on to them as I'd listened to her talk.

Unlike the Mortal Gods of the Academy, I'd never been given any formal education in a setting quite like this. All I knew came from Ophelia's books or the various members of her guild. An assassins' guild might not seem like the place for those of intelligent natures to convene, but good assassins—those that make it to old age and don't die on the job as many do—are scions of wisdom.

Newbies like Regis and I hadn't been officially welcomed, certainly not initially. Once we'd both proven that we wouldn't die so easily or fail Ophelia's harsh training, though, the elder assassins had taken us under their wings. We'd learned as much as we could from them. Street smarts. Book smarts—or at least how to fake book smarts if needed.

The kind of education the Darkhavens are receiving, however, is vastly different from what I experienced. It's colder and more detached. I'd appreciated my lessons with the other assassins and had mourned them when they hadn't made it back from jobs even if I'd gotten accustomed to losing people. The Gods of the Academy hardly seem to care about their students at all.

Save for this God—Caedmon. As if sensing my fixated interest, Caedmon reaches up to one of the shelves and flicks his fingers. A book wiggles against the wood and then shuffles out of its resting place high above our heads then slowly, it flutters down, floating right into Caedmon's waiting palm.

"*A History of the Hinterlands,*" he reads the title before tossing me a small smile. "I thought you might like to read this."

His arm arches out, holding the dusty leather-bound

volume out for me. "Me?" I say even as I take it from him. I hold the book between my hands, feeling the coating of ancient grime on its surface. The stiffness of its binding and the dusty feel of the pages poking out of its sides.

"You're from the Hinterlands," Caedmon states, not a question. "It's important to know where it is you came from."

"I—"

"As part of your punishment, I'll be giving you various reading materials while you assist me within the library," Caedmon interrupts, cutting me off before I can explain to him that I highly doubt either of my parents is from the Hinterlands. Certainly not my mother since she's a God much like him, but I doubt my father, who'd had no parents himself, had lived and survived the Hinterlands as a child. No, he'd most likely moved there because of me, to keep me safe and hidden.

"There will be days I won't be able to visit the library," he continues. "On those days, I will leave a note with the Terra who maintain this library when I don't request privacy as I have today. You are still to come and whatever I have written on those notes, you'll be required to do."

"Are you going to punish me if I don't get the tasks done?" I ask the question, not necessarily concerned with punishment, but more curious of his response.

Caedmon arches a brow at me. "I do not punish those who have not earned it," he states.

"If I don't complete your requests," I reply, "then wouldn't that mean I've earned it?"

He turns fully to face me, both brows drawing down as they furrow now. The expression on his face turns from surprised curiosity to deep confusion. "I know that you think poorly of Divine Beings, Kiera Nezerac—"

A breath shoots up my lungs and I bow my head instinctively. "No, sir, I—"

Caedmon holds up a hand, stopping my denial. "I humbly request that you refrain from lying in my presence, child."

I clamp my lips shut. *Fuck. Fuck. Fucking fuck.* Heartbeat galloping inside my chest, I bite down on my tongue and pray that whatever he decides to do isn't too bad. Though I'm nearly two weeks after the lashing, I still feel the phantom pain of Axlan's whip cutting through my flesh and muscle, almost down to my bone in some places. The skin might be healing, but the ache remains.

He knows. The harsh bite of fear claws at the back of my head. Vicious talons carve into my bones, ripping my insides to shreds as it consumes me. Bile rises up my throat, thick and hot and violent.

"Kiera, look at me." Caedmon's command is followed by a burst of his persuasion, the words wrapping around my head with invisible strength and forcing my gaze upward to greet his. "Calm yourself, child," he says. His eyes soften, but I can't allow myself to trust them. "Take a breath."

I gasp as I suck in air.

"Release it," he orders. I do, and the world stops tilting, the room no longer vibrating with the need to spin. "Good." He nods approvingly. "You're alright. There's no need to panic. Unlike my fellow Gods, I am not going to punish you for feeling anything such as resentment."

Shock, ripe and powerful, consumes me. *He isn't going to punish me?* Something of my thoughts must show on my face because his lips lift into a sad sort of smile—the kind of expression one might force upon oneself to comfort another but the brightness of it never quite reaches his eyes.

"I am old," Caedmon tells me. "Far older than many know, and I see much farther than even Tryphone knows. Past. Present. Future. They are all connected by the strings of fate. I understand why you feel the way that you do and I cannot comprehend the pain you must have suffered to get to where you are now."

How much does he know? My mind riots, demanding the answers I'm afraid to find. Cold beads of sweat pop up along my back and over the nape of my neck. My skin feels as if it's covered in a thin layer of frost. My heart, despite the breathing, is still racing in my breast, wild and uncontrolled. I continue to breathe evenly, forcing my body to maintain at least some semblance of control and calm, no matter how difficult it is.

"I asked you to visit me here, to help me with my research to give you time," Caedmon continues.

"Time for what?" My lips tremble with the effort it takes for me to voice the question. I'm not entirely sure if it's dangerous or not to ask it, but the need to know overwhelms everything else.

"Time to heal," Caedmon replies, unperturbed by my inquiry. "Time to consider what to do with the rest of your life—if you will rise to the challenges that will soon come before you or if you will turn away from them."

Challenges? What fucking challenges? Haven't I had enough of those? Haven't I done enough? Why can't I just be released from my contract and debt to the Underworld and disappear back into the Hinterlands? Scalding hot tears burn at the back of my eyes at the futility that weighs heavily upon my shoulders, warning me that this won't be as easy as I once thought. It's both a threat and a cruel tease just beyond my reach.

"I think that's enough for today," Caedmon says. "I merely ask that you read that and give me your thoughts on it when we next meet." He gestures to the book still clutched in my hands.

I'd forgotten it entirely, but at his movement, I glance down and squeeze my fingers around the side of the volume. "Yes, Your Divinity," I say, bowing my head again.

"Caedmon will do just fine when we're alone, Kiera," he states.

I don't know why, but whenever he uses my name it almost feels as if he's reminding me that I have it. Perhaps it's because the majority of the Gods and their children refer to the servants of the Academy as merely Terra—giving so few of them true identities even though they all have names. It's a kindness I didn't expect from one of his status.

With a frown, I give him a nod and back away a step. I wait, still half expecting him to chastise me for the action. He never does. Instead, he turns away and disappears down one of the aisles of bookshelves, the soft fall of his footsteps fading into the distance and leaving me utterly alone in silence and confusion.

CHAPTER 12

KIERA

Hinterlands: *the region from which all life formed.* I read the words, pressing the pad of my finger over the black script penned in what seems like old hands. The pages of the book that Caedmon had given me are worn, the edges cracked and yellowed with age.

The following events happened so long ago that there no longer lives any mortal or other being capable of remembering, but with this book, it is my greatest hope to share with all who may pick up this tome the beautiful mystery from which our world came to be.

I blink down at the words on the page and flip the book over, scanning the brown leather cover. Where I would expect there to be an author name, however, there is nothing. I reopen to the page where I'd left off and stare at the words once more.

"Other being..." I murmur absently. An interesting choice of words. Had the writer meant Gods? I wouldn't expect so. The Gods came along long after the start of our world or so the stories say.

Why would Caedmon give me this book? Was it a kind gesture to remind me of my home, of where I come from? Or is it something more from the God of Prophecy? I continue reading.

Humanity woke in the dark woods of the Hinterlands without any of the current weariness we now possess. The first of the humans were youthful, excited, and far beyond curious. They were brave.

A lump rises in my throat. *Brave.* No one now thinks that it's brave to venture into the Hinterlands. Everyone considers those who live beyond the edge of the Hinterlands foolish and too barbaric for civilized society.

Full of inquisitiveness, humankind left the Hinterlands to find a land devoid of life but not of beauty. The animals that had been born and raised alongside them crept out, following after the Brave Ones to find the new world welcoming to all. After some time, what we now know as the continent of Anatol became ripe and full of life thanks to the souls who were daring enough to leave their birthplace.

My eyes devour the page, scanning the contents, skimming long passages of how the first humans began to hunt and gather their sources of food. How they took saplings from the Hinterlands and carried them across the lands to build new forests. Hundreds of years of history pass in the blink of an eye as I consume the words on the pages of the volume in my grip, using nothing but the candle lit on my nightstand for reading light as the sky beyond my window had long since grown dark.

My education with the Underworld encompassed various subjects, but the Hinterlands are not a place for the Gods and my training was all about how to get close to them and kill them.

There are no dates in the introduction to the book,

which is written more like a conversation rather than textual or educational. That fact makes it easy to read and I can't stop myself as the flame of my candle flickers back and forth and the wick slowly melts away.

Though humanity may have left the Hinterlands behind to find solace in the new world they were to be a part of, the soul of life still resides deep within the forest beyond all that we know. Humans and animals were not the only creatures the Hinterlands gave birth to and there were creatures of dark and dangerous energies that refused to follow the young and reckless mortals.

Few are left to know of the truth beyond the mystical lands from which we were created. Few are courageous enough to dare cross its borders in search of those beings. Even the supposedly powerful fear what lies within.

Supposedly powerful? My eyes fall upon those words, pausing with incredulity. I'm more shocked that this book was gifted to me by a God, himself, considering the obvious distaste the author has for the Divine Beings— though they don't mention the Gods by name or title.

How in the world had this book not only been in the hands of a God, but on a shelf in an Academy dedicated to them and their offspring?

Centuries passed and the Hinterlands were forgotten by many. Once regarded as the holiest and most sacred of grounds, the Hinterlands and all that lay beyond it became a place of legend. The unknown hides within its groves and it is the unknown that all fear.

For those who wish no harm to befall the lands, however, there is nothing to fear as it will safeguard those that seek its protection and once you give yourself to the Hinterlands, they, too, will give themselves unto you.

A distant memory surfaces in my mind. My father's

ruddy face, gruff beard, and glittering dark coal eyes as he bent over the bed we'd shared, pressing a kiss to my forehead as he stroked my snow-colored hair away from my face. I'd never felt afraid of my homeland. Never once been filled with unease by the darkness that surrounded our small cabin. If anything, the forest had provided us with everything we'd ever needed—wood, food, and hope. Hope that my mother would return and that the three of us would be safe there.

I close the book, though I don't set it aside as I smooth a palm down the face of the leather binding. *Why had Caedmon given me this book? What was he hoping to accomplish?* I'm not so naive to think it'd simply been a gift. Gods did not give gifts unless they were indebted and the God of Prophecy had no reason to be indebted to me.

Perhaps this book has something to do with his research. What could he be researching though?

Glancing to the side, I note how low the flame of my candle has gotten. With a sigh, I finally give up my wayward thoughts and the bittersweet memories and decide to turn in for the night. I creep across my floor and place my book into the satchel that sits along the opposite wall, hoping for some reason that when this is all over, I'll be able to take it with me.

Once I'm back in my bed, it's a long time before sleep claims me.

CHAPTER 13
KIERA

Cold, wet slithery things crawl over my legs. I twist in my bed, the woolen blanket sliding down my torso. Something hovers just on the periphery of my consciousness. I shy away from it, pulling away from the odd sensation of the serpentine coils wrapping around my calves only to have more follow me. The scent of rain drenched soil and moss fills the air. My nose twitches as it grows thicker and heavier, twining around me with invisible hands that creep up my thighs and then between them.

With a gasp, my eyes shoot open and the world tilts as I'm jerked down the mattress, my legs split open and hooked over two thick muscular thighs. Instinct has me reaching over and ripping the dagger I keep hidden tucked between the stone wall and my mattress since the night Theos had snuck in. Before the shadow that falls over me can move, I have the sharpened edge of the blade pressed to his throat. I blink away the lingering effects of my sleep and stare at the face that comes into view before me.

Grinning wickedly and thoroughly amused, Kalix drops back on his ass. The movement causes my blade to nick his throat and a thin line of blood appears as it digs in. I waver between wanting to pull the dagger back and wanting to finish the job.

"Nervous, little mortal?" he asks, entirely unafraid of the knife I have pressed to his skin. I'm sure it's because he doesn't truly realize the depth of my secrets and how dangerous I am to him. It almost makes me want to show him. Then again, he's psychotic. No doubt, even if he did know, he wouldn't care. He seems the type to get off on pain.

Slowly, I pull back the blade, setting it to the side of my thigh on the sunken mattress before I lift my attention back to his face. "What are you doing in here?" I demand. My gaze flicks over his shoulder to my door and I follow up my question with a statement. "I locked my door."

Kalix's smile doesn't even dampen. "Yes, you did," he affirms.

I twist my head to the side and look over to the window. It's closed. The grate outside still in place. "Then how did you—"

My question is cut off as Kalix arches forward and his scent invades further. That dark fiery oakwood smell shrouding me, muddling my senses. "Do you always hide a dagger by your bed?" he inquires, his voice amused.

I press my lips together, gritting my teeth as I answer him. "Only when I worry that some pompous God spawn will sneak into my room without my consent."

Careful, I silently warn myself despite the anger curling around my throat threatening to voice the rage I've kept buried for days.

Kalix sighs as if my response is boring him. "You were practically devouring me with your eyes during sword practice today," he says. "What else was I supposed to do when you disappeared and went off to do *other tasks* for *other people?*"

I lean my head back. He really doesn't like me performing work for other people in the Academy. "What business is it of yours?" I demand. "I was commanded by the Gods themselves to—"

Kalix sinks down on me, once again interrupting me as he groans. His chest hits mine and his legs stretch over my thighs and calves as he presses his palms to the mattress on either side of my shoulders. "I don't care what those fuckers command," he mutters. "They should know better than to take what's mine."

Is he pouting? Even with Kalix's heavy form draped over me, I turn my head and peer at his expression. *He is* —his lip jutted out and his eyes gazing up at me from beneath the thick dark lashes that any courtesan or prostitute would kill for. *What the actual fuck?*

Bucking my hips beneath him, I strain to push my feet into the mattress and roll him off me. In response, Kalix merely settles that much deeper onto me, his hips trapping mine as our groins connect. I freeze.

"What were your tasks tonight?" he asks. The query surprises me far more than the feeling of the hard shaft against my thigh.

I roll my eyes up to the ceiling. There's no point in praying to Gods that don't give a shit anymore. Yet, still, I find myself sending out a hope—a wish—to the universe for Kalix Darkhaven to burst into flames. A moment passes and that wish goes unheeded.

Oh well, it was worth a try.

"Why do you want to know?" I ask instead of answering.

His hand reaches up and idly touches the end of my braid, his skin tan against the silver moonlight color of the strands. He plays with it for a moment, twisting the end back and forth before he pulls the leather tie free and the pieces unravel.

"I want to know everything you do," he admits. "Call it curiosity."

Obsession. That's what it is. A perilous obsession.

"Are you ordering me to answer you, *Master Kalix*?" I hiss out through still-clenched teeth.

He blows out a breath, the puff of warmth blowing over my collarbone. Tingles travel over the patch of flesh and goosebumps rise to dot my skin. My eyes slide shut as if needing to *not* look at him or else I'll lose the tenuous strain of control I have in my grip.

"No, I'm not ordering you, little mortal," Kalix grumbles. "I want you to tell me."

"And if I don't want to?" I shoot back, opening my eyes to find him grinning once again.

He shrugs. "Then I'll take a penalty instead."

I narrow my eyes on him. "What kind of penalty?" I demand.

His grin widens. "Deny me and find out," he offers.

No. Not just no, but fuck no. The feeling of his cock against my leg is all I can seem to think of. My insides clench and I temper myself, keeping my gaze steady on his face. He knows it too, the bastard. His hips shift forward, and coming from anyone else, it would be an innocent adjustment, but from him, it's anything but innocent.

Through the dark wash of his breeches, I feel him. The

hardness, stiff and thick and swollen. His lips spread ever wider, a hungry glint in his eyes as he gazes down at me. How fucked up would it be to fuck one Darkhaven brother only to jump into bed with another?

It would piss Ruen off so fucking much, an evil treacherous little voice murmurs in the back of my mind.

My tight muscles relax slightly at the idea and I find myself peering down at Kalix with a new interest. It *would* piss Ruen off, and I'm still holding a damned grudge for what he'd done. Fucking not just one but both of his brothers wouldn't be enough to pay him back, but it would be a start.

"Something on your mind, little mortal?" Kalix quirks a brow.

"Maybe," I hedge. I don't move to explore my sudden interest in him though. Not yet. I still need some information, starting with how the fuck he's managing to get into my room without waking me. This isn't the first time, but I damn well intend to make sure it's the last.

Kalix's breath brushes my cheek as he turns his head towards me and the feel of his lips touching my jawline has those goosebumps shooting up my neck as the baby hairs along my arms stand on end. I am a small creature caught in the claws of a predator delirious with the power he wields over me.

"Why are you here, Kalix?" I demand. "How did you get into my room when my door was locked?"

Out of the corner of my eye, I spot something at the edge of my room—the moonlight coming in from the window glinting off scales smooth and black as a tail slithers through a hole in the wall. Immediately, I jackknife into a sitting position. My jaw smashes into Kalix's head with the sharp movement and a burst of pain hits and then fades just as fast.

He rears back and blinks down at me, surprise etched into his features as his brows jump towards his hairline. "*What the fuck was that?*" Somehow, I already fucking know and I turn accusing eyes on the man above me. "Were you fucking spying on me?" Rage pours through me, red hot and volcanic. A molten fire that runs the length of my arms, causes my own power to slip free— just once, a bolt of current hissing between us.

Kalix sighs and leans back, putting a hand to the side of his neck and cracking his head to the side as he peers at me through lowered lids. "Of course I was," he says as if it's obvious.

My fingers inch back towards my dagger. He notices, and I freeze. Instead of being insulted, however, Kalix snatches the dagger up and flips the handle around, holding it out to me by the edge of the blade pinched between his fingers.

"Go on," he challenges in a whisper. "Show me what you've got, little mortal."

I want to. Oh, how I want to. If anyone could benefit from being knocked down a peg or two, it would be Kalix Darkhaven. The urge to be the one to bring him down from that pedestal of his rides me harder than his brother ever had.

Using the edge of the hilt, he tucks the grip beneath my chin and tilts my head back so that I'm forced to look directly at him. "What are you?" I demand.

His eyes glitter with delight as if he's been waiting for that question. The dagger falls from his hand and I catch it deftly before it can stab me in the thigh as I find the figure of a man above me suddenly gone and in its place is a snake. Not just any snake, either, but a massive green and black-scaled serpent with cold crimson eyes. The snake unlocks his jaw and a forked tongue flicks out.

I jolt as it flutters over the soft inner skin of my thigh, a gasp escaping me at the odd sensation of something damp, though not slimy, ghosting over my flesh. One moment it's there and the next, Kalix is back.

All of the air in the room is gone. I gape up at him in shock. It hadn't been a dream. The feeling of something slithering up my legs. The way he'd disappeared when I'd been taken to Dolos. For some reason, my mind had reasoned it away. I'd expected him to admit that he had familiars—I wasn't so naive as to think I was the only Mortal God with the ability—but not ... *this*. The ability to shift into a fucking snake.

This time, when Kalix smiles at me, I focus on the twin canines on the upper row of his teeth, slightly longer and sharper than the rest. Fangs.

"Any more questions, little mortal?" he taunts me, wrapping his arms around me and dragging me down the mattress until my back presses into the uncomfortable fabric. "Or perhaps you'll finally give me what I want and stop tormenting me by making me work for it."

I stare up at him. "Are you going to take it regardless of what I say?"

He pauses as if it never even occurred to him that I would refuse him. Still, my heart flutters in my chest at the sight I'd just witnessed. I take uneven, shallow breaths to calm myself, reaching for that place I'd trained myself to seek whenever I was too close to these kinds of emotions. Panic does nothing. Fear is only good in increments. If I let too much completely take me over then I'm as good as dead.

Cocking his head to the side, Kalix observes me with an unnerving intensity. The red gaze of the snake is gone and replaced once more by the jade of his green eyes. Another moment and my heart slows further until the repetitive *thud thud thud* of the organ reverberates in my ears and fades from existence. Quiet once more.

"You fear me," he states. A non-question. "But you don't run, you don't scream, you don't cry, you don't beg."

"No," I agree. "I don't."

He hovers over me, his face close enough to mine that his breath brushes over my lips. "*Why?*"

Because I would rather die than let my fear control me. I don't voice that thought.

Kalix is all dark Divinity and sensual threat. His very presence commands attention and I am helpless to do anything but look back at him and let him do his worst. No matter what that may be.

Silent seconds pass into minutes. Kalix angles his head lower. "Fine then," he murmurs softly, gaze falling over my face and then stopping on my lips. "Keep your secrets, little mortal. But I will have payment for my protection."

Protection? Before I can ask what he means by that comment, his head descends and his mouth pushes against mine, and I am utterly consumed.

It's only now that I realize that there's something decidedly lethal about Kalix Darkhaven and it has nothing to do with the excitement in his eyes when he holds a sword or is coated in blood. It's just ... *him*.

CHAPTER 14

KIERA

Kalix's kiss is a bruising, cruel action. There's no sensuality, no gentleness. Only hot, violent desire. I don't feel the pulse of his persuasion which means that when my lips part to allow him entry, I'm doing that all on my own. Once I decide to let this happen, all my inhibitions fall away and I kiss Kalix back with a ferocity I'm sure surprises him as he makes a little growling noise in the back of his throat. Suddenly, his hands are on me, around me, gripping my waist as he lifts me harder against him.

The hard ridge of his erection digs into my lower belly, a reminder of just how far this can go. How far I've already gone with one of them.

I don't bother trying to ask him why he's kissing me. I doubt he'd give me a rational answer or one I could understand. Kalix Darkhaven, I'm finding, is a man of little sanity.

My hand curves up and over his shoulder, pulling him down closer to me as I lift my hips against his and grind. A puff of air slips over my mouth as he pulls away and grins at me, repeating the action with his own body rolling against mine.

"Not fighting me tonight, little human?" he asks, nuzzling against the side of my throat even as he keeps his cock pressed tight to me. The only thing keeping us apart are the thin clothes we both wear, and I'm so hot, I feel as if I'm burning alive inside my own flesh.

"Would it do any good?" I counter, breathless.

The quiet laugh he emits is every dark, deviant thought I've ever had wrapped up into a single sound. It causes butterflies to blossom in my stomach and break free, fluttering up my abdomen and spreading out until they become tingles in my limbs.

"No," Kalix responds just before his head descends again and his lips crash into mine a second time. I close my eyes and lean into him, my nails digging into the shoulder I'm latched on to.

If he feels them, he doesn't react. No, all his energy and focus are solely on my mouth as he forces his tongue between my lips and then curls it around my own. The heat inside me is unbearable, but Kalix ... Kalix isn't hot at all. If anything, he feels cold. His skin is like frost as I retract my nails and skim down his arms and over his chest, pushing into the open neckline to feel his muscles.

He must have been outside before coming here, I think absently. It's the only excuse. Or ... wait, is it because he can shift into a snake? Snakes are cold-blooded. It's entirely possible that his body is—

My thoughts are interrupted as his hands rove down and curl behind my thighs. He twists the two of us, and my mouth rips away from his as the world spins and I'm suddenly sitting astride him, a massive male Mortal God lying beneath me. White flashes as he grins broadly.

Kalix cants his hips upward, rubbing himself against me in rough thrusts. Were we naked he would most assuredly be inside me. "Come, little human," he says. "Your heart is soft—you should put me out of my misery."

"By fucking you?" I gape down at him. This is a terrible fucking idea. Yet, I don't get off him. Maybe I'm insane too.

He lifts his arms back behind his head and threads his fingers together to prop his head up. The flash of tan skin beneath his tunic draws my eye. I liked feeling him, liked running my hand over his body and feeling his muscles and broad smooth flesh. As if they recall the memory, my fingers begin to tingle and inch towards the opening of his tunic.

"Why not?" Kalix asks with a slight shrug. "You fucked Theos. Wouldn't it just serve to get a little revenge on Ruen if you fucked me too?"

Definitely crazy, I decide. A part of me hates that Kalix is pointing out my own earlier thoughts, but at the same time … sometimes it feels like he's the only one who truly looks at me and understands. We're not all here to follow the Gods.

Kalix Darkhaven is dangerous in so many ways. I know I shouldn't, so why does it make me want him even more?

My core swells and wetness rubs against my inner lips, reminding me of the hot, hard cock pressed up between us. I swallow roughly, my eyes scanning down from his face to his throat. With his position, he's got his head reclined and it's open to me. It'd be easy to reach for my dagger and have it back against his neck before he could move. He wouldn't expect me to move as fast as him—or maybe he would and that's why he's baring his throat to me.

Is he testing me? My gaze flicks up to check his expression, half-expecting to find an amused, knowing look. There's amusement, for sure, but everything about his face reads hungry and uncaring.

I return to my perusal of him. There's still a smudge of blood from where I nicked him with my dagger. Thank the Gods for his quick healing ability because no doubt if Ruen were to see the wound, he'd have questions.

I blink. *Why the fuck would I care if Ruen has questions?* If I *do* decide to fuck Kalix, it will be because I want Ruen angry. I want to punish him for his betrayal.

"Penny for your thoughts, little mortal?" Kalix asks, lifting a brow. It's as if he's challenging me to follow through with this and regardless of how I ended up last time I fucked a Darkhaven brother—imprisoned and punished in front of the entire Academy—I'm stupid enough to still consider it.

What is it about these men that makes a woman lose all sense of reason?

Bending forward, my hair slides off my shoulder and curtains us between each other. "Why are you pushing me to fuck you so hard, Kalix Darkhaven?" I ask, tipping my chin with bravado I don't actually feel. "Can't get anyone else to do it?"

"Why would I want anyone else when I can have you?" The bastard answers my question with one of his own. He's playing with me like a cat with a mouse. Bite and retreat, watching and waiting to see how I'll respond. What I'll do. It makes me want to throw him out a window. Infuriating man.

"Who said you can have me?" I sit back up, moving

away from the temptation of his lips—lips that are still wet from our kiss.

His green eyes glimmer with a red hue, there and then gone just as fast. "You're a Terra," he says casually. "I can have any Terra I want whenever I want."

"Sure." He's not wrong and I hate that I can't deny it. The reminder that these God spawn can use and abuse their human servants leaves a sick feeling in the pit of my stomach. Would I have looked at human life the same way if my God parent had reported my birth?

"You can have anything and everything you want, Master Kalix," I state. "Save for a person's trust and heart."

Kalix, instead of being offended by my comment, merely unthreads his hands and drops them to my hips again. "Oh, little mortal." He breathes the words out as he sits up, putting his mouth right next to my ear as he speaks. A shiver rolls down my spine and I place my hands against his chest to keep him from getting too close. He already *is* too close—far too fucking close.

"If I want your heart," he continues, one of his hands leaving my hip to travel up my belly. I suck in a sharp breath but he keeps going, between my breasts until he pauses right over where my heart beats an erratic rhythm within the confines of my skin and bone. Storm and madness, that is who this man is. Who they all are. And I'm flying right into the eye of it. "All it would take is one second and it'd be mine."

Kalix twists his hand, fingers digging around my breast as the threat of what he means becomes clear to me. I can picture it too—my chest cavity ripped open and my heart sitting in the palm of his hand. The image is too clear to be anything other than my own survival instincts kicking into gear, warning me away from such a terrifying beast.

I don't give in to that fear. I pull away from him and stare into the forest depths of his gaze. "You can rip my heart from my body," I say, "but you'll never own it. You may take physical things from your victims, but there are pieces of them—of me—you will *never* be able to touch." The words are a hiss and I can tell that they confuse him because in the next instant, his hand falls away from my breast and he tilts his head at me.

With a furrowed brow, Kalix examines me, his eyes roving over my face to take in my serious expression. Even with the heat still throbbing in my core, I am not so weak as to let him get this close without ensuring that he knows just what kind of creature he's threatening. As much as I can anyway—because even if we're here in the secret darkness of my room, the both of us are still Academy wards. His decisions are not always his own and neither are mine.

"You truly do not want me?" Kalix's tone is rough with bewilderment as if he's never heard such a thing and thought that the other person was telling the truth. I note he doesn't react to my comment on his victims. It's as if the word rolled through his ears and off his shoulders, yet another accusation that he couldn't bother to concern himself with.

"What I want," I reply, answering his question with far more honesty than I know I should, "is freedom."

He blinks at that. A moment passes. Then another and another. By the tenth one, Kalix seems to have forgotten his earlier intentions entirely. He lifts me off his lap, and as he stands, peers down at me with frowning lips and a tight jaw.

I half expect him to say something caustic and demeaning—to insult me for confusing him so. He shocks me when he leans down and cups a hand around the back of my neck and brings me closer to him. Our faces are mere inches apart.

"Say no," he commands.

Fuck. My lashes lift as my eyes cut to his. There's no teasing glint there this time. Only seriousness.

"Say it," he repeats, his tone harsher and filled with power.

I don't. *I can't.* And that negates all that I just tried to tell him. Regardless of what I say and what I plan to do while I'm here in this Academy, there are some lies I cannot bear to speak.

Kalix sighs, and then finally, leans forward. His eyes remain open and so do mine as his fingers play at the back of my neck and his mouth touches mine. This kiss is nothing like the first. It's not harsh or mean but soft and curious.

Flecks of red and green play in his irises, distracting me from the sensual feeling of his lips playing against my own, plying my mouth open as his tongue touches me far gentler than ever before. My breath sucks into my chest and his hand stills on my nape. His eyes widen further and a bolt of fear shoots through me as realization hits where his hand had been.

It takes all my self-preservation not to cup my own hand over the back of my neck where his had been, *where the brimstone sliver is.*

Had he felt it? I hold my breath and lift my gaze to his once more as I wait for his questions. To my utter shock, though, his face gives nothing. His expression remains enigmatic. Even his furrowed brow has evened out and

Kalix just stands there for a moment more, looking at me as if I've somehow given him a riddle to solve and he's deciding if it's worth the effort or not.

A chill slides over my spine. I'm not entirely sure I want to be a riddle to Kalix Darkhaven. When he turns, unlocks my door, and walks out without another word a moment later, I'm left feeling like a broken piece of wood set adrift in the great wide ocean.

CHAPTER 15
KALIX

My eyeballs ache with a memory I'd somehow forgotten. The scent of the human sits in my lungs—crisp like a winter storm. Ice and snow and something else, something devious.

My little human, I call her. My little mortal.

My little liar is far more an apt name for her or perhaps one better, *my little thief*.

I walk through the corridors of the north tower back up to the chambers above hers as the darkened hours of the morning rest just outside these stone walls, and I think back to my time with Talmatia. The annoyance of one of our father's bedmates demanding one of us to service her, and to work in her pathetic excuse of a castle when we refuse, is nothing compared to the excitement I'd had when someone had stolen into her dungeons and freed the human prisoners she'd claimed had insulted her.

My lips twitch and I have to fight off the oncoming smile as I carefully enter our chambers, spotting a flash of light beneath Ruen's door. No doubt he's already awake and if he hears me and comes asking questions ... well, I have no problem telling him where I'd been—between the Terra's thighs—if only to see the battle of guilt and rage on his face. But I want to keep this new secret to myself a bit longer.

I make it up the stairs and into my room without ever hearing the creak of his door opening and when I've got my own closed behind me, I finally sag against the aged wood and let out a rush of breath. A chuckle erupts and I clamp a hand over my mouth as it shakes my shoulders and rumbles in my chest.

Oh, this is good. This is so very ... intriguing. When was the last time I'd ever had this level of interest in something or someone?

Never, I realize. Even the woman who had given birth to me had remarked at how indifferent I'd been. To her. To Azai. Only my brothers are impressive enough to keep me entertained. And now, *her*.

I push away from the door and snap my fingers as I stride across the room. All around me, fires flare to life, floating momentarily in the air before quietly drifting to their respective wicks. Casual Divinity allows these same small abilities to everyone with Divine blood.

Kiera Nezerac had used matchsticks to light her candle. Another giggle bursts out of me and I shake my head.

With another snap of my finger, the familiars I keep in the shadows slip from the cracks of my room. I push my thoughts into theirs, directing them to do my bidding, and they slither back, disappearing into the darkness as they follow my silent commands.

I bite down on my lip as I sink onto the end of my bed and put my hands back to prop myself up. There is a part of me—a small sane part that has constantly had to fight for space inside my head—that rears up and tells me I'm wrong, that it can't be possible.

It is, though. I know it deep in my soul.

Kiera Nezerac—the Terra assigned to my brothers and me—is not at all what she claims to be. She was there that night in Mineval, she was in Talmatia's castle. She was the one who'd slashed her blade over my eyes to hide her identity and now I know why.

My smart, wicked little thief. Sweet liar.

More laughter bubbles up out of my chest and this time, I don't stop it. I laugh and I laugh, letting the delight of this new piece of information clicking into place devour me.

I've never met someone quite as reckless as myself. Theos might attempt to assuage my need for companionship every once in a while—but he cares far too much for that to truly be the case. He cares if he lives or dies.

But for Kiera, *a Mortal God*, I think as her name echoes in my head—coming into a Mortal Gods Academy masquerading as a Terra, a human of all things ... this is beyond reckless.

I'd wondered at her scent. I knew somewhere, deep down, that I'd smelled her essence before. It'd been that night all those months ago in Talmatia's forgotten courtyard where Kiera had spirited away the imprisoned humans. Dangerous, audacious, and brash.

Now I know why it'd felt so wrong, why she'd seemed so much different—so much braver than any human that had come before her. She's a dichotomy like we are. Human and God.

That is why she seems to move so fast sometimes. The way she'd held the dagger at my throat lingers in the back of my mind and as my laughter finally tapers off as I run out of breath, I reach a hand up and finger the now dried blood crusted on my neck, my lips pulling into another smile.

A fresh rush of excitement buzzes through my bloodstream, vibrating the liquid in my body and spreading to my bones. Just as quickly, though, that surge of euphoria at this new puzzle I've found fades.

I lower my hand back to the bed and sit up straighter. More than simply being a hidden Mortal God and a lying Terra, Kiera is holding an entirely different kind of secret. The piece of brimstone I'd felt in the back of her neck shouldn't have been there—not just that, but it should be impossible for a Mortal God to live with the stone embedded within them.

For all the Gods have warned us, for all that we—ourselves—have dealt with the stone and its effects on Divine blood, to have a shard beneath the skin for long periods of time ... it would cause illness. A wasting sickness that she hadn't shown any symptoms of. Instead, she'd peered up at me, eyes wide and worried even if she'd tried to mask it.

I don't give a fuck if the Gods have forbidden hidden God children. Those old fuckers can all choke on their own cocks. Knowing that my brothers have no idea of the creature in our midst is by far the most amusing part of it all.

The brimstone piece in her neck, however, is one piece that perplexes me. Is it how she's remained hidden for so long? How had she done it? Someone had to have done it for her. The place my fingers had grazed it was in too specific a spot.

Dark rage blooms in my chest. The shard had felt like

a lock on her body, as if it was the back of a collar—one she could never take off.

Kiera Nezerac might be an undocumented Mortal God, but her secrets span further than that simple fact. And now that I know just how unusual she is, the allure of keeping her close won't be assuaged.

Whatever she came here for, whatever her goal is, she'll soon find that I have my own plans for the lying little thief.

CHAPTER 16
KIERA

S oft scratching noises follow the sound of quills against paper as they filter up to the vaulted dome ceiling of the Academy's library several days after that odd encounter with Kalix. I've managed to keep to the routine schedule that Dauphine gave me—including following the Darkhavens to their classes and returning after sword practice to this place. The only difference between the other days and now is the fact that Caedmon isn't here today.

In his absence, the Terra that run the library—compiling their volumes for any student or instructor who requests them and cares for the dusty collection—are my prison guards. Not that I'm considering this place a true prison. No, in fact, the Academy stacks, filled with various books and bits and pieces of knowledge gathered from across the continent, is more of a haven than anything else. I've grown accustomed to the scent of parchment and ink.

I turn another page, flipping through the books that

had been slapped down on the table in front of me when I'd arrived for my shift. The library Terra are vastly different from the ones that spend their days in the rest of the Academy. Most are older, with wrinkled hands and faces and cold eyes. They don't seem to be all that interested in me—not in avoiding or running away at least. They merely set about their tasks and give me the details of Caedmon's requests before flitting off to do whatever it is that they do. Returning books to their rightful places, cleaning the shelves, etcetera.

The sound of quill pens scratching against paper continues to fill the air and I stretch back, pushing away from the table as I bend a bit over the spine of my chair. I reach up and thread my fingers together, arching them above my head as I try to return the feeling to my limbs.

A book closes nearby with a loud and meaningful *thump*. I look over my shoulder, noting that the Terra that had given me these books and informed me that I was asked to read them all and write mini reports on each for Caedmon's research is eyeing me with a suspicious look.

Sylvis is her name and though she's closer to middle-aged than to youth or old age, her lean face is clean and unmarred by any makeup. Despite the sharp twist of gold and silver hair tied at the back of her head, creating a more severe expression than I expect she'd have without it, I have to acknowledge that she's a pretty woman. The coal-lined lashes flick up and then back down as she examines me from my stretching arms to my book stack —with more unread than read.

Her gaze narrows and she clicks her tongue before gesturing for me to get back to work. I blow out a breath, and a few strands of silver hair hanging in my face flutter up and then down as I turn back to the table and the remaining books. A grimace overtakes me as I look at all that I have left.

Either Caedmon is far crueler than I originally suspected or he's planning on being away from the library for several days. Otherwise, there's no way I'd be able to read this amount in the span of a single shift. I settle my gaze back on the book in front of me and re-read the passage I've already forgotten before making a note on the parchment that had accompanied the books.

I'm almost at the blessed end of the criminally dull book when a flurry of sounds distract me from my task. Lifting my head in the hopes of something to call me away from it, I feel them crash and burn as I catch sight of a familiar male walking through the shelves of books, heading in my direction. I have no doubt he's here for me, but I'd much rather shove my head into the book detailing the rise of farming and agriculture than talk to Ruen Darkhaven. Goat shit is far more appealing.

I flip back around and pretend to be absorbed into my book as he approaches. Distantly I hear the catering whispers of the other Terra, stopping and asking him if there's anything they can do to help him or if he's searching for something.

Damn it. *He is,* I want to yell at them. He's searching for me. *Why else would he come here? Had he found out about Kalix and me?* We hadn't crossed that line, but the almost still lingered in the air between us whenever I followed the Darkhavens between their classes. Perhaps Ruen had picked up on it.

My ears prickle with awareness as I listen for Ruen's responses to the Terra. Unlike their attitude towards me, they sound far kinder and even excited to see him here. I curse silently as he turns them all away, letting them all know that I'm fucking right. He's merely here to check on his Terra.

"How kind of you, dear," I hear Sylvis say.

Kind? Ruen? Ha. If only they knew. I fix my eyes on the passage in front of me and read it for what feels like the hundredth time even as my external attention itches to hear what they're saying.

"How are your hands?" Ruen asks.

Sylvis twitters and the sound of fabric rustling reaches me. I don't turn around. "I'm doing much better after visiting the Terra infirmary," she replies.

"Is it something the healers can fix?" My head tilts to the side. How well does Ruen know the Terra of the library? It sounds as if he's well-versed in talking to them if he's asking about things outside of books.

"No, unfortunately not." Sylvis sighs. "It is simply a product of age, dear. My hands are strained from all the writing, but I love it, so I will continue to maintain my position until my body gives out on me."

A moment of silence passes and I can feel my bones growing more and more tense as I wait for Ruen's answer. "I'm truly sorry to hear that, Sylvis," he finally replies, sounding for all the world like he means it.

I press my lips together as irritation floods me. He can offer kindness to Sylvis but not to his own Terra? *Asshole.*

Shaking my head in disbelief, I actually refocus on the book before me. I turn the page, watching the black letters on the yellowed parchment swim in front of my eyes before I reach up and pinch the bridge of my nose. A dull thud has taken up residence inside my skull.

The feeling is interrupted a moment later as a chair

across the table from me scrapes the floor as it's pulled out. I look up, not at all surprised to find Ruen Darkhaven there. I arch a brow at him as he peers back at me. Then, with careful and obvious intent, I lower my head and stare at the tome before me, not acknowledging his presence further.

Minutes pass. He clears his throat. I flip to the next page, keeping my eyes fixed even if I'm not reading a damn word. I'm not going to be the one to start a conversation. He's the one who came here, after all. I'm not on his time but Caedmon's.

A huff sounds from the most stoic and annoying of the Darkhavens and finally, he raps his fist against the table. "Are you going to continue to ignore me or ask why I'm here?" he inquires softly, lowering his voice to a whisper in deference to our location.

I don't lift my eyes as I respond. "Who said I was ignoring you?" I ask even though I definitely was.

"You saw me come in," he states. "I've been sitting here for minutes and you have yet to ask me why."

"Do you want me to ask you why you're here, Master Ruen?" I inquire lightly, closing the book and reaching for my quill. "I was under the impression that we were both content to just ignore each other." I scribble a few notes of what little I remember from the volume before grabbing another book and opening it up to the first chapter.

In my periphery, I watch him bristle. "I told you not to call me that."

I want to laugh in his face. "I'm aware," I say. "However, if you'll recall—the last time I was accused of disrespecting the Gods and their children, I was whipped to within an inch of my life in front of the entire Academy, and then I spent a week locked in my room to recover." I don't mention that had I been anyone else, I likely wouldn't have survived the punishment at all. I flip a page. "I *apologize* if it upsets you," I continue, biting the words out as heavy sarcasm fills them, "but I'd rather not suffer such a thing again. Therefore, from now on, you'll be Master Ruen and nothing else."

Silence greets me at that. It goes on for so long that when I glance up, I half expect the seat across from me to be empty. It is. But not for the reason I'd assumed. Ruen is up and out of his chair, crossing around the table as his booted, long legs eat up the distance quickly until he's standing right next to me.

The dark shadows under his eyes surprise me. I hadn't noticed them before because I was trying not to look at him too closely, but it's clear that he hasn't been sleeping, or if he has, not well. Without a word, Ruen reaches for me. Closing a hand around my upper arm, he pulls me from my chair and a strange buzzing sensation falls over me, like thousands of bubbles falling down my skin. He yanks me behind him until I'm almost stumbling to keep up—or rather I'm forcing myself to stumble just because it seems to irk him more.

Stay mad, Godson, I think snidely.

Once we've rounded a corner and he's stomped several aisles down until we're a good two dozen stacks away from the reading area where the other Terra and I have been for the last several hours, he releases me. I cross my arms and rub up and down—this far from the reading area and the subsequent fireplace, the library is far colder. I recline against the nearest bookshelf and blow out a long breath. A puff of white air dances in front of my face.

Ruen turns and strides one way, stalking several feet

from where I remain only to pivot back and fix me with a dark glare. Tipping my head to the side, I meet his eyes. "Something wrong, Master Ruen?" Then just because I know what he'll say, I reach for the strings of my tunic neckline and pull them out. "Would you like me on my knees or—" I begin asking as I widen the neckline and the curves of my breasts are uncovered.

"Stop!" In a blink, Ruen is there in front of me, gripping my wrists and halting me from finishing the rest.

I arch a brow. "You don't wish for me to undress, Master Ruen?"

He bares his teeth at me. "No, I fucking do not." Of course he doesn't. He's not the type, but that doesn't mean I can't torture him like this. Gods, I don't think I've enjoyed tormenting a man like this in so long.

Extracting my wrists from his hands with deft movements that take advantage of the weak point where his thumb and other fingers overlap, I take a step back, bumping into the shelves behind me. He eyes me warily. Good, he should be wary. I'm a wolf in sheep's skin and I'm angry enough to pounce if he pushes me too far.

Repressing a smirk, I slowly lower myself to my knees. "Duly noted," I reply. "I will simply pleasure you like this." I touch the ties of his breeches and once again, his hands capture my wrists.

"By all that is fucking Holy…" Ruen's curse is cut off as he yanks, using his hold on me to rip me up from the ground and shove my back against the books. A shelf juts into the center of my shoulder blades and I wince. He pauses, eyes locked on to my expression. A beat passes and then, he bows his head. "I am not asking for you to pleasure me, Kiera," he finally says.

"Then why did you drag me to the archives of the

library, Master Ruen?" I inquire, not at all impressed by the fact that he stopped at the first hint of my pain. Every time I call him 'Master' his expression grows thunderous and then guilty and then pained. Perhaps I would do to relax my biting tone a bit, but ... well, he brought my ire on himself with his conniving actions. Since I can't exactly punch him in the face and slit his throat without giving myself away, these small defiant little words and actions masked under the guise of *respect* are all I have.

Respect is like fear—it must be earned, not forced.

His head remains bowed as he replies. "I dragged you back here because you need to know that it's not just what you say, but *how* you say it that could be considered disrespectful. If the Terra here heard the way you just spoke to me—"

I roll my eyes. "What must they think of me right now?" I cut him off, giving up the pretense of politeness. "Do you truly think anyone would believe that I'm back here performing my duties for the one who was the reason for my punishment?"

Cool midnight eyes settle on my throat as he backs up a step, and then slowly, they lift up and up until they're level with mine. "Even if I were that type of man," he says, "which I can assure you, I am not, they won't think anything of the sort."

Another arched brow is my only response.

He sighs and takes a full step back and it isn't until he's leaning across the aisle against the other shelf that I realize how much heat he'd been emitting. A shiver steals over my shoulders and I cross my arms over my chest once again, staring at him as I feel my nipples pebble beneath my bindings and tunic. He waves a hand and a strange noise erupts on either side of me.

I pivot my head just in time to see the ends of the bookshelves extend outward, shooting down the room and disappearing into ... nothing. My lips part and I jerk my head around, but it's the same in the opposite direction. Just eons and eons of bookshelves with no end. I spin entirely and then look up, but the tops of the shelves are no longer several feet above our heads. Now they stretch on and on and on some more until the darkness above turns into the night sky. Stars glitter down, shining in a way that I've never witnessed before as if they're so close that they're providing us with their own light.

"What ... how...?" I feel breathless, confused, and utterly awed.

"It's to keep others from overhearing," Ruen's voice is quiet as he answers me. "And an illusion."

As if my head is being controlled by a puppet string and the thread has been cut, my gaze falls back to his face. "An illusion?" I repeat.

He nods once. "It's my ability," he answers. "I set an illusion back in the reading area to make the others think that the two of us were sitting there, talking quietly. Everything your illusion says will be nothing but respectful." And, no doubt, nothing of what I would actually say to him.

I stare at the man in front of me for a long, pregnant moment. I can't say what it is that's clued me in—the reveal of his ability or the look he's giving me. It reminds me of the same look Regis would often give me when we'd been kids and he'd stolen some of my favorite daggers to use for target practice. I'd caught him every time, and every time he'd had this same exact expression. I called it the guilty puppy look.

"You cast an illusion on me."

Ruen sucks in a breath and then blows it out. "It was necessary so that the librarians don't—"

"No." I shake my head. "Not today, during my punishment. That day in that arena, I thought I was going insane ... I couldn't feel the pain at first. There was a field and I felt like I was floating. It ... you illusioned me." My brow furrows, trying to comprehend. "Why?"

A vein ticks in Ruen's jaw, and normally I'd think it was a sign of anger, but he doesn't appear angry right now. That guilty puppy look is still there and then gone when he twists his head to the side and stares at the ground.

"Does it matter?" His question is nearly a whisper.

"It matters to *me*."

He grits his teeth, but still, I wait. I don't just *want* an answer, I damn well *deserve* one. After all that he did to put me in that position, why would he do something like that? Something else occurs to me and I eye him speculatively.

"Did you take away the pain or dampen it?"

"I can't ... take away pain," he says, sounding for all the world like he doesn't want to answer me. "I can only redirect it."

My heart stills. "I didn't feel it at all," I say, thinking back to that day. It feels like a blur in my mind, no doubt a consequence of the illusion I'd not even known I'd been under. "Not until the illusion was broken, so how..." The truth hits me as his eyes flash up to meet mine.

Redirect, he said. Someone had to feel the pain and since it wasn't me, it had to have been the one person in control of the illusion. *He* had taken my pain. Shock rolls through me.

But ... why?

No one has ever taken my pain for me. Sure, Regis might have helped to tape or bandage me after Ophelia's torture sessions or after a particularly rough mission, but no one had ever shielded me. The only person to ever do so is now dead. Why would he take my pain on himself if he truly sees me as nothing more than a nuisance and a danger to his brothers?

"You were right," Ruen says, breaking the silence that surrounds us as my words have drifted off into oblivion. "I played the game and I fucked up. I lost. It was one of the only ways I could think of to make amends. Unfortunately, the illusion didn't last as long as I'd hoped, and I'm sorry for that. I was..."—His face pinches tight as if he's searching for the words to use—"not quite fully in control of my abilities as much as I usually am." Because of his emotions or something else? I wonder. "Regardless, I never meant for you to get hurt because of my actions," he continues. "I simply wanted you out of the Academy and away from my brothers."

"Why is that?" I cock my head in the opposite direction, curiosity rising.

Ocean eyes flick to mine. "My brothers are dangerous," he bites out. Just like a wounded wolf might snap at anyone that comes near. "You rile them and you do it on purpose. I see the way you play with Kalix and Theos, after you..." He drifts off and then completely changes back to Kalix. "You excite Kalix's darker urges and I—*we*—can't let him lose control again. Any more and you'll find yourself broken and beyond repair."

"So, you tried to get me banished from the Academy for my own good then?" I deadpan, not quite believing it.

"Obviously, it didn't work." He glares at me as if it's my fault and in a way, I suppose it is.

"Do you think casting an illusion on me during my punishment would absolve you of your decisions?" I demand. Despite the harsh tone I use, I don't feel quite the same level of heat as I say the words. Damn him. I want to stay mad and he's making it far too difficult.

"No, of course not," he says quickly, "but..." He roughly shoves a hand through his hair, grabbing ahold of the dark strands and holding tight as he looks to the floor again, worrying his lower lip between his teeth. The skin around the scar that cuts through the side of his face tightens, growing white at the edges.

It then occurs to me why he'd sought me out and what he wants from me. A laugh erupts from my lips before I even feel it coming. His head jerks up at the same instant that I clap a hand over my mouth. The two of us stare at each other for long enough, but my amusement doesn't die. Oh, how fucking rich this is.

Ruen's guilt didn't just force him to cast his illusions during my punishment, but it's also forcing him to check on me. I can't believe it. The one Darkhaven I expected to not give a single shit about me is the one that can't fucking stay away.

I shake my head and drop my hand from my lips as another giggle pops free. I laugh and snort and feel tears in my eyes. Bending over, gasping for breath, I hold on to my knees, trying my best not to collapse under the weight of the ridiculousness of this entire situation.

And perhaps it makes me wicked—perhaps it makes me cruel—but I'm an assassin, not a true servant of the Gods and their offspring. I've had to kill and bleed to survive for half of my life. What's left of my soul is already shredded beyond repair. If he truly feels guilty then that's something I can use, something I *have* to use. Our lives aren't the only ones on the line.

"Do you want me to forgive you, Ruen?" I ask, dropping his 'Master' title.

Cool suspicion enters his gaze and he doesn't say anything, but that's alright. He doesn't have to. I already know the answer.

I straighten and move away from the stacks. One step and then another, I don't stop until I'm right in front of him. Our chests bump against each other and for the flicker of a heartbeat his eyes glance down to my cleavage before jerking back up, the edges of his lips turning down.

"I'm happy to offer you my forgiveness," I tell him honestly. "You know as well as I do that I'm the only one who can absolve you of the wrongs you've done against me."

Still, he doesn't say a word. Waiting. He might have made a good assassin, I think distantly. He knows how to be patient. That's always been difficult for me.

My attention drops from his eyes to linger on his lips. I wonder, dimly, if they're as soft as they look or if they're firmer like Kalix's. Does he cling to a woman as he fucks her like Theos or does he create distance even as he takes her in the most intimate of places? My lashes lift. I let all my curiosities fill my gaze and know the second his pupils dilate that he can read each and every one of them.

"I'll forgive you, Ruen Darkhaven," I say, lifting a hand and laying it against his chest. His heart thuds against my palm, pulsating in rapid beats. His mint scent is in my nose, filling my lungs. "And all I need in return is one..." I press closer. "... little ..." Our lips stop a hair's breadth away from each other. "... favor."

The second the word 'favor' rolls off my tongue, all

languidity in his limbs goes taut. I smirk, having expected that.

"What *kind* of favor?" Ruen demands gruffly as if he's waking up from a dream.

I meet his eyes. "I need you to help me get out of the Academy."

I need you to help me get out of the Academy. She wants to leave. I shouldn't be shocked by her statement. After all she's been through, were I in her shoes, I would want the same. I should be pleased by the thought of this girl finally out of my sight and away from my brothers, but I'm not. Quite the opposite. Before I can stop myself, I crowd her backward until her spine hits the bookshelf once more and my hand lands on one of the ledges, gripping it for dear life as I glare down at her.

"And just where *the fuck* do you think you'll go?" I grit through my teeth, the question coming out as more of an accusation. I don't give her a chance to respond as I catch sight of the mischievous twinkle in her gaze before I launch into my next words. "I'm sure Dauphine has told you what would happen to the rest of the Terra here should you make another mistake in Dolos' eyes. Leaving against the wishes of the Gods would be more than a mistake, Kiera. It would be a death sentence."

To her and everyone else—including ailing Sylvis. I put the Terra Librarian out of my mind and focus on the girl in front of me who tips her head back, silver hair sliding over her cheek as her gray eyes flash with some cool, dark emotion. There's no fear in her. No trepidation. If there is, she hides it damn well, and that only makes me more suspicious of her even as I want to bury my face in her throat and inhale that deeply pleasing floral scent of hers. Like the Elysian Fields of the history texts, she smells so divine that I worry one small slip and I'll be just as addicted to her as my brothers are. I'm already too close for comfort and I can't find the strength to pull back.

As if she knows what she does to me, the vile little creature before me tips her head back and grins. "Oh yes," she answers, confirming my assumption. "She told me." Then, as if she's not at all frightened of me—by the things I could do to her here, surrounded by one of my illusions with no one around to hear her scream—she pats me on the chest. *Pats me. On the damn. Chest!* Like I'm some wayward animal who just needs a good stroking to calm down. "I'm not going to be gone forever."

"No," I snap, ignoring her words. "Pick another favor."

She blinks those pretty stormcloud eyes at me and her grin widens. "So you *do* want my forgiveness."

I freeze and realize my own blundering fucking words. Damn conniving little—"If you want the favor," I say, cutting the words out through thin patience, "then I suggest you think of something else."

Kiera shrugs. "I don't want anything else."

This just gets worse and worse. I should've stayed away from her. Should have never let myself get so worked up by her. Yet, here I am, still contemplating the logistics of actually giving her what she wants if it'll mean relieving the guilt that has been tearing me apart inside each and every night until my ability to sleep has become nothing but a distant memory.

As if she senses my weakness, the vixen moves towards me. "I promise," she says, her tone soft and coaxing, "I have no intention of running away from the Academy and leaving the rest of the Terra to be cut down as recompense for my crimes."

"Then why?" I demand. "If you want me to help you, at least give me a reason."

Her mouth tightens, and I have to fight the urge to look at the petal soft rouge color of her lips. Instead, I study the barrage of emotions that flit across her face. She's not an easy one to read, that's for sure. Just as soon as she has an emotion—whether it be confusion, sadness, or irritation—it's there and gone. As if she's feeling them only briefly before shoving them back into their respective boxes. As if she can't allow herself to feel too much.

I consider her deeper than before at that thought. How much has a human from the Hinterlands been through to be so far away from her homeland, to have left that forsaken place to arrive here on the steps of the Mortal Gods Academy of Riviere?

Being so curious about one insignificant little human has already proven to be detrimental to my brothers. Theos wants her more and more. Though he doesn't think I know it, I'm well aware that he snuck out to see her during her recovery. The way he watches her as we walk the halls when classes are in session makes it obvious he's growing far too possessive. Kalix, too, for that matter, and even worse than Theos, if Kalix gets his hands on this girl ... well, I've never seen one make it out alive.

A beauty like hers doesn't deserve to be buried in a shallow grave, and all too often, that's exactly the end for young innocents. My one saving grace concerning Kiera Nezerac is that I know damn well she is no innocent.

"I need to see my brother," she finally says, ending my internal monologue after what feels like a lifetime.

I arch a brow. "That's why you want to risk your life and all the lives of Terra in the Academy?" To say I'm shocked would be an understatement. I almost expected something ... more from her, and not this disappointment.

Kiera's sharp gaze lands on mine and remains there for a long beat before she speaks again. "I'm not going to pretend to understand the relationship you have with your brothers, Ruen Darkhaven," she says, causing me to stiffen at the recalcitrant tone she slings my way. "What I do know—what I've gathered from watching the three of you, following you around, seeing how you interact with not just each other but with every other person inside this Academy—I don't think it's wrong to assume that you would die for them."

Even if it's not a secret she's revealing to me, her words are like daggers being thrown into my heart. I almost wince. She steps closer, unafraid, head cocked back as she glares up at me and our bodies collide. I hold my breath, refusing to inhale her intoxicating scent again for fear it'll drive me back to that brink of insanity that has me picturing what it would be like to rip her clothes from her body, turn her around, shove her head against the books, and slide my cock into her tight, warm, waiting hole.

"You tossed me to the proverbial wolves for the sake of your brothers," she continues. "You wanted to get rid of me to protect them." She rolls her eyes and whether she realizes it or not, it's certainly not the first time I've caught her doing that. It's strange considering I've never met another human with the same audacity. She has virtually no barriers around that attitude of hers, only when it seems to serve whatever silent purpose she has for being here.

Money, Theos had told me. A part of me hopes that isn't true though. As easy as it would be for her to be motivated by nothing more than cold hard denza, I think this woman is far more complicated than that.

"The three of you might have the same God parent, but it's obvious that you had different mortal ones," she states. "So, you're only half-brothers—and yet..." She taps a finger to her lower lip, drawing my eyes downward again before I can catch myself.

Fuck. I rip my eyes back up and she smiles at me knowingly. "Get. On. With. It." Each word is cut out from my tongue, sharp and deadly.

"What I'm trying to say," she finally concedes, dropping that tempting finger from her mouth to jab it into my chest, "is that you are not the only one who would do anything to protect the people you care about. I have responsibilities outside this damned Academy and I intend to make sure my brother knows about what's going on."

At her words, I close my eyes and inhale a long, steadying breath through my nose and exhale it out through my mouth. I do it a second time for good measure waiting until there's nothing left in my lungs

147

before I open my eyes and meet her gaze for what feels like the hundredth time.

"*Fine.*" The word is a concession and a death knell. She doesn't seem to truly understand the severity of her punishment and what will happen if we're caught so I have to make sure she doesn't do anything stupid. When her face brightens and she nods, taking a step back from me and turning to slip beneath the arm I still have locked on to the shelves, I stop her.

I grip her hip and push her back into the books, coming closer as she jerks at my touch. I flash my teeth at her—the facsimile of a smile as threatening as I can make it. "But there are rules to this favor," I tell her.

Her brow furrows. "I don't think you know what the definition of a favor is," she snaps. "They're not supposed to have strings."

I chuckle, the sound low and deep as it vibrates from my chest to hers. She shudders at the sensation and I have to hollow out my stomach and turn my thoughts to other things—such as that Second Tier vomiting in Narelle's History class—to keep my cock from reacting to the feeling of her body shivering against mine. It would be so damn easy to lean down and press my mouth to hers, to reach up and cup the breasts that are peeking out from beneath her tunic. I shove those thoughts back.

"Plenty of favors have strings, Kiera," I say, refocusing. "This one is only different in that the strings cannot be cut."

She glares at me and just as her mouth opens, I'm sure, to unleash a thinly veiled insult in my direction, I reach up with my free hand and press my fingers over her lips. "Take it or leave it," I tell her. "This will be your only chance. If I walk out of here without your agreement to my stipulations then you will not leave this Academy if it means I have to chain you to my bed and follow you around every single second of every day."

Her brows shoot up towards her hairline, and just because she knows what it'll do—I'm sure she must have some knowledge of what her proximity does to me, as hard as I've tried I've found it difficult to hide from her—she licks her lips. That pink tongue flashes out and touches the pads of my fingers, leaving a wet trail in their wake before they're gone again.

So much for keeping my cock in check. The damn thing springs to life within my trousers, swelling under the fabric until it becomes constraining and uncomfortable. My jaw tightens as I tear my fingers from her mouth and growl at her.

"Do we have a deal?"

Those glittering eyes of hers are twin pools of danger, enticing me deeper until I'm sure she means to drown me in them. Her lips curve into a cat-like smile. "Fine," she says repeating my earlier acquiescence. "We have a deal."

Gods help me.

CHAPTER 18
KIERA

Bird wings outside my bedroom window wake me the next morning and before I'm even fully cognizant, I'm up and out of bed. I rip open the glass frame and the familiar sight of Regis' messenger bird greets me with fluttering black wings. A breath shudders out of my chest as I spot the small, pale yellowed parchment scroll tied right above the bird's clawed foot.

The creature hooks its small feet onto the grate outside the window and I slip my fingers between the openings, untying the leather band before snagging the scroll and dragging it inside with me. The sun hasn't yet risen in the East, but the effects of the coming day have already begun to brighten the sky so I quickly unroll the message and read its contents.

Leaving for a job. Be back by the end of the week. No further word on C's arrival. — R

My fingers feel numb as I let the paper drop to my

nightstand and sag onto the rickety cot. The springs beneath squeal with age and I swear the smell of rust rises from under the bed. I close my eyes and pinch the bridge of my nose. Just when I got Ruen to agree to help me, Regis sends a message that he won't even be available.

"Damn it," I curse under my breath. I really must have fucked someone over in a past life—it's the only explanation I can think of for my terrible luck in this one. The dull throbbing ache at my temples that has been coming and going over the past few weeks now resurfaces, and no matter how hard I tighten my fingers against the bridge of my nose between my eyes, it doesn't ease.

I give up and let my hand drop. If Regis sent a note about his mission then that means he won't be in Riviere until his timeline comes to an end. I'm more surprised that he put an end to his mission in the note. He knows as well as I do that they can often take a wild turn that ends up lasting for weeks or even months. Exhibit A being my current predicament. Hopefully, his words mean that it's not a kill job and perhaps something else. I envy him for his ability to come and go as he pleases when I'm stuck here.

Regardless, I hop off the bed and grab a small blank scroll from my bag. I scribble out a note in response to his, letting him know I need to meet with him in person as soon as possible and to let me know when he gets back. I return to the open window and use the same leather band to tie it to his bird after setting the earlier note on fire and letting the ashes drop to the metal bottom of the candle holder on my nightstand. A quick stroke of the animal's wings sends it flying off, sailing first over the ocean's waves that clear the cliffs beyond before it circles back and disappears entirely from view, heading in the direction of Riviere's city proper.

With any luck, by this time next week, Regis and I will be face to face and he can help me get a message to Ophelia about the new complications of my current mission. I'm relieved, at least, to know that Carcel has yet to arrive. I dread seeing him even more than I do informing Ophelia of just how royally I've fucked up.

Scrubbing a hand down my face, I move over to the bowl of water I keep on my nightstand now and use it to wash my face clean of the oil and sweat of sleep. A light tingling sensation alerts me to a small intruder before I see my precious spider king peek its head out from beneath my bed. Stepping to the side to avoid crushing the creature, I give it space to skitter around my feet.

"I really should give you a name, shouldn't I?" I say absently as I pat my face dry and then pull my braid free, unraveling the strands as I finger comb the knots free.

The *Euoplos Dignitas* merely climbs up to the ledge of my window and stares back at me. "What would I even call you?" I ask it curiously, not really expecting an answer. Spiders, after all, don't have names like people do. Not to each other at least. "I haven't named a spider since my first familiars." And unfortunately, I'd not yet known that the average lifespan of most spiders is a year. My spider king, however, may live for a few decades if things turn out well.

The sensation of the spider's response flits through my head. I don't hear the creature's thoughts so much as sense its emotions. Right now, it seems quite interested in my words, though a bit confused by them. As if it doesn't know what I mean by offering to give it a 'name.'

Reaching out, I pat a finger over the top of the spider's

back, avoiding the eight black eyes that gaze up at me. "I'll think about it and get back to you," I promise before turning away to finish getting ready.

Less than a half hour later, I'm dressed in the black uniform that has the other Terra either gawking or running from me. I lock the door behind me as I head for the stairs, pausing when I see a shadow of a figure standing at the top. Coldness washes over me as I meet Kalix's stare and the small smile on his face. A moment passes, but he says nothing. Unease drifts over the back of my neck.

"Good morning, Master Kalix," I say politely, keeping my eyes locked with his as one might a dangerous predator that has found its prey in you.

He tilts his head to the side. "Yes, I suppose it is," he replies. "Do you know what today is?"

I blink at him. Was today some important day?

"No?" I rack my brain for information, trying to recall every minuscule detail of the Darkhavens' routines. It's been at least three weeks now since my punishment and though it feels as though the battles have long been forgotten, surely there can't be another one happening today. I haven't heard any bells ring.

Kalix holds out a hand with a cat-that-ate-the-canary smile gracing his beautiful lips, gesturing me forward. "Come," he says. "You'll see."

"Why does that sound like a threat?" The question leaves my lips before I can think better of it. Damn it. I've spent far too much time with the three of them. I'm growing comfortable and that's never a good thing. Comfortable means easy and easy means dead.

Kalix's smile only grows as he continues to hold his hand out for me to take. There's little other choice for me here, so I stride the last few steps that it takes for me to get to him and offer my hand in return. His fingers close over mine, warm and strong. It's a pretense, I know.

Of all the Darkhavens to fear, Kalix is at the top of the list. Not because his powers are somehow more unstable or stronger than his brothers', but because of his personality. Every time I look into his eyes, I wonder just what kind of creature lies in the deadened void that echoes beyond them.

Trepidation has never really served me well, but I feel it now as Kalix pulls me behind him, leading me up the stairs to the open door of the Darkhavens' chambers. My lips part in shock as I see not one, not two, but three elder Terra running around inside the main room. Their arms are full of fabrics and sweat clings to their brows as they rush between bedrooms. A few headless mannequins have been stationed before the big hearth in the main room and on each of them is a suit made of the finest fabrics. One of a deep indigo, one of a violent red, and another that is darker than the midnight sky itself.

"What..." My question drifts off as I slip my hand from Kalix's and a snarling Ruen stomps out of his room with a thunderous expression on his face.

He points a finger at Kalix, completely ignoring me as rage seems to sink into each of his features. "You could have fucking reminded us that the Day of Descendance was coming up," he bites out.

Kalix shrugs, unbothered by his brother's anger, and slides me an amused glance before returning his attention to the scarred and practically vibrating Darkhaven. Ruen doesn't even look at me as he shoves his hands through his hair and one of the elder Terra skirts around him with a length of lined tape.

The Terra's face is pinched as his lips pull down when he is forced to follow Ruen as he spins and stomps back to his room, the tape held up to measure the width of his shoulders. He stops when the door gets shut in his face with a resounding *bang*.

It's the Day of Descendance. Holy shit. I hadn't even thought about how the Academies would celebrate these Divine holidays. In the past, I'd never celebrated them myself. Only passed through towns as festivals had been set up and lights had been strung to perform the act of respect to the treasures of the universe for having come into our mortal realm to rule us all.

I turn wide, horrified eyes on Kalix and then look past him as Theos walks out of his own room, half-dressed as his trousers sag against the hip dips set very low on his abdomen. A very light, barely noticeable streak of pale hair leads down into the trousers right where his cock rests. I gulp down a breath.

"What does this mean?" I ask a little dryly.

Theos doesn't look nearly as amused as Kalix, nor does he look particularly enraged by the disruption to their morning like Ruen. "There's to be a party," Theos states coldly. "With everything..." He drifts off, gesturing around. I get what he means. Darius' death. The imprisonment. My punishment. Healing. Trying to get back to normal. It must have slipped their minds and it was never truly important in mine. "We lost track of the days," he finishes with a sigh.

I want to ask why the hell no one had told me, but then I remember, no Terra has had the nerve to approach me in weeks. The only one had been Niall and he no doubt hadn't even thought to warn me since he's likely under the impression that everyone knows about these things. He wouldn't have any clue that I've never even been to a Day of Descendance celebration. It was never something for me to celebrate beyond what it meant to my existence.

I'm not grateful to the Gods for coming here. Even if I'm only alive because they did. The harm I've seen them cause doesn't make my existence worth that sacrifice.

"Should I...?" I move towards the Terra female standing behind Theos, performing the same task that one of the males had attempted on Ruen. Her wrinkled hands jerk the measure across his back and then she circles to the side, wrapping it around his bicep as a strand of her graying hair slips out of the loose bun on the back of her head.

"No," Theos answers, guessing my question before I have a chance to finish it. "No, you don't need to help them. I'm sure most of the other students have already had their attire made for the event tonight. We were caught off guard when we got the invitation at midnight last night. Unless you can sew..." He looks at me with expectation.

I shake my head. Sewing up a wound? Fine. But clothing? I cast a glance at the mannequins and the luxurious glittering fabric of the suit coats sitting there. It's not my forte.

Theos nods as if he expected as much. "Then don't worry about it," he says. "Besides, you have to start getting ready soon too."

My head spins away from the mannequins. "What?" Me? Why would I have to get ready for a Day of Descendance party?

Kalix's creepy ass smile widens even further. I don't know how it's possible, but the damn thing takes up almost the entire lower half of his face. It's the most terrifying expression I've ever seen on him.

Theos blows out a breath and eyes me up and down as if he's measuring me the same way the Terra flitting around him like a honey bee is measuring him. "All claimed Terra are required to attend these kinds of parties," he explains and then tilts his head to the side.

Discomfort fills me, but I don't shy away or flinch from his narrowing gaze. "You of all people won't like it," he says. "But there are certain ... other requirements as well. Events held by the Gods, themselves, aren't like what you might be used to."

Even if I'm not necessarily sure what an event held by a God looks like, considering the only parties I'd ever been to were rough and tumble tavern brawls, I have to agree with him. Unfortunately, that only serves to increase my dread. That, combined with Kalix's unusually elated expression, means that this is nothing good.

I sigh. "What do you need of me, Master Theos?" I dip my head as another of the Terra men skirts around us to stop at Kalix's side. Though the man is taller than the average human and built a bit wider, his hands tremble as he holds up his own tape to Kalix's arm. Kalix, for his part, doesn't move.

Theos fixes me with those golden eyes of his, silently begging for my understanding. He waits until his Terra has finished measuring him and moves away, back towards the copious amounts of fabrics that are strewn throughout the room on lounges and even covering Ruen's reading table.

Kalix snorts, causing his Terra to jump in surprise. The scent of fear permeates my nostrils along with ... I wrinkle my nose and glance at the man, whose pale face is even more ashen, almost grayish. Did he just piss himself?

I glance at the man's trousers but note no stain. Still, my upper lip curls back in disgust. It's not showing, but even if it was only a little bit, I can smell the sharp, acrid odor. He, too, finishes quickly and hurries back to where the others are twittering around each of their mannequins.

Theos steps closer to me and my eyes settle on the expanse of naked male chest before me. Images of that one night we'd spent together circulate in my head. I drag my eyes up to his face, but that doesn't make them stop. No, instead, my gaze fixates on his lips, remembering the softness with which they slid over mine before delving down, down, down further until he'd sucked my clit and tasted my pleasure on his tongue before giving it back to me.

Heat crawls up my throat, choking me with a strange wanting that I've never felt before. One night. That's all it had been and it can't be anything more. I told him that, and I'd meant it.

"I need you not to unman me, *Dea*," Theos says, dropping his voice to barely a breath below a whisper. Something that only he and I—and maybe Kalix—can hear. His words hit me and force me back to the present rather than to the place behind his bedroom door where he'd taken me gently and roughly with everything I never knew I desired.

"That doesn't sound reassuring," I reply, matching his tone.

He closes his eyes, dark lashes lowering over his high cheekbones. A moment passes and then another. It takes Kalix's long breath for Theos to reopen them, shooting his brother a dark glare before returning his attention to me, expression softening the second he does.

I shouldn't feel the way I do at his easing tension when he looks at me. Like there's an opening in my chest, a hollowness that is waiting to be filled.

"You'll be attending the event with us as expected," Theos murmurs, "And Dolos is sending along the..." His words trail off, brows furrowing as he tries to figure out how to word whatever it is he's trying to say. "Ensemble," he finally decides to go with, "that you'll be expected to wear."

No, definitely not a good thing.

Then the door behind us opens and a new Terra enters, her face far more youthful than the other three as she bustles in with a mannequin clutched in her arms. She moves awkwardly, hefting the mannequin higher as she tries to keep the legs from scraping the floor as she sidesteps the three of us.

Her arrival doesn't cause a block of ice to sink to the pit of my stomach so much as the scraps of fabric that cling to the mannequin she's holding do. I gape in shock and horror as she walks across the room to set the damn thing up alongside the other three. Unlike the suits and jackets hanging from the guys' mannequins with the long sleeves and glinting, ornate buttons, this fourth one has no such coverage.

"That's not a dress." My words choke out as I stare at the sheer strips that curve down the female-shaped mannequin, pinned in various places.

Kalix snickers and shakes his head.

I can't punch a Darkhaven, I remind myself. If I tried, they would immediately know that I'm not as weak as a normal human. The desire to, however, doesn't go away.

It only grows as the new Terra flips through the fabrics and jewels that litter the ground and lounges. Picking up a thick golden neckpiece, she settles it on the neck of the mannequin before pulling the transparent fabrics up and doing something with her fingers that I can't see.

When she steps back, it looks like the strips of barely there material are coming from within the necklace. No, not a necklace, I concede. It might look sparkling and pretty, but I'm no ignorant innocent. That's not a piece of jewelry. No matter how many rubies, black diamonds, and topaz gems are encrusted into the piece—I see it for what it truly is.

It's a damn collar, and wearing it will be proof that I've learned my lesson for my disobedience and disrespect.

Now Theos' comment to not unman him makes sense.

Dolos wants me to arrive at the Day of Descendance party with a symbol of my submission not just to the Darkhavens, but to the Gods, themselves.

CHAPTER 19

KIERA

I stare at the dress—if it can even be called that—as it sits on my frame reflected in the tall standing mirror that had been brought in after the younger Terra had finished her duties. My fingertips feel ice cold as I trace the low neckline. I've been washed and primped and plucked like a damn chicken for dinner. My hair has been unraveled from its braid and rolls down my back and over my shoulders in long thick waves, curling at the ends.

The Terra that had been in the Darkhavens' chambers this morning have long since disappeared now that their jobs are done. My lips twist as I turn and a flash of long thigh appears as the sheer fabric splits all the way up over my hip practically to my waist. The only thing keeping the fabric from opening completely to reveal my intimate areas are the golden chains attached to either side.

The dress, itself, wouldn't be so damn offensive if it wasn't ostentatiously sexual. There's nowhere for me to hide any weapons. Reaching down, I finger the edge of one side, scowling at the shimmery light fabric. It's pretty, but the lack of appropriate coverage to hide a dagger or two leaves me feeling vulnerable. The collar encircling my neck is the worst part. It makes me feel like I'm choking despite its weightlessness.

Whatever metal it's made of, it must be painted. Real gold could never be this light. My fingers trail to where the metal arches up my throat on all sides, tied together at my nape by glimmering yellow stones that blend into the scale-like exterior. And as if the collar isn't enough to strangle me, there are matching forearm adornments in that same scale-like style starting from my wrists and moving up to just below my elbows.

It's half armor, half chains. All of it a reminder of my place.

I want to rip it off and throw it into the fire blazing in the hearth a few feet away. As if the sheer fabric wasn't enough to make me homicidal, the straps I'd used to bind my breasts beneath my tunics are gone, stolen away by the earlier Terra.

The only thing keeping me from complete and utter nakedness beneath the transparent cloth of the dress are the golden cups that dangle from the collar beneath the fabric and wrap around my back with the thinnest of chains. One wrong or too fast movement and it might snap. The matching golden thong on my lower half does nothing to curb my need for violence or make me feel the least bit covered.

I turn back around, lifting the long strands of my hair and pulling them forward as I examine my back. The markings of my lashes are still there—healing slower than I thought they would, but closed and now little more than white lines against my spine. In another few short weeks, they'll be completely gone. I pray that there will be no more surprises like this because should the Gods or the Darkhavens see that I haven't been scarred from that punishment, there will be questions that I can't answer.

"*Wow.* You look..."

Whirling around at the sound of Theos' breathless voice, I reach up, half intent on covering myself with my hands, but ... what would the point be? I'm about to walk out of these chambers the second the sun sets and follow the Darkhavens to whatever fucked-up party the Gods have decided to throw for themselves. I'll be open and vulnerable and very much on display for every person in the Academy to see.

I let my hands fall away and scowl—uncaring of how rude it is. "I look like a whore for the Gods," I snap.

Gilded eyes lock on to my body, traveling down over my longer than average legs and rounded thighs to the sandals that protect my feet from the floor. His perusal doesn't stop there, but instead slowly glides back up the length of my calves and then my belly, pausing at the place just below it. My pussy is barely covered by the scrap of gold satin that's the same damn color as Theos' gaze.

A hollowness sucks out of my stomach, emptying it completely as he finally drags his attention away from that place and up my breasts to stop at my throat. A dark shadow passes over his expression before he, at last, meets my wrathful eyes.

"I know you may hate being forced to wear this, but you *do* look beautiful, *Dea.*" The raw note of his voice strikes me deep. My mouth dries up. Theos' eyes can't seem to stop poring over me. The subtle way he shifts and reaches down to adjust himself in his pants should be disturbing.

It's not.

I'm still furious. My veins are full of the acerbic inferno of that emotion, but his words somehow manage to slip past my defenses anyway. As if he has a secret pathway only he knows to circumvent my rage. My shoulders slowly come down and I blow out a breath, a strand of my washed and curled hair fluttering away from my face as I do so.

"He's doing this on purpose," I say quietly. This is another punishment from Dolos. It has to be. One might think this is an ironic punishment for what I'd done with Theos, but Dolos doesn't care that I fucked him.

No one at the Academy does aside from Theos and his brothers and, maybe, me. Many Terra bend for their masters. My crime hadn't been doing the same, but in my actions that disregarded the rules of the Academy— entering courtyards where humans are banned and acting disrespectfully to those they deem superior to me.

Theos closes his eyes briefly and when he reopens them, the heavy arousal in them has been dampened. "Yes," he agrees. "He probably is. If it makes you feel any better, though, you won't be the only one dressed so..." he winces as his attention falls back to what can only be considered a sorry excuse for clothing, "lasciviously."

"There will be others dressed like *this?*" I gesture down to my attire as if he hadn't just spent the last several minutes eye-fucking me.

"That outfit is actually fairly tame in comparison to some of the outfits I've seen at these events," Theos admits. "The punishment is requiring you to attend.

Most Terra have tonight off and only favorites are required to attend."

As shocked as I am by his words, I have no time to respond as the door behind the reading table opens and Ruen strides out. His hand covers one of the glinting silver cufflinks shaped like a miniature wolf's head at his wrist, adjusting it as he moves. When he stops and raises his head, his gaze falls to me and all the casual ease Theos' presence brings evaporates. Red hot flames lick up my bare spine as the color in those deep oceanic eyes of his ripples with awareness.

My throat closes, but still, I try to breathe, breasts heaving with the effort. The vein in his jaw bulges to life, throbbing in time with my rapidly increasing heartbeat. Once again, I don't cover myself from his view. Unlike Theos, however, Ruen's eyes don't fall any further than the collar encircling my throat.

Dark blue and purple wisps appear at the edges of his hair as if his power is leaking out of him and he can't control its urges. The heat expands, trapped inside my body, as it swims through me, searching for somewhere to end its journey.

Theos glances between us, his brow puckering as he senses a change in the air. It isn't difficult to recognize. The tension is like a living current of lightning flowing between us.

"Ruen?"

At the sound of his name, Ruen shakes his head and sucks in a deep breath. As if his own breathing finally kickstarts my own, my throat reopens and air starts to flow again. Ruen turns away from me, practically turning his back to me as he glances up the stairs where the door to the third and final Darkhaven brother's room remains closed.

"Where's Kalix?" he demands.

Theos shrugs. "He hasn't come down yet."

"We're going to be late if he doesn't hurry."

I wasn't exactly expecting any sort of praise or compliment from Ruen which is why the irritation that skitters through me as he stomps towards the end of the staircase and completely ignores me is that much more frustrating.

My gaze slips back to Theos and skims down his attire. Both he and Ruen are dressed far more opulently than I've ever seen before. Their trousers are matching black, but that's where the similarities stop. Theos is dressed in a burgundy suit coat over a snow-white dress shirt that hangs open to reveal the expanse of golden flesh on his upper chest. The double-breasted jacket has two rows of gold buttons running up the front of his chest from where a corresponding belt rides at his waist. The upper right-hand side of the coat is folded back revealing the gold satin inside with a pretty thorn design creeping around the edges in red.

It's really not fair that he's allowed to wear so *much* whereas I'm being forced to wear napkins. With a scowling mouth, I leave off examining him further and glance to where Ruen stands, calling up for Kalix to hurry his ass up at the base of the stairs. Unlike Theos, Ruen's formal attire has no red at all. It makes me think that each of these suits were specifically created to match their personalities as well as their preferences despite the short notice.

A black shirt like I've only ever seen on fellow assassins from the guild peeks out of the collar of his suit coat.

It molds to his flesh like a second skin and arches up his throat stopping inches beneath his chin, hiding any extra flesh that would normally be bared.

What is he hiding beneath his clothes? I wonder absently.

Even as that curiosity fills me, my eyes continue their perusal. The jacket that he's donned for this eve is a rich violet indigo, a purplish-blue royal color. The wolf's head cufflinks sparkle from his wrists as he curses and then withdraws a pair of fingerless black gloves from his pockets.

He pulls them on just as the door above swings open and Kalix appears at the railing. My head tilts back and my insides clench. The Darkhaven I've always found the most dangerous simply because he's unpredictable and sadistic in so many ways moves down onto the top step and then descends the staircase as Ruen steps back. Kalix's lips curve up into a cruel smirk. He's enjoying it, the stunned silence that the rest of us can't seem to break.

He's wearing a skin tight black bodysuit underneath his clothes. It's not unlike the shirt that molds to Ruen's frame as it spans from the sides of Kalix's neck and only comes to a stop at his wrists. Unlike Ruen, however, the suit has been cut open from the neck downward, revealing tanned flesh and muscles that appear slicked with oils. The vest of pure onyx he's wearing gleams with blackened gems.

His booted feet hit the ground floor and they don't make a sound as he moves around Ruen, not stopping until he's in front of me. My head tips back further when he finally halts as his chest brushes mine. Emerald eyes glint with an open wickedness in them. *He's enjoying this.*

Kalix lifts a hand, just as he had that morning, offering it to me. My eyes fall to it and notice the silver and black chains crisscrossing over his chest and hips. It looks like a harness of some sort, dark and beautiful and simplistic. I blink as something else catches my eye. This close, I can finally see the embroidered image at the center of his chest just beneath where his neckline stops dipping at his collarbone. It's a snake. One of the venomous little creatures, not so little in the depiction, slithers up his chest and around to the back of his shoulders, reappearing on the other side and coming back to rest over his heart.

"Shall we, *little thief*?"

I've got my hand half raised to take his when his words hit me. I freeze. "What?"

Teeth flash and I swear, I spot fangs. Kalix captures my hand before I can pull it back and he drags me closer, dipping his head as he drops his lips right next to my ear.

"I know your secret, little thief," he murmurs, lower than I've ever heard him speak before. Quiet enough that I doubt even Ruen or Theos can hear. "Or should I call you my little liar now?"

My blood runs cold, but Kalix doesn't give me a true chance to respond. He laughs and uses his hold on my hands to spin me out of his arms and then back. "She looks good enough to devour, doesn't she, Brothers?" he asks, turning his attention to the others standing in the room with us.

I barely hear him. The dull roaring in my ears has taken over everything else. Horrible, bone-aching fear slides into me. My insides liquefy. My mind recoils.

No. No. No. This isn't happening. It can't be.

I'm spun again and my feet stagger. This time, it's not

an act. No pretending, just real unadulterated terror clutches at my throat.

He knows. He can't know, but he does.

When my eyes lift to meet Kalix's as he stops spinning me and the fluttering transparent fabric of my dress settles once more, he arches a brow as his smile stays in place. I should have known better than to think I could do this. I was arrogant. Cocky. Stupid.

Kalix brings me back to his side and lifts his free hand to my face, turning me to look at Theos and Ruen, both with tight expressions. It's clear they have no clue. Not yet. How long will that last? How long do I have left?

"Tell me, little *human*," Kalix says, the last word mocking. I close my eyes as his breath brushes my face. "How does it feel to be owned by three of the most powerful Mortal Gods? Do you feel powerful, yourself, having all of us surrounding you?"

My eyes reopen, but I can't make my lips move. No answer comes out. In this moment, none of them look mortal at all. They look like young and powerful Gods and I, their Divine sacrifice, am at their mercy.

CHAPTER 20
THEOS

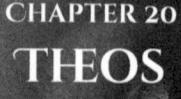

Day of Descendance parties are always full of rapture. I'd never been to one before coming to the Academy, but I'd lost my virginity at the first one, and ever since—I'd relished in the carnal nature of these gatherings. Until now.

Gods are old—ancient to humans and Mortal Gods alike—and in my time at the Academy, I've come to understand that with that age comes a loss of consideration for others. When you live eternally, few things bother you and even fewer entertain you. So, when they find something of interest, they latch on to it and drag from it all the enjoyment they can attain.

The Gods enjoy the avarice of power that the Day of Descendance brings.

If I could have prevented Kiera from attending this event, I would have. The idea of others looking upon her bare skin and knowing that all it would take is one small tear and she'd be naked before them makes me want to shove my fist through a wall. Unfortunately, however, the invitation that we received at midnight had specifically included her name along with a request from Dolos, himself. No matter my own wishes, no one disregards Dolos' requests.

The grand hall that's been prepared specifically for tonight's festivities hovers ahead like a specter of wanton abandon and danger. Echoes of moans and cries of both pain and pleasure slip from beneath the large ornate double doors as we approach. Laughter and clinking glasses are there too, but it's those moans that make my whole body go stiff. A searing sensation touches the back of my neck and creeps down my spine as I turn my gaze back to the Terra standing between Ruen and Kalix.

Cool, storm cloud eyes are fixated on those doors. Kiera's face is contemplative, as if she's completely forgotten her dress—or lack thereof. The sick stench of anxiety rolls off her in waves, though no one else seems to notice it.

Has she finally reached the end of her bravery? Does she think that Dolos intends to kill her in front of the Academy tonight? He's a cruel bastard, that's for sure, like most Gods—but once he's passed down a sentence, he's not the type to change his mind. Everything now seems to be designed purely to remind her of her place.

I wonder if his intentions have finally worked.

"Wait." Kalix draws Kiera to a stop and she stiffens as he reaches into his pocket and withdraws a long slip of fabric. Despite its dark color, the same onyx of his clothes, it's sheer, easy enough to see through. My mouth curves down at the sight of it. "All Terra are required to wear these."

My scowl deepens as Kalix slips the blindfold over her eyes. She stiffens but doesn't resist. He deftly ties it at the back of her head, trailing a finger through the spiderweb-colored hair there. His lips twitch as if this is all a joke to him. It makes my fists tighten at my sides with the urge to punch him in that stupid smug face of his. I repress the urge. The Gods will be gathered together today and they will be watching.

Kiera doesn't say a word as she blinks behind the lace, see-through fabric now hovering over her eyes. She looks like a depiction of the first Terra that served the Gods. Beautiful. Blinded. Chained. A captive of the ancient days and a stunning sacrifice to the desires of the Gods.

I look like a whore for the Gods. Her words circulate in my mind.

The blindfold is not meant to make her sightless, but to remind her that, without the Gods, mortals would still be ignorant to the blessing of the Divine Beings.

Her breath catches in her chest as Kalix leans close and kisses her cheek, his lips moving over her skin with deliberate slowness. His eyes lift and connect with mine. Teeth flash and unconsciously, I step forward.

"That's enough," I snap, reaching for Kiera's hand. Her fingers are cold against mine. "You're tormenting her."

Kalix offers me nothing more than a shrug as he lifts his hands in a faux innocent gesture. I narrow my eyes on him before switching to Kiera. "Don't stray from Ruen or I," I order her.

"You think I'm a threat to our Terra, Brother?" Kalix asks with a laugh.

"With the way you're acting tonight, I don't know what the fuck you are." I grit the words out, anger tightening the fists at my sides.

Still, Kiera doesn't say a word and with the lace fabric over her eyes, it's hard to tell what she's thinking. If eyes are the windows to the soul, then this stupid tradition has forcefully shrouded them. I hate it.

I cup her cheek. "*Dea?*"

She starts as if hearing me for the first time. Her chest rises and falls in a sharp inhalation. I focus on keeping my gaze on her face and not on the pale strips of white fabric that barely cover her. She looks like an ancient king's bride in this getup. Her breasts are full and round and the little slips of gold that cup them barely do anything but tease the memories of our single night together. I'd love nothing more than to rip them away and bend my head over her breasts, sucking one of her rosy pink nipples between my lips and hear her moans fill my ears.

"Are you okay?" I ask.

Her lashes flicker behind the lace mask as she glances past me over my shoulders to the doors we have yet to enter. "What am I supposed to do in there?" Her question is quiet.

"Nothing you don't want to," I assure her.

"Don't lie to her, Theos," Kalix snorts. "That won't do our brave little Terra any good. She needs to know the truth."

As if the sound of his voice reminds her of his presence, Kiera's body tenses. "Stop it," I hiss at him. "You're scaring the shit out of her."

"I'm fine." Kiera's hand touches my wrist. Her fingers encircle it and drag it away from her face. "It's fine. Just tell me what I am to do beyond those doors. Do I have to … I mean will the Gods expect me to…" Her throat bobs for a moment before she shakes her head as if clearing away cobwebs in her mind.

"You want to know if they'll be having a forced orgy beyond those doors?" Kalix appears at my side with that wide smile of his still in place. "And if you'll be expected to participate?"

Her fingers are still touching my wrist, holding it even though her head is turned towards him. "No one will touch what belongs to us," I tell her.

"Unless the Gods, themselves, decide that they want to taste her," Kalix shoots back.

The look I give him could wither entire fields. Kiera's lips twitch and curl back in disgust. "That won't happen," I reiterate. "Nothing she doesn't want to happen will happen."

"But…" Ruen steps up on my other side as he eyes the girl standing before me dressed like an erotic ghost, everything about her pale from the dress to her face save for the hints of gold and the black mask on her face. "It would be wise for you to follow our lead."

Kiera turns towards him. "Follow your lead how?"

I sigh as her fingers finally drop away from my wrist. She pivots her whole body to fully face Ruen. He doesn't move to touch her, but with how close he's standing, it's hard not to notice how fixated his attention is.

"There will be many people in there in various forms of undress," he admits. "Normally, attire for one's Terra is chosen by individual Mortal Gods. Many dress their Terra in something like this…" He lifts a hand, deftly fingering the slim curtain of cloth that spans over her breasts on either side. "When they wish to share."

Her lips part, but before she can speak, he goes on.

"No," he answers, somehow guessing her question, "we will not be sharing you with others. However … you may need to … *act* as though you are with us."

Kalix props an elbow on my shoulder and sweeps one

foot back, balancing himself on the toe of one boot with the other planted firmly on the ground. "What Ruen means, sweet little Terra," he says, "is that you'll have to sit there and let us touch you ... move you, *share* you as *we* wish."

She bristles and if she were a cat, I know by the wave of tension that ripples across her bare shoulders that she'd be on all four legs, back arched in the air, and hair standing on end at Kalix's less than subtle statement. Though, I can't say it's untrue because it's not.

Beyond those doors lies a night of salacious debauchery and violence. Walking into events such as these is like toeing a very thin line. One wrong move and aroused emotions can always turn violent. The possessiveness that the Divine feel over their servants and lovers is always taken to the next extreme. Cursing my own God blood, I know that if another aside from my brothers tries to lay hands upon her, I'll cut them from their bodies and shove them up their asses.

Kiera doesn't say anything for a long moment. When she clears her throat, she sounds gruff and only a little less nervous than before—as if she's coming back to that girl I know far better than this strange quiet one. "So, my duties tonight are to follow you and let you ... *do* things to me to convince the Gods that I am under your control?" she clarifies.

"More or less," Ruen agrees.

She bites her lip, teeth flashing white as they sink into the petal softness of her skin. My cock throbs in my fucking trousers. I should've asked for something with a little less fabric like Kalix. I'd hoped wearing this would reassure her when she found out about the types of parties the Gods host. Now, however, I'm regretting every single stitch that keeps me from feeling all of that naked flesh of hers against my own.

"Okay." Kiera jerks her head down in a nod. "Then let's do this. Let's get it over with." Her head turns to Kalix and to my utter surprise, she lifts her hand offering it to him. "Will you take me in?" she asks him.

Kalix freezes for a moment as if he, too, is stunned. He recovers far faster than I, though, as he removes his arm from my shoulder and takes her hand, lifting the back of her knuckles to his lips. He brushes a kiss to her skin and an ugly green monster surfaces inside me so swiftly that I nearly snarl out a curse.

Ruen catches my eye and shakes his head subtly.

"It would be my pleasure," Kalix answers Kiera's offer as he takes her palm and tucks it into the crook of his arm. Together, the two of them move to the double doors, and as if they're bespelled, the doors open, revealing all that lies beyond.

"Watch them," Ruen whispers to me. "Something is up with Kalix. He's playing a game with her and I think he's leaving us out on purpose."

My eyes shoot to his as Kiera and Kalix step up to the entrance. "Do you think he's planning on hurting her?"

Ruen is quiet for a long moment as we move in behind them. Just before our feet cross the border into the hall of pleasure and pain that is specially reserved for the Day of Descendance, I hear his reply. "I have no idea what he's planning," is all he says.

CHAPTER 21

KIERA

Flashes of skin on skin and gold drapery pass in front of my slightly distorted vision. With this mask covering my eyes—even if it is mostly transparent—I feel like a sightless fool. My fingers curve into Kalix's arm, my nails digging into the fabric until I hope he feels pain.

The action, however, only seems to amuse him. His smile hasn't waned in the slightest since we entered the room. "What are you planning?" I hiss quietly, low enough that no one else will hear.

In my periphery, Kalix's grin spreads. "Have you overcome your fear now?" he asks. "That was fast."

"You called me a thief," I whisper. "And a liar—what did you mean by that?"

He chuckles, the sound like two boulders crashing against one another and at the same time, so deeply sensual that it makes my thighs tremble. He's like a bad backstreet drug—addictive to those who need an escape and deadly to those who don't know how much they can take.

"You know exactly what I mean, little thief," Kalix says. "What you're trying to figure out now is how I figured it out—or perhaps you're wondering how you can convince me to keep your secrets."

"You haven't told anyone," I reply. It's an answer and a question.

"No, I haven't." The unspoken 'yet' hangs between us. Despite the uncomfortable sandals that adorn my feet, twisting up my calves, Kalix and I glide over the cold tile floor of the massive hall.

I recall Regis' map from months ago, going through the various blueprints in my mind until I come to where we are now. This side of the Academy is not usually open to students and Terra. It's part of the wing that houses the Divine Beings. A giant space that, for this auspicious day, has been draped in all sorts of finery.

Gold and red ribbons drift down from the beams above. I tip my head back and outright stare as there are several naked men and women tied up in an assortment of different positions. Some have had their arms and feet bound behind them, their breasts and genitals on full display as they dangle from the wrappings around their wrists and ankles—the only things keeping them aloft. Others lounge openly, legs swaying back and forth as they play within the ribbons as if they're swings for their amusement.

"Keep your head bowed," Theos' voice suddenly comes from behind me, a commanding whisper as we come to a stop at the end of the long hall before a trio of what I can only describe as thrones of old—the kind that ancient human kings and queens supposedly once sat upon before the Gods came to our world. In the center, upon the largest throne of them all rests a single dark crown made of black stone and metal. To the right, a second crown takes up residence, this one made of pearl and silver. No one is wearing them.

Kalix directs us to the left, where the only person upon the dais waits to be presented to. Dolos' shadowy frame sits casually against the smallest throne of them all. The shadows around the lower half of his body have pulled away to reveal a bobbing golden-haired Terra on her knees before him as she takes his cock into her mouth over and over again. I lower my eyes to the floor, not wanting to acknowledge the desperate noises coming from the girl's throat, as if she's doing her best to please the God of Imprisonment for fear he'll kill her if she fails.

Undisturbed by the awkwardness of coming up to him as he's being pleasured, Dolos doesn't acknowledge the girl as he speaks. "Darkhavens, come," he orders. In my periphery, he waves them forward with a swiping dark hand. "Bring me your Terra. I wish to see how she fares after her punishment."

I stare harder at the ground even as my nails sink deeper into Kalix's arm. As we graze the top step of the dais, the heat of the Darkhaven at my side fades as he pulls himself from me. Without knowing what else to do, the second Kalix's body is no longer in touch with my own, I go to my knee, bowing before Dolos. I never raise my gaze to meet his even when I hear the girl who'd been sucking him cry out in surprise.

My teeth grind down as a wave of heavy air slams into the back of my head, forcing my face lower until I'm nearly kissing distance to the stone underfoot. Dolos' shadows slip over my shoulder, lifting my hair and pushing the silver locks away from my back as he examines my spine.

An ice cold, skeletal finger slips down the ridges of my back, drawing the length of what I know to be one of the worst of my markings. I breathe out, slow and even, trying not to tense or turn and fight. Every instinct I've ever honed over these last ten years is demanding that I not show my back to an enemy. I close my eyes and sink into my position, forgetting all the aches and pains that it brings, ignoring the quiet but harsh breathing of the girl.

"She seems quite submissive now," Dolos says, his tone somewhat disgruntled. "Has she been this way since her punishment?"

I hear the words, let them slip through my ears, and don't respond. He's not talking to me. A beat passes and to my surprise, it's Theos who answers.

"She's learned the error of her ways, Your Divinity," he states. "This Terra has expressed how grateful she is for your mercy."

"Has she?" Dolos doesn't sound as if he quite believes Theos, and no one answers his suspicion as I feel the God of Imprisonment circle me again until he's standing in front of me.

My eyes squeeze shut even tighter. It makes me a cruel bitch, but I hope he doesn't replace the girl with me. I pray that I don't take her place. The thought of bowing before this God, of offering him something of my flesh to please the man who brought me such pain sits like a venom-filled capsule in my stomach. Tears gather at the back of my eyes and I push them back, fighting them with all my strength.

I've fucked for a kill before, but I was always the one in control. I was the one who decided which method would get to my target faster. I've never had to fuck for my life and I hope I don't have to contemplate that kind of sacrifice.

That icy finger touches the side of my face, making me jump at the suddenness of it as it slides down further until it curls just under my chin and slowly brings my face upward. My lashes lift and I curse the watery vision that blurs what is already a disrupted sight behind this damned mask.

"She does appear to have far better manners now," Dolos comments. He's so close that the weight of those invisible chains lock around my wrist and hold me down, clamping around me in ways that make it impossible to resist. His finger dips further until he touches the scale-like throat covering that I'm wearing. "I am pleased that the three of you accepted my gift for her now that she's been reintroduced to our Academy grounds."

"Our Terra is gratified by your words," Ruen replies.

"Is that true, Kiera Nezerac?" Dolos' head turns down to me. "Are you appreciative of my good will?" A single tear slips out of my eye and slides down my cheek. Shame rips through me.

"Yes, Your Divinity," I answer in my quietest voice. "Your benevolence is a blessing to one as lowly as I."

His finger taps under my chin, urging me to rise further. I do, not standing, but straightening my spine until my head is at level with his lap. I swallow and keep my eyes directed upward since that's where he's wanting me to focus. I can't see the expression he hides beyond his shadows, can only deduce from what I can see of him. Which is practically nothing.

"I am glad to hear it, young one," he says. "I shall look forward to your reform and seeing how you flourish within the Academy."

Dolos takes a step back and his hand falls away from my face once more. Air floods my body, and I don't even realize that I'm gasping as he takes his seat and motions for the blond-haired Terra that had been servicing him before to move back into her place. She doesn't hesitate, likely used to this kind of duty, as she crawls forward and locks her lips around the head of his cock and swallows it down, her cheeks hollowing out as tears stream down her face, coming from beneath the lace mask she wears that almost matches my own were it not for the different crimson color.

"Thank you, Your Divinity," Kalix appears at my side again, his tone far more polite than I've ever heard it even if it's spoken with a bit more bite than his brothers. His hand locks on to my bicep and he pulls me to my swaying feet, nearly ripping me off the platform as he drags me backward, towards the crowd and party-goers.

My head spins as I suck in breath after breath, trying to catch up to the instinctive fight or flight urge that's flooding me. Kalix continues to lead me through the hall, passing through an archway into another room that's been set up for even more Day of Descendance revelry.

More naked bodies are writhing. A dark-skinned Mortal God laughing and then groaning as two Terra males service her—one at her breast and the other at her cunt. I turn, my gaze sliding one way and then another. A red-haired, freckled Terra girl cries out as a female Mortal God slides her fingers down the girl's thatch of matching red hair over her pussy. I see why all the Terra now have to wear these masks—it marks them as servicers, as weak ones should Mortal Gods get too carried away.

"This way," Kalix grunts as he tugs me toward the back of the room and into a smaller hallway. Confusion swarms me. I glance back, thankful that I spot Ruen's dark head and Theos' white-blond head following close behind. On the blueprints, this place had looked like one large chamber. Maybe it is? Maybe the hallways are secrets that not even Regis could find?

"Kalix, wait—" Ruen jolts forward and grabs ahold of my other arm, stopping Kalix's stomping strides to keep me from being ripped apart between them. "Dolos is going to want to see us with her."

With me? My brows rise over the mask. "I thought you said all I'd have to do is act?"

A hand clamps over my mouth and Ruen's gaze flashes red before fading just as fast as it appeared. He sighs and drops his fingers away from my face. "Don't speak unless spoken to here," he says as if realizing that they had forgotten to tell me as much. "If another Mortal God or a Divine Being approaches you, keep your tone polite and your eyes on the floor."

"That won't be necessary," Theos snaps as he appears right behind me. "She won't be away from us."

A silent conversation passes between the two of them, but Kalix's hand remains locked on my upper arm. "I want her first," he finally says, tugging me back, and Ruen is forced to let go or bruise me.

"She's not a toy you can just claim," Theos sneers.

Kalix's other arm comes up and he pulls me flush against him with my back and ass to his groin and chest. Eyes are watching us, even here in this corridor. There are still plenty of Mortal Gods and their Terra moving in and out of rooms, some in states of undress and others completely clothed. If anything, the guys look more out of place than I do.

"That's exactly what she is," Kalix argues with Theos,

a derisive edge to his words. "As far as the Gods are concerned, Kiera is our plaything tonight. She is our prize for being their Blood."

I swallow against a suddenly dry throat. Something moves against my backside, thick and hard. Kalix, the prick, moves his hips against me, pushing his growing erection against me as he reaches down and grips my hips, digging his fingers into my sides as he holds me in place for his ministrations.

Both Ruen and Theos look as if they could cut him down right here and now had they any weapons.

"What?" Kalix taunts, his head moving forward as he rests his chin on my shoulder and looks at Ruen. "Are you so innocent that you don't want to see how she reacts to all three of us and not just *him?*" He nudges his jaw towards Theos who looks about ready to break his face.

I don't know what to say or how to stop this strange turn of events from barreling down the track of fucking no return, but what I do know is that I need to get Kalix alone and he and I need to *talk*.

I lower my voice into the barest of whispers. "May I speak?" I ask.

All eyes shoot to me. Ruen's throat moves and he jerks his head in a nod.

"I think it's best if I go with Master Kalix right now," I say.

Ruen's hands curl into fists at his sides, but he doesn't respond right away. Kalix blows out a breath right next to my ear, the sound whistling past. "Wow, little Terra," he says. "Choosing a favorite already?" He chuckles. "I'm impressed you could be so decisive."

"I am *not* choosing," I snap before I can withhold the bitterness in my voice and stop the second I realize it.

Sucking in another breath, I blow it out before I begin talking again.

"I am not choosing," I say again, this time far calmer. "I am yours—all of yours—but I believe that if I am to prove to Lord Dolos that I've learned my lesson then this is the path I must go."

Theos steps closer and Kalix moves back against the wall, drawing me away from him as he settles into the space with me now gripped firmly in his arms. Theos stops and glares at his brother for a moment before lifting those sunset eyes to meet mine.

"Are you sure this is what you want?" he asks me.

Not at all.

"Yes," I say. "Kalix is feared the most by Terra and other Mortal Gods. If Dolos sees me at his side, doing as he commands then he'll surely believe that I've been thoroughly punished and know my place once more."

Theos looks a bit ill at my words, but after a brief moment of uncomfortable silence, he nods. "Then we will respect your decision." He looks to Ruen, but when the midnight-eyed Darkhaven has nothing to say, Theos looks back to me.

"Ruen and I can't leave until the festivities are well underway," he tells me. "So, we'll be around, but we'll head to the green room where some of the more ... conservative Gods and Mortal Gods are. Find us there when you're done doing what you have to."

"Thank you."

Ruen doesn't say another word as he turns and stalks off down the corridor, not even bothering to wait for Theos.

Theos, to my surprise, turns back to me and leans forward, cupping my cheek in his hand as his mouth brushes against mine. The kiss is soft and gentle, far from that night we had together. It's nice, though, and sometimes nice is needed. So, I let him kiss me and I kiss him back, opening my mouth for him in a way that has him deepening our connection. His tongue slides over my bottom lip before slipping inside. Sparks dance along my nerve endings. A rough sound of feminine annoyance and rage hit my ears, but Theos doesn't look up and so neither do I. He continues to steadily kiss me stupid and the feminine noise of outrage fades as stomping footsteps echo back to us. I'm only dimly aware as Theos withdraws his tongue and then just as he'd started the kiss, he brushes his mouth against mine, one, two, three times.

He's gone far too fast. Disappearing in the direction of Ruen so quickly I didn't even get a chance to truly feel the bizarre sensation of having Kalix's cock rubbing against my ass with his arms wrapped around my hips, holding me pinned in his grip as his brother kissed me. The immoral action should have left me feeling disgusted, but it doesn't. Quite the opposite.

"Now, then," Kalix says, breathing against my neck as he reaches up and brushes my hair out of the way for him to lay his own kiss on my nape. "Shall we talk about your deceit before or after we put on a show for the Gods and Mortal Gods of our illustrious Academy, Kiera Nezerac?"

CHAPTER 22

KIERA

K alix Darkhaven is a prick, and he's toying with me. Now that I've been jolted out of my own damned head and fear, I find the anger rising once more. Hot and uncomfortable, like boiling alive inside my own hate, I let it fester as Kalix's hands traverse my body. Up and down my sides, his hands slip beneath the sheer fabric of my dress.

He never takes his fingers too far, which surprises me. I expect him to rip the cups of my bra away and even the tiny scrap of fabric between my legs and fuck me right here—standing against the wall. He doesn't. Kalix merely pets and breathes against my skin as he hums in the back of his throat. It takes several long minutes of this before I realize what he's waiting for. *Me.*

"Come on," I say, lifting myself away from his hold and knowing I'm right when he lets me go easily. "I want to get this over with."

Kalix's smile is blinding and even more irritating when he uses it on me, so I avoid looking directly at it, choosing instead to peer at the front of his throat or even at the snake embroidered on his chest. With a low chuckle that makes my stomach do strange flips, Kalix pushes away from the wall and stands to his full height as he reaches for my hand instead of my arm.

He tugs me back the way we'd come. I trail after him, letting him steer me this way and that. We move back through the rooms, the sounds of blissful moans echoing all around. Then behind them, there are a few startled cries—caused, I assume, by shock and pain. Each one slides into me like a damn poisoned knife.

How many of them are forced to be here? Forced to play out these twisted fetishes of the Divine? Those who wish for it, those who enjoy it, may have it all they like. I am not one to judge; if anything I am one to *be* judged for all that I've done. The idea, though, of being compelled enough, of having no other choice and no power over their own lives and bodies ... perhaps it simply hits too close to home for me.

Reminded of my own circumstances, my fingers itch to touch the back of my neck where the shard of brimstone rests.

Kalix stops abruptly nearly causing me to slam into his back as he whirls around to face me. His eyes are glittering, but the smile on his face has turned tight. "Do not push me away," he says with careful command. "No matter what I might say to anger you, do *not* risk your life in this place, Kiera."

I blink as he uses my name instead of one of his mocking and somewhat insulting nicknames. His fingers tighten on mine hard enough that I wince.

"I understand," I say quickly and they loosen once more.

"This way." Kalix begins walking again, but my foot

catches on something and I nearly go down to my knees. I'm saved by his arms as he lifts me against him and keeps striding, but instead of carrying me bridal style, he cups his palms beneath my ass. My legs are forced to spread and wind around him, locking on to his hips as we move through the rooms faster now.

My hands clutch at the muscles of his arms as I bounce with each hard step. A grunt releases from me and I feel something decidedly hard prod at that place between my thighs. Leaning slightly back, I arch a brow down at him. Kalix doesn't even bother to glance at my face.

His is focused forward as he says, "Don't risk it."

At that, I drop back against his chest, and even if I'd very much rather stick a dagger in his throat, I carefully lean my head against his shoulder. I close my eyes and hold on, feeling the world whirling around me. Something smokey and spicy lingers in the air. I hadn't noticed it before because it'd been such a subtle scent, but wherever we're going, it's only growing stronger.

My arms feel lax and languid, and soon enough, I'm finding it difficult to hold on as tightly as I once had. My head droops harder against Kalix's shoulder and I turn my face into his neck. The next time his cock bumps against the front of my underwear, a whimper is knocked out of me.

A wide hand comes up to cup the side of my face, holding me there, against him. "Just a bit further," he says.

It's so weird, I think. *Why is he being so nice? He is* not *a nice man. He's crazy.*

Air stops slipping past us and it takes me a few beats to realize that we've stopped moving. My eyes open just as Kalix turns and takes a seat on what looks like a backless couch piled high with a bunch of pillows. The room is darker with more golden drapes hanging from the ceiling. Unlike the great hall, though, there aren't any terrified naked Terra dangling from them.

All around us, I can smell that intoxicating smoke and spice. I hum in the back of my throat as I drift up, pressing my hands flat against Kalix's chest. A woman's distorted groan clears my head just enough for me to glance back over my shoulder and spot a couple towards the front of the large room. The same blond-haired Terra that had been at Dolos' feet earlier lies on her back with a Mortal God between her legs.

She's stretched out on another of the many luxurious couches all around the room, the only true furniture aside from the various cushions and pillows scattered everywhere. Kalix's hand slides up my spine, leaving a trail of sizzling heat in its wake.

"Take my coat off, *little thief*," he whispers to me.

I turn to him, head buzzing from whatever this scent is doing to me, and find my hands grappling with the lapels of his vest before pulling it off him. Then, before he can make another command, I touch the hem of his tunic with the embroidered snake and jerk that up and over his head. I'm met with a responding satisfied growl.

"We ... still have ... to talk," I try to say, my words so quiet I can barely hear them over the roaring in my skull.

"We are talking," Kalix replies.

"Not ... like ... *oh*—" I jolt as his lips touch my chest, just beneath this ridiculous collar.

"I'd love to take this off you," he says, "and sink my fangs into your pretty little lying neck—but we wouldn't want Dolos to get too suspicious."

"He's not ... even..." I'm breathless, fucking breathless and I can't seem to stop him. *Wait. I'm not supposed to stop him. Why did I want to again?*

"He's here," Kalix says, surmising what I was going to say without my needing to have finished it. "He's watching. Just because you can't see him doesn't mean he doesn't have eyes and ears everywhere."

Kalix flips me around and presses his chest against my back as he lifts both of my legs over either of his and widens his stance, forcing my legs to part. I lean back, my chest heaving for air as I try to swim through the soup that has become my thoughts.

A hand moves from my hip up to my breast. I cry out, shocked as my nipple peaks against his palm and he rumbles an approval that vibrates through my whole body.

"Tell me, Kiera," he whispers against the side of my face. "What is a hidden God child doing sneaking into a Mortal Gods Academy under the guise of being a mortal?"

Despite the strange smoke in the air, hovering over the room and clinging to my nostrils, I stiffen at the question. Ophelia had taught me how to withstand physical pain. She'd beaten and starved me, dunked me in frozen waters, and had burned awful, searing scars into my body —all wounds that had eventually healed even though the memory of the pain had clung to me for days, weeks, years. I'd never been particularly interested in the art of seduction. I'd only ever used it as an excuse to get close to a target, not to get information from them. In this game, I realize, I am wholly unqualified.

Instead of answering Kalix, I ask a question of my own. "Why haven't you told anyone yet?"

His fingers pluck at my nipple, twisting it between his thumb and forefinger to just the brink of pain. My back arches instinctively, chasing the strange sensations, and a rumble of approval vibrates in his chest. It occurs to me then that this is why he's so dangerous. Kalix is patient. He doesn't mind waiting until he gets his target alone and helpless in his grip. He doesn't have to torture me to get me to break, he just needs to get me to let down my guard.

I gasp as his other hand moves around and frees my other breast, baring me to open air as fingers pluck at my fresh, untouched nipple with exacting movements. My hips roll against him and I shudder as I repress a new whimper.

"You ... know they'll think you were in on it, too, if you tell," I say, gasping for air.

The low laugh that he releases is anything *but* appeasing. In fact, it sends a bolt of fear and dread through me. "I haven't told anyone yet, little thief, because I'm far too amused by you to get rid of you just yet."

As his hands toy with me, his attention fixed on my breasts as he cups and plays with them like they're his own personal entertainment, his words catch up with me. *He hasn't told anyone because he's enjoying playing with me? Does he not realize the danger he puts himself in by keeping my secret? The danger he puts his brothers in? Or does he simply not care so long as he gets his rocks off?* For some reason, that disappoints me. I thought he'd be more complex than that, perhaps a bit more loyal too.

"Moan," Kalix demands harshly as his fingers bite down on my nipples and twist abruptly.

I cry out, a shocked scream ripping from my throat.

My head snaps back and narrowly misses his as it slams into his shoulder and he grunts. I writhe beneath him, the pain of the sudden action making stars dance in front of my eyes. Dimly, I sense a fresh wave of heaviness settle over me, but I'm too lost in what Kalix is doing to me to grasp what it means until Kalix murmurs something in my ear.

"That wasn't a moan, but that will do," he says quietly.

The heaviness draws closer, and I recognize Dolos' shadows hovering nearby. His head is dipped down as he stares down at the Terra that had pleasured him earlier. Fear wafts from the girl, but she doesn't pull away as Dolos stands over her. The Mortal God at her cunt continues to thrust, sawing back and forth as he grunts with fervor.

"Thighs," Kalix snaps, jerking his legs out even more, forcing me to do the same.

Humiliation burns through me as I feel a bead of wetness ooze down the crotch of my underwear. "Don't try to close them," Kalix warns as his hands suddenly leave my breasts and move down my stomach, slipping beneath the transparent dress. "Put your arms up and around my neck."

Closing my eyes, I follow the order, reminding myself that this is all an act. We're putting on a show and since Dolos is now in the room, it's even more imperative that I don't fuck this up.

The first stroke of Kalix's fingers between my thighs has me biting back a pathetic noise. My nails scratch at the back of his neck and he groans, pushing his hips up into me as he lets me feel just how hard he is.

"Tell me the truth, Kiera," he whispers in that too low

voice of his, erotic and enticing. Like he's not really there, but just a whisper on the wind. An old fairytale that mothers used to tell their daughters of great and powerful beings coming from another land to carry them away to be their brides in giant gilded castles. "Who are you? Who do you belong to?"

"I-I'm just..." It's heady, intoxicating, the feeling of his fingers over the satin fabric between my legs. "Kiera," I breathe out my name.

He makes a growling sound and then pushes his fingers beneath my underwear. A moan bubbles up out of my throat as two fingers slide right into my wetness, dipping into my hole and then retreating before thrusting even deeper. All the while, his other hand moves in circles around my clit. Those stars dart back and forth behind my closed eyelids, dancing faster and faster. I'm getting dizzy.

"Who is your God parent?" Kalix's question sinks into my mind, but I can't answer, I'm on the verge of something great and powerful. It sparks up in my belly and floods outward, growing larger and larger like a tidal wave until it comes crashing down all around me.

I cry out again, sobbing as I clutch on to him. The stars burst into a million little lights. No more dancing as they just all suddenly stop and erupt at once. Everything feels *alive*.

He says something, a massive rumble in his chest, but whatever it is, I don't hear it. His cock burns against my backside, rocking into me in slow thrusting motions even as his fingers never stop their circling or thrusting.

"Stop." My eyes pop open. I'm sweating, panting, and wet slick is dripping down my thighs onto his trousers. "Stop," I say again. I release his neck and whimper as my clit becomes sensitive, but still, he keeps toying with me. "Stop, *please!*" I grab ahold of his forearms, nails sinking deep as tears crest at the edges of my eyes.

"Not until you come again for me, little thief," Kalix says. "Let me feel your cunt clamp down on my fingers just like it'll clamp onto my dick when I finally take you."

I shake my head, those tears spilling forth. Dolos' Terra and the Mortal God aren't the only ones here with us. Neither is Dolos, for that matter. There are several couples in all states of undress and wantonness. My skin feels cold and pebbled, but at the same time, my breasts feel heavy and aching. There's something wrong with me, I decide, as I've never felt this way—not even when I enjoyed sex. Not even with Theos. This scent in the air, it's not natural. It's messing with my head. With all of our heads.

A female Mortal God is lying back on one of the couches, her legs splayed as a female and male Terra both lick at her pussy while she cries out in utter ecstasy. A male Terra is on his hands and knees in a collection of pillows with his ass turned up and his head to the ground as a male ... oh Gods, that's Axlan, the God of Victory, driving his cock into the younger male as he whimpers and whines under him.

A flash of that same man holding the whip that streaked fire down my back hits me and I push back into Kalix's chest, unintentionally seeking protection. As if he senses my vulnerability, Kalix's fingers still beneath my underwear pinch down on my clit and those stars return in full force—slamming into me.

My body shakes and the fresh scream locks in my throat as my eyes roll back into my head. The sex. The scent in the room. The threat of sitting in this place so casually as something that should never have existed rolls through me all at once, the terror heightening the experience of my second orgasm of the night.

Kalix leans closer to me, finally withdrawing his fingers as he drags them up my body, painting a trail with my own juices over my stomach and breasts. He pauses to swipe both of my nipples, stroking them with the wetness before he finally lifts them to his lips and sucks them deep.

I turn my head and stare at him in a mixture of horror and arousal. His pupils have grown far thinner than I remember, turning into vertical slits that resemble the eyes of a snake as he gazes back at me, licking the taste of me from between his digits. When he's done and appears somewhat satisfied that he's gotten all my wetness off his hand and into his mouth, he drops his hands back to my hips and squeezes.

"This is what the Gods do to those that please them," Kalix says, and despite the earlier teasing glint in his gaze, his eyes are very much serious now. No hint of taunt or amusement. I don't have to look around to know what he means. I gulp down another breath.

"Despite what my brothers may think, you were not invited here as *punishment*," he states, "but as a reward for surviving the Gods' mercy."

This *was my reward?* A fresh shudder works through me, this one coming from a very different place than before. If this was what the Gods saw as a prize for bending to their will ... then Ophelia was wrong. They won't just torture me to find out who kept and hid me for my entire life. They'll rip me apart, put me back together, and do it all over again for the answers they seek. There will be no running and no hiding in my own mind to get away from them.

"If anyone finds out what you are, *little liar,*" his eyes drop to my cold lips and he leans forward, nipping them with incredibly sharp teeth. "Don't expect your death to be quick."

As we seek out the others, Kalix is beyond relaxed. It's as if *he's* the one that just got back-to-back orgasms and not me. All the while, my stomach is tied up in knots, and despite the heat pouring off the copious number of bodies all through these rooms and the great hall, I feel cold down to the marrow of my bones.

I don't know how Kalix knew Dolos would be in that room, but considering how accustomed the Darkhavens are to all things in the Academy and how well they seemed to know what to expect before we'd even entered, I wouldn't be surprised to find out that things like this happen regularly throughout their years at the Academy.

Kalix leads me through the rooms and great hall. Now that the night has waned, there are fewer people amidst the crowds, and those that had been strapped and tied above the great hall have either disappeared entirely or been replaced by new faces and bodies, all rapt with sexual fever. I cross my arms over my chest, shivering as I trail behind Kalix. There's no need for him to hold on to me so much anymore. He seems content to let me follow, confident that I have no intention of running away.

Step after step, I move behind him like a shadow as Kalix steps into a darkened hallway. I blink and he's gone, disappearing completely from my sight. My feet come to a standing halt and I glance back, wondering if perhaps I'd just missed him turning around and moving past me at some point. But no, there's no one here. No one up one side or down the other of this deserted corridor. My heart starts beating rapidly, pounding against my chest.

I've never felt so much fear in my life, and yet, now it curls around my throat, wrapping long tendrils of fury and dread over and over until I swear I'm covered in the sickening emotions.

Don't panic, Kiera. Never panic. Instead of Ophelia's voice in my head, I hear Regis' calm gruff one. I close my eyes and breathe deeply, holding it in and counting down from ten. The fear doesn't dissipate immediately, but it does lessen if only a small kernel, just enough for me to reopen my eyes and calmly lower my hands back to my sides as I take in the space around me.

This corridor is long, but it's close enough to the rest of the party rooms that I can still hear people—moans, cries of pleasure, and even some of pain. I swallow thickly. Kalix had told me not to leave his side or no, wait, that had been Theos. Theos had told me not to leave their side—but Kalix hadn't said anything. He simply told me not to push him away.

My upper lip curls back in irritation. I sniff delicately, sensing something beyond that odd smoke and spice scent from earlier. It's not as powerful in these back rooms and hallways, not as invading. My head feels clearer and my mind sharper. My eyes fall to the wall alongside me, roving down the dark stones and then ... I pause.

A shadow of a man darts out of a side alcove I hadn't noticed before and I jump back, hands coming up and balling into fists at the ready. The shadow comes mostly into view a moment later and Kalix's cold, snake-like eyes watch me with keen intelligent interest.

He doesn't say anything and neither do I. Then he sighs and reaches back the way he'd dived out of the wall and slides a hand behind the stones there. My eyes widen as the wall moves, shifting slightly, just wide enough for one person to pass through. He nods for me to continue. I lower my hands back to my sides and glare at him through the lace mask still covering the upper half of my face as I take a step forward before turning and sliding into the space he's opened for me.

Almost as soon as I enter the darkened nook, the heat of his chest is against my back again. Darkness encroaches, dimming the view around me and though I suspect my senses are stronger than an average mortal, I still find it difficult to move forward without putting my hands out to ensure I don't run into another wall.

Skimming my fingers along either side of the walls in this small space, I take a hesitant step ahead and then another and another. All the while, Kalix's presence remains a steady constant at my back. The hairs on the back of my neck and along my arms rise.

I don't like how close he is—especially after what just went down. I cough, clearing my throat as I seek my way through the darkness. "So," I murmur quietly, "why do you think Dolos will assume I've learned my lesson just by treating me like a common street whore in front of him?"

Kalix's chuckle is deep and intimidating. "A common street whore?" he repeats, amusement lifting his voice from the laugh that seems to settle somewhere low in his chest, too low for anything light to touch because every time he does it, it sounds like a monster's laugh.

I stumble a step and a hand reaches out—*his*—grabbing hold of my hip and helping me to right myself. With a curling scowl, I reach down and slap at the hand that's still touching me. Now that I no longer have to pretend to be human with him, it feels ridiculous to have him treat me as if I'm weak and fragile.

"That is not how I treat common street whores," Kalix says at last. "In fact, I don't treat common street whores at all since I rarely leave the Academy unless called upon by one of my father's associates." His hot breath touches my ear as he leans closer than before. My spine stiffens. "If you wanted me to treat you rougher, all you had to do was ask."

I pull away from him, stomping a few steps ahead in an effort to get away from him. It doesn't work because, in the next instant, he's right there once again, invading my space as if it's his right. A growl rumbles in my throat and I shove it down. Now is certainly not the time to antagonize a psychopathic Mortal God who can kill me just as easily as I can kill him.

"You're sidestepping my question," I snap. "Why was *that* necessary?"

Kalix doesn't answer immediately and as the end of this dark tunnel grows slightly brighter, a dull glow of something in the near distance makes me blink my eyes as our surroundings come into clearer detail. This damned mask is driving me crazy.

"Dolos needed to know we have you under control,"

Kalix whispers finally. "He likely sensed your rebellious-ness when you were first taken to him, and he needed to see you broken. Dolos is the God of Imprisonment for a reason and he sent you these clothes because he wanted to see his prisoner in chains—*pretty chains*, but still chains nonetheless. It was better that I did it than one of the others."

My breath fogs in front of my face, coming out in a white cloud in front of me. I didn't realize the tempera-ture was dropping so much, but now it makes sense. It must be why I'm so viscerally aware of Kalix's heat as he stands so close to me.

"Keep going," he urges and I do simply because I don't think I have any other options. The light gets brighter until the two of us step into an open space with dirt ground and I look up, seeing the dark glittering jewels of the stars above. We're outside.

"Finally." I jerk my head down as Theos' voice slams into me a second before his arms come around me and practically rip me away from Kalix. The white of his hair flashes in front of my face for a brief second as he dips down and moves his palms down my arms and over me, I think, checking for something.

"She's fine," Kalix says as he moves away from my side. A chilling wind whistles through the ten-by-ten space here. There are three tall stone walls on either side, one curved outward, and as I glance up and up, I realize it's because we're outside near one of the towers of the Academy.

Theos straightens away from me and then cups my cheek. "Are you okay?" he demands.

I'm so stunned by this show of concern that I just nod in answer. His face darkens and he curses before ripping the mask away from my face. I blink and reach up, touching the skin just below my eye as the rest of the world comes into clearer view. Even if that damned mask hadn't been meant as a blindfold, it had done enough to hinder my sight that now that it's gone, it feels like everything is filled with a new sense of clarity.

"The party should still be going on," Ruen says as Theos drops his hands away from my face to undo the buttons running up his coat. "We should get going."

Theos slings the jacket around me and I'm not stupid enough to refuse it, since I'm fucking freezing. Putting my arms through the too-long sleeves, I wrap it tighter around me and inhale the scent of spice and rum that seems to be his natural brand. He puts a hand to the small of my back, the heat of it slipping past the fabric and into my skin as he does.

Kalix doesn't say anything as he looks back at me from where he's now standing in an opening passage that leads from the small alcove that is protected by the walls of the Academy's building. I swallow sharply, waiting, but he says nothing. He merely smirks at Theos' protective hold on me as his brother glares at him accusingly.

Ruen sighs, casting a glance between all of us before he moves towards where Kalix is standing. "Did you take care of things with Dolos?" he asks quietly.

A quick decisive nod is the only answer Kalix gives and Ruen takes it before slipping past him. A moment passes and then Kalix turns to follow, leaving Theos and me alone either to stay or trail after them. I don't see much else to do so I step forward as well, slipping out of the opening with Theos at my back.

"Are you sure you're okay?" Theos asks as we fall into line behind his brothers, the four of us walking back through the Academy grounds to where I assume their tower is.

I'm not okay. Not even a little. Kalix Darkhaven knows my secret which means that he knows the Guild's secret. Even if he doesn't know what I'm doing here, just him knowing my lineage is enough to have me on edge. I don't want to lie to Theos, not anymore. I'm tired and I'm cold and I really wish I had an idea of what the fuck I'm supposed to do. So, instead of answering, I simply lean into him, stealing his body heat as his arm moves up from my lower back to hook around my shoulders and bring me closer to his side.

I close my eyes as my head throbs and more cool wind smacks me in the face. I should have never come to this Academy, I decide. It was a fool's errand to think that one mission would be the key to my freedom. Now, I'm paying the price for my idiocy and my own greed.

CHAPTER 24

KIERA

Two days pass and Kalix doesn't say anything to the others. There are no further conversations or interrogations on what I'm doing here or how I even came to be after the party. No Mortal God guards come to drag me back to the dungeons. I don't wake with a sword to my throat, and yet I almost wish there was something to break up the monotonous dullness that fills the time after the Day of Descendance party. Waiting and patience have never been my strongest suit even if I've had to learn to accept it in the last ten years. It almost feels like Kalix is tormenting me with it.

A part of me wishes someone would slap a pair of brimstone shackles on me by the end of the third day. At least then I wouldn't be stuck with all this unnerving *waiting*. Kalix disappears immediately after classes are over and I shuffle through the hallways of the Mortal Gods Academy, my head throbbing harder than ever before as I've been staying up each and every night in anticipation of something—anything.

The doors to the library come into view, cracked open with the sounds of quills scratching and papers shuffling as I grow nearer. I pause as the soft, low timbre of Caedmon's voice echoes back to me from within.

"Take this twice a day for the next week and I assure you, your limbs will feel much better, Sylvis," I hear him tell the head Terra Librarian who had acted as if she knew Ruen well that one day he'd come to me here.

"I cannot accept such a gift, Your Divinity." Sylvis, for all her pride, sounds like she's about to cry, her voice trembling with the effort it takes to speak.

"You can and you will," Caedmon insists. "You are a favorite of a God, Sylvis. This is for me just as much as it is for you. I cannot bear the thought of seeing you leave this place before it's your time."

Sniffles escape the library. Surely, they're not speaking in front of all the other Terra? Or are they? After all, most Gods only see Terra as convenient tools to be used and discarded. They seem to forget that the Terra they employ all have thoughts and wills of their own. That they're people.

Deciding that this isn't necessarily something I need to be eavesdropping on, but also wanting to hurry into the library to get this shift over with, I press against the door and enter. Several feet away from the various tables and desks of the reading area, Sylvis and Caedmon stand with their heads bent toward each other.

Sylvis raises her eyes over Caedmon's shoulder and spots me before quickly ducking down. It's too late, though, I've already seen the red rimming her eyes that definitely tell me she's been crying. I scan the area and note that there are far fewer Terra than usual, only about two or three of them remain at some of the desks and Caedmon and Sylvis are far enough away that they likely thought themselves safe from prying ears. Not me, though, since exceptional hearing is part of my own increased abilities—which just makes Kalix's ability to intrude into my room without waking me that much more frustrating.

Pretending that I'm not interested in whatever little conversation that Sylvis and Caedmon are having, I move across the library until I reach the desk that sits next to Sylvis' and the Terra there. The older man has a protruding nose and eyes that are far too close to be attractive, but he looks up at me with no hostility despite the marked uniform I'm wearing.

"What are my tasks for the day?" I ask him.

He directs his gaze to Sylvis' desk as if to tell me that I should ask her, but then he realizes she's not there. Guess he'd been too absorbed in whatever he was writing to notice when she got up. His head turns and he spots her some feet away.

"You'll have to wait for her to give you your duties after she's done talking to Lord Caedmon," the man says. "Unless he has use for you." He gestures to an empty table across from him. "You may sit there and wait." And then, belatedly, as if he reminds himself he should say it, he tacks on a, *"quietly,"* in a harsh breath before going back to his writing.

I sigh and turn away, striding the few feet it takes me to get to the table. I plop down into my seat and set an elbow on the table, leaning my chin into it as I look around the reading area. It's so quiet in here that it lulls me into a sense of peace. No wonder Ruen likes this place so much. I've never been one much for reading—beyond what I had to for education—but I think losing oneself in a story not my own, in a life that is not my own, would be nice right about now.

Seconds pass into minutes and I avoid listening in any further to Caedmon and Sylvis' quiet conversation in the corner. I breathe evenly, counting the breaths as boredom gets the best of me, needing anything to focus my thoughts on lest I start thinking about other, far more complicated matters that only serve to make my head ache. My eyelids droop lower and lower until I cannot keep them open any longer.

I don't realize that sleep has claimed me until a hand touches my upper back and I jolt up out of my seat. I automatically reach for the blade that I keep at the small of my back, stopping when I recognize the man standing in front of me with an amused quirk to his lips.

Caedmon looks me up and down as I shake myself and peer around the library, but all the other Terra are engrossed in their work and no one has seemed to notice my near blunder or the fact that I fell asleep while waiting for my shift duties to be relayed to me. I shuffle awkwardly, adjusting my stance as I glance at Caedmon, who still looks pleasantly occupied by my uncomfortableness.

"You're with me today," is all he says before turning around and walking away.

I blink and pause for a beat before I jump into gear and start after him, my shorter legs hurrying to catch up with his longer ones until I'm a few steps behind him and I can slow my gait to match his.

Caedmon leads me down the library's multitude of

shelves, past the point that Ruen had dragged me to before and around a corner. Statues appear at the end of a particularly thick shelving unit. We walk in silence down the row of statues for several long minutes until the sounds of the other Terras' quiet working fades from even my own ears and nothing but echoing quiet lingers all around.

We come to a stop in front of what I think is the final statue only to find that the wall curves and there are several more just around the bend. I look up and up some more at the woman peering down from the inset into the wall. Down the side, there are several other similar niches, each of them holding a different statue. The one I'm standing in front of depicts a woman in a long flowing dress, her hands cupped in front of her, one facing down and one facing up as a spider dangles from a string on the top one onto her waiting palm.

I peer at her curiously. She's beautiful, with long hair that flows down over her shoulders and curls around the ends of her breasts. Her figure is voluptuous with wide hips and a small waist. But that's not why I find her interesting. I find her interesting because of the expression she has. Her lips are parted, slightly curved up at the corners, and her eyes are softly lidded as she gazes down at the creature in her palms.

"Tell me, Kiera," Caedmon says, his voice dispelling the quiet that had flowed around us so suddenly that it makes my heart leap within my chest for a beat or two before slowly steadying out once more. "How much do you know about the Gods and how we came to this world?"

I look at him like he's crazy, my brow furrowing in confusion at such a random question. "I know what I've been taught, Your Divinity," I say. "That the Gods came to us and shared their knowledge and—"

"I thought we'd been over this," he stops me, dark ebony eyes turning my way. "My name is Caedmon, and I'd prefer it if you called me as such."

"I—Caedmon," I amend, lowering my eyes as the sight of his own seems to make dangerous vibrations arise in my stomach. Not arousal, not interest, but something more ancient. Like a warning.

"I didn't ask what you have been taught by the classes here at the Academy," he continues. "I want to know how much of our truth you know."

"Your truth?" I ask.

He returns his attention to the statue of the woman. His features soften as he gazes upon her. "We did not come down from the skies like many believe we did," he states. "We came from somewhere else." He glances my way once before returning to the statue. "Did you read the book I gave you?" he suddenly asks.

Heat steals over my cheeks and I duck my head. "A little," I admit, "but I wasn't able to finish it."

He nods as if expecting that answer. "What did you think?"

My breath catches in my throat. Is he asking me my opinion? A God to a seemingly mortal girl?

My lips part and I answer him. "It was interesting."

"In what way?"

I consider the book he'd given me to read as I stare at the statue of the woman, my eyes roving up and over her face again to the crown that looks half like a sun and half like a dozen spikes sticking out of the back of her head.

"There was no author," I say, "but it was clear to me that whoever they are, they don't consider the Divine

Beings as anything more than interlopers in this world."
These words feel dangerous, especially to speak them to a
God, but Caedmon doesn't grow angry or chastise me.
He's the one who gave me the text, after all. I assume he's
already read it himself.

"The author wrote that humans came from the
Hinterlands and that the Gods are afraid of that place,"
I say.

Caedmon remains silent as I talk and I take that as my
cue to keep going. "They said that the Hinterlands were a
place of refuge and safety." I peer at him out of the corner
of my eye and decide to give a little truth of my own since
he already knows that I'm from that place due to the fake
last name I'd chosen when I entered this Academy.

"I remember it being a brutal place," I admit to him.
"The winters were colder than any outside of the woods,
darker too. The summers were hot and the autumn and
spring were mild. More than anything, though, I
remember it being so quiet…"

An old memory surfaces, a day like any other. An
image of my father and I walking down to a local stream
appears in my mind's eye, both of us carrying heavy pails
as snow crunched underfoot. The sun bore down from
the sky and it had made everything seem so much
brighter as it reflected off the white glossy surface of the
stream we had gone to. It hadn't been too cold that day,
merely chilly after the storm had passed. In those woods,
my father had learned to hunt and he'd learned to build,
he told me.

He had shown me ways to set traps for the smaller
animals and had instructed me on offering thanks for the
lives they gave for ours. It hadn't been easy, living in the
middle of nowhere with no friends and no access to the

outside world and how others lived, but it had also been simpler.

"Quiet?" Caedmon prompts me as my voice trails off.

Shaking my head and the old memory away, I turn and look at the God at my side. His eyes fall to mine as I answer him. "It was *peaceful*." And maybe that's why I want so badly to return. Because the Hinterlands, to me, are not a place of darkness and fear and the unknown. The Hinterlands are a place of beauty and peace.

Caedmon tilts his head as if considering my words before he slowly pivots to face the statue. "It is important for you to understand this, Kiera," he says, his voice growing quieter as he talks. "The world is made up of different stories, different points of view. The ones that get taught and learned, though, are only one side. History is not written by the farmers or the peasants. History is written by kings and gods, by conquerors and rulers. The true history lies somewhere in between what is written and what is not."

I frown, confused more than ever now by his strange cryptic words. "Why are you telling me this?" I brave the question, feeling very much like I've somehow been picked up by a much larger being than myself and put into a small pond with other fish, all of whom are curious if not a bit hungry—trying to decide if I'm food or friend.

The smile he gives me is a bit sad, but when he answers, it's not what I'm expecting. "Even Gods lose people too," he tells me. "Divine Beings are only Divine so long as their blood remains untainted. Nothing ever remains the same eternally. Time changes all in this mortal world of yours, Kiera. I want you to be prepared for the challenges you will have to face in the future."

"What chall—"

He doesn't let me finish as he continues. "Both you and those boys you find yourself growing more and more attached to will need to overcome what is to pass. That is … if they wish to overcome their own monsters."

I stiffen at his words. "I'm not—" The denial leaps off my tongue before I can stop it, a refusal to believe what he says because the second he starts talking about 'the boys' my immediate thoughts drift to the Darkhavens.

Caedmon stops me with a raised palm, and the darkness of his eyes swirls, the ebony color receding a bit to reveal the warmer depth of brown there. "I am the God of Prophecy," he states. "I see far and I see much, but I can only see what may come to pass, not what will never come to pass. Remember that."

I don't know how I can forget it—his words resound inside my head, spinning around and around even as I struggle to truly understand their meaning.

Caedmon moves back slowly as if he is forcing himself to pull away from the statue of the woman. I glance from him to her, wondering who she is to him and whether or not she's important to him or important to me since he brought me here to talk to me of history and pasts and futures.

"You're dismissed from the rest of your shift today," Caedmon announces as he turns to go. "And from all future shifts in the library."

"What?" I gape at his back.

Without turning back, Caedmon doesn't halt his departing footsteps even as he calls back to me over his shoulder. "The library will always be open to you for research," he says, "but your requirements have been fulfilled. You may use it to your content, but you're no longer under forced duties. Use your time wisely, young one. I will be available if you need me."

With that, he disappears, leaving me standing in front of a curved wall and a row of strange God-like statues that I don't understand with words I *also* don't understand echoing in my head.

CHAPTER 25

KIERA

Caedmon's words linger in my head, making the ache present there pound ever greater as I enter the small bedroom below the Darkhaven chambers later that day. I'm so absorbed in the God of Prophecy's words that it takes me a moment longer to realize that I am not alone.

A small figure steps out of the corner of the room just as my head lifts and the scent of something wet and familiar hits my nose. The attack comes a split second later, and I react purely on the instinct that I've been repressing since the moment I set foot on Academy grounds.

Hands close over my arms and lift me from the ground. I let them. Dropping my weight and throwing them off. They stumble, meeting not just feeble resistance, but no resistance at all. My heartbeat, which under normal circumstances would soar, evens out. I blow out a long breath and count down from ten.

Ten. My attacker's leg collapses as my weight shifts. They grind their teeth—the sound like rocks clanking together as it's right next to my ears—and attempt to adjust their hold.

Nine. I rear back and slam the soles of my feet into their legs, kicking off and catapulting myself out of their arms.

Eight. Whirling back to face my opponent, the world fades away as I finally see who they are. My vision narrows. There's no mask or even masking spell to hide their identity—as if she knew no one would care if she got caught.

Seven. Rahela's face twists into a veil of rage and disgust. She's red with fury. *Fuck*. I should have known better than to think she would let things be after all, but it's too late now for regrets.

Six. I take another breath as I slide into position, feet apart, hands raised, fists at the ready. Two more breaths. Three. They come faster and faster. That's not right. They should slow down. I should be calm. I've done this many times before.

Five. Rahela dives for more, lifting her fingers as the water sitting on my nightstand shoots up, coming to her call and she throws it at me. It freezes in the air, turning into shards of sharp ice. With a muffled curse, I duck and weave out of the way of the onslaught. Her face grows more and more angry every time I glance at her.

Four. Rahela cracks her neck to the side and sneers at me. Her fingers twist into the air, recalling the water droplets and shattered ice all around the room, its chill sinking in past my clothes. A puff of white air snags in my throat and then rushes out. She lifts her hand and the water reforms into a giant ice spear, which she then takes and slings at me with all her might.

Three. My eyes widen, but my grin grows. It's been

too long since I've trained and I've gotten rusty in the months I've been in the Mortal Gods Academy of Riviere. Turning as it rushes towards me, I lift my elbow and bring it down hard just as the spear moves past me. The ice shatters mid-air, falling at my feet. I stomp my boot on a particularly large piece of it.

"Is this really necessary?" I grit out the question, frustrated as my back bumps into the wall opposite my bed. This room is far too small for close combat.

Two. I dart to the side, my calf slamming into the side of the bed, as the ice under my boot shivers and the particles still left lying across the wooden planked floor begin to tremble in what I assume is a response to Rahela's rage as she lifts her hand once more, drawing the ice and water around the room to form a ball next to her head. Spinning and spinning, it lingers like a weighty threat. I hiss out a curse. *Fucking bitch*. She really is trying to kill me.

"You should have just fucking died, you stupid human whore," Rahela snarls, teeth bared so much like an animal that I blink twice, wondering if I missed something.

"Died when?" I ask. "I don't remember almost dying any time in recent events." I pause and reach up, tapping my chin as I pretend to think about it.

Her upper lip curls back, exposing more of her teeth as bright blue flashes in her eyes, glowing with that Divine power within her. Then, just as suddenly, her expression evens out and she begins to move. I drop my hands back to my side, balling them back into fists.

Rahela slowly circles me and I—skirting around the thin bed frame of my cot—do the same. I can't fucking kill her, but if she's intent on trying to kill me, what choice do I have? I'm not about to let myself fall to someone like her, a barely trained Mortal God who knows nothing of the plight of the world outside these walls, nothing save for what she's been taught by the very beings that have kept her trapped here.

If anything, I pity Rahela. She makes me seem so much freer than I've ever felt outside of this damn contract that keeps me prisoner to the Underworld.

"Axlan's whip should have killed you." Rahela's words start to make sense.

Ah, so that's what she meant. Almost as soon as that realization comes to me, she sends the spinning ball of water towards my face. I dodge it, ducking and rolling across the floor only to pop back onto my feet and crash into the wall facing out towards the hallway. Seeing how close I am, I dive for the door only for the water in Rahela's power to collide with the handle and frame, turning to ice in an instant and freezing it shut.

"*Fucking cunt,*" I mutter, annoyed as I rip my hands away from the burning ice that's far colder than it naturally should be. Otherwise, I'd be able to rip the door open with my extra strength, but just touching that shit makes my skin feel like it's been sliced off. I can handle pain, but that doesn't mean I *like* it.

"There's the real you—disrespectful little human whore," Rahela spits at me.

I roll my eyes and face her again. "Respect is earned," I say, "and you certainly haven't earned anything but ire from me."

I crack my neck to the side and slide a hand toward the small of my back. She's made it clear that if I'm going to make it out of the room, it'll be at bloodied hands.

"You're a greedy little thing," Rahela tells me as the

ball of water spins and spins above her palm, streams of the leftover liquid not freezing the door shut are gathered and sucked back into its orb. I don't know what she's waiting for—perhaps my speedy reaction to her initial attack has thrown her off. "You just couldn't have one, you had to have all of them."

"What?" I blink at her. "Have *what*?"

"I saw you on the Day of Descendance!" she snaps. The water orb above her palm spikes out and then begins to spin faster.

Interesting, I think. *Her divine power is controlled by her emotions.* I had to work for my power, to strengthen it, but I've never felt that my emotions influence it to *this* degree.

"You walk in with that outfit, practically proclaiming that you're being shared between them. The three Darkhavens have *never* shared one woman between the three of them. Sure, perhaps Theos and Kalix, but—"

"Whoa, hold on." I lift my hands, palms facing her, but it seems my words only spur her into action as she takes my sudden pause as her cue to leap forward, thrusting her palm and the water ball from her grip. The spikes shoot out, stabbing into me as water splashes down my front before I can skid out of the way.

"Motherf—" My dagger is in my hand in the next second, yanked from its hiding place at the small of my back and I let my own power infuse it, darkness curling around the blade as I lift my eyes to meet hers.

Rahela's smile falters and then her eyes widen. "No ... you can't be..." She gapes at me, shock disrupting her momentum as she stumbles.

Her body slams into mine and I use the movement to turn the two of us. My blade lifts and I slide it up her body, the cut going straight through her middle up her breasts and then trailing off at her neck. She cries out and cups her hands over her throat.

Blood gushes down her opened tunic. "You're a fucking mortal!" she shrieks. "You can't be—"

Frost has already begun to form over my shaking limbs. A gasp escapes me as the little ice chips spread from my clothes to my skin, burning into me. I try to bat them away, but they cling even harder, like living creatures doing their Mistress' bidding. I clench my hands tighter around the hilt of my dagger.

One. No more stalling. The countdown has ended.

I raise it once more, intending to slice through her throat and end her miserable fucking existence. Ice crawls over my hands and when I tighten my hold, it flakes off.

The brimstone in the back of my neck heats, fire trailing a path down my spine. My knees hit the floor as a shocked and pained cry echoes out. It's not the ice but the fucking stone. It vibrates beneath my skin, every movement sending ricocheting tendrils of agony up and down my back and through my skull until I swear it'll explode. My vision fades for a moment and then a heavy *crack* lands and it clears again.

I blink my eyes open, not realizing I'd closed them, and glance up to see Rahela staring down at me with a vile twist to her lips. Her eyes are no longer glowing, but normal and dull as her hair flutters around her face in long dark tendrils. Her hands shake as she latches them into my hair.

Where the fuck is my dagger? The brimstone heats again and I bite down on my tongue, tasting blood to keep from screaming as it arches up and through me.

"You shouldn't exist," she says. "You're forbidden.

You have to be." It sounds like she's talking to herself more than me. She keeps repeating herself over and over again, the noise of her words like swords through my eardrums.

She rips my head back as water continues to ice down my body, crawling down to my limbs and sinking into my flesh. Were I human, I likely would already be close to hypothermia by now. A shiver overtakes me and tears leak from the corners of my eyes. The pain stems not from her pathetic powers, but from the damned brimstone shard.

Work, damn it. I urge my fingers even as my whole body seizes with the pain in my neck. The brimstone has never reacted this way—not since the day it was put in.

*Hold her down! Grab her legs, get her arms. Don't let—*I can feel my mind wanting to go back to that horrid night, but I bite down on my tongue harder, sending a wash of blood towards the back of my throat and the fresh pain makes the memory recoil until I'm firmly in the present.

"Even if you are a forbidden child," Rahela spits the words at me as she pulls my head back further. "This is a mercy—if I tell, *they'll* kill you. I want that right. It's my right to kill the whore who took what was mine." I barely feel the strands of my hair ripping free. By the Gods, it feels more like a massage compared to the torture of the brimstone's flames stroking through my bones.

I don't understand what's happening to the inside of my body, but I do know that if I don't fucking move, if I don't do *something,* I'm going to end up dead.

More water forms at Rahela's outstretched palm and begins to ice over once more. She curls her fingers around the beginnings of a hilt as the water extends, frost crawling down the hovering droplets to form a blade.

Shit. Shit. Shit.

I squeeze my eyes shut. Thunder rumbles overhead, louder and louder. My eyes pop open once more. Rahela flicks her gaze skyward and then her lips curve upward when her eyes connect with mine.

Son of a motherfucking bitch. After everything I've survived, I am *not* going to die like *this*. I extend my hands out to the floor, seeking, searching. *There!* I curl my fingers around the handle of my blade, fighting past the pain as my gaze narrows above me. The line cut through her tunic, making the fabric hang on either side of her breasts, is already starting to heal.

Thunder rumbles again. My dagger is in my palm before Rahela can even blink and I use my own pain as a force, fighting not against it, but pushing it beneath me to help me stand as I launch myself up. More hair tears free as she tries to keep her hold but fails. The metal of my blade slices through her ice as it darts between us to protect her, cutting it clean in half and then slicing through something with more warmth.

For a moment, time stills. I stand there, panting as the painful fire recedes from my mind with dizzying speed. Rahela's staring at me, her lips parted and gaping like a fish gasping on land. She chokes and then the line of red appears at her throat, coinciding perfectly with the line up her middle. Blood dribbles out like the perfect necklace without a back just as the door to my room slams open and three incredibly powerful and incredibly pissed off Mortal Gods arrive.

Rahela puts her hands to her throat and turns to them. Blood flows over her fingers and between them. Theos' face goes slack with shock, the fury dropping away to reveal stark confusion. He gapes at Rahela as she stumbles away from me and towards him. Ruen's brow is creased and his eyes flash from Rahela to the blood-coated dagger in my palm.

Kalix takes action though. The first one to do so, he strides through his brothers, half shoving them to the side as his gaze connects with mine and then with a wicked grin, he takes Rahela's head in his hands and snaps her neck to the side with a loud, sickening *crack!*

My stomach threatens to expel everything in it when her body sags and he doesn't just stop there. I watch, wide-eyed and horrified, as Kalix grips her shoulder with his free hand and clamps his other over the top of her head. Then, as if it doesn't take more effort than one might exert in rending a shirt, he tears her head from her shoulders, where it's connected to her spine ripping away as well.

I thought flesh would make a sound when it's being torn, but it doesn't. It's almost quiet, far quieter than paper or fabric. Blood drips and pools onto the floor and the scent of shit and urine hits my nose. I've seen death, caused it enough times not to be shocked by it, but I am not brutal. I am quick. I am clean. I kill with precision, not with the barbaric savagery that Kalix commands.

Rahela's body finally collapses to the floor between us, her legs and arms a tangle of limbs, and then, as if her head is an afterthought, Kalix tosses it next to her body and sighs. He places his hands on his hips and stares down at the merciless crime he'd just committed, and guilt blooms inside me because I know why. He did it for me.

"*What. The. Fuck.*" Ruen's quiet wrath is an ominous warning.

Kalix tips his head back, letting it fall onto his shoulders as he stares up to the ceiling above.

"What have you done, Kalix...?" Theos still sounds more shocked and confused than particularly angry or upset.

When Kalix lifts his head again, his moss green eyes meet mine. A silent understanding passes between us. He's waiting to see what I'll do. What my decision will be. Right now, I don't fucking know.

"You just killed another Mortal God," Ruen says the words and Kalix turns to face his brother with a casualness that I certainly don't feel. Quickly, I lower the dagger in my hand to the floor, turning and dropping onto the cot. It squeaks, the noise loud enough to make me flinch.

"So what?" Kalix asks with a shrug. "She attacked our Terra. She would've told the Gods that Kiera fought back —and then where would you be? Don't you want to keep some of your favorite servants in the Academy still breathing, Brother?"

Crimson fills Ruen's features, turning his normally stoic expression into one of sheer rage. I close my eyes, not wanting to see it, not wanting to acknowledge that it's my fault. He just doesn't know it.

"She would've healed from a throat cut," Theos says. "We could have reasoned with her to stay si—"

Kalix laughs, the sound unrepentant. "You thinking you could reason with Rahela is what put our Terra in this mess," he replies. "She was obsessive and wouldn't have stopped until she put our Terra in the ground."

"You wouldn't have given a shit before!" Theos' yell makes me bury my face in my hands. I don't know why I expected him to be on my side in this. I'm the one who told him that the sex hadn't meant anything.

"*Kiera.*" I raise my head and lower my palms, turning as my name slips from Ruen's poisoned lips. His eyes are glowing a dangerous red. The color pulsates in his irises. The room swells and shrinks, the walls growing and then shriveling back and forth as if he's losing control of his abilities as his emotions surge. "*Explain,*" he orders.

Kalix doesn't turn around now that Ruen is focused on me and I don't glance at him as I meet Ruen's stare. "I came in my room," I say, surprised by the evenness in my tone, but pushing through nonetheless. "And she was here waiting for me. She attacked me as I came in and I ... defended myself."

"That's all?"

I stare back at him and then push up off the bed. "What do you mean 'that's all?'" I ask. The sharp instincts that had me reacting so quickly have returned to where they came from and my heart rate has lowered, but the sound of his voice is grating on my ears. "Are you asking me if I fucking provoked a Mortal God into attempting to kill me?"

His face clears briefly as if he's shocked by my response, but then just as quickly his brow furrows again and he steps closer, just past Kalix. "Did you?"

I want to punch him. No, I want to do something worse. I want to take the dagger I used to slit Rahela's throat and I want to dig out his eyeballs and throw them into a fire.

"*No.*" If anything, since my punishment, I've been a perfectly acceptable Terra. I might have allowed myself to be a little more mouthy to them, but outside this tower, I've been submissive and obedient. I let Kalix grope me and finger fuck me in front of Dolos, for fuck's sake!

"Ruen, don't put this on her," Theos says. "She's just a human—"

Kalix snorts and shakes his head. "Enough of this," he says, dragging their attention back from me. "We need to let the faculty know and take care of the body." He gestures to the corpse still lying on the ground, her blood soaking into the floorboards.

Ruen growls right before he lets loose a long stream of curses, some in a language I'm not sure I understand. Perhaps the ancient Gods' language. I knew they had a class that studied it—not that I paid attention—but I didn't know their education allowed them to learn curses in that language.

"They're not going to be happy about this," Theos says.

"Tell them I killed her for overstepping," Kalix replies. "It wouldn't be the first."

Bile rolls against the back of my tongue. It's not the first time? Was that why he'd torn her head from her shoulders so easily? To ensure that she wouldn't be able to heal from the slice I'd made to her throat? What will he ask for in return?

"They're going to want punishment," Ruen states, sounding far too cold for the fury he'd just been ready to unleash. My gaze shoots to his and he's staring at me *hard*.

"A week or two of imprisonment?" Kalix laughs. "That's fine. I can handle it."

My hands ball into fists, half expecting Ruen to say something to me about that, but he doesn't. Instead, he turns away and disappears out the door.

Theos curses. "I'll go help him gather the supplies,

you—" He glances at Kalix before turning worried eyes on me.

"Go," Kalix huffs as if he can read his mind. "I just killed one of our kind to keep her alive. I'm not going to fucking hurt her."

Theos lingers regardless, as if Kalix's words aren't quite enough for him, but when I nod to him that I'm okay, he finally sighs and stalks out. Once more, I collapse onto the bed and cover my face with my hands. All is silent, but the smell of blood just gets stronger and stronger.

"Well, that was a fun scene to walk into," Kalix muses as he, too, drops onto my bed. The rusty springs beneath don't just squeal like they do with me, they scream loud and long as if the pressure of his body is torturous to them. "Guess you owe me a favor now, huh?"

"Owe you a favor?" I whip my head towards him. "You just fucking killed someone and they're going to blame me for it!"

He arches one dark brow and swipes a hand over the top of his head, pushing back the shaggy, wet hair there. It's then that I notice how he's dressed. Body half naked with only a pair of trousers pulled up his long thighs and calves, not even laced properly. No shirt. No boots. His hair is dripping with water. He must have just come out of the bathing chamber.

"They would have blamed you regardless had you actually killed her," Kalix replies coolly, those green eyes flicking to me, then to the body in front of us. He toes her arm with his foot and grimaces. "To be honest, though, she's been getting annoying for a while. I've been looking for a reason to get rid of her. You just gave me that reason."

"Killing ... comes easy to you, doesn't it?" I find myself asking.

His answer is little more than a noncommittal shrug. "I don't really care about the things that don't bother me and I don't care about things that don't matter to me. If something bothers me, though, then..." His hand moves over the evidence of what happens that's sitting right in front of us.

He really is deranged, I decide.

I don't have another moment to question him about that, however, as the door opens and Theos and Ruen appear carrying ... I stand up at the sight of the crates and the swords and saws sticking out of them.

"I can't watch this," I say.

Ruen and Theos drop the crate with a loud thunk. "Fine." Ruen nods to the open doorway and steps out of the way. "You should get cleaned up anyway, you're covered in blood."

I'm ... I glance down at my front and am shocked to see that he's right. I bite back a curse as I feel the blood dripping down the front of my throat and even if my uniform is now black, it's soaking in the crimson color of Rahela's blood, and I can smell it. I shoot a dark glare at Kalix, who doesn't even bother to get up off my bed.

"Come with me." Theos holds out his hand to me. I move around Rahela's body, my booted foot stepping through her blood since there's no path I can take around it—blood that I highly doubt will ever truly be cleaned out of the grooves of wood.

Just as I hit the doorway, I hear the springs of my cot squeal again as Kalix stands. "Not you," Ruen barks. "You're going to help me clean up this fucking mess."

My eyebrows rise as I glance over my shoulder and

see Kalix give Ruen a bland look, but instead of arguing or simply walking out, he moves to the crate of supplies. Theos' hand touches my arm and I jolt, looking up at the concerned expression on his face. I press my lips together to keep myself from apologizing. He'd come down—they all had. Was it because they'd heard the fight? Would they have done that for another if I hadn't been their Terra?

"Let's get you cleaned up," Theos says, ushering me towards the stairwell.

I go simply because there's nowhere else for me to go. I'm not a scared ten-year-old girl anymore. I'm a twenty-year-old woman with half a lifetime of experience handling pain and killing others for survival. These three are just obstacles in my way. I should not feel guilty for keeping Ruen and Theos in the dark about my identity. I should feel ashamed that I've failed Ophelia and Regis and the entire Guild by letting Kalix find out.

Theos is quiet as he and I move up the stairs and through the open door to the Darkhaven chambers, which looks like someone had nearly taken it off its hinges to get it open. Theos leads me up the stairs to the bathing chamber I've been in quite a few times before—just to clean it, of course—and opens the door, urging me through and into the still steamy room.

The mirrors along the wall are still coated in condensation and I stare at the blurry outline of my black and white figure in one of them as Theos goes to the bathtub that sits in the center of the room. He rolls up the sleeves of his loose-fitting tunic and then bends to mess with something inside. Faucets shriek and water spurts out as it begins filling the tub.

When he stands again and looks back to me, his

golden eyes fall to my throat where the droplets of blood I suspect are starting to crust to my skin. Keeping his gaze there, he strides forward, not stopping until he's standing right in front of me. His hand rises towards me deliberately and only when he touches the first button below my collarbone do his eyes lift to meet mine.

Whatever he sees has him undoing the button and then the next one. His pace is unhurried as he carefully undoes them all and then prompts me to turn and face away from him towards the mirror as he slides the uniform's jacket from my arms. Beneath it, I wear a small cream tunic and my bindings under that.

A shuffle of fabric reaches my ears and I close my eyes, breathing deeply into my lungs. I expect Theos to leave then, but to my utter dismay, he comes right back after disposing of my uniform coat. This time, he takes my hand and leads me back towards the tub where he has me stand next to it as he then undoes my trousers and pulls them down my legs, stopping when they refuse to move over my booted feet.

I perch on the tub's edge and he flashes me a grateful smile as he carefully unlaces my boots, pulls them off, and then my trousers. Once he's done, he stands back up and stares at me, specifically at my tunic still covering me from shoulder to upper thigh.

"You know you're going to have to take that off too," he tells me.

My lips twitch into a smile. "I know how to bathe." I've just never had anyone do this for me—take care of me like this, remove my clothes, or start my bath. Not since my dad...

"Lift your arms." Theos' command is followed by his hands at the hem of my tunic and I suck in a breath as he sweeps it up and off me, dragging it over my head and tossing it over his shoulder.

His nostrils flare as he takes me in, from the tops of my still marked shoulders—where there are a few of the lash scars—to the reddened, fast-fading bruises on my knees from where I'd fallen during the fight in my room. Absently, I reach a hand up, fingering the place behind my neck where the brimstone had heated up and nearly made me lose myself—and my life.

"Take the bindings off." Theos breathes the words, eyes fixed on the place where my breasts are restrained against my body.

Leaning forward, keeping my eyes upon his, I take my fingers away from the brimstone shard and move them to where I'd tucked the end of my bindings—new ones that I'd had to find in the Terra infirmary since I was starting to run out of clothing here at the Academy. Pulling it free, I unwind the first piece and then continuously loosen the bands of fabric until more and more of my skin is revealed. All the while, Theos' gaze never leaves my flesh.

Wrong. So fucking wrong.

But I almost just died, I remind myself. *It's not wrong to want to feel a little alive, is it?*

Theos takes my bindings from me, wrapping them up without glancing away. My nipples pebble against my flesh, tightening at the tips of my breasts. "Underwear." The word comes from him on a nearly silent breath.

Swallowing down the emotion in my throat, I stand and shuck my underwear, kicking them away until I'm standing before him in nothing but the air that flows over my skin. His eyes catch fire, turning from liquid pools of gold into a dark void so vast and deep I could fall forever within them. He blinks and the darkness fades before the sunset returns.

"Let me help you get in," he murmurs, tucking the bindings into his pocket as he turns me and takes my hand. I stiffen but lift my leg anyway and step into the piping-hot water. A hiss leaves me and he curses. "Hold on." He rips his hand from mine so fast I nearly fall and have to reach out, catching hold of the lip of the tub as I hear him turning the faucets and adjusting the temperature.

"Okay, now ease in," Theos orders as his hands move over my shoulders and I slowly sink further into the water until it laps at the sides and comes up and up over my legs and knees. I close my eyes, sinking back as the heat—once painful—becomes soothing against my sore and aching muscles.

You're getting too close to them, I hear Ophelia tell me, her voice ripe with disapproval. I fucking know I am, but I can't seem to stop.

I'm no longer a spider winding my own web but another insect caught in theirs.

Kiera's face is flushed from the heat of the bath and she moans softly as I grab a washcloth and douse it in soap, bringing it to her shoulder and rubbing my thumb into her muscles through it. The sound she makes does bad things to my insides. It makes my cock stand at attention, craving a taste of something it's already had once and wants, very much, to have again.

I wash her gently, moving the cloth over her upper back and down her arms. Her pale breasts bob in the water, the pink tips visible even in the murky water salted with some of the herbs we keep in here for when we've had a damn rough day in training. The little red dots that speckle her front and face catch my eyes. I can't stand the sight of them, so I slide my hand up through her hair, taking a fistful of the silken strands, and tug her back.

Her lashes lift, such a different color than her actual hair, and those dagger-silver eyes of hers meet mine as I lightly touch the cloth to her neck and cheeks, wiping away the blood that still lingers there. Her pupils dilate,

233

blowing wide and dark, taking over the gray hue of her irises as if she wants to take in each and every detail as she watches me clean her body.

"Why are you doing this?" Her question is spoken so softly that I almost miss it.

"Doing what?" My voice is a whisper as my hand stills at her collarbone. I want to reach down and lift her breast above the water, flicking that perfect little rose-colored nipple, and see if she shudders or moans. One night certainly hadn't been enough for me, but since then, I haven't had an opportunity for round two.

Right now is not that opportunity, I remind myself, pulling my hand back.

Hers shoots out of the water and latches on to mine, fingers wrapping around my wrist. "Why are you bathing me?" she asks. "I'm not a child. I can take care of myself. You know that." She peers at me with a furrowed brow as if she truly cannot comprehend that someone would offer this for any other reason than another's inability to do so.

"Has no one ever taken care of you?" I ask curiously.

She flinches, but just as quickly erases the action as if it'd never happened. I blow out a breath. She doesn't seem nervous about her nudity anymore. In fact, she appears more comfortable in her own skin now than she did when she was still somewhat—a term I use incredibly loosely—covered on the Day of Descendance. It's driving me insane with wanting to touch and taste and take.

Before that, though, I'll have my answers.

Tipping my head to the side, I keep my hand in her hair. "Do you want me to stop?" I ask. Her eyes flick down, lashes shielding the emotion that I might read there. I tighten my hold and her lips part on a gasp.

"Answer me," I command as her lashes fly back up and her gaze collides with my own.

Her lips purse. "It's not that..."

"Then what is it?" I wait for an answer I'm not entirely sure I'll receive, but then after several minutes of silence, as the water cools significantly, she finally gives in.

"No one does anything nice without expecting something in return," she murmurs. "That's the law of the world. I'm not sure if whatever recompense you ask for will be something I'm willing to give."

"You think I'm doing this to ask something of you later?" Maybe I am. No, I *know* I am. She's hiding something and I want to crack her open and find it. I want to know everything about her. Kiera nods with a jerky movement, and it burns something in my chest. What kind of life has she lived?

My eyes slide shut as I contemplate how to respond. Even if all I've ever had are Ruen and Kalix—and at one time, Darius—I still had people that I knew would care for me should I need them. There is no record between my brothers and me. No idea or count on who has cared for whom more or how often. We do what needs to be done because they need it and that's the end. There's no tit for tat.

Exhaling, I reopen my eyes and fix them on the beautiful woman lying in the bath before me. I don't say anything as I urge her to sit forward, letting my fingers release her hair as I reach down and unplug the tub. The water starts to drain and she stands, the water sluicing off her limbs in smooth movements. My mouth dries up, but I force my body to turn and move away from her to grab one of the towels laid on the table near the door.

Unfolding it, I stride back to her just as she's stepping from the tub. In a blink, I have her wrapped up and swept off her feet. Not a single sound escapes her lips as she latches on to me, staring up at me from my arms with incredulity.

"Open the door, please," I ask her as we get there, and with a frown, she follows my command.

Neither of us says anything more until we're down the stairs and in the privacy of my personal chambers with the door closed between us and the shared rooms. Only then do I let her legs slip from my arms and her feet touch the floor.

"This can't happen, Theos."

My lips twitch as her eyes settle on my throat and just because I know what it'll do to her, I raise my arms over my head, stretching back until I fist a handful of my tunic in my grip and then rip it up and over my head. The fabric falls down my arms to my wrists. I toss it away as I advance on her. Kiera's eyes widen and she takes a hasty step back, keeping the towel up with her hands clamped tight to where it's tucked above her breasts. I don't slow down, don't give her a chance to run.

"Theos—"

My hand is in her hair before she can finish whatever denial she's about to utter and my mouth takes hers before it can fully be voiced. Despite the chill in the air, her skin is warm and the inside of her mouth is molten. My tongue dives in, touching against hers and in the next second, she relaxes against me.

Her hands come up around my neck and I rip her towel away before she can try to break the kiss. A gasp echoes from her mouth into mine and I swallow it down as I back her towards the bed. I know when we hit it because she halts and groans in what I suspect is a mixture of frustration and hunger.

"I remember how you taste," I tell her against her lips, "like the sweetest fruit on my tongue."

"We really shouldn't—"

"Let me taste you again," I cut her off, not afraid to beg. I want it more than I want anything right now, even my next breath, and I fear if I don't have her, I'll turn into a monster that might just take her without her consent. "Please..." I kiss her throat, dragging my lips and tongue down and down some more. Her nipples are hard little buds and I pinch one between my thumb and forefinger before licking the other and sucking it into my mouth.

She gasps, going up on her toes as she bows into me. Her hands find the back of my head, spearing through the strands. A cry leaves her lips and I switch positions, toying with the nipple that's now wet with my saliva and moving my mouth to the other.

Her hips writhe against me and my cock strains against the front placket of my trousers, demanding to be released. Not just yet though. I want her mindless with pleasure when I slide into her waiting warmth. I want her crying out, my name on her lips, as the world crashes around her, and then, only then, will I finally get what I want from her—the truth.

She might have thought she hid it well enough, but Kalix wouldn't just step forward and kill another Mortal God just because she attacked our servant. That's nothing like him—even if he's far more interested in her than he should be. I know I can't crack him, so it'll have to be her that breaks and if this is how it has to happen then so be it.

"Theos!"

LUCINDA DARK

That's a start, I think as I pull away and grab her around her thighs, hands cupping her as I jerk her up and onto the same bed where we last did this. One hand—so much smaller than my own—cups my shoulder as she exhales sharply. I go to my knees, one at a time, and then use my hold on her legs to drag her to the edge so that her cunt is right at the perfect height in my line of sight.

Pushing one thigh outward to reveal the pretty pink flesh of her pussy, I blow a soft stream of air over her quivering clit. She jolts, squirming on the bed even as her nails stab into my shoulder.

"Tell me that you want me," I whisper, getting closer and closer to that soft, wet secret flesh of hers.

"Theos..."

"*Say it.*" I lift my gaze to hers, feeling lightning in my veins. Too close, my powers tremble along my limbs, shuddering in my bloodstream. I tamp them down, needing them to stay under control. She's far too fragile for me to lose it in the midst of this, but I'll have her regardless. There is no stopping now, not when I'm close enough to see the way her pussy twitches for me.

"*Say. It.*"

We're both reckless—she and I. Two lost souls adrift in a wild world that never meant to house us all. Yet, still, we're here. Unwilling to die. Unwilling to fade from existence.

"*Tell me that you want me.*"

Her eyes collide with mine and her brow puckers, her lips forming the words and struggling as if she is scared to voice them even if the evidence is sitting right before me. Then she says it. The magical words.

"I want you, Theos."

I unleash the monster and descend upon her.

CHAPTER 27

KIERA

With a leg over one of his shoulders and the other pushed out so that he has full and complete access, Theos devours me. A shudder works through me, running up my spine and down my limbs. My hands clench into the soft fabrics beneath me as I writhe under him. He licks up my center, tongue swirling through the wetness gathered there. He's on his knees for me, lips on me, sucking my clit into his mouth as he fucks me with his tongue. I moan for him, my hands sliding into his hair, tangling there as I push it back and away from his face so that I can look down my body and meet his gilded gaze.

I'm so damn fucked.

That's possessiveness in those eyes. I've seen it enough from Gods and Mortal Gods alike but never towards me. I've never seen anyone look at me the way Theos Darkhaven is looking at me right now. Like I belong to him.

Will he still look at me like that when he learns the truth?

He settles his lips over my clit again and my back bows as lightning tears through me. I scream, arching up only to have one of his hands smooth up my belly and press me back down, holding me in place. I gasp, struggling for breath.

Somehow, I'd managed to convince myself that it wasn't this good, that it couldn't ever be this good. I'd overblown the sex between us in my mind and I'd been so wrong because it's not just this good, it's *better*. My memories dim in comparison.

Warm fingers span outward, stretching until he's nearly engulfing the entire width of my stomach, from hipbone to hipbone, from thumb to pinky. Wetness gushes down below, soaking my thighs and his chin. My lips are parted, but the noise locks in my throat as Theos finally pulls back.

Unlike the last time, though, he doesn't make me come with his mouth and he doesn't feed me my own juices. Instead, he lifts me off the bed and turns, sitting down with me on top of him, straddling his lap.

"Kiera." My name is a prayer on his tongue and I close my eyes as pain hits me in the chest, the sound more akin to the wishes and hopes our mortal ancestors once sent up to the Gods. Before they answered. Before they came down and ruined everything.

Shit. "Don't look at me like that," I warn him, covering his eyes with one of my hands even as I tremble in his arms.

His lashes flutter against my palms. The hands holding my ass in his grip slip away, tearing open the front of his trousers and freeing his cock. It juts up from the light dusting of hair. My eyes lock onto it as my fingers fall away from his eyes. I swallow and bite down on my lower lip as Theos takes himself in hand, gripping the base of his shaft and stroking it up once and then back down.

"You said the words," he whispers.

I had ... simply because I'd seen the need in his eyes and the hurt that would happen if I refused him again. Gods, I'm a fucking idiot.

"Theos, there's no future here," I tell him, still trying to be honest—or at least as honest as I can be. *There is no future between us,* not with the brimstone shard in my neck, the contract containing my blood, the debt hanging over my head, and the fact that I'm here in this Academy under false pretenses.

"I don't care."

Oh, Theos...

I close my eyes, blocking out the image of him staring up at me beseechingly.

"Even if this is all we have," he murmurs, leaning forward to touch his lips to mine. I feel so cold inside, crueler than I ever have been before. "Let me have it. I'll mourn you later."

He'll mourn me ... because he still thinks I'll die far sooner than him. Because Kalix is right, I'm a fucking liar.

Hating myself for being unable to deny him again, even if I want to shove him away, I bend my head and kiss him back. His cock throbs against my lower belly and lifting up onto my knees, I let him guide it towards my opening.

The moment I feel the head of him at my entrance, I press down, lowering myself onto his lap. His cock fills me, the slide of him into my inner depths slow and even.

A whimper escapes me and flows into him as his hands move back to my ass, gripping, kneading.

"All the way, *Dea*," Theos grits out, using his hold on me to slam himself all the way to the hilt.

I cry out as the feeling of him hitting somewhere deep within me coils up through me. With one hand on my ass, and the other snaking up my back to slide through my hair, gathering it into a fist, Theos directs me up and down. Much like riding a horse—only naked and on a Mortal God male—I ride Theos until sweat sticks to my skin, eradicating all the good the bath had done before.

"Yes, just like that," Theos urges, thrusting his hips up into me harder. "Fucking take me deep. So good." He kisses my lips, my jaw, my throat.

My skin feels too flushed, hot, and heating further. I can't breathe. My body is tingling all over. Little zings are shooting up and down my spine, collecting in each of the places he's touching as if the strange sensations are drawn specifically to him. The room blurs at the edges and I cling to him.

"Can you feel it, Kiera?" he asks.

Feel it? I can't feel anything—nothing save for him and the way he's driving my body into the fiery surface of the stars.

The room spins and for a moment I think I've finally lost it—that my head has cracked and I'm falling—but then my back hits the mattress and I realize that's not the case. Lifting my leg over his shoulder and standing at the edge of the bed, Theos thrusts into me, powering forward as his hands fall to my hips, dragging me to the edge and keeping me captive on the precipice.

Air saws in and out of my throat, raw and painful. Still, I cry out in the most blissful agony I've ever felt.

"So sweet for me," Theos hisses through his teeth, thighs still moving. When his thumb touches my clit, right above where we're connected, my entire being seizes. When he eases off, I nearly sob in desperation. My nails scratch the blankets and I arch up, locking onto his forearm, ready to drag him back.

"You want to come?" he asks.

Delirious, I answer. "Yes, yes, I—"

"Then tell me, *Dea*," he says leaning forward as he bottoms out, his cock cutting through me until there's no more room for anything else and my lower belly starts to ache. "What are you hiding from me?"

"What?" I gape at him, my mind trying to catch up with this sudden turn.

He flicks my clit and I jolt, nails biting down harder. Blood begins to flow and we both ignore the streaks dripping from his arms. He'll heal soon enough without a healer.

"*What. Are. You. Hiding. Dea?*" Each word is punctuated by a fresh withdrawal and thrust.

I realize that I've been fucking deceived. Conned. This bastard. My nails rake down his arms, slicing his arms open like ribbons and I don't care. I want him to bleed.

"Get off me," I snap.

He ignores me, fucking into me even harder. "Answer me," he demands.

"No!"

A hand lands on my throat and Theos' gilded gaze hovers over mine. "*Answer. Me.*" The effects of his persuasion slip under my skin and I shut my eyes, shaking my head as I try to shove it off. It's ruthless, wrapping around me, especially when he speaks again.

"*Look at me!*"

I do, and I fucking hate him for it.

Don't trust anyone, Kiera, Regis' warning sounds much like Ophelia's. They echo in my head, both of their voices combining into one as an unnatural burn itches at the back of my eyes. *Trust only yourself. No one will save you like you will.*

I should've known better. I should've been smarter than this. One fucking kind deed and I fell to his plot like an addict in need of a good hit. I want to throw up because it still feels so good having him inside me.

"Tell me what you're keeping from me," Theos orders.

I stare back at him and bare my teeth. His hand clamps down harder, his fingers tightening at the sides of my throat. I can hold out for as long as he can, probably longer.

"Fuck. You." His eyes widen as I grit the words out through clenched teeth.

He curses and finally slides his free hand from my hip to my clit, thumb moving over the little bundle of nerves at the apex of my thighs with sharp precision. I bite down on the scream that threatens to spill out, not wanting to give him the satisfaction of hearing my body lose control as my insides clamp down around him. His hips stutter against mine before he stills and holds himself deep inside me. The hot wetness of his release fills me and when his hand eases from my throat and his cock slips from my cunt, I feel it leak down my inner thighs.

I roll over and shut my eyes, pretending as if the man standing at the edge of the bed with his gaze boring into me doesn't exist. I press the heels of my hands into my closed eyelids as if doing so will keep the tears at bay.

The world is a cruel place, I've always known that.

I thought coming to a place like the Mortal Gods Academy would be no different, but it is.

It's far worse than the cruelty of the rest of the world. It's lies and secrets and damnation—no matter who you are. And you can't trust anyone.

I don't know how long I lie there, but I do know that Theos cleans himself up and leaves after a while. Still, I lie there. The door opens and closes again and I don't open my eyes, not even when I feel something warm and wet against my inner thighs, cleaning me. I pretend to be passed out—I'm certainly tired enough to be.

When I'm lifted from the bed and carefully placed under the sheets, I half expect Theos to crawl into the bed alongside me. He doesn't. Instead, I sense his body heat and presence just there for the longest time. Watching me. Waiting for something, I'm sure.

I don't give up the facade, and after what feels like hours of pretending to be unconscious, when I'm sure I'm truly about to fall asleep, his presence fades. The door to the bedroom opens and shuts, and then, so subtly that I'm sure he doesn't think I hear it—the lock clicks.

My eyes pop open and I sit up, turning to stare at the large oak door.

My first rule of survival has always been to never trust

anyone and I almost fucking broke it. For *him*—for a pompous manwhore of a spoiled God child. Mortal Gods Academy is far more dangerous than I think even Ophelia suspected. Mission or not, I'm not sure how much longer I can keep this up.

Creeping out of the bed on silent feet, I go in search of clothes. Finding Theos' wardrobe is easy work, but finding something that doesn't slide right off my frame is a bit more difficult. I manage to tug on one of his darker tunics and a pair of trousers that are obviously several years old and far too small for him as they're tossed and covered in a thin layer of dust at the very bottom. Pulling them on and lacing them up extra tight to keep them from falling, I go to the door and try the handle.

Yup. Locked.

I mentally flip Theos my middle finger. I take a step back and close my eyes, seeking out the minds of my familiars. The *Euoplos Dignitas* answers first, but it's too big for this task, so I send it off on another errand as a new plan forms in my mind. Once the creature is on its way, I seek out a closer spider, finding a small one at just the right size. It comes skittering under the door within minutes.

I open my eyes and bend down, holding my hand out as it crawls onto my palm. Spiders, unlike people, can be so loyal, I think with a bittersweet note. I relay to the little creature what I need from it as I turn my hand and press it close to the lock. The spider flutters off my fingers and crawls sideways over the door frame until it gets to the lock before disappearing inside.

As I wait for it to figure out the mechanics, carefully giving it a nudge here and there with the details I've learned over the years, I glance around the room. The dagger I usually keep on me had been dropped after the fight with Rahela, so now I'm weaponless.

Unlike Kalix's room which was adorned with numerous weapons, so much so that I half wondered if most of them weren't trophies he collected after defeating others instead of his own personal collection, Theos' room is far more normal. There's the bed and the nightstands. A window with a sitting bench in front of it. A trunk and ... *there!*

I dive across the room at the sight of the small short sword. There's a larger broadsword leaning against the bed, nearly hidden by the folds of the sheets, but I know I won't be able to take it with me—plus I've never been much good at longer ranged weapons. The short sword isn't a dagger but it will do better than nothing at all. I grab it and thank whatever luck I might still have that it's attached to a belt and sheath. Wrapping the leather at my waist and tying it off before I flip the tunic over it to hide its presence, I hear the telltale click of the lock and whirl around.

My hand goes to the hilt of the short sword but doesn't go any further as my little spider friend crawls out of the lock's hole. I send my thoughts to the little creature and sigh in relief as their proud emotions flood my mind.

"Thank you," I whisper to the little thing as I pick it up and set it on a nearby table. "If I ever come back, I'll be sure to leave out some good bugs for you to eat."

The spider lifts its front two fuzzy little legs as if it's responding and even with my shredded emotions, I can't help but smile. The smile is short-lived, though, as I turn back to my only route of exit. I press my ear to the door for a quick beat, listening hard to the other side for any sign that the brothers are out there in the shared spaces. A moment passes, but there's nothing except silence.

I decide to take my chances, carefully twisting the knob of the door and holding it until I ease it open and away from the frame. Peering out into the shared living area, I glance from the large arching windows to the door that leads out into the corridor. There's only one way out of this tower unless I feel like scaling and I'd really rather that not be my current option.

The short sword is a problem because it feels conspicuous but I didn't feel safe without a weapon before Rahela attacked me again—I certainly feel even less safe now. I hold my breath and creep out of the room, my feet slipping along the hardwood floors with practiced steps. I move towards the door that leads out into the stairwell and perform the same thing I had previously, checking the lock, twisting the knob completely, and easing it open to look out into the hall.

My heart nearly jumps out of my throat when I see a shadow cross the wall.

No, no, no, I plead silently. *Not now.*

Ruen appears at the top of the staircase, the shadows under his eyes seeming deeper than they had hours before—had it been hours? It couldn't have been longer than that. I glance back over my shoulder. The sun has definitely set now outside the windows across from where I stand. My fingers tremble lightly and I slowly blow out a breath and open the door wider, stepping out into the hall.

Ruen freezes when he sees me. His eyes move over me from head to toe, no doubt noting whose clothes I'm wearing. When his gaze gets to mine, it's hard to read whatever he might be thinking. For a long moment, he doesn't say anything and then, as if he's far too exhausted to do much of anything else, he exhales a breath and moves the rest of the way up the stairs, not stopping until he's standing in front of me.

"If you're going to run, just tell me right now," he says.

"Why? Planning on locking me up?" Like Theos had?

His nose wrinkles and his pupils dilate for a moment before he curses. "Are you fucking serious?" His midnight eyes narrow on me as he glares.

I blink and realize what he's referring to. I hadn't bathed after Theos and I had ... well, after what had happened, and there was only so much cleaning with a cloth could erase.

I hold up a hand before Ruen can launch into a scolding, well aware that I'm acting contrary to how a normal Terra would at this moment, especially to him. "Believe me," I tell him. "I already regret it and I can assure you that I have no plans to ever let it happen again." He stares at me, that vein in his jaw bulging again. I shrug. "I just want to leave before he gets back."

Ruen's brow eases slightly and he tips his head, staring down at me as if he's trying to read my thoughts. I'm confident by now that none of them have that ability, so I wait imitating patience for him to release me. Finally, he shakes his head and steps out of the way.

"He and Kalix are reporting to Dolos," Ruen says as I take that first step towards the staircase, pausing as Dolos' name leaves his lips.

Cold dread swallows my insides.

"They're explaining to Dolos how Rahela attacked Theos and Kalix stepped in," he continues. "Her absence would have otherwise been noted."

I turn back to face him. "They're taking the fall?" Numbness spreads through my limbs, down into my fingertips as my brow furrows. Theos had just fucked me to get information out of me—that much was clear—so why would he take the fall for me now, after I refused to give it to him? Why had he watched me after I'd pretended to fall asleep for that matter?

Ruen's gaze moves over me, from my face to my body and back again. In that one quick glance, though, I feel thoroughly scrutinized. As if he knows everything that just transpired between Theos and me and not just the sex. I press my lips together and force my expression to ease as I wait for his response.

"*We* are taking the fall, Kiera," Ruen states, clarifying. "Darkhavens do not let one fall without the rest. Technically, Kalix did kill her. We're just keeping your involvement quiet. Any more problems from you and I fear what will happen to the other Terra—even if Dolos has seemed to lose interest in you, I never trust that the Gods ever truly stop watching for long."

"I'm sorry." Despite how terribly things have gone between us, I mean the words. "I was just trying to defend myself." As I had been taught because no one would ever do it for me. Except for them. Because they are defending me, now, I realize. They're stepping between me and the Gods to ensure that my attacking a Mortal God, even if she had attacked me first, never comes to light.

The last vestiges of the instinctive fear and apprehension that had flooded my body slowly dissipate as does the tension. It releases and my shoulders sag slightly.

Eyes strong with the current of the midnight sky peer back at me, assessing. "Just ... don't run, Kiera." Ruen blows out a breath. "It would make my job far harder than I care for it to be. I only came back to inform you of the story we've decided to run with as well as some evidence that will help our case."

"Evidence?" What kind of evidence could they possibly have had for something that had occurred only hours ago?

"We're going with Rahela attacking Theos because she's been obsessed with him for a while."

"Why?" Theos was attractive, that much was obvious, but what woman would go as far as she had—or as far as they're trying to make it look like she went—just for a man?

"I'm sure you've noticed that Theos makes sport of going after females he shouldn't." I stiffen at what I assume is an unintentional insult but say nothing. "Rahela's mother is not exactly fond of our father. She was forbidden from playing with anyone of Azai's line. Theos took that as a challenge and when he abandoned her, she felt betrayed."

Because she had been, I think darkly. *Fucking Theos.* It's hard to feel bad for her, though, since she had tried to kill me first.

"She's been sending him love letters for a while. Theos wanted to burn them without opening them, but I kept a few of the more threatening ones on the off chance she actually went through with some of her promises."

Of course he kept them. Ruen is calculating and the letters would be evidence for him.

"I see." I deadpan. It doesn't make me feel any better to know that I'm not the only woman to have fallen for Theos. In fact, I was the reason we'd slept together in the first place. I'd felt sorry for the bastard. Now, I just want to shove his dick so far up his own ass that he tastes his own cum.

When Ruen doesn't say anything more, I give him a small nod. "Thank you for letting me know." I pivot back to the stairs.

"I meant what I said, Kiera," I hear him say at my back, voice hard. I take the first step down and the second. "If you run, I will find you," he continues.

I pause on the third step and look over my shoulder. "I'm not running," I tell him, making my new decision in a heartbeat. "You still owe me a favor, remember?" I just want to be away from the north tower and away from Theos when he returns. "I'm not leaving or running anywhere until I can collect."

Ruen's glittering eyes watch me with that ever-present wariness, but I don't say anything more and neither does he as I face forward and descend the steps, moving past my room until my feet carry me all the way to the end and then out the door and into fresh, cold air.

CHAPTER 29

KIERA

Rahela's death is taken in stride by the other Mortal Gods of the Academy. It makes me wonder if the girl ever had any actual friends.

I stare across the training grounds, the arena, as Theos takes a sword to the arm—the blade slicing clean over his bicep as blood dribbles from the wound. Perhaps it's dealing with Ophelia's training, but walking into the arena after my experiences is far easier than I'd expected. Despite the fact that I haven't spoken to Theos in days— not since I snuck out of his bedroom—even he had looked me over, likely for signs of distress, as we'd entered. I'd kept my face unmoved, my attention straightforward. Even if being in the arena did disturb me, I don't want to disrupt the invisible line we've drawn, though I'm not so foolish as to think he's dropped the matter for now. He knows that I'm hiding something and likely suspects that Kalix knows. Theos hadn't said a word, not even to ask me how I'd managed to break out of his room. I assume it's because he must think Ruen released me.

I don't care. I've made enough mistakes with Theos. There are far bigger and deadlier problems that lay in front of me.

As that thought runs through my mind, I swap my stare to the being of that bigger and deadlier problem. Kalix grins widely, his intense eyes narrowing and his pupils sliding into thin slits, as his opponent trembles before him.

The poor Mortal God that has unluckily drawn the short straw of sparring with him during training is a rather buff looking male with a shorn head and an aristocratic nose that seems to dominate his face beneath his too closely set eyes. He's not as beautiful as most Mortal Gods, so I assume he must be a Third tier—someone with more mortal blood than Divine.

Kalix has, like most of the males that have separated from the rest of the group with their sparring partners, removed his shirt for battle and circles his opponent like a predator with a helpless victim. He's enjoying frightening the male too much and with as excessively aware of the eyes in the arena as I am, I resist the urge to roll mine as he fake dives for the other male, nearly making his opponent scamper back and fall on his ass.

I turn my gaze to the final Darkhaven. Ruen stands still in the invisible ring of his own sparring area, his eyes flitting side to side as his opponent makes a zigzagging motion, cutting through the ground as he approaches. One moment Ruen is there and the next—as his assailant leaps, sword overhead—he's gone. The opponent then cries out and falls, face down into the dirt. There's no spray of blood, but he doesn't get back up as Ruen appears right over him, looking at the flat side of his sword before lifting his gaze from the metal and meeting mine.

It's been well over a week now since eliciting my favor from him, but I've still yet to receive word from Regis to let me know he's back in Riviere. My experience tells me it's normal to go several weeks, not just several days without hearing from him, especially when he's on a job. My mind, however, settles on the fact that he'd given his own mission an end date and that end date has come and gone.

This is why we don't give end dates to missions. It's almost like a jinx. He had to have thought it would be easy, and now is finding that it's not. *Regis is talented*, I remind myself. He was raised just like me, and in a lot of ways, he's a far superior assassin than I am. If it weren't for his aversion to filth and grime, he'd likely be ahead of me in terms of Ophelia's best killers. My only claim to fame is the fact that my Divine blood gives me better senses and certain abilities.

A feminine curse startles me from my reverie as a familiar body strides past me. She turns, letting her back hit the wall first as she tosses her blade into the sand at our feet and slides down to sit on her ass, knees folded up.

Maeryn's fiery red hair is pulled back into a series of intricate braids—some beaded and some free of adornment—on the top of her head as one long thick rope of hair hangs down her back. She's flushed from head to toe, her normally pale freckled skin pink due to the sun that has decided to come out from behind the wintry clouds. It no longer feels like winter is hovering overhead, but that spring might be on its way. I've been here for nearly a full semester when I wasn't even sure I'd make it past a few weeks. I surprise even myself sometimes.

"This is ridiculous," Maeryn mutters as she stares out over the arena, watching her classmates go at each other with dagger, sword, and fist.

Across the way, I spot Niall hurrying toward a large water barrel, set up for the Mortal Gods, no doubt, because the Gods often forget that Terra have needs as well. He waits in line to gather a mug of the water most likely to bring it to her.

I glance down again. What is she doing sitting over *here*?

"Do you know how many Mortal Gods die in those battles?" She snaps the question out so fast, I'm not sure if she's just talking because she's frustrated or if it's because she wants someone to listen. I keep my mouth shut, not saying a word.

Maeryn tips her head back and looks at me pointedly. "Well?" she prompts.

Fuck, she does *want a response.* I offer her a shrug. "No, I don't," I admit.

"Most of them," she tells me, looking back to the arena. "More survived these past battles because Maladesia had been selected as the original reigning judge." She flinches. "It's rare for that many to survive and advance."

"Have you battled before?" I ask before I can think better of it.

Her head slumps back against the stone wall and she blows out a breath. "Once," she confesses, eyes growing distant. "And it's something I'd rather not repeat. It took weeks for me to heal and I barely made it out with my life ... much less the nightmares."

The last part of her admission slips out quieter than the rest. *Nightmares,* I think. *Something we share.*

I, too, had nightmares for years after my first kill, after Ophelia's training. If I clear my mind enough or exhaust my body, then, sometimes I can outrun them, getting a few hours of sleep before they find me again. It makes sense that she would have them as well if she was forced to fight to the death in this very arena.

Maeryn fists the sand at her sides, lifting her hands and opening her palms to let the grains run between her fingers and back to the ground. A moment passes and I glance to see where Niall is in line. Two more Terra stand before him. He'll be over soon.

The Second Tier healer blows out a long breath. "Do you know what it does to someone like me," she starts again, drawing my attention, "to know that I've hurt someone, killed them, because I had to survive?"

I don't answer as she pulls her hands in front of her and stares. "I'm a healer," she says. "That's what I do— what I was meant to do. *Heal.* Not kill." Her hands drop again and I avert my eyes as her head turns up.

I shift on legs that feel numb. *How long have we been out here?* In my periphery, I see Maeryn's sad smile and hate myself for feeling relieved when she stops looking my way.

"Most of us have never had any other choice but to be here," she says. "I always wondered why humans wanted to be here too. What would drive them to these walls as if it was something to be revered to be allowed inside?" Maeryn glances across the arena and I follow her gaze just as Niall gets to the front of the line and excitedly dips his mug into the water, filling it up. "He's so sweet," she murmurs, lower than her earlier words. "Innocent in ways I likely don't deserve."

At that, my head jerks and I can't stop the way I whip

my eyes down to find her staring at me again. *Damn it.* A ruse? But no, there's no trickery in her eyes.

"Niall is kind," she says. "He's hard working. He's here because being a Terra at a Mortal Gods Academy will bring his family not just money but some prestige and out there"—she gestures above and beyond the walls currently surrounding us—"that means something." She sighs and drops her arm again. "Here, being a Mortal God means nothing because that's what *everyone* is. Being strong and destructive means more." She looks to where Kalix is standing over his unconscious opponent. I avoid looking at the Mortal God at his feet or at the blood streaming down Kalix's blade.

"That's why people fear the Darkhavens, because they realized that the second they entered the Academy," she confesses. "Most Mortal Gods don't band together, but most don't meet anyone like themselves until they've been taken from their mortal parents or from the facilities of the failed Mortal Gods—if they don't present their powers upon their birth."

"Why are you telling me this?" I ask.

Green eyes connect with mine, framed by red lashes. "They were smart. They used their already pre-formed unit to divide themselves, to make them stronger." That makes no sense. They were together to be apart? My confusion must be evident on my face, because her next words work to clarify. "They fought together and made everyone else stand up and take notice. Now, they don't have to be so close. They can separate and people still fear them even when they're not in a unit because they recognize that they are only as strong as their weakest link, and they have no weaknesses."

My brow furrows. In the distance, Niall moves away

from the water barrel and begins the trek towards us. "You've still lost me," I tell her honestly.

Maeryn groans and then slaps her hands against the sand, using it to stand up before brushing as much of the stuff from her ass and thighs as she can. "Dangers hover over the Academies like secrets," she states, slapping at her sides. "And secrets have a way of coming to light sooner or later, Kiera."

She stops moving and looks directly at me. Niall is only a few yards away. So whatever she has to say, it'll have to be now unless she wants him to hear, and considering she waited for him to be away before saying anything, I doubt she does. She strikes me as an intelligent woman. She must be if she, a healer, survived the battles.

"Gods imitate mortals," she whispers the words, eyes darting to the sides and back to me. "Just as mortals imitate Gods, but remember, no one can pretend forever and eventually—just like secrets—the masks come off."

My brow furrows and my arms slacken from behind my back as I turn to face her fully instead of remaining with my back pressed against the wall like I know I should. "What—"

"I got your water, Miss Maeryn," Niall hurries up between the two of us, an exuberant grin on his face.

Maeryn turns away from me without hesitation and smiles back at him. "Thank you so much, Niall," she says, taking the mug from his hands to chug it down like I'd seen men in Taverns chug mead and ale. She releases the lip of it with a gasp. "I really needed that."

I glimpse the lingering half a glass left and eye her with speculation. "Here, you can have the rest," she says, shoving it back into Niall's hands. "I'm good. I think my next sparring match is about to come up."

"Good luck!" Niall calls as she grabs the sword she'd dropped earlier and heads back across the arena.

I watch her go. A woman as slender as her and as ill-equipped to do battle would have needed that entire mug if not more. She could have walked over and gotten it herself, but she hadn't. She could have ordered him to get her more but she hadn't. To not make herself look like she needed it? Or too weak? Both likely answers. Along with a third...

Niall looks longingly down at the half-drunk mug of water. He considers it for a moment before looking back to me. "Do you want some?" he asks. "We can have it since she offered."

I close my eyes. Cunning little healer. My mouth stretches into a tight smile. "My Masters offered me water earlier," I lie easily. "You haven't had a drop since we came out here. Drink it."

Terra cannot have anything they have not been permitted. So, while their Mortal Gods sweat and train under the unusually warm sun, their Terra stand to the sides—eyes glued to that barrel of water that is only meant for them and can only be had if the hand that offers it is one of their Masters.

Yes, Niall's little Second Tier healer is far more intelligent than most give her credit for, I suspect. Which begs the question ... what the hell was she trying to tell me?

CHAPTER 30

KIERA

Training ends and Terra are released at the sound of the bell tower's echo across the Academy grounds. Niall and I head out and away from the arena, back towards the buildings meant solely for Terra usage. We separate and find our individual bathing chambers as most of the Terra move towards the dining hall in search of water and food after their long day outside.

Niall is softhearted enough that he doesn't want to leave me to eat alone, and I'm trying to get a bath in before the others come up to use the chambers lest they see my now nearly completely gone lash marks.

I spend no more time than necessary washing my body, wrinkling my nose at the hardened cakes of soap Terra use. Theos' bath salts had smelled so much better.

This is exactly why you shouldn't let people do nice things for you, a little voice in the back of my head chides. *You get too used to it.*

That voice isn't wrong.

Regardless, I quickly move through the motions,

dunking my head beneath the water and then rising back from the large open bath meant to hold dozens of Terra at once with a gasp. As I'm wiping the shadows from my eyes, a shadow streaks past the far wall and I freeze.

Without moving my head, my eyes go from one side of the wall to the other, picking over each and every piece of furniture there—from the benches to the stacks of bathing sheets to the extra soap cakes placed on a wooden tray—searching for another sign of the shadow. There's nothing, but that only makes me even more suspicious.

Restarting my movements with slower, more methodical motions, I duck my head, peering out through the curtain of my hair as I lift a leg out of the water, soaping it again and then picking up a nearby bucket to wash it clean. My heart slows to a steady beat as I breathe evenly, watching and waiting.

I perform the cleaning ritual on my second leg and then my arms and shoulders—still no more from the shadow. Something is here, though, I can sense them in the room—a quiet sort of presence. Curious, perhaps.

Once there's no more for me to clean and I'm sure I've taken far longer than I wanted to, I climb out of the bath and walk naked over to the stack of towels towards the back of the large room.

"Sssssssss."

I don't stop this time. I don't show any reaction at all as that hissing noise reaches me, just quiet enough that I'm sure it wouldn't have reached a human's ears nearly as quickly or as clearly. I pick up a bath sheet and whip the long strands of my pale silver hair over one shoulder, squeezing the water out with strong fingers before patting the locks with the sheet.

"Sssssssss."

My fingers continue their ministrations, moving over my hair and then the rest of my body. It isn't until the distinct sound of a rattle hits my ears—like the small child's toys I'd seen in marketplaces—that a true bolt of alarm slams into me. I glance over my shoulder, noting that I'd locked the inside of the door to the bathing chambers on the off chance that one of the other Terra had thought to come up during dinner and wonder how fast I can reach it and get out of the room before he attacks.

I take a step towards the doors, the bath sheet clutched in my fist, but not wrapped around me. Nudity means nothing in the face of knowing whether or not you can outrun a very specific sort of monster. My second step follows as I prepare to take off. That distinctive rattle echoes off the walls, closer than before, and just like that, I dive forward.

My bare feet slap the wet tiled floors. I only distantly worry about tripping on the slick surface as I focus the whole of my attention on the doors within my line of sight. I make it to within five feet of the damn lock when the hissing and rattling grows louder and then abruptly stops a split second before wide, strong arms with telltale markings from his earlier sparring come around my middle and pluck me off my feet.

Not fast enough is the answer apparently.

I bite down on the instinct to scream, throwing my elbow back into his face so fast that he grunts and his hold loosens. Just like breaking the hold of someone's hand—always go for the weak point. I jam my nails into the still healing wound in his forearm and throw myself forward, forcing him to break his grip on me.

"Shit!"

My lips curve up as he hisses in pain, but I haven't won yet. Not by a long shot. Those doors are still locked and I'm not on the other side. Even though he hasn't spoken a single word, I have the sense that he's playing a game with me. If I make it to where there are other eyes present, he might just let me go.

My feet hit the ground running. So close that I fling my arm out, hand reaching for the handle. It turns under my grip, but the door doesn't open. My other hand reaches for the lock but before my thumb and forefinger can grapple with it, Kalix's arms are back around my middle, hefting me up and turning me over one solid shoulder, ripping me from the literal door to my freedom. The bath sheet I'd had in my hands when I started running is on the tiles beneath us and he strides right over it and back into the warm water.

I bounce, cursing as I shove still wet hair out of my face. I can't kill him because then it reveals everything I've worked so damn hard to keep hidden, but that doesn't mean I won't put up a fight.

Curling my fingers into a fist, I bring it down hard against his lower back and relish in the grunt of pain he emits as soon as I strike his kidneys. For anyone else, that blow might've sent them down. For Kalix, however, all it does is make him chuckle darkly right before he sends me soaring into the center of the pool.

I bite down on my tongue, tasting blood, and squeeze my eyes shut as water closes over my head. The feeling of weightlessness overwhelms me in an instant and my eyes reopen to see murky depths all around. I turn, my hair floating near my face. I shove it out of the way as I spot the Mortal God cutting through the water towards me. With gritted teeth, I stroke backwards, arms pushing up and legs kicking as I resurface, gasping for air right before a hand locks on to my ankle, yanking me back under.

A mouthful of water invades. Kicking against Kalix's hold, I grit my teeth and slam my heel into his face. Cartilage crunches and his grip releases me. I spot the tendrils of dark red blood lifting up from his nostrils. Even under water, Kalix looks like a cruel king when he smiles.

My heart pounds unnecessarily in my ears. So loud that I swear he can hear it even through the water surrounding us. I bare my teeth at him as he waves his fingers at me, taunting me. Asshole. But I need air, so I tear away from him and race for the surface once more.

Lungs burning, I shove my head above water and gulp down the air for several long beats, waiting for Kalix to surface near me or to grab ahold of my legs once again. I turn in a circle, realizing just how far he'd managed to throw me. Unlike some public baths I'd been to before, the Terra bath is a big and deep circle with steps that start at the edge and go down the further you get to the middle—which is right where we are. As far from the lips of the bath as possible.

Is he trying to drown me?

Something touches my foot and I jerk my head down, peering into the somewhat clouded water. I don't see a hand on my ankle, though, but a tail. A black, scaly tail. It tugs, not hard, but insistent enough to tell me that it wants something.

What the fuck?

I try to kick the thing again, but it doesn't release me and then another finds my other ankle. Two scaly tails wrapping around my legs moving up. Bubbles rise from beneath the surface of the water a few feet away before Kalix comes up, slicking his hair back with both hands.

I gape at him. More blood leaks down the front of his face from both nostrils, and his nose is completely crooked. Without flinching, he takes it in a solid grip and snaps it back into place with a sickening squelch. Then with his thumb, he swipes at the blood from under his nostrils and lifts water from below to clean his face with.

"Done running, little liar?" he asks, arching a brow as he treads the deep water.

I continue to kick, but the tails never release me and if it's not him then ... shivers dance up my back. "What's touching me?"

He grins and spreads his arms out, sluicing through the water as he propels himself closer until our chests are nearly touching. I feel flushed, hot, and not at all clean like I had been after my bath.

"What is touching me, Kalix?" I demand, repeating the question as I try to kick the things off once more to no avail.

Kalix reaches for me and I try to send myself backwards only for the things latched on to my ankles to move towards him. My head dips back, hair going under water before I can right myself. His hand touches my waist and the second his fingers are on me, the creatures underwater release me.

Cutting my gaze to the side, I watch as twin little water snakes slide through the top of the water's surface, hurrying away from the two of us. I flip accusing eyes on the Mortal God smiling at me with a little blood still on his lip and a wild look in his eyes.

"Cheating much?" I ask.

"All is fair in war, sweet little thief," he says. "It was cheating for you to blind me back in Mineval, but you don't hear me complaining."

I go still, my legs no longer kicking beneath the water to keep me afloat as he pulls me more firmly against his profoundly *hard* body. Just like me, he's naked, and I can feel the evidence of all that hardness pressing right against the skin beneath my belly button.

"Mineval?" I repeat, forcing a casual and confused tone into the word.

He chuckles. "Don't try to deny it," he murmurs, head dropping against my throat.

I swallow as he presses a kiss right where my heartbeat throbs, smiling against the delicate flesh as if he knows what I'm thinking. Kalix Darkhaven is an enigma. He's difficult to predict and he likes it that way for a reason. I don't know if he's going to fuck me or kill me or perhaps even both.

"You sensed me before you ran," he whispers against my flesh. "Just like you did that night." Teeth scrape up the side of my neck and I gasp for breath as I arch up, feeling tingles racing down my chest. "Why did you set those humans free?"

"I didn't—"

His hand tangles in my hair, the strands curling around his fingers as he does so. My neck strains as it's ripped back and I'm forced to stare up into snake slitted pupils surrounded by jade green. "*Don't lie.*"

I press my lips together for a beat. "Then I can't tell you anything," I say. "I won't divulge anything I've done before coming to the Academy."

He arches a brow, the violent expression on his face easing somewhat in mollification. So fickle, this Mortal God. "But you'll tell me anything from the time you entered?" he asks.

I blink at him. Considering I haven't necessarily done

anything that would unveil my purpose, I don't see why not. If I give him bits and pieces that make him feel like he's getting what he wants, he might stop asking the kind of questions that won't end well for either of us. Because I'm not sure if Ophelia would command it of me, but if she does—I don't know if I'd even survive trying to kill Kalix Darkhaven, much less what it would do to his brothers or my soul if I manage to succeed.

The hand in my hair loosens its hold and Kalix drags it downward, around to my throat as it strokes a thumb over my fluttering heartbeat there, eyes glued to where it thrums. "How did you stop from healing so fast after your punishment?"

The question is a bit surprising, but after a beat to think, I decide that the truth wouldn't necessarily hurt. "Poison."

He tilts his head to the side. "Poison? You weren't poisoned in the dungeons, were you? Did someone—"

"No!" I say quickly as I see darkness expanding in his gaze, anger filling the green color and turning it sinister and dangerous. "I poisoned myself because I knew I would heal, but I didn't want anyone to notice that I wasn't healing as slow as a normal human."

The clouds hovering over his eyes recede slightly and I breathe a sigh of relief. "I see." Kalix kicks his legs, turning us in a circle. "Interesting." He peers at me as if he's trying to figure out the image I'm supposed to present, as if he sees all these pieces but isn't quite sure how the puzzle fits together.

I swallow roughly. "Niall is waiting for me—"

"Your human friend can keep waiting," he says, cutting me off. "I want you to myself."

I gape at him. "You can have me to yourself all the

fucking time," I snap. "Why now?" And why did it *have* to be in the bathing chambers?

Instead of answering, Kalix turns, keeping one arm solidly locked around my waist, and propels us towards one of the edges of the pool. I kick my legs awkwardly, trying not to hit him as I do, but end up feeling as if all my movements are useless while he carries me until I feel steps beneath my feet. Once there, he releases me abruptly and my hand shoots out, slapping into the water as I catch myself from going under at the sudden change.

I shoot him a glare that he doesn't notice as he takes the steps out of the water two at a time, not stopping until only the lower half of his calves still remains beneath the surface. I look up and up some more, taking the full length of him in all his glory.

Kalix is tall and broad shouldered, like an ancient warrior of old—back when humans were the only beings on the land and they fought wars against each other to lay claim to the various territories. His thighs are strong and powerful, and his abdomen is shredded with muscle. When I get to his cock, my mouth goes bone dry.

Where Theos' was long with a mushroomed head, Kalix's cock is far thicker. But there's one major difference between him and Theos that I've somehow missed even with him rubbing against me on the Day of Descendance. My cheeks heat as I gawk at the bars that line the under-side made more evident by the erection he's sporting. There are at least five pieces of metal that pierce the skin there. I'd heard—in the backstreets—that there were such things done, but I've never seen it myself.

Kalix, noticing my expression, looks down at his cock and then grins before fisting his shaft and turning back fully to face me. "Like what you see, little liar?" he inquires, cocking his head to the side as he strokes himself before me like he's displaying the piercings for my viewing pleasure.

My eyes crawl up from the massive length between his legs over the shadowed ridges of his stomach muscles and then his pecs to his face. He looks proud, almost smug that he's stunned me, and I truly am so fucking shocked that I can't hide it from him.

"Why would any man ... do that to themselves?" I ask honestly.

He laughs, the sound more honest than I've ever heard it. Not calculated. Not deep and throaty and seductive. But real. That laugh is even more treacherous than his psychotic mind.

"Pain is fleeting," Kalix says, taking a step back into the water, deeper until it rises above his knees. He only stops at his thighs. I suspect it's because he doesn't want to shield his cock from my view. After all, I'm struggling to tear my eyes away from it. My gaze keeps going there. I've never felt so damn *innocent* before in my life—not since the night my father died and I was taken to the Underworld. "Pleasure can be whenever you want, little thief."

"I do not want it," I say, ripping my attention back to his face. "Not with you."

His smile doesn't dim even the slightest bit. "I thought I told you not to lie," he reminds me casually, hand slipping away from his cock as he takes another step into the water towards me.

I inhale sharply and move back. "I'm—" I see the water move before he does, but that can't be possible. Regardless, he's there in a beat, arms closing around me, lifting and turning me until it's my back against the steps as the water sloshes around our bodies, sliding between us like a third lover.

"I'll have to punish you for lying to me again after I warned you not to." Kalix's words drift over my ears just before my head closes under the surface. I release a scream, bubbles erupting at the muffled sound.

I fight against his hold, dragging my nails against the steps of the bath as I try to clamber backward and up. He drags me further, back into the center, deeper and deeper. I kick at him, but all Kalix does is catch one leg and wind it around his waist before grabbing ahold of the other and doing the same. Then I'm pounding on his chest with closed fists and struggling to get him to let me up.

He can fuck me if he wants, but if he doesn't let me surface soon then he'll be fucking a corpse. Kalix pushes his lips into mine, licking at the seam of my mouth with his tongue. A shudder works through my limbs.

How? I want to ask. *How is he doing this? How is he not struggling to breathe?*

Kalix shoves his mouth against mine harder, demanding. And just because I hope it makes him release me, I finally open mine. The second my lips part, he's there, thrusting his tongue over mine like an invading army, taking and pillaging.

Kissing Kalix is raw and violent. I scratch his chest and when still he doesn't let me up for air, I snap my teeth down, biting the shit out of his tongue until blood rushes into my mouth. He pulls his head back and grins down at me before kicking his feet, sending the both of us upward with strong strokes.

Black dots are dancing in front of my vision, blurring everything at the edges. When our heads break through the water, I cough, water spewing from my lips.

"You ... fucking ... *asshole!*" I bite out, gagging as more and more water comes up. How the fuck was he able to kiss me with so much damn water in my mouth?

"I warned you," Kalix says, not sounding the least bit upset. My legs are still around his waist and I find that I'm so exhausted by fighting him that if he's going to let me cling to him and use him as something to keep me afloat, then that's his problem.

I suck in breath after breath, panting even as my hands lock on to either side of his arms and I press my face into the bare chest in front of me. I close my eyes and just luxuriate in the feeling of fresh air in my lungs. It's almost peaceful. *Almost.*

It's always almost a lot of fucking things with these Darkhavens.

Kalix's cock bumps against my ass and I immediately release him and tread water a few feet away. He arches a brow at me as I glare back at him, not even trying to pretend to be his Terra in this moment. "If I wanted to fuck you, I would have you, little thief," he tells me. "Running only makes me want to force you."

I ignore his words and gesture to the bath around us and below with a big splash. "What the fuck was that?" I demand. "How are you able to hold your breath for that damn long?"

He tips his head to the side, lifting a hand to stroke back some of the wet black strands of his hair once more. "Some snakes can hold their breath underwater for ten minutes or even as long as an hour," he says. "My familiars' abilities can become my own. As a Mortal God, I would have thought you'd—"

I dive for him, slamming the heel of my palm up until it cracks against his nose, shoving the cartilage up as

273

blood spurts with a satisfying spray. Glittering green eyes flare wider and the smile he sends me, coated in his own blood, is anything but angry. *Fucking psycho.*

Kalix rolls his eyes and lifts his hands, gripping my wrists and pulling mine away. "No one else is here," he assures me.

"You don't know that," I snap. "Forgive me if I don't necessarily trust the man who's been chasing me around this fucking bathing room like a randy fucking Lord God with a mortal housemaid."

"I do know that," he insists, ignoring my other comment. "My familiars are keeping a watch." His hands slip down my arms and back to my hips and I find him grabbing the backs of my thighs and lifting me against him until my legs are around him once more.

I blink. *How did that happen?*

He nuzzles against my neck, breathing warm air over the quickly cooling flesh. "You fight me so beautifully, little liar," he murmurs against me. "You never give in even if you're overpowered."

His cock bumps against my ass again and I bite down hard on my lower lip as I lift up and away from it. I squirm in his arms, uncomfortable. And in true Kalix fashion, he grips my hips and brings me down with great force. All the air I just replaced rushes back out of me as the head of his cock sears into my entrance and then just *slams* inside.

I cry out before I realize what he's done—what I've *let* him do—and then slap a hand over my mouth. The bars of his cock rub against my inner walls, scraping through my insides and setting off little fireworks throughout my body.

This was what he'd meant, I realize belatedly, when

he said that pain was only temporary but pleasure could be whenever I wanted it.

Those piercings are stroking places in my pussy that I didn't know could be stroked. Moving over them with each thrust as he pulls me up, nearly removing me from his cock before thrusting back in. Tears pop into my eyes. I drop my palm away from my mouth and hold on to his shoulders.

"You're squeezing me so tight," he says, sounding pleased by the fact.

I want to punch him in the face ... after I can get my legs to stop trembling.

It feels like every time he plunges into my core, those metal piercings of his are setting off a thousand little mini-orgasms that have me unable to control the rest of my body. When he starts kicking his legs, driving us across the bath back towards the steps, I cling to him for dear life, feeling bright lights flash behind my closed eyelids as I slam them shut.

There's only so much a woman can handle and as proud as I am, I'm not sure I can handle Kalix Darkhaven when he has his mind set on fucking a woman senseless.

My ass connects with a step and drops down. Kalix stops—likely because his feet have found purchase a few feet down. Releasing his shoulder with one hand, I reach back and grip one of the steps above my head, holding on as Kalix uses his newfound position and ground to slice through me with his cock. His thrusts grow harder and increasingly more violent.

Water laps at my sides, splashing me in the face. I shake my head, gasping for air as I slip and it covers my head. I reach for him, intending to drag myself up and out again as his face hovers above mine. Just when my hands lock on to his now healed forearm, though, he pulls away, giving me no chance to use him as leverage.

Asshole! I mentally scream.

Rage pours through me and in retaliation, I set my nails to the sides of his abdomen—the parts I can reach and dig them in, breaking the skin. The pain only seems to push him harder though and above the surface, I feel the low vibration of a groan come from him.

Using my new hold, I burst out of the surface, water sluicing off my face and my hair sticking to my cheeks as Kalix laughs. He drops his own hand down over his face, wiping off the spray I'd just sent directly at him. His cock never leaves me though as he continues thrusting, keeping me pinned to the steps of the bath with a palm over my belly, pressing down.

He leans closer, dropping his voice until the low timbre rumbles against me. "Did you know," he whispers conspiratorially as he shoves his dick so far in and holds it within me that I swear he's coming up my throat, "that when I'm inside you this deep, I can feel my own cock right ... here." His palm presses harder and my eyes widen when my muscles all tighten as I try not to unleash my bladder.

I glare and bare my teeth at him, feeling like an animal caged in his grasp. "Is this all you have, *Dark-haven*?" I spit at him. "Or are the bars there to help with your poor performance?"

His head snaps back and his eyes narrow once more, the pupils becoming those slits. His palm slips away from my belly, but before I sigh in relief, he's dragging his dick from my cunt and flipping me over. My knees hit the steps with too much force despite the water slowing down the momentum and I know I'm going to have bruises later.

A moment later, Kalix's fingers tangle into my hair, gripping me at the scalp as he uses his hold to yank my head back and his cock fucks back into me in one long stroke. I release a choked moan as those bars hit a new place, setting off more of those mini-orgasms.

"I'll show you poor performance, *little liar*," Kalix hisses in my ear right before he takes the lobe between his teeth and bites down. Hard. I cry out, pain cutting through the flesh there, and feel something wet fall on my shoulder as it hovers above the water's surface. When he releases me, I turn my head and see the blood there and know that he did that on purpose.

Kalix thrusts into me so hard I nearly slam head-first into the next step. I slap my palm against the step and lift my leg, trying to ease the force of him, but it's not enough. It had been an offhanded comment, something meant to punish *him*. Now, it's backfired and I'm the one being punished anew.

Each shove into my pussy makes me feel like I'm being forced forward. My knees scrape against the steps beneath the water and it isn't until I feel cold, hard ground under them that I realize, he has been forcing me forward. He's been leading me with his cock out of the bath and onto the tiled floor surrounding it.

My skin tears against the rough surface and I grit my teeth as the pain hits. Kalix grunts, his low animalistic sounds echoing in the chamber just like the wet, slapping sounds of his hips against my ass.

"I like your rebelliousness," Kalix says, sounding as if he's breathless. His cock throbs inside me, the feeling of him swelling making me shudder as sparks dance against my spine, up and then back down. "I'll even encourage it from time to time."

I rake my teeth over my lips, tasting more blood. My hands try to hold my own body up and steady, but it's hard to do. I'm sure my legs are scratched to shit and I blame him as much as I relish in what he's doing. He makes me feel like I could just put my face to the cool tile and arch my ass up and just let him take me like we're two wolves in the darkest parts of the Hinterlands—violent animals mating under a full moon. Yet at the same time, he makes me want to wrap my hands around his throat and throttle him.

Kalix groans. "Gods, your fucking cunt is perfect."

No longer able to use the water as an excuse, now that we're on semi-dry land, I can tell that the wetness dripping from between my legs is my own. There's an ache in my abdomen and with a whimper, I clench around him, eliciting another groan from his lips.

I feel taken. I feel marked. I feel owned.

"Theos might have had you first," Kalix says, his words growing tighter and more clipped as he gets closer to his own release, "but I intend to keep you, little thief. So long as you amuse me, your body is mine. Continue to amuse me and no one ever has to know about your dirty little secret."

My eyes cloud over with tears as my fingernails dig into the grout of the tiles. A loud *smack* reaches my ears and I bite back a sob as lightning pulses through me at the sharp pain on my right asscheek as it heats and then spreads into something else. Another *smack* lands on the other asscheek, louder in the otherwise silent bathing chamber.

Those damn bars rub at a spot inside me so sensitive

that the tears run down my face, breaking free from my eyes as that lightning returns at the second slap. This time, it completely consumes me.

Kalix's hips still, and he pushes in one last time, his cock driving so deep he hits something and the ache there *throbs*. A low, erotic groan full of masculine pleasure unleashes from his lips as he spills himself inside me. His cum collides with my own, mixing and when he pulls back, it drips out of me onto the floor beneath us, the sound like light tapping.

Drip.

Drip.

Drip.

Panting, sweating, trembling, I stare down at my arms which seem to refuse to lift me up and then peer at my legs. They, too, are having a hard time. I close my eyes as humiliation slams into me far harder than anything ever has before.

What ... am I doing?

Before I have long to contemplate that thought, a pair of rough hands grip my hips and bodily lift me up. "I swear to the Gods if you try to fuck me again after that, I will slit your throat while you're sleeping," I growl.

Kalix's amused chuckle is his only response as he carries me the few steps back to the bath. I'm probably a wrinkled prune at this point, but I don't argue as he slides me into the warm water and washes away the blood on my hands and knees.

He sets me on the final step and as my eyes reopen, I watch him march across the room in all his tan, naked male flesh, unashamed of himself. But me—I have much to be ashamed of. Quickly scrubbing one of the bathing sheets over his head to dry his hair and then over his body, he drops it to the side and retrieves a fresh one before stalking back over to me.

This time, I keep my gaze on my bruised and cut-up knees. The bathing sheet is dropped next to me.

"I had my familiars leave a note for the Terra boy that you weren't hungry and had gone back to the north tower," Kalix says. "Return when you're done with the rest of your bathing rituals."

The shock of Kalix's admission has me whipping around just as he shifts into his snake form—his body collapsing in on itself as his skin stretches and his bones melt away into the new form. A long, thick, black serpent blinks at me once, twice, and then turns, slithering away, back into the dark—likely one of the various vents that air out this chamber when the steam becomes too much.

When I'm sure he's gone, I drop my back to the floor and stare up at the curved ceiling. My head is a mass of emotions and confusing questions. This game we're playing—the Darkhavens and I—it feels like I'm the one that started it, but I'm also the one missing half of the pieces.

"Where have you—" Theos freezes as he gets a whiff of my scent as I enter our shared chambers. His nose wrinkles. "Why do you smell like wet dirt?"

I'd have to agree with him. Those hard cakes I'd watched Kiera wash with had smelled like soil and herbs, not at all like the bath salts the healers sent us after training sessions. My own senses found the damn stuff repulsive as well which was why I'd ended up covering her in my scent, rubbing not just my body over hers, but my cock and seed into her core as well.

I grin in remembrance. Fingers snap in front of my face as Theos appears there, brows drawn down tight in annoyance. "Kalix!" He barks as if he's been saying my name on repeat for several minutes now. "Are you going to answer me? Why do you smell like that?" He frowns at me, still looking over my body with his upper lip curled back in disgust. Now dressed in a loose tunic and a new pair of trousers and boots, I stalk towards him with that shit-eating grin.

I can't stop the curve of my mouth even if I tried to. The feel of my little thief's cunt wrapping so tight around my cock still lingers on me like a phantom touch. Even with her temper, she's a fantastic fuck. Something I'll definitely be sampling again in the very near future.

"I shared a bath with our favorite Terra," I tell him honestly, smugly. Now the bastard can't say he's the only one to have had her. His jaw drops in stunned shock and I step past him and head for the stairs.

"Wait a fucking second!" Theos gathers himself much faster than I anticipated and I pause on the first step, glancing over my shoulder with an arched brow.

"Problem?"

He seethes. "Yes, there's a fucking problem. You can't fuck her."

I shrug. "Already did." I take the next step and keep talking as I move. "Besides, isn't it a little hypocritical of you to say that after you had her not just once but twice?"

"Ruen—"

I get to the final step and then lean over the railing, staring down at him. "Ruen does not dictate to me what I can or cannot do or who I can or cannot fuck," I state coldly. "You might follow his orders, but he knows better than to command me."

Whether they choose to acknowledge the threats circling our precious forbidden little treasure or not is up to them, not me. The two of them—Theos and Ruen—are already behind in terms of information. I've found out her filthy little secret and even if Theos was the one to play with her, he's an idiot for not seeing why she's such a temptation.

A forbidden God child masquerading as a human servant. The idea is laughable. Yet, she's a reality that none of us can deny. My smile grows as I imagine the reaction Ruen will have when he learns of her deceit. Oh yes, that's when true storm and madness will reign. There's a reason Ruen is seen as the de facto leader of our little family—outside of the pompous God sire we all share.

I'm not so naive like my brothers to think that Rahela's death will be the end. Dolos had taken our excuses with little more than a slap on the wrist once Ruen had produced those letters the damn bitch had been sending Theos. Always the planner and manipulator. But Rahela's mother will likely want recompense when she, too, joins us at the Academy for the God Council and I don't want anyone connected to the spiteful Sigyn, Goddess of Strife, thinking Kiera doesn't have protection.

Theos moves for the end of the stairs, stomping as if he means to come up to meet me. I turn and fold my arms across my chest, staring back down at him. "Ruen sets rules in place for a reason," Theos grits out. "If I have to follow them then so—"

"But you *haven't* followed them," I cut him off. "You fucked her immediately after Rahela attacked—were you feeling so bad about your nasty ex going after the Terra that you felt the need to give her a few orgasms as recompense?" My grin turns lethal. "Shall we compare notes?"

Theos' eyes flare with anger, going straight black before fading immediately back to gold. When he loses himself to his divine rage—that's when he becomes so much stronger. "What? Afraid I pleasured her more? Would that wound your arrogant pride?" I prod him a bit further.

He growls at me, baring his teeth in a way that only

serves to amuse me. I chuckle a bit and cock my head to the side. "Did I strike a nerve?" I ask.

He blows out a long breath and shoves a hand through his hair, pushing back the white strands, but they only spring forward once more, falling back into his face the moment he takes his hand away. "You're antagonizing me on purpose," he surmises, the glare and scowl fading a bit as he catches on.

I repress a groan. "Why must you always ruin my fun? I thought that was our eldest's job." Even if his position is only what it is because of a few months' difference.

"Ruen is the only one of us who seems to plan ahead. He got you out of the trouble you caused by killing Rahela," Theos replies. "The Gods need to think that we are under control—"

"The Gods do not understand systems without a hierarchy," I snap, cutting him off as my smile falls away completely. "I am my own hierarchy, Theos. Do not push me on this."

"This is fucked up, you know that, right?" he demands. "She's mortal and she's hiding something. If you did anything to break her—"

I hold my hand up, halting him. "You need not worry about our Terra's physical constitution," I assure him, recalling just how hard she'd fought both on land and underwater.

It makes my blood race just thinking about it. I reach up and touch the side of my nose in fond memory of when she'd kicked it so hard, she'd broken it. I wonder how she'd fare against me and my familiars. I shiver just thinking of the pleasure it would bring to see her fight against the hold of my snakes as I pinned her down and fucked into her sweet cunt.

"She's just fine," I tell my brother.

Gold eyes narrow on me, suspicion curling in their depths. "She's not hurt, then?"

I cock my head to the side a little bit, my lips twitching with remembered amusement. "She's well," is all I say.

Theos stares at me for a moment and I wait, expecting him to say something else and he doesn't disappoint. "Ruen thinks that once everyone has forgotten her punishment, perhaps in another semester or two, we can request a new Terra and she'll be reassigned. He's spoken to the Terra Librarian about having her work with—"

A snarl releases from my chest before I can hold it back. My fangs punch out of my gums and I have my hand wrapped around the railing, the wood creaking under my grip. "She is not leaving," I snap. "It is not an option."

Theos' eyes widen. "Kalix."

"Not. An. Option." I repeat the words, even as the lisp from my fangs makes enunciating them a bit harder than it usually would. My vision flashes blue and green, my serpent's sight, and then quickly flickers back to normal as I take a breath and settle the rage in my blood. I inhale deeply, pulling on the excruciatingly fresh memory of her skin, of her blood dripping as I fucked into her hot, tight little cunt.

My fangs retract and when I look back at my brother, calm has settled once more. I release the railing.

"Fucking shit." He gapes at me and stumbles a step back before pointing. "Tell me you didn't."

I straighten and stare down my nose at him. "Tell you I didn't *what?*"

"You fucked her, but did you scent mark her?"

I don't answer.

"You did, didn't you?" He brings his fist down on the railing at the end of the stairs and the whole thing groans. "No, Kalix. You cannot do this. You fucking can't scent mark her unless you intend to keep her and you don't keep—"

"I'm keeping her."

"You fucking snake." Anger bleeds into his expression, but so, too, does jealousy.

"Yes, I am." I offer him a shrug. "And you're an idiot for pissing the little Terra off with whatever you said to her."

He stiffens and his hand drops away from the railing. "I don't know what you're talking about."

I roll my eyes. After all these years, does he truly believe I don't know his tells as well as I know my snakes? The dart of his eyes to the left even as he tries to keep a stony face. "Is that so?" I deadpan.

"*It is.*"

"Then you have nothing to worry about," I tell him. I let my grin grow as I take a step down. "In fact, since you've fucked her and now so have I—perhaps we could share just like we used to. Do you think the Terra would like you in her cunt while I opened her pretty ass for my cock?"

Theos is up the stairs in a blink, hands fisted in my tunic and shoving me against the wall so hard that something cracks. I laugh, unafraid. I could turn him, flip us both—by the Gods, it would be easy to send him sailing over the railing to break his fucking legs. He'd heal, of course, but not as fast if I don't immediately take him to a healer and let his bones knit together wrong so that they'll have to be re-broken before they're set and healed again.

I do nothing, though, simply content to have a front row seat to my brother's downfall as he realizes that he wants her just as much as I do and that I'm not backing down. He knows he wants her, but ... what he said? She's hiding secrets? Perhaps Theos isn't as much of an idiot as I once thought.

"What's going on here?"

Theos releases me the second he hears Ruen's deep rumbling question. I arch a brow, silently daring him to tell our brother, but all he does is shoot me an angry look and then turn on his heel. I smile, taking two strides to reach the railing as I watch him stomp back down the stairs, bypass Ruen without so much as a word, and slam the door to his bedroom behind him.

A laugh bursts out of me and I shake my head. She truly does make things interesting.

Ruen's brow puckers in confusion as he stares at Theos' door before he switches his attention to me. "*Kalix.*"

I wave my hand in his general direction, pushing off the railing. "Don't worry about it, Ruen," I say, still chuckling. "I think our baby brother is just experiencing his first case of blue balls since losing his virginity."

Something hard slams into Theos' door from the inside in response to that. I go into my own room and close the door, leaving Ruen to deal with Theos' rage tantrum.

Yes, Kiera Nezerac is far more interesting than any Terra we've had before. Perhaps because she's not really a

Terra, but a Mortal God masquerading as such, and even if she hasn't told me why, I have every intention of taking a note from Theos' bag of tricks and fucking the answers out of her. I'll get it sooner or later, and by the Gods, what a true labor of lust this hard work of mine will be.

CHAPTER 32

KIERA

Two weeks after Rahela's attack, I wake to a bird's insistent tapping on my window. A mixture of excitement and relief has me out of bed in an instant, hopping over the new rug that had appeared in my room the day after the attack—no doubt to hide the blood stain I knew for sure wouldn't come out. No one ever visits a Terra's room, though, certainly not in the north tower, so no one would suspect that Rahela was killed here unless they came in and either scented the blood or searched for it.

I swing open the window and the bird lands much as it had the last time, little clawed feet on the crossing metal grate. I snatch the scroll on its leg and absently pet its beak with the tip of my finger as I unroll it with my other hand and read the short note written there.

Returned to Riviere. Urgent meeting requested. — R

I frown at the words written. Urgent? That's basically Regis speak for 'get your ass back to Madam Brione's before I come hunting for you myself.' Is it because he'd heard what happened at the Academy? I release a breath and stop stroking the bird's beak long enough to walk over to my nightstand and light the candle sitting there. The flame flares to life and I hold the scroll over it, letting it burn to nothing but ash as I scribble out my reply. It only has one word:

Sunday.

That'll be the only day Ruen will have completely free of training or classes and so will I, now that my duties in the library have been discontinued. I'm ready to call in my favor. As I roll up my note and attach it to the bird's leg, I spot my spider king crawling across the top of my mattress.

The bird flaps its wings as it leaps away from the window and catches the wind in the perfect gust that allows it to coast along back to Riviere. I shiver as I close the glass and take a step back. That one warm day we'd experienced seems to have been the last one of its kind for quite a while. From the slit of a window in my room, I can spot a light dusting of ice and snow on the ground.

Turning away from the disgusting sight, I drop onto the mattress and hold my hand out for my little familiar. The spider king crawls right into my palm with a new ease that we didn't have the first time we'd met. I smile and pat its head.

"I think I've got a good name for you," I tell it. "Just let me know what you think of these."

In response, the spider tilts its little head, bumping it against the pad of my fingertip in a request for more stroking. My smile widens.

"What do you think of Ragno?" I ask, peering down at the creature with curiosity as I send my thoughts to it. I wait, but there's no responding emotion.

"No?" I sigh. "What about ... Xaxis?"

Still, there's no emotion. Neither negative nor positive. I press my lips together, my slight strokes pausing. "Lacerta?" I ask. "Lacerto?" I glance down and wince. "I don't know if you're a boy or a girl," I admit a bit sheepishly.

The spider's emotions darken and then it pushes an answer back into my mind. "A girl?" I blink. "A spider queen then, it seems." The guilt at not recognizing her gender pangs in me, but I overcome it quickly enough as I swap my name ideas and begin rattling them off one after the other.

Each one either gets me no response or a negative one and on one that sounds a bit too close to that of a bird's name, my little spider queen nips at me.

"Okay," I say, shaking my hand out. "Definitely not that one then." I blow out a long breath and set my little friend on the bed next to me. "Let me think a bit more as I get dressed," I say.

She sits there, my form reflected in eight black eyes as I slip out of my sleep shirt and into the black uniform that I'm still being forced to wear most days. Binding my breasts down and tucking the last thread into the top, it comes to me. Slowly, I look over my shoulder at the spider that sits on my bed as if it's basking in the warmth of the room and the small kernel of sunlight that streams inside.

"Aranea?"

At the sound of the name, the spider turns and glances at me. She lifts her front two legs and rubs them together as her emotions pour into my mind. Sweet. Comfortable. *Right.*

I smile. "You like it?"

She rubs her legs together again and I finish dropping the tunic over my head before tucking it into the waistband of my trousers and snatching up my jacket, buttoning it up to my neck. "Then Aranea you shall be," I tell her. "I think it's a beautiful name."

I wonder if she knows, too, what it means. One of the few books in the old language that Ophelia had kept in her personal library was what seemed like a dictionary. I'd been horrid at old language, but I had been curious about what the word for spider had been, and thankfully, someone had drawn the little creature right next to that word and it'd been in the front of the book.

Aranea simply meant spider, and that's what my spider queen is. She is herself, a spider, a queen, and that's as simple as it gets.

"I'll be away this Sunday," I say quietly as I sit on the bed again and tug on my boots. I push my thoughts into her mind, directing her to see what I need from her while I'm gone. After a beat, she lowers her front two legs to the mattress and then scuttles away, disappearing behind the bed and into another hole in the wall. She'll likely be off to find herself some breakfast and then after, she'll gather the other spiders.

Just as I think of Aranea catching her breakfast, my stomach rumbles with hunger. Scrubbing a hand down my face, I stand and move towards the door, ready for the rest of this week to finish so that Sunday may come all the sooner.

I head to meet up with Niall in the droves of Terra moving like the living dead, their eyes half closed and heads hanging low as they all trudge towards the Terra dining hall through the cold. He's bundled in a dark gray jacket with his arms crossed over his chest and hands tucked against his sides as he walks.

Despite my different uniform, no one seems to care today who they're walking next to as I slip into their masses until I make my way to Niall and nudge him. He starts and swings his gaze around, wide-eyed, but when he sees it's me, he calms considerably and even offers me a small, tired smile.

I frown. "Are you okay?" I ask, curiously.

He nods, but the response is interrupted by a loud, jaw-cracking yawn and he blinks a moment later as if it'd startled him. Shaking his head, we move into the dining hall and sigh in relief as the cold goes from biting and harsh to only mildly uncomfortable.

"I'm okay," Niall finally answers me. "I'm just tired."

"Everyone seems that way," I note, glancing around pointedly before refocusing on him. He looks exhausted, but he always seemed far more accustomed to the work as a Terra than I. What could be causing him distress?

"Winter means shorter daylight hours, but no less work," he says. "The dark, I think, makes us all sleepier than we realize."

"Are you sure there's nothing else?" I insist. "Do you need help?"

Niall avoids looking at me as he stares straight ahead and shakes his head. "No, nothing else. I'm fine. I don't need any help."

Lie.

He's definitely not fine. There are deep bruises beneath his eyes and they match many others. "Did you receive extra duties?" I ask.

He stiffens and then blinks, as if remembering something. He turns and looks at me. "What makes you ask that?"

Answering a question with another question. One of the oldest tricks in the book for evasion. "Niall." I level him with a look. I stop walking and because he doesn't want to leave me—because that's just the kind of man he is—he stops walking too. Even as other Terra move around us, some shooting us dirty looks and most scowling at me openly. I'm surprised no one has been mean to him because of me, because he and I seem so— realization hits me.

"Have the other Terra been asking you to do their chores as well?" I demand.

He flushes and ducks his head. "I'm really hungry this morning, Kiera," he says. Another evasion. "Can we please hurry before all the good stuff is gone?"

I grab him by the shoulders. "Who?" I demand.

Niall immediately flicks his eyes up to someone over my shoulder and then back down. "No one."

I look behind me, but there are too many Terra here for me to know which one he'd been seeking out with that telling gaze of his. I flip back to him. "Tell me who is harassing you, Niall," I order, squeezing hard enough just to show how serious I am.

"It's not a big deal," Niall argues. "I'm just helping out a few Terra who've been falling behind—"

"A few? How many?"

Niall pinches his eyes shut as more pink travels up his face to fill his cheeks as well as his neck. "It's..." He opens his eyes and gives me a pleading look. "Really nothing. Please, can we get in line? I was too busy to eat dinner last night, so I'm hungry now."

Too busy to eat dinner? My upper lip curls back in irritation.

Before I can say no and argue, Niall pulls back and I have to release him or risk hurting him. He gives me a small sad smile and then turns, following the last remaining Terra who have made it into the dining hall. I stare after him as a sinking feeling spreads in my gut.

I watch him go, feeling like it's the wrong thing to do, but I don't know what else I *can* do. My hands clench into fists and I glance over my shoulder once more, scanning the room from side to side as I try to seek out any faces or any clues as to who might be responsible for those dark circles under Niall's eyes.

This is why I don't make friends on missions. This is why I don't care. Because when I start, I care too much.

I DON'T FIND out which of the other Terra are responsible for Niall's obvious exhaustion, but I do convince someone to tell me where the Second Tier residence building that Maeryn lives in is and which room is hers. A few denza I'd snuck into the Academy with me and the female Terra that had been straggling inside as the last of the line for the food was diminishing had been all too happy to take my coin and offer up the information. I'd slipped out before Niall had gotten his food or seen who I'd been talking to or where I'd gone.

For one, I need to tell her what's going on with Niall, and as a healer, there's something else she might be able to do for me.

Now, as all the rest of the Terra are eating their breakfast in the relative warmth of the dining hall, I'm sprinting across campus to the dorm building. Of course, it would be just my luck that she'd be in the south tower, as far from the north tower and the Terra buildings as possible.

Though I push my legs into a jog, I don't afford myself any of the luxury of my extra abilities. Not this out in the open. The south tower comes into view, and unlike the north tower, it appears far more well-kept, with vines growing beneath the ice up the circular stone that appears regularly washed and maintained. There are several more windows on this tower too, not just the massive ones at the top and the slits for the rest of the north tower storage rooms that I'm used to.

I wait and wait for a bit, hovering just out of sight of the doors that lead into the tower and when a few Second Tier females that I don't recognize come out in a pair, I sneak along the side of the stone walls and dive for the door before it shuts.

Fourth floor. Seventh room to the right. Fourth floor. Seventh room to the right. I chant the words in my mind as I take the stairs two at a time. I pause on the third floor as female voices sound in the hallway around the corner, but there's nowhere for me to hide.

Shit. I close my eyes and suck in a breath. Sweat collects at the back of my head and the dull aching throb that almost always accompanies me now begins to start its rapid *thud thud thud* at the base of my skull.

I open my eyes and straighten my back, lifting my head. If there's nowhere to hide then I won't hide, I decide. Most people ignore those around them and if you act like you belong then, in their eyes, you do. Keeping my head high, I move up the stairs, one at a time now, slowly and deliberately. Only one more floor to go. I act as if I've done this a million times—traveled up these stairs, walked these halls—and as the girls come around the corner, my breath catches.

Neither of them looks my way, though, as they dip their heads closer together. The one on the left is dressed in a cream-colored gown and says something that has the other who's dressed in a pair of black trousers like my own and a dark green tunic laughing as they pass me without ever lifting their gazes in my direction. I still hold my breath, though, until I make it down the third floor hallway and then to the fourth floor stairwell.

Releasing that breath, I start again taking the steps two at a time and once I'm on the fourth floor, I scan the doors on either side of the hall. Seventh room on the right. I race for it and pause, my hand half raised.

Wait! The voice of logic stops me. *What are you doing? You can't be here. You're not a Terra for the south tower. You're not Maeryn's Terra, Niall is.* But ... Maeryn would want to know if Niall was being harassed. She'd made it clear how much she values him that day at training and I'd seen the way she looks at him. She doesn't see him as just another human, as a servant.

I grit my teeth as I argue with my inner voice. Then, before I can think better of it, I knock three times on the seventh door. Footsteps sound on the other side and then the door creeps open and fiery red hair fills my vision a split second before Maeryn's stunned expression is there as well.

"Kiera?" She looks out into the hall, glancing up one way and then down the other. "What are you doing here?" she asks. Her gaze goes down to my uniform and before I can provide an answer, she asks another question. "Are you hurt?" She steps forward and places the back of her hand on my forehead. "You're flushed, come inside."

I'm still trying to drag air into my lungs as she pulls me into her bedroom and shuts the door behind us, my throat feeling raw from how fast my breaths are coming. The warmth of her room is vastly different from the chilly air outside or even the slightly dampened version in the corridor. It seeps into my bones and makes me sigh in relief as my muscles relax. I crack my neck to the side and peer around the Second Tier Mortal God's room.

The walls are stone like the ones in the north tower, but the differences between Maeryn's bedroom and the Darkhavens' chambers are vast. Instead of one large shared room and separate bedrooms, Maeryn's room appears more like the usual Lord bedroom chambers I've snuck into plenty of times before. It's rather large for a room with an arching window—only a single one that's of average size with a bench in front of it saddled with a stack of books. My gaze moves from it to the four-poster bed and the green tapestry on the only wall that doesn't boast a window, bed, or fireplace.

"Come in," Maeryn urges as she moves across the space to a cart near the fireplace, not as large as the Darkhavens', but not as small as the one in Hael's office. "Take a seat." She gestures to the bed, the only other place aside from that reading bench by the window.

I drift further into the room. A crystal chandelier hangs above with little cups for fire lights to illuminate the room after the sun has set. The scent of herbs and sandalwood permeates the space. It's relaxing. Maeryn pauses in front of the cart and glasses clink as she moves things around, opening bottles that don't look like liquor and sniffs them before setting them down and reaching for another.

"It should be far too long after your whipping for your wounds to be infected now," Maeryn murmurs. "Did something happen to them? Did they reopen? I can take a look, let me get you something to ease the pain—I might need to prod the lacerations to see if they—"

"No," I say quickly, correcting her. "No, I'm not ill. There's no fever. I'm not here for healing."

Maeryn lifts her head and slowly turns to face me, wide-eyed. "You're not?"

I shake my head. "I'm here because of..." Shit, Niall would definitely not like this, but there are very few people I actually like much less care about enough to go this far. I'm already here. It's too late. I suck in another breath and level Maeryn with a dark look. "I think the other Terra are harassing Niall," I inform her.

She blinks and then her gaze, too, darkens. "Harassing how?" She enunciates the two words slowly, with retribution in her eyes. There's no question of whether or not she believes me. Which must mean that I've already missed other signs as well.

"You suspected," I guess.

Maeryn is quiet for a moment, but then she nods. "He hasn't been sleeping well and he stays..." She bites down on her lip and glances to the side.

"He stays in your rooms for long hours, like he doesn't wish to return to the Terra dorms." I'd say it was another guess if I wasn't positively sure I'm right.

She nods. "I healed his arm a few days ago," she admits. "He never asks for healing—says it's not his place, but I could tell he was in pain and I pressed him until he revealed the wound. He swore he'd fallen while carrying a bag of laundry, but it took me longer than a simple bruise to heal. I'm pretty sure his arm was fractured at the very least. I suspected someone had pushed him and he was just too proud to say as much."

Pride or not, whatever Niall's reasons for keeping his problems to himself have my insides churning with violence. "I—" I stop talking as I realize the words that are about to come out of my mouth. *Fuck.* I turn away. *Was I about to tell her my plans to leave the academy?* I shake my head and smack the side of my temple with my palm. I need to get it together. This isn't even about the Darkhavens, so I can't blame it on them and the way they mess with my equilibrium.

"Kiera?" Maeryn's soft voice is confused when she calls my name.

I bite down on my next breath and turn to face her again. "Sorry," I say. "I just wanted to let you know my suspicions and ask—since it seems as if you care for him —for you to keep a lookout since ... well, I don't live in the dorms like the other Terra so I can't—"

"You don't need to explain," Maeryn says, holding up a hand to stop my embarrassing spew of explanation. "Of course I'll look after him. I *do* care about him, Kiera." Her brows crease as she slowly lowers her hand back to her side. Half of me wants to simply nod and walk out, but there is a reason I snuck into the female Mortal God's dorms. A reason I chanced getting caught where I know I'm not supposed to be and the least I can do is listen to whatever she so obviously wants to say if I'm going to ask for a favor anyway.

"You know not all Mortal Gods are like our parents," she says quietly. I stiffen, for a split second thinking she's talking about me, but then she keeps going and I relax once more. "I can understand that you're cautious—I'm surprised there aren't more humans like you, but I promise ... I truly do mean no harm to Niall. He's good." Then, below her breath, I hear her mutter, "far too good for someone like me."

I almost snort in derision. It must be part of a Mortal God's genetics to either be too pompous for their own good or self-loathing. There never seems to be any in between. Unless you're me that is because even I can admit that sometimes I'm far too prideful and self-loathing in the same instance. What had she said at her training class? That we're not all that different? She had no clue how right she truly is.

"Thank you," I say quietly, not letting on that I'd heard that last part. No doubt, she hadn't meant to say it aloud as she had and perhaps, if she still thinks I'm human, she didn't expect my ears to pick up on it.

Maeryn gives me a nod and then tilts her head to the side, curiously, as if finally realizing that it seems unlikely of me to come here and risk being caught and questioned all to ask her to look after my friend. "What *else* are you here for, Kiera?" she asks a moment later, confirming my suspicion.

Locking eyes with the stunning jade color in hers, I take a step further into the room. She moves away from the cart, the two of us striding in sync, circling each other until we're near the edge of her bed. "I might need a favor," I tell her.

She tilts her head in the opposite direction. "Is it about healing?" she asks.

I nod. Though I can't be sure, Regis' sudden departure from Riviere has me concerned. With Carcel on the way here, Regis wouldn't normally take on extra jobs. The fact that he has can only mean one thing—it has something to do with his missing brother, Grell.

Even after nearly ten years, Regis' dedication to finding his brother remains as strong as it was the day I'd met him. But if he had, then there would no doubt be things that even my Divine blood couldn't help Regis' brother with. Grell, if he's still alive, will no doubt need an experienced healer, and if I was right then a Divine healer like Maeryn might be able to do more than heal external wounds, but potentially emotional ones as well.

Both Regis and I know what kind of deviant and cruel things the Gods do with their toys. Perhaps it would have been better, merciful even, if Regis' brother died a long time ago rather than live through it all. Under the constant thumb of some wicked God who liked to break already too-breakable humans for pleasure.

"If I need your healing," I begin slowly. "What would it cost for your silence?"

Green eyes speckled with light flecks of gold and brown deep within their pools of emerald glimmer in almost—I pause—no, that can't be hurt, can it? Maeryn blinks and the emotion, whatever it is, disappears instantly.

"My silence can't be bought," Maeryn states coolly.

"If it's denza—" I have enough, hopefully. Surely even Mortal Gods have use for the coin, but Maeryn holds up her hand once more, halting my words.

"Like I said," she levels me with a hard look, "my silence can't be bought. It's earned."

A kernel of respect swells in my chest. Even if I had a good defense to her statement, I'd swallow it in this moment. I nod, understanding. "I see," I say simply because I have no idea what else can be said.

"I will keep a look out on Niall regardless of what you do, though," Maeryn says quickly as I turn to go. "My friendship with him does not affect you just as his with you doesn't affect me."

I pause just before I reach the door and turn back, glancing at her over my shoulder. My lips part and before I can think better of the words coming out of my mouth, they are already there. "I think in another life we would have been good friends, Maeryn." Perhaps if my mother had reported my existence, we would be more than good friends, but the best of friends. Living together in these very buildings that now feel like a prison to me.

Maeryn's attitude on the training grounds reminds me, then, though, that they are a prison to more than just me. Not every Mortal God thinks that they shit gold here. Some recognize the precarious position they're all in. They might be treated better, but at the end of the day, we're all carrying around the invisible shackles the Gods have placed on us.

I pivot back to the door and turn the handle, sneaking a look up and down the hall to make sure the coast is clear before I slip out. Hopefully, whatever Regis' immediacy is about, I won't need to come back for Maeryn. I don't know yet what will earn her silence and I'm not sure if I can chance another in this Gods forsaken place learning of the truth.

CHAPTER 33
KIERA

The rest of the week passes by rather quickly. I'm hoping that when I see Regis again, I'll perhaps gain more information on the details of this damned mission that brought me to the Mortal Gods Academy of Riviere to begin with. My boots crunch the snow that fell overnight under my foot, and I pause to glance up at the darkening clouds.

It's been well over a month now since the last update and I'm more convinced than ever this was one of Ophelia's tests. Surely, by now she'll have convinced herself that I can be trusted. The loss of the two million denza sits heavy in my stomach despite everything. Even I hadn't been aware of just how much hope I'd had for this job, for what it could do for me.

Now, I don't know what to believe anymore.

What little optimism had remained after a decade in service to the Underworld is dying a slow, painful death. I want to see Ophelia again, to demand the reason she would do this to me. Dangling a carrot in front of my face and pretending as if my goal was near is something the

Gods would do, not Ophelia. And yet, if I find out that my suspicions are, in fact, true—I sense no surprise.

I start moving again, catching sight of a familiar head of dark hair and a straight back. *Ruen.* Just the man I wanted to see. He's alone, and since receiving Regis' letter, I haven't had a chance to tell him that I'll need his services this weekend—two days from now, in fact.

"Master Ruen!" I call out when it appears that he's about to slip around the corner. I huff a breath as he stiffens and turns back, eyebrows rising to find me trailing after him. He turns entirely, eyes darkening as I approach. Still as cold as ever. That's just fine by me, though, so long as he keeps up his end of our little bargain.

"Kiera." He nods down to me as I come to a stop in front of him, panting slightly. His gaze travels down to the not-uniform I'm wearing. His lips turn down at the edges, but the rest of his face remains placid and expressionless as he speaks. "I don't believe I've ever seen you wearing a gown before."

I withhold a grimace. Yes, the true reason for my breathlessness. Although I don't mind gowns and dresses as a whole—they are warm enough with all their layers—walking around in them and even fighting in them is particularly difficult. How a few had been placed in my room as the tunics and trousers I preferred slowly disappeared, I had no idea. I had a sneaking suspicion, though, that a certain Darkhaven was behind the sudden disappearances.

Dauphine hadn't even questioned me when I'd gone to her this morning and requested more uniforms. Perhaps she had expected that my things would be stolen eventually. I look down at the dark woolen dress that reminds me of the blanket I'd been given upon arrival. It's thankfully not fancy, but a solid brown that makes any mud splatters on the skirts easy to hide. I'd still prefer trousers, but it's better than going around naked.

"My uniforms are missing," I tell Ruen without another thought.

Midnight eyes sharpen. "Missing?" he repeats.

I wave my hand dismissively. Discussing my attire is not why I stopped him. "It doesn't matter," I say. "I've already informed the head Terra and she's ordering new ones for me. *This*—" I gesture down to the heavy mass of skirts. "Was all I had left. It'll do until I get more trousers."

His scowl deepens. At this point. I think it's permanently fixed on his face. I don't know if I've ever even seen him smile. I step closer before he can say anything and lower my voice.

"I need you this weekend," I murmur quietly. Those deep ocean eyes of his widen a fraction and I repress a snort. "For an excursion," I say, "not for whatever you're thinking."

Ruen's face goes carefully blank. Ophelia would approve, I think absently, if he weren't a Mortal God anyway. "What day?" he clarifies.

"Sunday," I say. "Early."

He nods. "Meet me by the southern courtyard at dawn," he tells me.

I open my mouth to reply, but he's already turning and walking away. "Oh-kay," I huff out, watching him stride off. Despite his agreement in the library to help me see my 'brother,' I half expected him to back out when the actual time came. Hopefully, he has a plan for this Sunday, but if not ... I glance to the side, across the vast courtyard towards the front of the Academy's main entrance.

My head tilts back and I scan the walls above the gates that lead closer to the God city, Riviere. At least two older Mortal Gods stride back and forth with weapons strapped to their hips. Yes, I think. Just like prison guards.

I blow out a breath. I always have a backup, but I'd rather not use the sewers if necessary. Those are my last resort, even if they are practically a sure-fire way to get in and out unseen. I turn away from the sight of the older Mortal Gods managing all who go in or out of the Academy grounds and head for the Terra dining hall as the bells ring throughout the campus announcing the end of the class day.

Just as I'm entering the Terra courtyard outside the dining hall meant for servants, I feel a tingle race up the back of my mind. Pausing, I scan the surroundings, passing over all the Terra in their gray uniforms as they hurry toward the open doors and the warmth and food that waits inside. The statues that surround this court-yard stand like silent guards, watching them all as well.

Drifting closer to one of Danai, Tryphone's wife and the Queen of the Gods, as she stands with her hands lowered to her sides, but her gaze riveted on whatever is in front of her, I stop and scan the length of her stone dress. A smile threatens to break free and I feel myself softening as I spot my little spider Queen, Aranea, as she clambers around the side of the chiseled skirt.

Eight big, black round eyes gaze up at me and without hesitating I reach out and touch the top of her tiny little head. Small by comparison to me, but much larger than my other familiars. I shift closer, lowering my head as if I'm praying to Danai as I'd seen many other

Terra do, blocking anyone passing by from seeing the spider.

Aranea's mind reaches for my own and my eyes slide shut as images are passed from her to me. I'd asked her to do a search of the north tower for Kalix's potential familiars the morning before I'd spoken with Niall. When she'd later come back with a less than helpful report on Kalix's serpents, all of whom had slipped away whenever she had drawn near as if they could sense her powerful connection with me, I'd then given her a different task— finding out who was harassing my friend.

Dark corridors and smooth voices. Ara's memories record the sight of two far taller Terra, one boy and one girl, hovering over the form of a smaller one, though it's clear by the emotions she passes along with the images that she is confused by their language. The language of humans and Gods. She might understand me, but it's only because of our connection. To this little creature, humans, Mortal Gods, and Gods are all alike. Larger life forms that threaten her very existence.

It's the very reason she and her brethren hide, why they burrow into the ground and only come out when they feel it's safe. It is okay to be scary if one is large, but never when one is small and easily destroyed. My body stiffens when the memory shifts and the face of the smaller Terra comes into view.

My upper lip curls back and a growl rumbles low in my throat. Maeryn and I were right. I watch with sick helplessness in my gut as Niall's face is scrunched with confusion and resignation as the taller boy shoves him into a wall. He leans closer, hissing something I don't hear in the memory.

After a moment, I take my finger back from the spider

queen and blow out a breath, letting my growl trail off as I glance behind me to make sure no one has spotted us. Most people hate spiders and I've already caught enough attention as it is.

"Thank you," I whisper quietly to my little spider queen. "Keep a look out for him, too, if you don't mind."

Ara doesn't nod, but I feel the kernel of her agreement in my mind before she skitters on, disappearing around the back side of the statue and back into the shadows. Anger rises hot on the edges of her departure. I squash it, tamping it down as I turn to enter the Terra dining hall just like everyone else.

I spot Niall almost immediately, hovering at the back of the room, and when I approach, I step a little louder so that he hears me coming. His head lifts and his face brightens instantly, though the evidence of the dark shadows under his eyes remains. I offer a small smile in return.

"Evening," I murmur as we shuffle forward, the two of us, into line as we wait our turn to approach for food.

Niall opens his mouth to say something, only to freeze as he spots something over my shoulder. A cool grin slides onto my face, replacing the smile from before as I turn and see the man from the spider's memory. "Who's that?" I ask Niall, feigning casualness as I peer at the tall Terra that looks as built as a bull with his wide shoulders and square head.

Niall glances at me with trepidation before he ducks his head and murmurs an answer. "Th-that's Rodney," he says.

Rodney. A plain name for a plain looking man. I hum in the back of my throat. "Is he the one who's been bothering you?"

Niall's head shoots back up. "W-what? How—I mean, no, of course not. I-I told you the other day that I was fine."

I roll my eyes. "I'm not stupid, Niall." And I am also not forgiving of those who pick on the weak. "Why's he been targeting you?"

Soft brown locks swipe across Niall's forehead as he shakes his head. "H-he hasn't—"

I sigh and turn fully, giving Niall the brunt of my dark glare. "You stutter more when you're lying," I tell him. "Just give in. I already know that something is going on. Answer me. Why is he targeting you?"

Niall bites down on his lower lip and for a moment, I'm sure he's going to refuse me again, to deny what I can clearly see is fear and sorrow in his eyes. Then his eyes widen and he reaches out, grabbing ahold of my arm so fast I'm surprised by his speed more than his strength as he yanks me forward and I go.

"Whatever you're thinking, Kiera, don't," he whispers to me, his voice growing higher in pitch despite his attempt at quietness.

My grin grows. "I don't know what you mean," I lie.

Niall's brows lower and his lips part, but before he can say anything a shadow falls over both of us. "Well, well, well, if it's not Niall and the Godless whore."

I close my eyes and suck in a deep breath. Niall straightens immediately. "D-don't c-call her that," he squeaks out.

It's sweet, truly. Which only pisses me off more. I turn to face the brute known as Rodney. Up close, he's even uglier than in Ara's memories. His eyes are far too close together, his lips are thin, practically non-existent, and at the crux of his brows is a furrow of hair that draws them both together. I cross my arms over my chest and look up at him, quirking a brow.

"You certainly don't mean me, do you?" I inquire lightly.

Rodney ignores me. Instead, he reaches out to shove at Niall, his big meaty hand hitting my friend in the shoulder and sending him sailing back a few steps. My hands curl into fists beneath my elbows. I step in front of Niall as Rodney laughs and goes to shove him again. The big, stupid meathead stops and arches a brow at me.

"Godless whore," I state. "You don't mean me, do you?" I repeat the question.

He chortles, the sound half choking and half mocking. "Who else would I mean?" At his back, there's a girl who shifts closer. Despite her feminine features, she looks similar enough to Rodney for me to recognize that they must be related. Brother and sister, probably. Rodney grins down at me. "Heard that to make up for your disrespect before, you were led to the Day of Descendance and shared with plenty of our Masters. Bet that pussy of yours is well-used by now. I tried to ask my friend here"— Rodney gestures behind me to Niall—"if he's had a taste yet."

I let my light grin turn razor-sharp and bare my teeth. "If my body was accepted by the Gods, then how am I Godless?" I ask curious as to what his stupid little pea-sized brain has come up with.

To my pleasant surprise, the girl at his back steps up to his side and answers for him. "If you truly respected the Gods then you would never have disrespected them in the first place," she sneers at me. "Your remaining presence here is an insult to all Terra."

"Is that so?" I turn my attention to her and stay there.

Rodney shuffles back a step so that the girl stands in front of him. It's clear now who the brains of their little harassment is and who is the brawn. "It is," the girl sniffs in my direction, raising her face and crinkling her nose as if she smells something foul.

I nod as if I'm agreeing with her. "I still don't understand, though." I tap my chin thoughtfully.

The girl rolls her eyes, short stubby lashes twitching with the movement. "Of course you don't," she grouses. "You're too stupid to—"

"If I'm an insult to all Terra, why are you harassing this one?" I ask, cutting her off and gesturing to Niall who stands behind me somewhat dumbstruck as he gapes at me and then at the two in front of me.

I can sense the attention of several Terra in the dining hall. Some are pretending to eat their food, but plenty more have lost all pretense and are openly gawking at the four of us. There really is little by way of entertainment for the servants of the Academy if they're focused on this mess. Though I suppose I shouldn't really be surprised.

"Because he obviously doesn't understand the disgrace you made of the rest of us and continues to associate with you," the girl states matter-of-factly.

If this were the Underworld, it would be simple enough to grab the back of her head and help her meet the top of my knee cap. I imagine it now, locking my fingers into the thick, greasy looking brown mass piled at the back of her head and using it to direct her head into my knee again and again and again. Until her nose was broken and bloodied and her eyes were swollen with tears.

But this isn't the Underworld and despite my rising temper, I have to deal with this delicately.

"I see." I step closer, covering the girl's front as Rodney glares at me over her head. "Well, I should remind you that every Terra here is under ownership of the Mortal Gods and the Divine Beings. Fucking with one of them is, just as you accused me of being, *disrespectful* to the Gods." Her shoulders go back and she lifts her chin, though I see by the nervous glint in her eyes that she hadn't considered that. "I would absolutely hate for Niall's owner to find out that you harassed her servant without permission."

"We have permission," Rodney blurts.

Shock rolls through me, but I temper the reaction and slowly lift my gaze to his. "And just *who* gave you permission?" I demand.

"That doesn't matter," the girl says, coming back to herself. "It's not disrespect if—"

My hand snaps out, my folded arms falling away as I grab ahold of her wrist as she waves a hand through the air. She sucks in a shocked breath as I contract my fingers around her wrist. Tighter and tighter. "*Who* gave you permission?" I repeat the question, clearly articulating each word.

"Our Mistress," Rodney snaps. He reaches for my hand, but I step back out of his reach, dragging his sister with me. "Let Laria go," he demands.

Laria stares at me and tugs at her hand. I don't release her. "Who is your Mistress?" I already have a feeling I know, but I want to hear the confirmation.

"Rahela of the Goddess Sigyn's line," Laria whimpers as I contract my fingers harder.

"Your Mistress is gone." Dead. "You were given to a new Master." Laria tugs without success as she tries to get me to release her. I step even closer until our chests touch and I lower my voice. "If I hear that you're harassing Niall again," I warn her. "I will report you for *disrespect* and I can assure you, his Mistress is not as kind as she seems. She, after all, let me suffer with my wounds without healing for weeks." I don't mention that she had offered her help or that she had allowed Niall to bring me food when no one else had been brave enough to.

Laria's eyes widen and I let go just as she jerks her hand. She stumbles, falling back into her brother's arms with a yelp. I lower my hands back to my sides and stare at her, waiting for her reaction. If I'm right, she'll finally notice the eyes all watching us and embarrassment will make her bark something vile only to storm off.

Rodney glares as he helps her straighten. Laria, however, merely brushes him off and glares at me. Her cheeks redden. Right there. Just as I predicted, humiliation burns over her expression and she sneers at me. "No God would believe a Godless whore over the exalted and dedicated Terra."

I tilt my head to the side and offer her a confident smile. "If that's so, then you're welcome to test your theory. After all, I'm sure you were welcomed with open arms to the Day of Descendance party and allowed to dedicate your body to the Divine Beings and their children as well ... right?"

No. She wasn't. The Gods and their children are shallow people. Even if my own features and Divinity are dampened by the brimstone in my neck, compared to a girl of short stockiness and plain features ... the fury on her face makes it clear she understands my assumptions.

Without another word, she turns and stalks off. Rodney stays behind for a moment, his unibrow furrowing in confusion as he glances between me and his quickly departing sister, then he too, turns and follows. At my back, Niall releases a sound of relief.

"Kiera, you shouldn't have done that," he says, stepping to my side.

I turn to him and fix him with a dark look. "Don't ever lie to me again," I snap.

His brows arch up, nearly reaching his hairline, and his lips part in surprise. "I-I didn't want to burden you."

I shake my head. "I don't care. Don't"—I suck in a breath—"please don't hide shit from me again. Whatever it is, don't lie." I already deal with enough deceit that it's liable to one day drive me to madness. I can't stand more, especially not from him.

Niall ducks his head, and his brows lower at the same time. "I'm sorry," he murmurs and I believe him. I *want* to believe him.

Whether Ophelia realizes it or not, with this stupid test of hers, she's sparked the desire for freedom that has been slowly building since the night she bought me from those bandits. It felt so close, the reality of being free of the shackles of servitude and the contract that binds me to her. The fire inside me slowly kindling over the years is now aflame and I don't think anything can put it out now.

CHAPTER 34
KIERA

The light outside my slender bedroom window is a blurry dim ray on Sunday morning. No birds sing. No footsteps sound overhead, but I find a pair of dark trousers and a matching tunic—both too large for me—waiting outside my door. Quickly grabbing the clothes, I scan the corridor before closing the door, and quickly change out of the brown gown I've been wearing for days. It's starting to smell.

The trousers are loose on my hips and I use one of my daggers to cut slits in the waistband before weaving the dress's belt through the holes to keep them from falling down. Tucking the tunic into place and shoving my feet into my boots, I grab my cloak and hurry from the room within minutes.

The hallways are quiet as the sun peeks through the windows and I walk faster, practically racing through the slowly receding darkness until I'm sweating beneath the new clothes and panting for breath through raw lungs. The cold air slaps my cheeks when I reach the outside and I flick my hood up as I rush towards the southern gate.

I spot a figure dressed in dark fabrics waiting for me. Ruen turns as I approach. I don't know how he's tipped off by my approach, my footsteps are quieter now that I'm actually trying, but his expression doesn't change when he spots me.

"How are we doing this?" I ask as I come to a standstill beside him. I glance beyond him to the locked gate and frown up at him. "We are getting out through this gate, right?"

Ruen holds up a hand and quiets me with the movement. The sound of footsteps further back alerts me to an approaching third person. I glance at him with outrage and betrayal. *Again?* Before I can say anything, however, Ruen's hand reaches out and he snags my arm, jerking me into his body.

Rippling muscles beneath soft clothes and heat permeate my thoughts as my side slams into his chest. Wrapping his arms around me, Ruen lifts me off my feet and slides a few steps back and into the shadows of a large, perfectly propagated bush. With one hand still wrapped around my hips, keeping me pinned with his chest to my back, he lifts the other and clamps it over my mouth to keep me from making a sound.

Together, we stand in silence as the third person curses, their footsteps stuttering slightly over the snow-covered ground and the cleared stones underfoot. They're unaware of our presence, I realize a moment later as they bypass us and march toward the waiting gate. My head tips back and I scan Ruen's hard features, pinched with tension as he leans out of the shadows and looks towards the back of the person's head.

It's wrong, I know it is, but as his chest bumps against my spine, I close my eyes and can't help picturing how he'd looked in his sword training classes. Ruen is paler than both Theos and Kalix, but no less cut. His abdomen is carved perfection beneath the fabric of his tunics, but on those oddly warm days, when he does feel the need to remove them, all the women and even a few men in the vicinity are enrapt by the dips and valleys of his frame. Ruen might enjoy books and solitude, but his body is a work of art.

Even now, I can feel the outline of his hips as they press into me. Something thick and long presses into my asscheeks. *Fuck.* My eyes pop open as if that can disrupt the memory of Ruen panting in front of an opponent, sword in hand as sweat gleams on the powerful mass of his shoulders and chest. It doesn't. The memory continues with the sight of a bead of sweat sliding along one of the two deep lines at his hips that carve an arrow right for his...

"Let's move," Ruen whispers, disrupting my wayward thoughts.

He releases me and my body sways with disappointment. Thankfully, though, Ruen reaches back, snagging my hand. I blink in surprise and he turns, lips frowning. "It's better for the illusion if I touch you."

Is it? I want to ask. *Then how was he able to show me an illusion during my punishment?* I don't comment though, and neither do I pull my hand from his grasp as he leads me towards the gate. When his words hit me, I understand his intentions. We're sneaking out under the guise of his illusion and somehow, Ruen had known that someone here would be using this gate.

More questions fill my head, but as I spot the figure ahead—Hael, I recognize—I go silent. Hael unlocks the gate with what looks like a long metal key and then struggles to push one large iron side out of the way. The rattling of a cart sounds in the distance, coming from inside the Academy grounds. I glance back but see nothing, turning just in time to see Hael get one side of the gate open. Once it's set firmly in place, he kicks a larger rock to hold it and then hurries to the other, and once again, it's another struggle for him to move the heavy metal with his scrawny arms.

The rattle of wheels and the sound of a horse huffing get closer until a gray-bearded man clicking his tongue at a horse hauling the open cart at his back comes into view around the corner of one of the Terra residences near the southern gate. I lean up on my toes, squinting as I try to see what the cart contains.

Ruen flashes me an annoyed look and shoves me back down, stepping in front of me. A ripple of air moves through the space between us, and my eyes widen as it shimmers. Divinity, I realize. He's cloaking us in an illusion.

Hael puffs out cloudy breaths in the cold air before blowing into his bare hands and standing to the side as the cart rattles through the opening. Ruen tugs and the two of us are circling the side of it as it slides right past us. Neither Hael nor the driver glances our way even though we're now very much in the open.

Something gray falls out from beneath the tarp covering whatever the man is leaving the grounds with. I narrow my eyes. It's a stick ... I think. A long, grayed stick that's almost shaped like a hand with gnarled fingers curled inward. As the cart moves in front of us, the smell of something rotten hits my nose and I clamp my only free hand over my nose and mouth, blocking out the foul scent with a choked nose.

Ruen doesn't glare at me this time, but his expression changes too. His nose wrinkling and his face blanching as his eyes land on the stick jutting out of the cover. I choke down another breath, turning away as I drop my hand and try to breathe through my mouth more so than my nose. It doesn't help. It's like a lingering piece of whatever those sticks are is permeating the air and I can almost taste it.

"Hurry." Ruen's whisper is followed by a sharp jerk as he grips my hand tighter and pulls me along behind him. Together, we slide out of the southern gate behind the cart just as Hael quickly closes the iron bars behind us and re-locks it.

I half-expect Ruen to suggest we get onto the back of the cart and ride it into the city and fuck, but I really don't know if I can stomach sitting on that cart with the acrid scent of ash and shit in my lungs. I've smelled dead bodies and slept in urine-drenched cells beneath the Underworld's headquarters, but something about that dusty odor full of decay leaves me feeling light-headed and sick to my stomach.

I sway on my feet as the cart gets further and further away. I realize why Ruen doesn't say anything about hitching a ride a moment later as the driver of the cart takes a turn and starts heading *away* from the city and down to the cliffside. Small miracles, I guess.

"Come on, it's a long walk." Ruen strides in the opposite direction that the driver and the cart went, the ripple of his Divinity moving over both of us. Smart, since there are still sentries standing on the walls of the Academy and they could see us heading into Riviere. He doesn't release my hand.

"How did you know Hael would open the southern

gate today?" I ask, curious. How much about the Academy does he know that he doesn't mention? How can I find out that information and use it to *my* advantage?

Ruen doesn't look at me as he responds. "I just did." Well, that's not at all helpful.

"Does Hael do that a lot?" I can't help but press for more. "How often? Every week? Once a month?"

The hand around mine tightens and Ruen jolts as if realizing he never released it. Suddenly I'm free and cold air washes over my palm. I sigh and tuck my hand underneath my armpit, folding both arms and doing the same for each hand to keep them warm as we continue walking.

"It's not always Hael," Ruen replies, "but they send out garbage a few times a year."

"A year?" I gape at him. That hadn't just been garbage. The smell of garbage was nothing compared to the disgusting rot of whatever Hael and the driver had been carting around. They hadn't seemed to notice the smell though. How odd. "How did you know they'd be there today?" On exactly the day we would need them.

Ruen doesn't answer me and just keeps walking. I eye him speculatively. Since it's clear he's not willing to say more, I should stop him here. "Okay then, well..." I jog to catch up to his side and then bypass him. Flipping around and stopping, I glance back over his shoulder. "You don't need to come with me. Thank you for getting me out of the Academy so I can go see my brother. I'll see you when I get back."

The big man stops and just looks at me. I crane my neck back so that our eyes collide. I wait. His gaze narrows. "I am not about to let you traipse off into the city after you used me to get out of the Academy grounds," he tells me, glaring down his nose at me. The shadow of a beard grows over the underside of his jawline as if he'd meant to shave it this morning but had woken too late to do so. I hate to admit it, but he looks rather attractive with it. More so than when he's clean-shaven. With the little pinpricks of hair dotting his chin and jawline, Ruen looks almost ... animalistic.

"You can't come with me," I tell him. "People would notice a Mortal God walking through the slums."

He blinks. "You're from the slums?"

"I'm from the Hinterlands." I rock back onto my feet. "My brother is staying in the slums, so that's where I'm going today." And I doubt bringing along a big, six-foot-plus hulking mass of Mortal God who still doesn't know what I am will make Regis feel at all like telling me what the hell his urgency had been about. I shoo him back towards the Academy. "So, run along. I'll be fine. You go back to the Academy."

Ruen arches a brow. "And how do you expect to get back into the grounds before nightfall?" he asks.

I shrug. "I'll figure something out." Sewers if need be. "Don't worry, I won't implicate you in your assistance. Your job is done though. You've fulfilled your part of the bargain in getting me—"

Ruen steps closer to me and my words dry up in an instant. I stare up at him, at the glittering midnight sky that lingers in his gaze. "If you wish to see your brother today," he states, "I suggest you start walking, Kiera Nezerac."

He's not backing down. This is not good. I curse silently and turn, trudging towards the city. I'll have to think of another way to lose him. No, that would simply make him more cautious and wary of me. I bite down on my lip and try to think of what to do as we continue towards the city in the near distance.

It takes a solid hour for us to walk to the city's edge and hail a cab. The second we step onto the streets of Riviere, however, I notice Ruen lifting his hood to cover his face. I suspect he's used to this. How else would he have known Hael was going to be there today, opening one of the few gates? Though it had been unguarded this morning, I dimly remember that when I'd scoped the area myself there had been a few older Mortal Gods stationed at that gate. Had they been in the middle of a shift change? The old guards usually didn't leave until new ones came.

More and more, I'm starting to wonder what Hael and that driver had been doing. What had they been sending out of the Academy?

Ruen and I ride in silence, stuffed next to a few other passengers. I'm half sat on his lap and in the sliver of seat left for me after he hauled his big ass shoulders into the cab of the rickety carriage. The wheels whine under the weight of us plus the other passengers as the horse clomps onward, down the cobble-stoned streets. I glance up at Ruen's face, but it's mostly shadowed in the dim interior. I have to convince him not to follow me to Madam Brione's, but ... how?

Minutes pass into yet another hour and, finally, the carriage rolls along the edges of the slums. I tug on Ruen's cloak to let him know it's our turn to get out. Cold wind slaps my cheeks and nearly pushes my hood off my head as we step out of the carriage onto a street corner. Strands of my silver hair drift in front of me and immediately, Ruen is there, yanking the hood back up and scowling down at me.

"Careful you don't show your face," he snaps.

I roll my eyes. "Careful *you* don't show *yours*," I reply testily, adjusting my hood. "You're the one with Divinity shining through your skin like a candle in the darkness."

As the carriage pulls away from the curb, I spot the answer to my problems across the street. A tavern. I grab ahold of Ruen's hand as he's pulling away and start dragging him behind me. He stumbles, clearly surprised by my strong hold, but falls into step behind me and I feel confident letting him go because I know he'll follow me.

Entering the tavern, I pause on the threshold and take in the odd interior I don't recall seeing in other taverns across Anatol. The inside is dark, but that's to be expected with the only windows being a row at the front corner of the building. Instead of drunkards, however, the various tables cloistered together are filled with men in suits and hats, talking in low tones as they drink steaming dark liquid from mugs that are shaped similar to tea cups, but a little deeper. This isn't a tavern at all.

"What's that smell?" I ask, sniffing at the bitter, but not unpleasant scent drifting through the air and ridding the last memories of that decaying scent from the cart.

"Coffee." Ruen's voice rumbles at my back and he shuffles forward, forcibly moving me out of the threshold and further into the place. "Have you never had it?" he inquires, sounding bemused by the fact.

"Of course not," I blurt. "It's—" I glance up at the board that hangs above the bar with the prices listed. *Expensive,* I silently finish with a wince as I look at the denza these men are obviously willing to pay for the dark liquid in their cups.

Ruen steps past me and moves to the counter, and though it'd been my plan to convince him to stay here and wait for me to travel to Madam Brione's, curiosity has me following him to the counter. A bustling man in a white tunic and black vest wipes down the bartop as he makes a beeline for us.

"Morning," he says, beaming brightly. "What can I get you, folks?"

"Two coffees," Ruen says, holding up two fingers and nodding to an empty table towards the back of the sitting area. "We'll be sitting over there. Please have someone bring it to us." He drops a dozen denza onto the counter-top, adding two denza as a tip on top of the price of the two coffees. Then without waiting for the man's response, he reaches back and snags me by the waist and steers me around the various tables towards the one he'd indicated.

Steam lifts off the cups the men drink, making the smell permeate the entire room. A soft green couch backs the wall at the table Ruen stops aside. He pulls out the chair across from the couch and I frown, slipping around him and the chair to take a seat on the couch with my back to the wall. His mouth twitches before he frowns deeply.

"This chair is for you," he states, gripping the back of it as he glares at me from beneath the hood of his cloak.

"I like having my back to the wall."

"So do I," he says.

I shrug. "Too slow then. You can have this seat when I leave."

Instead of answering me, however, or commenting on the 'when I leave' bit, Ruen grits his teeth and shoves the chair back in before rounding the table. My eyes widen and I scramble out of the way as his ass sinks onto the couch next to me.

"*What* are you doing?" I hiss at him, irritation clear in my tone.

He ignores me. *Bastard*.

The man from the countertop stops by our table a moment later, dropping off the two cups of the black liquid. If he finds it odd for two people to be sitting on the same side of a damn table, it doesn't show on his face. He sets down a small matching porcelain plate with a little pitcher of what looks like milk, a handleless cup that has cubes of sugar, and tongs onto the surface of our table. Once he's gone, flitting back to another table, I grab one of the cups and drag it towards me. The outside of the porcelain is warm to the touch, not surprising considering the steam lifting away from the rim.

After the icy wind outside, I cup the mug in my hands for a minute, letting it warm my palms. Ruen immediately reaches forward and lifts his to his lips to take a sip. I watch him for a beat before lifting my own cup to my mouth and taking a sip. I cough and set it back down immediately.

"It's bitter!" I turn accusing eyes to the man next to me.

The corner of Ruen's lips twitch upward, but he doesn't say anything as he sips at his drink a bit more. How is he doing that without any expression? I scowl at the mug in my hands. How can something that smells so good taste so ... awful?

"Try the milk and sugar," Ruen murmurs quietly.

I eye the two things skeptically. How could they make this foul-tasting liquid any better? How are there so many damn people in this place still drinking it? With a sigh,

Ruen sets his cup down and then reaches for the milk. He lifts the mini pitcher and dumps a hefty amount in and then grabs the tongs next, dropping at least three cubes into my cup until the liquid, now a light brown compared to the black from before, is at the rim. He stirs with the tongs until he seems satisfied and then sits back.

"Try it now," he commands.

I lift the mug back to my lips and take a hesitant sip. The note of bitterness is still there, but not nearly as over-whelming. A soft breath escapes me though as the warm liquid pours down my throat and warms me from the inside out.

"It's good," I admit.

He hums in the back of his throat and goes back to his own drink. After a few beats, I chance another look at him. "Look," I begin, "I know you and I don't get along —"

He snorts. The first sound of amusement I think I've heard from him. "Understatement," he says, setting his half-drunk mug down, "but go on."

"You can't come with me to meet my brother."

Cool eyes meet mine. I expect him to tell me 'too bad' or 'tough shit,' but instead, he tilts his head to the side and looks at me. His eyes don't glow like they have in the past. Today, they're a simple clear blue. He doesn't exude the natural Divinity that usually sits at the surface of his skin. Instead, in this darkened coffee room, he looks almost normal. If someone like him could ever be called something so pedestrian.

"Why is that?" he finally asks.

I release a breath I hadn't realized I'd been holding. "My brother doesn't like Mortal Gods." I decide to stick with some truths. Lies are easier to warp when they're based on fact. "He's uncomfortable around them and I want to make sure that he knows I'm well after ... everything that's happened." I pause before that last part, subtly reminding him of his part in my punishment and why he thinks we're here.

Long moments of silence descend between us. Sweat gathers at the base of my neck and slips down my spine beneath my borrowed tunic. I wait, curious to know what Ruen will say, what he will decide. At the end of the day, I truly cannot take him to Madam Brione's so if he refuses to listen, then I'll have to call this whole trip off and getting out of the Academy will have been a waste.

Ruen lifts his head away from mine and gazes across the room. Unlike true taverns, there are books on the walls. Some patrons at the tables are drinking along with papers strewn in front of them or books of various types spread on their laps. I'd meant to bring him into a tavern and get him a little drunk before disappearing on him, but I think this place suits him far better.

"How far from this coffee house does your brother live?" he asks.

I stiffen, debating on how to answer. Truth. Lie. Or half and half. I go with the truth. "Several blocks," I answer. "Deeper into the slums than the edges, but I can run there in under thirty minutes."

Ruen seems to consider my words. Several more silent moments pass and I reach for my coffee, drinking down more of it as it cools. When my cup is nearly empty, Ruen sighs. "Go," he says quietly, "you have exactly three hours until I come looking for you."

I straighten in my seat. Three hours only gives me two if we're including the thirty-minute run there and back. "I'll come back," I assure him.

Those unsettling eyes of his, deep and vast as the powerful seas and like a storm on the horizon, meet mine. "I know you will," he tells me. "Because if you do not, I will come for you myself." He leans close to me until the heat of him is pressed into my side and all I can think of is his half naked body covered in sweat and how fucking dangerous he is simply because he is the one who turned me in to Dolos and had me punished.

Unlike other Mortal Gods, though, and their Terra, Ruen had felt guilt for what he'd done. It hadn't been his intention to see me hurt, and when I'd been punished, he'd tried to take the pain away. He's here, helping me because of that guilt.

"If you leave me here and disappear, I will spend the rest of my life searching for you, Kiera Nezerac," Ruen threatens in a low voice. "There will be nowhere you can hide, nowhere you can run from me. There are more powers at my disposal than mere illusions, secret keeper. Remember that. I will be waiting here." He holds up three fingers. "Three hours." His head turns and I follow it, spotting a clock hanging between two bookshelves on the wall. The hands of the clock hang onto their respective numbers, marking it the beginning of the hour. "Your time starts now."

CHAPTER 35
KIERA

"Three hours." I repeat the words to Ruen as he stares at me with that enigmatic expression of his. He'll never know how unsettling he can be. I'll never tell him and I'll have to be tortured for the information if he wants it. He nods to the clock on the wall again and that's the only further indication I need.

I leave him and the half-drunk mug of my coffee and flee the coffee house. It's been so long since I've been outside the walls of the Mortal Gods Academy—and more specifically, away from the prying eyes of the Dark-havens—that it feels as if I've come up for a breath of fresh air the second I step beyond the doorway. Once I've been freed from Ruen's attentions, I don't waste any more time. I take off in a sprint, curving around the building and diving for a side alleyway.

It hadn't necessarily been a lie when I'd told Ruen that Madam Brione's was less than a thirty-minute run from the coffee house, but that was considering a human's speed.

The alleyway I enter is a dead end, but I spot a series of cracked and thin wooden planks set up against the far wall and I pick up speed, racing towards it. My booted feet fly across the cobblestones and for the first time since I put them on this morning, I'm grateful for the clothes Ruen had likely placed outside my room this morning. This would have been impossible to do in skirts.

My foot connects with the flat edge of a plank and I race up their angled faces. One cracks further under my weight and then breaks entirely, but I've already got it. My hands reach up and out, one catching the lip of the building's slanted rooftop. The fingers of my other hand scramble to latch on also and I use my hold to drag my body up from the broken wooden planks on the ground.

My chest hits the hard shingles first and I roll the rest of my body sideways as I lift my knee and hook it over the edge until I'm lying flat on the surface. Then I drag myself to my feet and start running. Racing over the roof of the building—closer to the middle where the shingles don't seem as loose and likely to cause me to slip and fall—I leap from one roof to the next, a blur of speed.

It's early enough in the morning still that very few people are milling about in the slum streets. Every once in a while, I spot the slumped over body of a man snoozing in a doorway, empty bottles clutched to their snoring chests. With a roll of my eyes, I hang a right when I see the rooftop I'm on ending and dive onto the next.

It's a zig-zag of streets and alleys that I move over, casting a glance down every so often to ensure no one is watching me. The outer streets of the slums, closer to where I'd left Ruen, fall further back and the ripe stench of piss, ale, and horseshit lingers in the air.

When I spot the scarred wooden door of Madam Brione's shop and boarding house, I take a great leap from the edge of one rooftop and drop into the alleyway across from it. Scanning the street up and down, I breathe a sigh of relief when the only person I see is a woman sweeping her front porch, her hunched back turned in the opposite direction as I dart out of the alley's shadows towards my goal.

Just like the first time I'd entered, the door chimes upon opening but no one comes rushing out to greet me. Not that I expected Madam Brione to, but at the very least, Regis should be. He is, after all, expecting me.

Throwing off my cloak and draping it over one of the hooks lining the wall at the bottom of the stairwell, I glare up the narrow path. "Regis?" I call out. "I'm here!"

Thudding footsteps followed by the sound of a door creaking open meet my shout. Regis appears at the top of the stairs looking disheveled and paler than normal. My brows arch up towards my hairline as he hurries down the stairs and stops in front of me. "Kiera." His face splits into a wide grin as he takes my shoulders into his hands and draws me into a sharp hug.

Confusion slides through me at the odd excitement with which he embraces me and the relief. Though I consider him to be my closest friend within the Underworld, we've never exactly been touchy-feely people. Carefully, I draw one hand up and pat him awkwardly on the back.

"It's … good to see you too?"

The strands of his hair appear to be wet and they smack against my cheek as he pulls back. He smells of fresh soap. No doubt, he's been miserable living with Madam Brione's level of cleanliness.

"You must be starving," he says, pulling away from the awkward hug and brushing past me to head down the side hall along the stairs leading into the kitchen area. "I'll make something and you can tell me all about your time in the Academy."

"Regis?" His exuberant tone is strained, forced.

I eye him as I trail him into the small kitchen, glancing to the door just off the room that I suspect leads to Madam Brione's personal chambers. I've never actually been inside, but for the short time I lived here between receiving this mission and getting into the Academy, I'd seen her go inside time and time again, disappearing for hours when she wasn't 'cleaning' her shop that never seemed to actually change.

Few people in the Underworld get privacy and as long as she doesn't give me a reason to suspect her, then I'll stay away. My eyes span away from the door to the rest of the kitchen, seeking out some reason for Regis' edgy attitude. The back window is open and Regis stops before it as he takes something from the sink and moves to the fireplace—putting a metal kettle above the fire before he flips back to me.

There's a fresh bruise poking out from the back of his collar, spanning over the side of his neck and disappearing beneath the fabric of his tunic. I pause when I realize that his shirt is wrinkled. Not just wrinkled but *dirty*. As if he's been wearing the damn thing for several days now. Now that we're in better lighting, I can see the sweat stains under his armpits, darkening the fabric there, and ... is that blood on the hem?

My eyes snap back to his face. Dark circles line under his eyes and now that I'm taking a closer look the roots of his hair appear greasy. His jawline is unshaven, the golden shadow of a beard growing in.

Regis *hates* wearing dirty clothes. He's grown used to it over the years—assassins often have to get the dirtiest before they get to their target—but once he's off the clock and back in a place with an accessible washroom and fresh clothes, he never remains in his mission clothes. Something is most definitely wrong.

I sniff the air and focus on listening, but all I hear is his rapidly beating heart and the scraping of metal, and the *glug glug glug* of water being poured into the kettle.

"How about some tea?" he asks.

"Tea?" I stare at the side of his face harder, but he doesn't look at me. Not yet.

He nods. "Yes, Madam Brione just received some good rosebay flower leaves."

Everything in me goes quiet. "*Rosebay?*" I repeat the word, sure I must have misheard him, but his expression when he turns from the window towards me changes in an instant.

When he speaks again, his tone is the same and it does not match the darkness glittering in his eyes. "Yes, *rosebay*," he repeats. "I know I told you I didn't quite like rosebay, but it's here and it's worth a try."

Already, I can feel my throat closing as agitation takes over, but I keep my face placid. In my mind's eye, I recall one of the many books we'd been forced to read during training—something we'd pored over though never understood why until it had become necessary. The language of flowers—a secretive, but seemingly innocent way of communication when it was clear we were either being watched by those who couldn't know the truth or followed.

My gaze darts to the open window and then back to him. That window being open isn't a mistake. Someone must be near—someone that has Regis on edge. Is it Carcel? Regis is being cagey and not straightforward. He hadn't come down when I'd entered. We both knew that Carcel was due to arrive, and yet ... he still isn't here. My mind races as I try to come up with answers.

Whoever might be listening, it's not Carcel. Carcel would know that all assassins in the Underworld are trained to speak in this code. So, why would Regis mention rosebay? In the language of flowers, all I recall of its meaning is 'danger, beware' or 'we are not free.' I have to choose my response carefully and gather more information from him.

Forcing a smile, I reach forward to take Regis' hand and lift it. "Perhaps if you'd like, I could make some Rhubarb pie to go with your tea?"

Meaning, *do you require my aid or advice?*

Regis shakes his head slightly. "Oh, I'm not that hungry, darling love." The kettle over the fire begins to whistle and he pulls his hand free of mine. "Madam Brione brought in some broken straw and it's begun to mold—it's made my nose turn and it's hard to eat anything anymore."

It takes considerable effort not to let my face show my reaction to his words.

Broken straw—a broken contract. Whose? Mine? Does Ophelia already know that I've been found out? No, she can't know. That's the whole reason I'm here—to inform him of my fuck up. Unless ... Ophelia can't have a spy in the Academy, can she?

Was I right and this has all been nothing more than another of her ridiculous tests?

My heart begins to race within my chest as Regis busies himself by setting up a tray with bumbling fingers and too-hurried movements. I've rarely seen this side of him. He's an exceptional assassin who leaves little to no evidence of his kills; in every other aspect of his personality and life, he is the same. Clean and methodical.

Right now, he's anything but.

Once he's done, though, Regis practically races from the kitchen and up the steps and I follow just as quickly. He doesn't speak again until the two of us are alone in his room. The curtain is drawn shut and no doubt the window has been latched. We are, for all intents and purposes, safe from anyone looking to peer into the building. If that person is human, of course. If they're a God, then ... we might as well give up this pretense, but if they were a God, then ... Regis and I likely wouldn't even be here.

At least, that's what I tell myself. Regis sets down the tray he'd brought up onto the desk pressed against the wall. Then, he steps over to his bag and withdraws a long slender piece of stone. I can't withhold my flinch when I see it. The stone is a deep smokey gray color, but I know it well enough that if I stepped closer and settled my eyes upon its surface, I'd find little glittering particles in it. Like stardust on an earthen rock.

Brimstone.

Regis moves to the window sill and lays it flat on the edge. A second later, the stone begins to vibrate, shaking against the wood it's laid upon. The sound is quiet but noticeable. *Spelled* brimstone. I swallow my surprise even as the noise stabs through my eardrums. I flinch and breathe slowly through my teeth. After a few moments, the sound eases—not necessarily getting quieter so much as I'm getting used to it. I've experienced it enough before that it's not hard, but still unpleasant.

There are few items in the world spelled and sold to humans, but spelled brimstone is the rarest of them all. I'd seen it before because Ophelia is nothing if not willing to spend any amount of coin for things she finds useful. She must have lent it to him.

Once the curtains fall back over the spelled brimstone, the noise is light but there enough that if anyone is listening outside, they'll find it hard to hear. Divinity or not, that spelled brimstone will be like a beacon of white noise that will make eavesdropping on our conversation incredibly difficult. We're in as much privacy as we can manage.

"What's happened?" I demand the second I'm sure we're alright to speak freely.

Regis sighs, the sound long and drawn out. "I received a mission request last week," he says before turning and sitting on the bed to his side. The mattress sags under his weight, springs squeaking. He doesn't seem to notice. "At first, I thought it normal—but then I ... found that it was not."

I frown and march forward. Now that the pretenses have been dropped, Regis appears much more haggard than before. The fake smile hid just how worn his face actually is. His skin is pale and almost sallow, as if he's been sick. The shadows I'd spotted before are darker, deeper, and more prevalent without the feigned cheerfulness.

"What made it different?" I ask, stopping in front of him.

Regis doesn't move his head from where it hangs, chin tucked into his chest. He looks up at me through his lashes and brows, his lips thin and bloodless. His sandy blond hair is scooped back from his face and tied at the nape of his neck, but the roots dark and unkempt.

"It was a routine job," he says, almost as if he wants to convince me of that before he continues. I nod and gesture for him to go on. "I was to terminate a servant of a God that lives a day's ride from here." He lifts a hand to his head, not noticing how it disrupts the tie at the base of his skull as he scrubs at the top of his hair. "Nothing about the mission was unusual. I found the servant. He seemed fine, a pompous asshole. At first I thought he was a human—he *looked* fucking human, Kiera."

Dread coils in the pit in my stomach. *No.* I take a step closer to him as Regis lifts his dull blue eyes to mine. "He wasn't human?"

Regis' face crumples and he ducks his head once more, shaking it. "When I was keeping track of him during his duties for the God he was serving, I had my suspicions, but I'd never get a job to kill anyone with Divinity—I can't kill the Divine! I'm fucking human!" Both hands spear through his hair, shaking the knot free.

If Regis had thought the man human, then he must have been a Mortal God. Perhaps one whose bloodline was long removed. Not half-blood like me, but someone with a grandparent who had been a God. Still, the Divinity would have made it impossible for Regis to complete his task. No one with Divine Blood can be killed by those of Mortal origins.

"What happened?" I press.

Regis' face pales further and he swallows heavily. "On the third day, I saw my opportunity," he says, voice low.

Ominous. "The servant had been with his God for the duration of the night—it was a location I couldn't get to, not without being noticed. So, I waited outside the building and when he emerged the next morning, I noticed how gray his skin had become. He looked ill. He was stumbling as if he were drunk. I-I assumed he'd been —" Regis makes a choked sound and I find myself at his side in an instant, cupping his shoulder as I crouch before him.

"It's okay," I tell him, hoping like fuck that I'm not lying as I say the words. "Keep going."

"He wasn't human." Regis rocks back and forth, head in his hands. "He wasn't ... how ... why ... he wasn't human."

My own mind tries to catch up with his words and their meanings. "Why would they give you this job?" I ask, trying to switch tactics since it appears he's falling apart.

Regis shudders and when my hand tightens on his shoulder, he lets out a sound of pain. Immediately, I rip my hand away from him. *Shit.* Standing, I turn away and stride across the small sliver of floor between the wall and the bed. I pause when I reach the wall, turn, and stride back to the bed once more, repeating the process as I speak my thoughts aloud. "You surely didn't complete it. I mean, how could you? What could Ophelia be think—"

"I did."

Ice fills my veins at those words. I stop pacing and turn to face my friend. My *only* friend, I remind myself. Though I do like Niall, Regis is the only one who knows *everything.* He knows my past, my present, and my hopeful future. Niall doesn't know my birth or my abilities or my blood-stained past. Regis does. He shares it. And right now, he looks as if he's swallowed a poison that's eating him from the inside out. His cheeks are ashen and his lips are nearly white as he chews upon them.

"Regis."

His chin jerks to the side, but still, he does not look at me. I step towards him and his hands reach for each other, clasping in front of him as they hang between his slightly parted legs.

"Regis, look at me."

He shakes his head. "I can't." He starts rocking again, back and forth as the bed beneath him squeaks. "Kiera, I —" He shakes his head again, jerking it side to side. "I don't know how I managed it or how it ... was so *easy*." Droplets fall from his face, little dark wet spots hitting the floor between his booted feet.

"Easy?" Killing a Mortal God has never been easy. Not for me and it certainly should not even be possible for a human like Regis.

If there are three facts in this world, they are these:

The Gods are Cruel.

The Gods are indestructible to those who don't possess Divinity.

And Mortal Gods are the same.

I crouch before Regis once more, knees hitting the floor and digging in as I take his hands in my own and lift them to my face as I seek out his eyes.

When one does not see terror in a person's eyes for so long, they start to forget just how strong of an emotion it is. Right now, Regis' face is full of it. As well as confusion and panic.

"You need to tell me *everything*," I say. "How it

happened. Who the mission came from. How he died. Don't leave out a single detail."

Regis sucks in a shuddering breath and his hands clamp onto mine. His skin is cold, but as I settle my gaze on him, he nods. Then he opens his mouth and what he tells me ... is the reality of the impossible.

CHAPTER 36
RUEN

I do not trust easily, and even if I do still feel the tendrils of guilt wrap around my throat when I look at the silver-haired vixen that has seduced not just Theos, but both of my brothers, I know I cannot trust her. So, when she tells me the story of her brother disliking Mortal Gods, I let her go. Not because I don't believe that there are humans in this world that hate my kind and the kind of my sire, but because it's easier than trying to fight with her.

Three hours. That's the timeline I give her, but really it's a ruse because the moment she's out of the coffee house where she'd tried to leave me, I finish my drink and follow her. Casting an illusion of invisibility over my body the moment I step out into the street, I trail the lingering scent of Kiera Nezerac to an alley just off the street to the side of the building.

I watch her cast a look around before taking a sprinting leap. Her limbs are agile and she's faster than most humans I've met—too fast, my mind suggests—as she climbs the planks of wood lying against the end of the alley. One cracks and then snaps in half under her slight weight, but she's already catching the lip of the roof and clambering onto the surface. She jumps to her feet and sprints off without even seeming winded.

Suspicion grows as I trail her. She's a cautious creature, glancing down and back several times as if she knows I'm following, but she never spots me. Once, her cloak hood falls back and the silvery strands of her hair spill out, glinting under the morning light. Just as quickly, though, she lifts it back into place and dives for the next roof.

For several long minutes, I follow the Terra as she leaps from roof to roof, and then finally, she slows down and then drops into an alley. Quickly looking up and down the street, where only a single plump woman with a broom brushes at her front step, Kiera flits across the street and into what looks to me like a shop.

Lifting my head, I sniff at the air. My nose wrinkles automatically. She hadn't been kidding when she'd said her brother lived further into the slums. The stale scent of garbage and urine drenches the area. A curtain flutters in a second-floor window above the shop, catching my eye. I lean closer from my position perched on the roof across from it, narrowing my eyes as I try to catch a glimpse of the figure there.

Brother, I remind myself. Kiera's papers had said she had family in Riviere. One brother, no parents. There is so much intrigue about this woman, though, that I wonder if her papers are even real. I drop into the alley that Kiera had and stride across the street. My ears prick at the sound of her voice calling out for a man named 'Regis.' Something dark curls in my gut at the familiar way she says his name, but I shove the feeling down.

The front windows of the shop are coated in grime so thick that it would be too obvious if I were to clean some off just to peer inside. Instead, I look down the narrow street and decide to round the back. Just as I do, though, the curtain above shifts again, and a pale face peers out glancing around as if the man inside senses something amiss.

His eyes never land on me, but instead move over me —through me. My illusion is still holding strong. The man's instincts, though, are telling him that something is wrong. Interesting.

The curtain closes once more and I move down the street, fast enough that were I not under my illusion, the woman sweeping at her stoop would likely gasp and scream if she saw me. I round the row of shops and slum houses until I spot the entrance to the back alley behind them. For most of the buildings, there is simply another right next to it and no yard or garden, but a few have a square of land, unkempt as they are with unplucked weeds and littered with laundry hung out to dry.

I count the back doors until I find the one that must belong to the shop that Kiera's brother—Regis—lives in. This little shop doesn't necessarily have a yard, but the stone-laid little plot in the back is overrun with cracked pots filled with dying foliage. Even with my illusion, as I hear the sound of a man's voice join Kiera's through the open window, I duck down and sit propped against the wall, listening. The mortal man is too keen for my preference.

Their voices are quiet as I listen to them discuss various teas and ... did Kiera offer to bake a pie? Does she know how to bake? I'd be surprised if she did. The conversation is normal and my lips purse as I tilt my head. Despite the actual words, the sound of the man's voice is tight, more pitchy than I expected. When I'd caught a glimpse of him in the window, he hadn't looked anything like Kiera. With dirty blond hair darker at the roots and a more angular face shape, but that could be due to his masculinity versus her femininity.

A warning clings to the back of my mind as I continue eavesdropping on their conversation as Regis gathers supplies and then Kiera follows him down the hall back towards the front and up the stairs. With a silent curse, I stand and step away from the wall, glancing up.

I take several steps back and pull my illusion closer just before I leap and catch the roof edge. I haul my body up and pray for silence as I slip over the top of the building and to the other side. Peering over the side, I watch the curtain flutter in that same room again. Hopefully, now, I'll be able to get a—

A shrill noise stabs into my ears, cutting off that thought. It's so sharp and unexpected that my foot slips on a broken shingle and I nearly go sprawling over the side of the building. Cupping a hand over each of my ears, I stumble back and land hard on my ass. Another shingle cracks.

I pause for a moment and sigh in relief when I realize the sound of my fall was swallowed by my illusion. The noise continues, though, when I pull my hands away. Whatever they're saying is interrupted by the vile thing. I grit my teeth, my short nails stabbing into my palms as I shake free the pain in my head.

Mother fucker. What is *that?* The sound isn't loud but remains a constant ringing in my ears. I'm sure with time and exposure, it wouldn't be so bad, but it makes listening to whatever they're saying in that damned room impossible.

More curses fill my throat, but none come out. I wait. Minutes slide into an hour. Half the time I allotted Kiera passes in an instant. That noise continues, but finally, by the start of the second hour, it no longer makes me want to take a knife to my ears to stop the horrendously annoying sound. In fact, if I focus through the pounding headache that's started up, I can pick out a few words here and there.

"—Ophelia will want to know—"

"—isn't the time, Carcel—"

"I'll take care of it. Don't—"

The snippets are giving me virtually nothing save for a few names. Ophelia and Carcel, I record those and listen harder.

"—impossible, Kiera." That from the man, Regis. *But what is impossible?* I strain my hearing, annoyed by the fact that I have to do so.

"There has to be an explanation," Kiera replies. "I will look into it. I swear. It's going to be okay, Regis." Despite my own skepticism over Kiera's background, it's clear in her voice that she cares for this man whether he's her brother or not. "There's something else I need to tell you. We have more issues in the Academy."

I sit up straighter, leaning over the side of the building. Anger pierces my skull when a door slams in the distance and a loud man yells, cursing in such a way that the sound reverberates up the street. As the minutes have passed into hours, the sun has risen higher and what was once a quiet morning in the slums has quickly turned into a far noisier space, making listening that much more difficult.

"What's happened at the Academy?" I hear Regis ask.

"I had to use the poison you gave me last time," Kiera says.

"Already?" The man sounds shocked.

Poison? What poison? I think.

"When I came back from my last visit, I was taken to the Dean of the Academy. One of my ... *Masters*," Kiera's voice turns sour at the last word, and I already know where this is going and who she's speaking of. I tamp down the guilt. "Reported me for disrespect and I was punished. There's too many eyes on me now and I don't think I could be pulled out even if Ophelia wanted it."

"*Fuck.*" The human male's one word encompasses a plethora of emotions ranging from anger to fear to apprehension.

What does she mean by 'pulled out?' Just who is this fucking woman and what is she doing in the Academy?

This very well could be my only chance to find out and I'm more pleased than I'll ever admit aloud that I accepted her bargain that day in the library.

"They didn't find out who you are or else you wouldn't be here right now," Regis says, his voice rumbling over the noise still assaulting my head. I close my eyes and blow out a slow breath.

Fucking focus, I order myself. Something tickles at the inside of my nose and I reach up, eyes opening as I press the pad of a finger to one nostril. Blood. *Just perfect.*

"Well..." Kiera's voice is followed by a long moment of silence.

"You are still safe, right?" Regis asks. There's a sharp noise such as a bed squeaking and booted footsteps shuffling against a wood floor. I can just imagine the man taking Kiera by the shoulders and shaking her as he says his next words—there have been plenty of times I've wanted to do the same. "Tell me that you've not been found out, Kiera," the man demands.

"One of them knows." *Knows what?* I want to shout and pound my fist into the shingles beneath me. "He's keeping it a secret for now. He—"

"We're dead." The human male gasps out the two words as he interrupts whatever she's about to say next.

"No, we're not," Kiera insists. "We're fine. Regis, he won't tell. I'm close to him and if he were going to say anything, I'd know. He's one of my Masters in the Academy. He said he's—"

"You cannot trust them, Kiera!" Regis snaps, cutting her off once more.

Like a damned bug, I lie flat on the roof and press my ear even closer. More blood trickles from my nose. No Mortal God or Divine Being would still be here listening to this. Whatever that noise is, it's clear that it's affecting my head and causing this throbbing migraine. But this is too important. I have to know what secret this woman has been keeping from me and ... who knows of it.

"Mortal Gods are just like their sires," Regis says, scolding her. And though I understand the man's position since it's one I've been in many times myself, the thought of someone else doing so to the woman who's been a thorn in my side since the second she stepped through the door to my chambers makes a violent creature blossom in my chest.

"They are not kind and they are not forgiving," the man continues, not stopping. "Even if you think you can trust them, you fucking can't. They're all monsters. Evil, wicked, vile creatures that would kill us if they find out that we're a threat."

"I already *am* a threat to them, Regis." Kiera's voice is so quiet I have to strain harder to hear it. "Don't forget, *I* am one of those evil, wicked, vile creatures."

What.

I sit up and away from the rooftop. Still, her next words are as clear as sunshine on a cloudless day, as if the strange noise that has been impeding my ability to listen to them is suddenly overwhelmed by the shock that hits me.

No.

"I'm a Mortal God, too, Regis."

I close my eyes, blocking out the rest of the world as those words slam into me. She continues talking, but I don't hear her. The truth slips in on the heels of this realization. She'd said one of her Masters knew. That means one of my brothers knows this secret, and I already suspect which one.

Three things are now clear.

One. Kiera Nezerac is a Mortal God.

Two. One of my brothers knows.

And three. He. Didn't. Fucking. Tell. Me.

CHAPTER 37

KIERA

I step out of the front door to Madam Brione's shop without ever having seen the old crotchety woman leave her bedroom. My eyes burn with the brightness of the sun that's risen since I've been inside the dark cramped space of Regis' room. A dull throb has taken up residence at the base of my skull and slowly grows in both intensity and volume.

Turning, I start my jog down the street. I'm going to be late, I think, as I hit the end of the narrow road too slender for carriages to pass through, avoiding the eyes of those who've come out of their doorsteps and alleyways to beg for food or denza from anyone in their vicinity, even if those passing by look hardly well off enough to feed themselves, much less offer to others.

No sooner has the thought struck me that Ruen is going to be particularly angry at me for my tardiness than a hand snakes out from the shadows of an alley and grabs ahold of me. The move is so quick and silent that even my trained instincts are frozen for a moment. Those instincts, however, come roaring back to life an instant later.

I stomp my foot into the kneecap of my attacker, whirling around. My assailant makes no sound as strong, masculine arms corded with muscle I can feel through the dark shirt they're wearing come around me. They pluck me off my feet as easily as if they were lifting a bag of laundry. The urge to shout rumbles up my throat, but I stifle it.

I'm the fucking trained one here. This man is no one. Likely a robber or drunkard who got too tired of begging and decided to try his hand at crime instead. He'll learn, though. He'll learn today that choosing the wrong victim will get him killed.

My fingers inch down my thigh and around my hip to the dagger I strapped at the small of my back. The assailant carries me further into the darkness of the empty alleyway. Rage thrums in my bones. I truly don't have time for this. I'm going to piss Ruen off enough as it is. I call for my power, dark threads dripping from my fingertips as I do.

Strangely enough, though, it feels like the darkness is surrounding us, closing off the end of the alley that leads out into the street. It's as if there are far more than the little strings of my own darkness moving around us. A low, rumbling vibration at my back tickles my ears. A growl.

"You've made a very lethal mistake, Kiera."

Oh. Shit. I know that voice. I don't *just* know that voice—that voice belongs to the man that is waiting on me. The one that absolutely should not be here.

"Ruen..." I breathe his name, and suddenly we're spinning and my back is slammed into the side of a stone wall. Bits of rock and dust flutter down around my face and on my shoulders. My hand slips away from the dagger I'd been mere milliseconds away from unleashing and using to slice his throat wide open.

The Mortal God that had brought me into the city is there, hovering over me, his face a mask of fury that I've never seen on him. Oh, I've seen annoyance on those perfectly sculpted features of his. I've seen ire, but I have never seen Ruen Darkhaven in pure, unadulterated rage. The sight of it stops my heart dead in my chest.

How much does he know? How much had he heard?

"What are you doing here?" I demand. "You agreed to stay at the coffee house."

The muscles in my thighs bunch and jump, dancing beneath my skin as the urge to fight him off and flee rises from my belly. I press it down. No, not yet. I need to know what he knows.

Eyes that were once a calm sea have become a stormy ocean, full of wrath and madness. They start to glow, the blue color receding as something vicious comes forth. The crimson color of blood seeps through the exterior colors, swallowing them up until there's nothing but the red of his irises and the black of his pupil.

Ruen glances down, his eyes seeming to glow brighter as they snag on ... my hands. I follow his gaze, noting that the shadows are still clinging to my fingers. I shake them free and they disperse. Accusatory eyes rise back to meet mine. I swallow roughly.

"I can explain," I start.

A hand clamps around my throat and I lock my gaze on Ruen's as his fingers squeeze until the air stops slipping in through my lungs. Had it been just hours ago that he'd pressed his front to my back and I'd wondered what it would feel like, him with all that power and repressed strength thrusting into me just like his brothers had? It feels like a lifetime ago now.

I don't try to remove his grip, though I could if I truly wanted. Ruen might have trained in the Academy, he might be versed in swordplay and survival in the battle arena, but I am versed in the simple act of the kill. Not the spectacle he was expected to perform. I try not to think about the fact that both of us merely did it for survival. That piece of information won't make slaughtering him if I have to any easier.

"You think I would trust the word of a forbidden God child after you lied to me?" Ruen's question is a hissing arraignment. I'd blow out a breath if I could, and as if he senses that desire, his hand contracts even tighter around my throat.

My lashes flutter as more dust rains down around us when he slams the flat of his other hand against the stone over my shoulder. Something sharp digs into my spine. I keep my gaze trained on the man above me.

"Are you going to kill me?" I manage to get out when his grip eases the slightest bit to allow the smallest amount of air in. Despite that, my voice still sounds choked as he bares his teeth at me and my words.

His eyes flicker between both of mine and then, as if he can't help himself, they fall to my lips for a brief second before shooting back up and narrowing. "I haven't decided yet," he states.

My fingers curl into fists at my sides. "I'm not fighting you," I tell him. Not yet. Not until he makes his decision. My heart has restarted and thrums in my breast, galloping faster and faster with each passing moment that my fate hangs in the balance. It clings to a string as slender as a spider's between the two of us.

And I wait.

"You fucking lied to me," Ruen growls, repeating some of his earlier accusation.

I nod. "I did."

"Kalix knows."

I close my eyes. Of course, he would figure that out. Ruen is no idiot. Yet, already I can feel my freedom slipping further and further out of my reach, if it'd ever truly been within reach in the first place. Ice fills my veins, colder than even Rahela's water Divinity. I reopen my eyes and fix Ruen with a flat look. "Yes."

Another curse tumbles out of his mouth. My lips twitch in amusement despite my current predicament. "Is *that boy* even really your brother?" Ruen demands. Furious red eyes settle on me once more.

That boy? "Regis?" I clarify. I hadn't heard anyone call Regis a boy since he'd reached fifteen and had shot up a good six inches taller than all of those of his same age group. Ruen jerks his head down in an affirmative, his grip on my neck easing a bit more and I gulp down another breath.

Ruen can be a good ally if I can keep him from spilling my secret. More than an ally, he can be a good partner. He's powerful. It's clear from the looks I've seen others send his way at the Academy. Theos might be the playboy who seems nonthreatening, but Kalix is the one everyone fears. Ruen is the one they look to in order to keep someone like Kalix in line. If I can't convince him to keep my secret, I'll have to kill him. I know I will, and I really don't fucking want to kill someone that doesn't deserve my blade.

"Regis is my brother in every way that matters," I tell him honestly. "He knows me the best and he's a good person, Ruen. If you tell..." I let my voice fill with trepidation and a little bit of pleading. He doesn't need to know that the second he openly decides to go to the Gods is the moment I'll gut him. "They'll come for him and they won't just kill him. The Gods will torture him for keeping my existence a secret." They would torture and kill everyone in the Underworld if only to set an example of what happens to those who don't worship the Gods properly just as Dolos had done to me in the Academy.

"Is he—"

I'm shaking my head before he's even finished the question. "He's completely human." And just to add a bit more to the heaping plate of what I'm hoping is uncertainty on his shoulders, I add, "he's fragile, Ruen. He wouldn't survive whatever they do to him."

The red in Ruen's eyes fades slightly and I glimpse spots of blue rising forth. Hopefully, that means his anger is lessening. A beat passes and then another. Ruen releases my throat to grab my arm and he begins dragging me after him.

"Come on," he grits out. "We're going back to the Academy."

"Are you going to—"

He doesn't allow me to finish my question. "No," he bites out, flashing me his teeth and furrowed brows before he amends, "not fucking yet anyway."

It's as good of an answer as I suspect I'm going to get from him right now. So, I let him drag me through the slums—our pace much slower than the one I'd set to come here from the coffee house. He's trying to keep a low profile in Riviere as much as I am. I consider that as well as all the ways this could go wrong.

If I re-enter the Academy with nothing more than Ruen's word that he won't betray me—*again,* my mind reminds me snidely—there's no telling when he'll decide keeping my secret is too much of a risk for him and his brothers. But if I don't go back with him now, then I'll most certainly have to kill him. I bite down on my tongue and keep walking.

Trust does not come easy to a woman like me. I've been hurt and captured and sold. I've been tortured and trained. Raised in shackles and bound by the damned blood contract that keeps me beholden to the Underworld in spite of the ways I've tried to prove my loyalty to them, to Ophelia. Yet, something is telling me to trust this man. To trust Ruen Darkhaven.

Both you and those boys you find yourself growing more and more attached to will need to overcome what is to pass. That is ... if they wish to overcome their own monsters.

Caedmon's words come back to me from that day in the library. They hadn't made any sense at the time. A realization slams into me so suddenly that my foot catches on the lip of a street corner and I stumble. Only by the hard grasp that Ruen still has on my upper arm do I manage to save myself from sprawling out, face down, on the cobble stones.

"What is wrong with you?" Ruen grits out, yanking me up onto the corner of the street. His words are harsh even as his eyes scan me, looking for wounds, I think.

"He knows." I breathe out the words, shock and confusion rippling through me.

Ruen scowls. "Yes, I've already figured out that much," he snaps. "When I get my hands on Kalix, I—"

"No." I cut him off, lifting my eyes. "Caedmon."

Ruen goes still. The God of Prophecy knew all along what I am—perhaps even ... who I am. Whose God child I am.

The rattling of a street cab comes up the street and I glance up to find that we're right in front of the coffee house from earlier just as the public carriage with its black exterior and scuffed door comes to a shaky stop in front of us. I stare at the door that opens as a pair of men in gray suit coats step out. The men are well dressed, but the wrinkles on their brows and around the edges of their mouth make it clear that regardless of clothing or style, they are in fact human.

"Are you two getting in or what?" the driver shouts from the seat up front, turning his squinty little beady eyes on Ruen and me as he clicks his tongue in annoyance.

Ruen settles a glare on the man and he flinches, quickly turning back as if he suddenly has important business adjusting the reins in his lap. I barely notice, my mind too full of my sudden revelation to pay the man much mind. If Caedmon already knows what I am then it's pointless to run.

What else must he know? I wonder. Does he know about Ophelia? If he's the God of Prophecy, has he already seen the future? Had he seen Kalix and Ruen finding out about my heritage? Does he know what will become of me?

"Kiera." I jolt at the sound of Ruen's voice and I look up as he holds the door to the carriage propped open with a hand reaching out for me. "Come."

I stare at that offered hand. If I take it now, there will be no going back. If there ever even was a job in the Academy, I likely won't be fulfilling it. Because if I take Ruen's hand and follow him back to the Academy, I know that there will be one more person to reveal my secrets to. Theos. The final Darkhaven had already made his suspicion about me clear the last time we'd...

I bite down on my lower lip, interrupting that memory with a shake of my head. It hurts more than I care to admit. Theos was the first man I'd ever fucked that hadn't been for a job. He'd given me pleasure again and again and then, he'd ripped it all away for information. Fresh burning opens up at the back of my eyes. In front of me, Ruen's brow creases in confusion.

Mistaking my watery gaze for something else, he steps down from the opening of the carriage and reaches for me. His hands touch my shoulders and I stiffen, not sure if I should bat them away and make a run for it or just let him.

"Kiera, look at me." Fire races through me as the persuasion in his tone has my face immediately rising until our eyes clash.

"Don't," I grit out, "use your Gods damned Divinity on me." The words are spoken so softly that I know none of the men or women passing by, nor the cab driver, can hear me. But he can.

Ruen's face slackens. "I-I didn't realize I was. I'm sorry." If I had the energy to laugh right now at the uptight Ruen Darkhaven *apologizing* to me, I would.

He sighs as I simply continue to glare at him, daring him to say whatever words he'd been about to. "If Caedmon knows," he says, dropping his voice level with my own, "then you have to come back to the Academy." It's as if he can see right into my mind. I want to wrap my hands around his throat and squeeze. "Caedmon is feared by the other Gods for a reason, Kiera," he murmurs. "If he knows what you are and never said anything even knowing the laws, then there's a very good reason."

I try not to think of the risk I'm taking about being so honest with him as I speak my next words. "I can't risk going back to the Academy if there's even a chance that you could betray me again."

He blinks, reminded of the fact that he'd been the reason for my punishment all those weeks ago. With a groan, Ruen thrusts his head back and stares at the sky. He mutters something that might sound like a prayer to the Gods—that is, if I believed he would ever pray to the beings responsible for what he and his brothers have been through. Then, before I can react, he's lifting me off my feet and shoving me into the cab.

"Drive," he barks at the man sitting before the horses. "Bypass your other stops and take us to the north edge of Riviere."

"Now, just you wait a minute," the driver sputters. "I can't—"

The man goes silent as my ass hits a seat and I hear the tell-tale jingling of denza clanking together in a coin purse. I have no doubt that whatever amount Ruen handed the man, it's certainly more than the driver would ever make in one single day of driving the passengers on his normal route.

"Strap in, young man," the man says suddenly, his tone shifting immediately as Ruen hefts himself into the interior of the thankfully empty public cab that he's somehow commandeered for his own personal use. "We'll be there in a jiffy!"

The door snaps shut and Ruen sits across from me, the two of us staring at each other for a long moment as the carriage pulls away from the street curb with the snapping sound of a whip against a horse's rear end. I barely maintain my calm and unbothered face as the noise cracks through me. I hate that fucking sound.

"I'm not going to bother asking you not to hold that against me for however long we're together," Ruen starts.

"Good," I snap. "Because as a Mortal God like you, my life is just as long and my grudges will hold all the same."

His lips twitch. That can't be amusement, can it? Not after what he just discovered. If it is, though, it's gone in the next instant.

"We have a lot to discuss when we get back to the Academy and—no, don't start spewing your vitriol, secret keeper," Ruen says, stopping me as I open my mouth. "I'm not done."

I huff out a breath and cross my arms, shifting back against the swaying cab's wall as I glare at the man sitting across from me. Now that it's just the two of us in this space, I wonder just how he and I had managed to sit in one seat while another couple had sat across from us on the way here. He takes up the entire side that he's currently sitting on, his massive shoulders nearly spanning the length of the narrow cab. Even his parchment, ink, and mint scent seems to overwhelm the musky scent of body odor that lingers inside.

"You have a lot to explain to me, Kiera," Ruen continues. "About who you are, why you're at the Academy, and how the fuck you've managed to last so long out of the eyes of the Gods."

I snort. "They're not as all seeing as they'd like for you all to believe."

The red is completely gone from his irises now, but the stormy seas of his eyes settle on me. "Oh, I am well aware of that," he tells me. "That still leaves much to be discussed between us, and I do mean all of us, Kiera. You will explain yourself to me and Theos, and then Kalix will tell me how he figured you out."

Ruen is nothing if not loyal to his brothers. What would it be like, I wonder dimly, to be the recipient of that kind of dedication. The closest I've ever managed would be my relationship with Regis and Ophelia.

Yet, I know beyond a shadow of a doubt, that if it came down to me or Ophelia—she'd sell me out in a heartbeat if it meant she would survive. She'd never made that a question. She never promised loyalty where there was none and she never lied about her priorities. Regis is far less jaded than her, but I'm not stupid enough to wish for him to give up his future for someone like me, to give up the chance to find his brother—his *real* family.

"What are you thinking?" Ruen's question jolts me out of my reverie and I blink, glancing at him sharply.

"Why?" I demand.

"I don't like the look that just crossed your face," he answers. His brows furrow as he stares at me as if he truly can see into my mind with little more than his own force of will. "I want to know what caused it."

"None of your fucking business," I snap defensively, huddling further into the corner of my seat as if doing so will keep him at bay.

A glimmer of irritation flashes across his expression. "Everything about you is now my fucking business, Kiera Nezerac," he informs me. "As of this moment, your fate is intertwined with my own."

And just like that, I know for certain that no matter what happens—whether I follow him back into the Academy or not—Ruen isn't planning on revealing my secret. I can't say what tips me off, what makes me so sure. It could be the hard, flinty look in his eyes or the words that leave his lips.

Fate. A word I've tried not to think about for the last ten years. Fate is what killed my father. Fate is what saw me at the hands of the Underworld. Fate had irreparably stained me in the blood of those I'd murdered. But fate has also brought me to this moment, to this man. To Ruen Darkhaven and his brothers, and I have a feeling that it hasn't even begun to show me what it has in store for me.

CHAPTER 38
KIERA

Sneaking back into the Academy is a far simpler task than sneaking out. I would be confused by the fact that the security of those wishing to get in is far more lax than those wishing to get out if I didn't know the insidious reason behind it. Much to my surprise, however, instead of leading me towards the same southern gate we'd previously used, Ruen guides me around to the northern part of the Academy walls. The two of us move in quiet sync under the cover of one of his illusions, but my eyes continue to trail him, watching his stoic face and the shadow of beard growth that seems to have gotten darker as the morning has waned into early afternoon.

Ruen looks over his shoulder at me as we come to a junction between two walls where a large swath of deadened ivy and foliage covers the stones that make up the wall before us. His deep midnight-blue eyes rove over me, as if examining me for a clear threat. Now that he knows my secret—one of them, at least—he likely understands that I don't need to be holding a dagger in my hand to be a threat. Still, he looks me up and down and then turns away as if what little Divine power I have is nothing compared to his and he can just turn his back on me without concern.

There's a not so small piece of me that's insulted by his obvious dismissal. I grind my teeth and, instead, refocus my attention as he steps up to the dead foliage covered wall and presses two fingers into the dried vines and brown leaves not yet dropped despite the cold air around us. Something slithers through the air as he whispers a few words in the ancient language. To my utter shock, the vines begin to unravel and move apart, and a small sliver of an opening appears. A crack in the wall.

I gape at the opening he's created. "*What* ... why didn't we use this before?" I demand, glaring at him as he gestures for me to go in first. It would have been far easier than waiting for Hael to unlock the gate. "Is it because you didn't trust me then, but you do now?"

Ruen levels me with a dark look. The indigo swirls of his irises parting as little pin pricks of black and red surface. "I *don't* trust you now." His reply is cold. "But it doesn't matter. This is a long-term illusion spelled to my blood. You won't be able to find this place without me or one of my brothers."

I flinch but recover quickly. "That still doesn't explain why we didn't use this method this morning," I remind him.

He sighs and reaches out, grabbing on to my arm and hauling me closer. My hand moves back, palm covering the hilt of my dagger still strapped to the small of my back, but he pauses, not moving, and just because he freezes, I do too.

"I will find out what you're doing here, Kiera Nezerac," he warns me testily, the tightness in his tone making his displeasure obvious. As if the glare and ice practically dripping from his gaze wasn't warning enough. "You don't get to ask any questions, not until you've answered some."

My lips part, a retort at the ready, but then his palm squeezes against my side. Hard fingers digging into my waist and flashes of silken sheets and naked flesh flash through my mind. I close my eyes immediately and shake my head, warding those images off. When I reopen them, it's to find that Ruen has leaned even closer, narrowing his gaze.

"Get. In. The. Fucking. Hole."

I bite my lip, not wanting to snort since this is truly not the time. When he releases me, I follow his command. Not because I'm afraid of him. Oh no, Ruen Darkhaven might think he's the most terrifying creature in Anatol, but I know what fear is. I've lived with it pressing its boot against my throat for a decade by now. To an extent, I've become somewhat immune.

I duck my head and scamper through the hole he's opened for the two of us. When I come out on the other side it's in a small alcove between the wall and the rounded stone of the northern tower where his rooms reside. A moment later, the dead vines and leaves shift and Ruen appears, glowering at me. It's a bit more of a squeeze for him, but he lowers his head, turns to the side, and slips through with practiced ease. How often must he or one of his brothers use this secret entrance for it to look so effortless with his massive body?

The second Ruen is through the opening, the vines and deadened leaves move back over it and the hole disappears entirely from view. Catching my look back,

Ruen reaches out and grabs my arm with a snarl. "Don't even think about it," he growls at me.

I roll my eyes and deftly twist out of his grip, breaking the hold easily. If he's surprised, he manages to hide it well. Now that I'm no longer pretending, I find that my attitude comes far faster than it would have had I not been stifling for the last few months. "I know," I snap back. "You said it's spelled to your blood only."

He narrows his eyes as if he doesn't believe that I won't try something. He's right. If given half the chance, I will. Instead of saying as much and not waiting for him to start barking orders once more, I turn and stomp around the side of the tower, scanning the grounds and pathways for any onlookers. Thankfully, we've arrived at a good time. No one is here.

A hulking shadow falls over my frame as I move towards the doorway that leads into the tower and I resist the urge to come to a halt and force him to slam into me. Biting down on my tongue, I open the door and slip inside. Ruen catches it as it swings shut and follows me in. Together, we ascend the stairs, moving past the storage rooms at the bottom of the tower and then my own door until we're all the way at the top.

Reaching past me, Ruen unlocks the door and shoves it open. A moment later, his heavy hand lands on my spine and pushes me inside. Two familiar figures stand across from each other at the massive arched window across from Ruen and me. Kalix and Theos turn their gazes back. Kalix's lips curve upward as he takes in the sight of his elder brother's furious expression when the illusionist, himself, moves around me and stalks the floor towards him.

Theos stands with his arms crossed over his chest and

his brow furrowed as he glances between Ruen and Kalix before his eyes land on me. Something shutters his emotions then. Pulling back as his expression drops away and so, too, do his arms. I narrow my attention on him, my upper lip curling back slightly. I haven't forgotten what he'd done after Rahela had tried to kill me.

"So, cat's out of the bag, huh?" Kalix grins wildly, a glint of pure insanity in his jade eyes as Ruen shoots across the room and has him slammed against the glass of the window so suddenly that the whole room seems to shake.

My eyes shoot up when the chandelier overhead clinks as it trembles and then back down. Kalix's laughter echoes into the otherwise silent room. "Do you know what kind of danger she presents?" Ruen demands. "And you decided to keep it to yourself?"

Discomfort creeps up, hot on my back and then neck. Theos' golden gaze settles on me rather than taking in his brothers as Ruen shakes Kalix, the rage on his face so different from his normal indifference and aloofness.

I shift awkwardly from foot to foot before sucking in a breath and then blowing it out. "Do you really think fighting will change the facts?" I ask.

Kalix's eyes glitter with amusement as he holds up his hands, not even bothering to shove Ruen off him as he glances my way. "Didn't think you cared about being the voice of reason, little liar," he murmurs, gaze moving down over the dusty trousers and dirty cloak I'm still wearing.

With a sigh, I reach up, unbuckling the pin keeping the cloak closed around my shoulders. The heavy fabric slides off my frame and I catch it before it can collapse to the floor completely, setting it over a nearby chair as I stride further into the room. I ignore Kalix's comment and make a beeline for the liquor cart and cabinet that I think I'm about to become even more familiar with than I did the night I fucked Theos for the first time.

"I need a drink," I mutter. And a moment to gather my thoughts and figure out just how much I can tell these three without risking Regis, Ophelia, and the rest of the Underworld.

I make it to the crystal decanter full of amber liquid and yank down a glass before filling it to the brim, shooting back several mouthfuls, and refilling it a second time. When the burn of the alcohol moves down my esophagus and seems to do the work of easing the tension in my muscles, I finally turn to face the room again.

Ruen releases Kalix who straightens his casual tunic, as dark as his hair, without a single hint of displeasure at his brother's reaction to this news. Theos, however, has moved closer as I'd been pouring myself a drink, and I start at how close he is. So quiet I hadn't even heard him.

Before, only Ophelia and Regis had ever managed to throw me off. Now, I know Kalix is capable of the same, but I never expected Theos. My fingers tighten around my glass and for a moment, golden eyes flick to it before they rise again. Settling his attention on my face, Theos calmly and without speaking reaches around me to grab the decanter and a glass of his own. It isn't until he turns and walks towards the lounges in front of the fireplace that crackles with flames spreading over dried wood that I realize I'm holding my breath.

Immediately, I release it and suck back another. My chest aches. Fuck. Everything does. I want to cover my face with both hands and sink into the ground and curse until my lungs dry up and turn to dust. I'm so Gods damned tired. Down to the marrow of my bones, I feel as if I'm on a carriage with no brakes. The horses lost to madness as they careen down dangerous paths, closer and closer to a cliffside that's guaranteed to kill me the moment we cross over that last threshold.

Ruen moves away from Kalix and into the center of the room towards Theos. "Theos..."

The white haired Darkhaven lifts the hand holding his glass. "I assume this is about the secrets she's been keeping," he says calmly. Too calmly. "You and Kalix obviously know, but I..." He glances over his shoulder at me and for the first time in a long time, my conscience prickles. I resist the urge to look at my feet and avoid his stare. "I'm always the last to know, aren't I?" The question leaves him, but no one answers. I have the strangest feeling that he doesn't just mean this—me—but I don't know how to ask him what else he could be referring to. I don't know if I have the right to even ask.

Ruen is the one to respond. With a long drawn-out breath, he shoves a hand back into his hair, pulling the dark strands, longer at the top, away from his forehead as he cuts a dark look to both me and then Kalix before fixing his attention on Theos. When he does, however, the tension in his shoulders eases a bit.

"This isn't the same, Theos," he says quietly.

My fingers contract around the glass in my fist and the sudden urge to put it to my lips and drain it presses into my mind. For once, I listen to that compulsion without question. Setting the rim to my mouth, I tilt my head back and swallow mouthfuls of the spicy, sharp liquor until it burns its fiery path down into my belly and my head isn't quite so full of guilt anymore.

Kalix steps off the ledge by the window with a casualness I don't feel. I eye the decanter in Theos' hand as he finally sits onto one of the couches by the fireplace, setting it onto the table before him and pouring himself a hefty glassful. I know I shouldn't. I'm going to need all my wits about me to figure out this mess I've gotten myself into, but I'm going to have another fucking drink because the thought of facing these three sober really isn't one I want to contemplate.

Moving swiftly, I take up residence in a wing-backed chair and reach for the decanter. Ignoring Theos and Ruen's collective look of disapproval, I pour myself another and throw it back as all three Darkhavens approach and take their own seats. Three sets of eyes linger on me and I cup cold fingers around the empty glass in my palms.

"Well, what is the big secret?" Theos finally demands.

I bite down on my tongue. "Kiera." Ruen's cold tone makes me want to throw this glass at his head. Instead, I set it on the table before me and I close my eyes. Calling my power to me, I feel the tug of dozens of little responsive minds pulled towards me. Each spider is its own creature with various emotions and thoughts that I can never quite see. The brightest of them, though, is Aranea. My spider queen moves faster than the rest, the connection between the two of us the strongest.

A masculine sound of shock echoes into the room, and I know without opening my eyes that the three of them sense it. Either that, or my power has collected like dust, moving into swiping shadows at my fingertips. I've never been able to control them so much as they've been drawn to me. Dimly, I wonder if things will be different when the brimstone in my neck is removed. It's likely obscuring much of the power I should've been born with. A shudder works through my system.

"Fucking ... Gods..." Theos' breathy words have my eyelashes lifting and darkness has encompassed the room. No. Not darkness. Spiders.

What I thought was a few dozen is far more than that. Hundreds of thousands of little creatures have crept out of the stone work, called from not just this building but the entire Academy. Across the grounds, anywhere in the vicinity of my signal, they have come.

Kalix sits with a bemused smile stretching his lips as he gazes around. When his eyes fall back to my face, he licks his lips, a promise in his gaze. Ruen has paled, but remains otherwise completely unreadable. Theos, however, is no longer sitting, but standing and turning as he stares at the mass of spiders that have suddenly appeared, blocking out the light of the window behind us. The light of the fire appears that much brighter and hotter with the sunlight from the window diminished.

A heavy weight crawls up my back and onto my shoulder. Without looking down, I lift a finger and touch the top of Ara's head. She nuzzles at the digit before casting her attention and curiosity to the fact that I'm introducing her to others of my race. Mortal Gods ... just like me.

Theos' golden gaze, full of horror and wonder, meets mine.

Now he knows too. All three of them know one of my deepest secrets and as such, my life is in their hands.

CHAPTER 39
THEOS

Since being recognized as one of Azai's sons, since being removed from the facility for failed God children—the place of my childhood—I have not found myself surprised by much. When you don't expect anything from anyone, no one can truly shock or disappoint you. But this ... as Ruen had warned me, is an entirely different matter.

Who could have guessed that the beautiful and biting little Terra that had entered our chambers and announced herself as our new servant and we, her masters, would end up being that which we all have hated ourselves for being. A Mortal God. A child of the Divine Beings and, with as many spiders as she has called to her, a powerful one at that.

Ruen was right again. She is dangerous. Her very existence and the fact that we now know ... if we don't turn her in to the Council, it isn't just her life at stake, but all of ours. I turn my gaze to the woman that has just damned us all. The very same woman that had come to me in one of my darkest hours. I knew she had been hiding something, but ... I'd never anticipated that it would be of this magnitude.

The spiders lingering around the room, blocking out the window light, begin to slowly disperse. It's not necessarily noticeable at first, but soon enough the sun pours back into the room and when I glance up, there are only a few skittering here and there as they disappear. My gaze returns to the woman sitting before us.

The look in her eyes—as deep and wide as a storm and as vast as the world itself—is followed by a fine tremor starting up in her fingers. I watch her, curious and astonished, as she clenches her hands around the glass and a crack forms along the crystal's side. Quickly realizing her mistake, she sets it down with a hard and heavy *thump*.

"I know that this complicates things," she begins, "but I think you can understand why I kept it from you."

Despite the silver hair that is pulled back and away from her face, hanging in a thick rope down her back with soft tendrils broken free at her temples and against her neck, her lashes are charcoal dark as they lower against her cheeks and rise again. "I can't tell you much," she continues. "My life isn't the only one at risk if anyone finds out about my existence."

"Then why tell us now at all?" I demand. As much as I tried not to feel the bite of disappointment in my brothers for hiding this from me, I know I failed earlier. I'm angry with them. Buried in that anger and hurt because for so long, it has felt as if I was the addition to the two of them. Kalix might find me more amusing to play with because I'm not as fastidious as Ruen, and Ruen might find me far more tolerable and controlled than

Kalix, but they had been together years before they'd found me. *Before Darius had helped them find me.*

That last thought stabs into my chest, a violent, cruel reminder of the life unnecessarily lost. Kiera's response is the only thing that keeps me from falling into my darker emotions.

"I wouldn't have told you at all," she admits. "Kalix found out weeks ago." She gestures to him with a curl of her lips, obviously displeased by that fact. "Ruen found out just this morning by eavesdropping on my conversation with..." Kiera pauses, eyes flashing to Ruen before shaking her head. "It doesn't matter."

"With her brother," Ruen supplies, glaring at her for trying to keep yet another secret. Her head turns slowly in his direction, gray eyes flashing with promised retribution.

"Is he—"

"*No.*" Kiera's snarl, cutting off my question, echoes throughout the chambers, causing Kalix to thrust his head back and bark a laugh. She turns her furious gaze on him.

My eyes, however, fall onto the creature perched on her shoulder. Although the other spiders have receded, disappearing back into the crevices and walls to go only Gods knows where, the rather large brown and black spotted spider remains. I tilt my head and the creature follows the movement. When introduced to Kalix's familiars, the serpents hadn't shown nearly this much curiosity. The slithery beings were content to sunbathe in the open or follow his commands, but rarely did they gaze back with this much interest.

Pausing her eyeing insult fest with Kalix, Kiera lifts her head and glances down at the spider on her shoulder before looking back to me. Confusion mars her brow as she reaches up, almost absently, patting the head of the spider before she looks to me. "Would you..." Kiera's lips twitch as if she's not quite sure how to phrase her question. I wait.

I might seem the patient type, but I'm not. It's like driving daggers beneath my nails to hold myself back from throttling her and demanding to know what thoughts cross her mind. Still, I do.

Kiera clears her throat uncomfortably and then casts another odd glance between me and the spider. "Would you like to hold her?" she asks.

I blink. That had not been what I'd expected. "Hold her?" I inquire. "How do you know it's a female?"

Kiera shrugs, the movement jostling the spider slightly. I bite down on my urge to crack a smile when the spider's head turns towards her and I get the sense that the creature is annoyed. "She told me," Kiera replies. "Her name is Aranea."

"Spiders have names?"

Kiera sends me a dull look. "I named her," she answers.

"We don't need to discuss holding your damn familiar. What we need to do now is—" Ruen's demand is cut off as I lean forward in my seat and set down my glass.

"Yes," I say. "I'd like to hold her."

Curiosity burns bright within me and before Kiera can overcome her shock, the spider decides that my request is now up to her to fulfill. Aranea practically leaps down Kiera's shoulder, sliding over her arm to her lap and then skittering off the tops of her thighs to the lounge cushion and then its armrest. From there, it's a short hop for her to land in my lap.

The spider is quite agile for its size. Though small, merely two inches or so in diameter, it's far larger than most spiders and when it props itself up on my thighs, it lifts its head to me. Eight pitch-black eyes land on mine, glittering with quiet intelligence.

Silent surprise permeates the room. It does make me feel a little better to know I'm not the only one who can still be shocked. Lifting a hand, I hover it over the spider's head. She tilts it at me, waiting. Unlike me, she seems far more tolerant and patient. With gentle movements and careful not to hurt her eyes or go near her mouth, I stroke the back of her head. Little fuzzy legs twitch and she shudders under the movement.

"She ... likes you." Kiera's voice is ripe with bewilderment. "Most spiders don't like humans or Mortal Gods."

I hum in the back of my throat, continuing to stroke Aranea. Doing so seems to calm something inside me in a way I never knew I needed. This creature, so fragile and yet so fierce, finds me ... likable. The honor I feel should be preposterous. I don't need the affections of something I could easily kill, and yet, the fact that Aranea is sitting here, in my lap, allowing me to caress her fuzzy spine and twitching with pleasure, eases an ache in my chest.

"Start talking," I say quietly, continuing to repeat my motions over and over again. "Tell us everything from how you came to be here, why you've remained undocumented and hidden for so long—I assume you are undocumented?" Without stopping my strokes of the spider's back, I lift my gaze to Kiera, who nods her answer. "Then tell us how that's possible and why."

"Are you going to turn me in to the Gods?" she demands.

"It depends on your reasons," Ruen answers.

Kiera shakes her head, unsatisfied with his response. "Then I can't tell you everything. I need your word that you'll keep this secret and I won't say a damn word until we've performed a blood contract solidifying your silence."

All three of us stiffen automatically. Aranea bumps against me when I stop the petting to lift my gaze back to the woman staring at the three of us with violence and something else in her gaze. A muscle jumps in Ruen's jaw. Kalix yawns, unconcerned. He's already bypassed the news since he was the first to know and doesn't seem all that interested in the reasons behind her deception.

"And just how do you know about blood contracts?" Ruen's question is as dark as his expression.

Kiera turns her head and doesn't flinch away from him as many before her have when prompted with his anger. It's so rare when he shows it like this. Aranea prods me with a tapping leg, clear annoyance in her insistence. I start stroking her once more, using the spider's furry body and the repetitive motions to lull my own mind back into the present without the coil of riotous emotions filling me.

"I'll tell you when the four of us have made one in order to keep these secrets," Kiera replies.

And before Ruen even says a word, I already know that we'll do it. I don't appreciate the lies or the falsities, but I can understand the obvious protective instincts she feels towards those she considers her own. Her brother—as Ruen had said—knows of her identity, and I know beyond a shadow of a doubt that were the Gods to find out a mortal had kept her existence hidden, his death would not be quick or painless.

The Gods are cruelest to those they feel slighted by,

and deceiving them into believing a Mortal God with the power to call thousands of spiders at her will was little more than a human Terra is certainly a trickery that would prick at their damned pride. Kiera would die and so, too, would her human family. Whoever they are.

"I'll do it," I say quietly. All eyes land on me. Kalix in boredom. Ruen in shock. And Kiera in ... Gods, I pray that is not hope in her expression. The anger I still feel towards her might be dampened at this moment, but it is still there.

A curse slips from Ruen's lips, but then, after a long moment, he nods. "Fine," he bites out the word, glaring at Kiera. "We will do it, but once we sign the blood contract—you tell us everything, and I do mean everything. I want your name, *your* fucking name, I want your identity, who your God parent is. *Everything.*" He repeats the last word with emphasis as if that will force more meaning into it.

Kiera nods, her head bobbing with the movement. Kalix pops up from his seat with a grin replacing his look of dullness. "Be right back," he announces before disappearing up the stairs.

Moments later, he returns with a stone bowl, a blade, and a small satchel of herbs. Of course, he would be ready for something like this. As the first one to know of her truths, no doubt, he'd been expecting this turn of events. I tamp down the urge to growl at him and punch him in his smug face as he sets the stone bowl onto the table between us, dropping the blade and satchel next to it.

"Let's get this party started, then, shall we?" he says, clapping his hands gleefully.

CHAPTER 40

KIERA

Blood wells up from the slice I make through the center of my palm. Pain radiates outward. Pain I'm used to. Pain I can handle. The consequences of these actions, however, are another matter entirely.

Not for the first time I ask myself if I'm making the right choice. Am I giving in too easily? It feels like I am, but what choice is left? I am a piece of driftwood set afloat in the vast ocean, pulled along by the currents beneath. Did I ever even have a choice to begin with or was this inevitable?

Did all the torture Ophelia put me through mean nothing? Was it all in vain?

Someone would have found out about my existence eventually. I should be grateful that it's the three of them. The Darkhavens, at least, are willing to make this blood contract to keep my secrets.

The blood that leaks from my hand fills up the crevices of my palm as I curl my fingers inward. I turn my fist to let the blood drip into the stone bowl, coating the inside before I pass the blade to Ruen and he does the same. Then Kalix. Then finally, Theos.

My gaze lands on the third Darkhaven brother and more specifically, Aranea, who has been casually propped up in his lap since I offered for him to hold her. I hadn't expected him to be so willing, but when she'd prompted me to ask, the curiosity and interest in her mind supplying the desire of hers more than words, I'd asked. To my utter surprise, he'd accepted and now, she seems more than content to remain on his thigh, waiting for him to finish contributing his blood to the contract we're all about to make.

By the time Theos is finished adding his blood to the stone bowl, I open my palm to a completely healed cut, nothing but the vestiges of my own wound left. Ruen's eyes fall upon my hand with a deadened expression that he just as quickly turns away as I wipe the blood clean on my dark trousers. Kalix leans forward to tear open the satchel of herbs he'd brought with him. I don't even bother to ask where he'd found roots from the Hinterlands or brimstone shards that he upturns and dumps into the blood.

The blood contract that had been made between Ophelia and me nearly ten years ago now is tied to the brimstone in my neck, and as if in response to this new power it feels, I can practically sense the stone's shard throbbing in response. I grit my teeth against the fresh wave of prickling pain.

All four of us lean closer, scooting to the edges of our seats as the blood in the bowl begins to bubble. The herbs catch fire and melt into the red sticky liquid, but the brimstone doesn't. It heats, glowing red as if it's been put into a kiln. My skin grows slick with sweat and I swallow roughly, tamping down the desire to vomit.

Kalix groans, cracking his neck to one side. He lifts his gaze to mine and grins wickedly as if the pain is pleasurable to him while both of his brothers catch their breaths and refuse to make a sound. *Prick.* I glare at Kalix as if to let him know exactly what I think of him. His smile merely widens.

More heat radiates from the bowl, the shards shake, trembling with some unseen force. I don't know when blood contracts were created—no one but the Gods can say for certain—but I do know that they were once used long ago when the Gods first came to our world to control the first generation of mortals and keep them from rebelling against their new overlords. The amount of blood and power it would have taken to force a blood contract upon an entire society of people astounds me even now.

"Now," Ruen grits out the word as he leans forward and dips his finger into the blood. Kalix goes next, then Theos, and then me. The second the mixture of blood and burned herbs touches my fingertip, fire blazes a path up my arm, shooting lightning through my veins. Though the blood sits on the outside of my body, it is still a piece of me, connected by the Divinity it holds.

Vomit threatens to scorch a path up my throat. I swallow it down and turn towards Theos. He bows his head. My hand shakes as I push his hair out of the way to draw an ancient rune with the blood on my fingertip into the skin of his brow. The red liquid turns brown and then black almost immediately as soon as it touches him. He feels colder than he should be, or perhaps it's simply that my skin is on fire.

Theos nods to me and turns to Kalix, doing the same for him. Around the circle we go, until it's my turn and I press my head downward to allow Ruen to draw the rune upon my own brow, now sticky with even more sweat. The burn of the blood sears my forehead. I squeeze my eyes shut as my hands clamp into fists on my thighs.

Soon it will be over, I promise myself. *This is the only way to ensure their silence, the only way to ensure the Underworld stays safe in light of my failure.*

Once the ritual is over and each of the four of us are sitting there with a rune painted upon our heads, we—as one—whisper words of the ancient language that will ensure our bond in blood will remain long after we have washed the runes away. Though most humans don't know the language that has been long dead, they know it because of their education here at the Mortal Gods Academy and I know it ... because of Ophelia.

Flames erupt within my head, and despite myself, a cry of pain emerges from my throat. I cut it off a second later when I see Ruen reach for me, pain clear on his face. I jerk away from him, shaking my head. Seconds pass, feeling like an eternity and then it's done.

Breathing out a sigh of relief, I shoot to my feet and flee up the stairs to the bathing chamber. No one follows. I don't expect them to. I wash the blackened blood off my flesh quickly, still feeling as if the rune has been burned into my skull despite the fact that when I look into the mirror to see my own reflection nothing but cool, pale skin remains. Then I grab a few cloths and wet them, carrying them back out into the main room.

Theos and Ruen take theirs without comment and wipe away the blood on their foreheads, but Kalix is mysteriously missing. I glance down to the table, realizing that the blood contract supplies have disappeared. So, not so mysteriously missing anymore, I guess as I hear the door above creak and he appears out of his room for a moment, glancing over the rim of the railing before he disappears into the washroom.

I toss his wet cloth onto the table and sink into the chair I'd occupied before with a heavy breath. A minute later, Kalix appears at the railing again and descends to the bottom floor to retake his seat.

"Now." Ruen leans forward and props his elbows on his knees as he fixes me with a dark, expectant look. "Tell us the truth, Kiera Nezerac," he demands. "Who are you?"

I take a long breath and then another and another, none of them feeling as if they are truly reaching my lungs. No turning back now. The three of them agreed to the blood contract and it's the only assurance I'll get that once I open my mouth and tell them the truth, they won't immediately drag me before the Gods to be punished and executed.

Still, I spent years under Ophelia's tutelage. Years, trained to keep my mouth shut. The words don't come easily. "I," I begin, annoyed by the slight tremble in that single syllabic sound. "I was born in the Hinterlands."

Starting at the beginning, I feel, is the best choice. From the night my father died, to being sold to the assassination Guild, to the deal I'd made with Ophelia, and, finally, the job that had led me to the Mortal Gods Academy. I tell them *everything*.

Each word feels like hot vomit spilling from my throat. They scorch my insides and if I didn't know better, I'd say that Ophelia was a Goddess, herself, who had a spell upon me that made revealing these secrets painful.

I tell them about what little I know of my abilities and

my God parent—my mother—whom I never actually knew. The three of them remain silent as each admittance leaves my throat like broken glass crawling up from my insides. Each truth, however, leaves me feeling less and less burdened. As if a weight I hadn't known was sitting on my chest is being lifted away.

I've never unburdened myself like this. Never admitted everything to someone that didn't help keep me silent. When I'm done, there's an emptiness within the chambers of my ribcage that I've never had before. As if my own body is a bird cage that's held dozens of the fluttering little animals for years and now I've let the door open and they've all flown away.

Exhaustion clings to every piece of me. Aranea scampers off Theos' lap and returns to my side. I lay my palm flat on the cushion of the chair and she crawls onto it, tapping her fuzzy leg as I lift her up to my shoulder. Sympathy and care brushes at the edges of my mind— her emotions pushing into me. I close my eyes and push back my gratitude. She responds by nuzzling the skin at the side of my neck.

Theos is the first to speak, his gaze directed to Ruen. "What now?" he asks.

Isn't that the million denza question? I think snidely to myself. What happens to the four of us now that they know my secrets? Now that they're bound by the blood contract to commit treason and keep it to themselves?

Before Ruen can respond, though, bells ring out. Ruen and Theos both leap to their feet, their gazes turned out to the window. The sound of the bells echoes as Kalix slumps back against the lounge he's on and groans, loud and long.

"Battles?" Theos asks, glancing at Ruen.

Ruen shakes his head. "No, it's been too soon since the last one."

My muscles coil with tension. The bells are a warning, a signal of something. "They're calling us to the arena," Kalix murmurs, sounding put out as he lifts his head and pouts—actually fucking *pouts*. The damned psycho.

"How do you know that?" I demand. Why would they be calling the Academy to the arena if it's too soon for another battle?

Kalix cracks his neck to the side as he pushes one hand flat to the cushion beneath him and leverages up. "Because," he says, "that's where we always go when they have an unscheduled announcement to make."

An unscheduled announcement? Fear bolts through me and I pass a glance to the door. Before I can take a step towards it, Ruen is there, flashing by me in a blink and blocking my path. "Do not run, Kiera," he orders, eyes flecked with sharp spots of red. "It will only be worse for you in the end. If they knew then they wouldn't have called the entire Academy."

His words ease the tautness in my limbs but only marginally. "What do we do then?"

"We have to go," Theos says. "It would be suspicious otherwise."

I don't like that. I don't like it at all. Ruen turns his gaze down to my dirtied clothes. "You should have a uniform delivered to your room by now," he says. "Go change. Hurry."

Theos moves, shaking off his earlier emotions as he moves away from the lounges and the roaring fire that now feels too hot. "We should change as well, just in case," he says.

"It's not the battles," Kalix comments absently, repeating Ruen's words without moving from his spot.

I bite down on my lip to keep from snapping at him, but stand from my seat and move towards the front door. "I'll go see if Dauphine had my uniform delivered," I say.

Ruen steps out of the way. As I go to pass him, however, his hand shoots out and sparks light up along my flesh beneath the fabric of my tunic as he grips me by the bicep, halting my forward momentum. "Remember what I said, secret keeper," he says, his voice dropping. "Running will only make things worse."

My body goes incredibly still, as if even the vibrations of my beating heart have quieted in the face of Ruen's low spoken warning and reminder. Each day I live, others' lives are cast into the fires of danger. Each time I open my mouth, I make wrong choices. Again and again. When will I ever learn?

Months ago when I'd first arrived on the steps of the Mortal Gods Academy of Riviere, I'd taken one look at these three brothers—powerful, strong, cruel—and assumed the worst. Since then, I'd learned things I never wanted to know. I'd born witness to Theos breaking under the weight of his loss. Felt the heat of responsibility and guilt that clings to Ruen like a cloak he can never take off. Of the three of them, Kalix seems to be the only one who feels no such *mortal* emotions. Yet, beneath his ease of life and wicked behavior, he remains with them. He'd agreed to the blood contract without complaint. He's an enigma, perhaps even more so than Ruen Darkhaven.

I shake off those thoughts and give Ruen a nod of understanding. A moment passes and he releases me. My footsteps lead me from their chambers, out into the hall, and down the stairs until I'm standing in front of my own room.

Aranea taps my neck as I open the door and step inside, letting the wood swing shut. Just as Ruen had predicted, a bundle of new clothes sits at the edge of my bed, the black woolen pattern of my uniform stark against the gray sheets.

Something else pulls my attention away from it, however. Aranea jumps from my shoulder and despite the distance, she seems to glide easily to the floor. I don't ask her where she's going as she disappears beneath my bed. Instead, my gaze fixates on the book I'd almost forgotten about. The book that Caedmon had given me.

The dull, worn cover is the same, but ... I stride across the room until I'm standing at my nightstand where it lies. Of all the collection of things that have taken up residence on the tiny space—there and gone—this one has remained for quite a while. Yet, something is different.

I pass my fingers over the roughened surface of the leather-bound pages and frown as I read the title. *The History that Which You Must Know,* it reads. That isn't the title of the book Caedmon had given me. Is this a new book? It can't be. The color of the cover is the same sullen brown with black lacing. The book is just as thick and the author's name is still absent.

Despite the bells still ringing in the near distance, calling the entirety of the Academy to the battle arena, I lift the book into my hands and open it to the first page.

CHAPTER 41

KIERA

I spread my fingers over the etched-in gold foil title, feeling the dips and ridges for some physical evidence of trickery. The title I took from Caedmon at the library was *A History of the Hinterlands*. That book had been a dull leather-bound brown tome with rough edges and no author's name.

Other than the title now glimmering back at me as if telling me to trust it, nothing about the book has changed. I open the page to the last one I'd read, finding the corner of the paper folded over in the same exact way I'd done in order to mark my place. The words inside, however, are just as different as the title on the outside.

The History that Which You Must Know is not a book at all, but a diary. The contents have changed entirely and I would swear that someone has snuck into my room and replaced the older one were it not for the obvious signs of my usage. I scan where the indentations of my nails are left where I'd pressed them beneath certain words. Now, the words are entirely new, different. I read them.

The Gods would have all believe that they came from the

skies, blessed beings capable of a great many new things. They, dear reader, are liars. Just like you.

I swallow roughly, casting a look at the door and then the window before I keep reading. For some, unknown reason this book seems to know something. As if the writer is a God themselves. I stiffen at that thought.

"Caedmon..." I breathe the God of Prophecy's name before shaking my head and continuing to read.

The Gods did not come from the skies, but from a place far out in the ocean of this new world. The Gods as you know them are not Gods at all. Beings of incredible power, yes, but not all-powerful. Not all-seeing.

Somehow, I knew these words to be correct. The Gods were not all-seeing. If they were, then my existence would never have been a question. I would not have been hidden because they would have known. My heart stutters in my breast, my breaths coming in shallow pants. I sink onto the bed and flip the page.

Off the coast of Ortus, within the depths of the ocean, there is a stone capable of withstanding all elements. Fire. Water. Lightning. Divinity. The mountain of Brim. From it, the cursed stone came. From it, the Gods came.

The cursed stone? The mountain of Brim? My thoughts clamber over each other as I reach my own conclusions brought about by the book's words. I'd never thought to wonder where brimstone came from. I had only ever been grateful that there was some sort of stone in this world capable of wounding or even killing a Divine Being. But if the Gods came from Brimstone and the stone came from a mountain off the coast of Ortus ... where the original Mortal Gods Academy still lies...

A hard knock sounds on the door, jolting me from the

pages of the book and my thoughts. I jerk my head up, realizing that the sound of the bells has faded.

"Kiera?" Theos' voice filters through the closed door. "Are you ready? We have to go."

Shit. Shit. Shit. Fumbling with the book in my hand, I snap it shut and jump up from the bed. "Hold on!" I yell, stripping out of my tunic and loosening the self-made belt from the loops of my trousers.

As fast as I can manage, I dive for my uniform, ripping the fresh black trousers up my legs and buttoning them as I adjust my dagger holster. The knob turns and I whip towards the window just as Theos steps inside.

"Theos!" I snap.

The door clicks shut behind him. "Sorry," he says. He doesn't sound sorry, though, as I hear him approach, the soft footfalls of his steps bringing him closer to me. I look to the side as his hand appears in my periphery. He lifts the new tunic to go along with my uniform.

Slowly, viscerally aware of my bare flesh, I turn to face him. I'm still wearing the band I keep around my breasts, but with each breath I take—harsh and unbidden—I swear they're going to spill out. Golden eyes settle on my face for a brief moment, meeting mine before descending to the rounded mounds of my chest.

There are no flushed cheeks. Not from Theos. No, he's seen far more than enough naked females in his lifetime. Heat, however, is a different matter entirely. His golden gaze catches fire, flaring out like the sun itself is blazing out from beyond his eyes. He lifts my tunic and then drops the top part over my head.

Numb and confused, I let him move my arms as he helps me to weave my limbs through the holes of the sleeves and then tuck the hem into the waistband of my trousers. He doesn't say anything about the dagger he'd no doubt seen at my back.

"Theos?"

His lips are pressed together in a flat line that doesn't reveal any clear emotion. It's only the fire still crackling in his eyes that gives me any sort of indication that he's not as calm as he appears. Despite the fact that he'd mentioned our need to hurry before coming in, it's as if time has stopped for us. He lifts one hand, fingers grazing the side of my jawline.

"I think I knew," he whispers, "that whatever you were hiding would be a danger to my brothers and me."

I don't know what to say to that. My words seem locked behind my lips, unable to move or voice themselves. Theos' attention never leaves my face now that he's settled firmly on it.

"Ruen wanted you gone the moment you got here and showed an ounce of spine. He's not used to that, especially not from humans, but I suppose it makes sense now why you were so..." He doesn't finish the comment, shaking his head instead as he moves on. A thumb touches my chin, forcing my head back in the gentlest of motions.

"Kalix wanted to play with you," he continues. "People are toys to him. Objects that he owns and breaks when they fail to live up to his expectations—if he even has those." The corner of his mouth lifts ever so slightly as if he's amused by that. It falls in the next instant.

"But me..." He leans closer until his face, those sunset eyes of his, become all that I see. My heart stutters in my chest, beating wildly and incomprehensibly. "I thought I'd be like Kalix. Play with you and see how much it took you to break." His eyes flash between mine before falling to my mouth. I lick my lower lip on instinct and his lids lower ever so slightly. "Imagine my surprise when you didn't break at all but outsmarted us."

What was a few short months in the past now feels like a lifetime ago. My breath catches as his thumb and fingers tip my head back further and he steps closer until the heat of his chest is right against mine.

"I didn't want you gone, and after Darius," he cuts himself off with a cruel twist of his lips and a low chuckle that is more caustic than amused, "I just wanted you," Theos finally admits. "I wanted the girl who looked at me like she understood my loss and knew what it felt like. Who looked at me and didn't see a being that could threaten her and take her life in an instant, with merely a word. You were so unafraid and I wanted that. Someone who didn't want to fuck me to claim some relation to my father or to just say they had. I wanted someone who didn't have ulterior motives. I guess that was never my fate because you did have them, didn't you?"

The smell of him, rich in spice and rum as if he'd just downed an entire bottle, is heavy in my lungs. It weighs me down, pressing into me and I have to withhold my desire to press into him further and rub my face against his chest. My own breath hitches at his words. Slowly, I shake my head. His fingers don't fall away. They remain locked onto my jaw, gentle, but unyielding.

"Fucking you was never in the plan," I tell him honestly. "I won't lie to you and say I've never fucked for a job before, but you weren't ... part of that job."

He tilts his head to the side, examining me with careful inspection. I don't know what he sees, his face is a mask of calm I'm certain he can't truly be feeling. "Is that because your Guild never gave you the name of your target?" he inquires.

I flinch. My, how far I've fallen. So many years I'd been tested and trained not to give up a single molecule of information and yet, here I am now, standing before one of three outsiders I've given everything to. The blood contract, however, is the strongest vow anyone can take —stronger for those with Divinity because of the power in their blood. So, even if I can't trust anyone in this world, I trust that power. I trust that they will keep my secrets. I have to because if I don't ... then I just damned an entire organization, the woman who raised me, and my best friend.

The thought of Regis brings me back to reality and the man standing before me. I shake my head again and sigh. "I didn't fuck you because I was going to use you," I say.

Theos waits, as patient as I've ever seen him. Cool indifference plastered on his face when I know it's so much deeper than that. *He* is so much deeper than that. "I just wanted, for once, to choose." My words are a whisper in the silence that hangs like a pendulum between us. "You were hurting and I didn't want you to hurt anymore."

"So, it was a pity fuck then?" Theos frowns. "I've never had that before. No one's ever bothered."

Gods, I could slap the shit out of him right now. "It wasn't a damned pity fuck," I bite out, pulling away. Or at least, I attempt to pull away. The moment I step back, however, Theos moves as fast as lightning. His hand comes down hard on my waist and he spins me until I slap into the wall opposite my bed.

"Then what was it for?" he demands, baring his teeth at me. "You don't get to come in here and wreck my life or our carefully laid plans and give no explanations. I want fucking answers, Kiera."

I curl my hands into fists, digging my nails into my palms to keep from beating him senseless. "I just gave you answers," I snap back. "Do you have any idea the things I've done in my life? The people I've killed?"

He waves my words off as if they mean nothing. "That was for survival," he replies. "You didn't have a choice. You had a choice about me and you decided to take me to your bed and you took Kalix too."

Technically, it was his bed that we'd fucked in, but I don't think he's worried about semantics at this point and I'm certainly not. What I'm focused on is how easily he seems to disregard my past actions, my kills.

"There was a choice when killing and I chose to kill because it was easier." The words are like knives ripping up my throat. I hate them, revile them, but admit them because they are the truth.

Theos glares at me. "Why. Did. You. Fuck. Me?" Each word is cut from his lips like diseased flesh from the body. Rage fills me. It's so damned obvious, how can he not see it?

"Because I wanted to, Theos!" I scream at him. "Because for once, I didn't want to kill or hurt. I just wanted to make you feel better, but I wanted to feel better too. It wasn't damned pity." Maybe it had started out that way, but it certainly hadn't ended as pity. "It was desire," I spit at him. "Plain and fucking simple. Are you happy now? Can we go?"

Black spreads from Theos' pupils, consuming the gold in an instant. "No." The denial is cold and hot all at once, a fire coated in ice. "I'm never happy, Kiera."

Then his lips slam down on mine.

CHAPTER 42

KIERA

This is not the time to fall into Theos' kiss. We have to leave the north tower and we have to go to the battle arena to find out why the Gods have called everyone. And yet ... when Theos' mouth touches mine, I don't shove him off. I don't push him away.

No. Instead, I lean into him. I uncurl my fists and wrap my arms around his neck, pressing myself against his body as I part my lips for his tongue to enter. *Desire.* That was the reason I'd given him for our first night. It's the truth. I've never desired to be so important to him as I was that night. He had needed someone to understand him, to distract him from his sorrow and loss, someone to just be there in spite of his vicious tongue intent on driving everyone else away, and I had needed to be that person.

Tears gather in the back of my eyes, but I squeeze them shut as Theos' hands grasp my hips. He drives me back into the stone wall, his chest smashed against mine as he devours my mouth. A moan bubbles up my throat and he swallows it down as my fingers dive upward, into the locks of white gold hair at the top of his head. His hips encase mine as he rubs the evidence of his arousal, trapped within the confines of his trousers, against my stomach. Then, as if he can't help himself, Theos shifts and drives one knee between both of my legs.

"I'm still angry," he murmurs against my lips, "fucking furious with you, *Dea,* but I understand why you kept your secrets."

I *really* don't want to talk about all the secrets I've kept right now. What I want to do is divest both of us of our clothes, throw him back on my cot, climb atop him, and sink down onto the rigid erection straining between us. But I can't. We can't.

"We have to go," I breathe the words out, hating them even as I know how important they are.

My words, however, aren't what stops Theos. Instead, it's the rapid pounding against my door that gives him pause. Black eyes shoot to the door with biting fury. I suck in breath after breath, trying to fill up my lungs as I shake the strange sensation from my mind caused by Theos.

He steps back and cold washes over me. His black eyes fade to a dull yellow once more. "Finish getting ready," Theos bites out the words, practically vibrating with unspent energy.

I don't argue. I grab up my boots, shove my feet inside, and tie them up in record time. Then, we're both leaving the room and meeting Ruen and Kalix in the hall as I snatch up my uniform jacket and pull it on. Kalix's lips twitch in amusement. I don't even bother commenting on the fact that Theos had been well aware of what had occurred between the Kalix and I. What little extra time we'd had is gone now.

The three of us descend the north tower and head for the arena. The closer we get, the more bodies we see. Mortal Gods mill about at the entrances to the arena seats, trailed by their smaller and far more nondescript Terra.

By the time the Darkhavens reach their seats, I'm half-convinced that Ruen and Kalix are wrong and that a battle is about to be called into session. The situation feels much too similar to the first time. The Gods of the Academy are gathered in their own section, separate from that of their children, at the far end of the arena, right above the tunnel entrance that leads into the sand and dirt covered circle below. My heart beats at a rapid pace against my breast as I scan the crowd for signs of Niall.

Despite the chilly winter air, the sun beats down on us all and sweat begins to collect beneath the fabric of my clothes. My palms are sticky with it as the Darkhavens take their padded seats and paste disinterested and bored expressions upon their faces. I take my position at the end of their bench and clasp my hands behind my back, fingers encircling one wrist tightly.

My eyes move over the heads of the students as they, too, take their seats, collectively gathering before the Gods. A heavy pressure settles on my shoulders and slowly, so as not to appear suspicious, I turn and face forward. Dolos is there. Cloaked in his usual darkness, sitting far back beneath the shade as someone leans close to him and says something I can't hear from this distance. With the shadows of whatever he uses to dampen his abilities clinging to him, I hate that I can't see his face, can't read his expression. Being able to read him might have given us some sort of hint as to why we've all been brought here.

A crimson color catches my attention and I yank it away from where Dolos is to spy Maeryn cutting through the crowd, stomping in, to my surprise, a pair of tight trousers and a loose tunic with a brown vest laced up in the front. I've only ever seen her wear pants when training, so it's startling to see her so casually attired as she stalks through those surrounding her to the Second Tier section she'd sat in during the battles.

I cast my gaze behind and around her, but there's no sign of Niall. My eyes shoot back to Maeryn as she slams herself into her seat, waving off another Terra who's carrying a tray and offering her a glass of water. Her expression is puckered and dark. A pit of unease opens up in my belly.

Finally, when it seems that everyone has gathered and taken their seats and Terra line the back walls or stand alongside their Masters' seats, Dolos rises from his chair and moves to the edge of the balcony overlooking the arena. Prickles of awareness crawl over my spine. A collective breath is held as he approaches and pauses, letting everyone get a good look at him before he speaks as if this is some forsaken dramatic play in which he is the main villain.

No, the Gods don't think of themselves as villains. That's what makes them so dangerous. To them, they are the heroes. Saving the little mortal creatures from their own misgivings. I close my eyes and tighten my fingers around my wrist. I count backward from ten in my head, pleading for patience.

Slowly, I fall back into that place I know so well. The same place I go to when Ophelia is teaching me one of her lessons. It's a small piece of myself that I've kept away from her, away from everyone. My safe place. Once I'm firmly ensconced within it, I open my eyes and stare blankly across the arena and I wait.

"Welcome students," Dolos calls out, his voice echoing across the sky, loud and booming. "I'm sure you are all wondering why you've been called to the arena. Unfortunately, we are not about to hold our battles again so soon." The tension within me eases but only marginally. If this isn't a battle, that doesn't necessarily mean it can't be something far worse. Knowing the Gods as I do, it is better to keep my expectations low. Kindness is as rare in this place as hope is.

My skin itches, growing taut as Dolos continues to speak. "Our illustrious Academy will soon be hosting the God Council. As such, any and all permission for requested trips outside of our walls have been denied and canceled."

At my side, Ruen stiffens at the mention of the God Council. I want to turn my head and demand answers. *What is the God Council? Why is the Academy going on lockdown? What does this mean?* I don't say a word, though. I don't even flick a glance his way. I keep my gaze trained steadily ahead.

"Tryphone, himself, our King will be arriving within the next few days." Dolos' words punch through me in an instant. Tryphone, the King of the Gods.

Oh ... Gods. I may have managed to fool the Dark-havens, even the Gods here at the Academy, but Tryphone—the King of the Gods is the most powerful of them all. Surely, even with the brimstone dampening my Divinity and power, he'd be able to see right through me.

Panic claws at my throat. The safe place in my mind calls to me.

Somehow, I have the strangest sensation that Dolos is looking at me from beyond the shadows that surround him. The dark copse of fog that keeps him from being fully visible and keeps his power from shattering the minds of everyone around him under his mental imprisonment tilts slightly to the side, as if he's canting his head as he speaks again.

"It is your duty to prove to the God Council that you are the most powerful of their offspring and therefore, the most worthy of their presence," he states. "The mercy I have shown over recent months has now ended. Indefinitely. Should any of you—Student or Terra alike—betray the rules we have set forth, your execution will be swift. Classes will be put on hiatus for the next two weeks as we prepare to welcome our King and his entourage. Any questions of assignments may be directed to your instructors. You are dismissed."

All of this fanfare, and Dolos calls an end to his summons with a speed that leaves me feeling as if I've been whipped off a horse and thrown over a cliff's edge. The sound of roaring winds and water fills my ears. Tryphone is coming. The King of the Gods is coming *here*.

Dolos fades back from the balcony and then leaves the Gods' section entirely. The other Gods and instructors get up, talking amongst themselves, some appearing excited and others appearing bored by this announcement. They don't care. Of course, they don't. It's not their lives at risk. I rove over their faces, each of them—spotting Narelle, Maladesia, and even Axlan.

Where's Caedmon? I don't spy him anywhere. His figure is missing from the stands ... just like Niall's.

Niall. The reminder has my head turning back to where Maeryn had been seated before. She's gone now though. It takes me a moment, but my eyes catch on her retreating back as she storms up the stairs of the stands, moving with grace and speed. I have to catch up with her. I will make sure that Niall is fine and then ... then I'll figure the rest out.

Perhaps, it's time for me to leave this Academy. To leave the Darkhavens.

"Kiera?" Panic and fake calm are warring within me and despite my attempt at hiding it away, the panic is winning out. I turn to face Ruen as he stands from his seat and peers at me, brow furrowed. "What's wrong?"

"I have to go," I say. My voice is so slight that I think he doesn't hear me at first because now that Dolos' announcement has ended, everyone is talking. The roar of the students' voices rises as they begin to file out.

"You—" He reaches for me, but I back up a step, shaking my head.

"I have to find my friend," I tell him.

He narrows his gaze on me and Kalix peers around his side, curious. "The Terra boy?" he inquires.

I nod, swallowing roughly.

"You can find him later," Ruen insists. Once again, he reaches for me and once again, I step out of his range. A cloud of darkness descends over his features. "Kiera—"

I don't wait for his refusal. My heart is thundering in my chest. "I'll be back," I swear just before I turn and sprint off.

The curse that follows me is low and vicious. I ignore it as I take the stairs two at a time, diving around Mortal Gods and Terra alike. *Where had Maeryn gone? Was she looking for Niall or does she know where he is?* She had seemed upset, her face a mask of frustration when she'd sat through the announcements.

I hang right and skid past a familiar face—Malachi—but he doesn't see me as he boasts that the God Council would only ever come to Riviere because they are the best Mortal Gods in the realm. Even his ridiculous pompousness isn't enough to give me a reason to snort. I'm too focused on finding the red-haired healer.

Minutes pass by, each stretching longer than the next as I scour the crowd that's flooding out of the arena for any sign of Maeryn or Niall. Niall would never be the kind to miss an announcement from the Gods. If anything, he would have been one of the first ones here, helping to set things up if needed or offering waters to the Mortal Gods and Divine Beings.

I slam to a stop when Maeryn's red ponytail catches my attention. Lifting a hand over my head, I wave to her, hoping she sees me. Her head turns and pauses, eyes narrowing. When she spots me, some of the tension drains from her expression. Clear relief etched onto her features. She cuts through the lines of Mortal Gods and Terra towards me and I do the same.

"Where is Niall?"

"Have you seen Niall?"

My question and hers overlap and unfortunately, they answer each other. "You don't know where he is?" I ask, peering at her as her expression scrunches once more.

Maeryn shakes her head, the long curve of her ponytail swaying at her back. Little wisps of red curls have broken free and linger around her rounded, freckled cheeks. "I haven't seen him since this morning," she says. "He would have been here but he wasn't."

Fuck. The curse is on the tip of my tongue. Unfortunately, we're currently surrounded by other Mortal Gods and Terra, so I have to bite it back. Maeryn seems to recognize the issue and before I can say anything, she reaches out and latches onto my wrist.

"Come on, this way," she orders.

Maeryn pulls me behind her and dives into the mass of bodies. A few people curse—Mortal Gods, of course—some even threaten to skin me when my sides bump theirs. Maeryn doesn't stop. She ignores them all and so do I.

The two of us make it out of the arena and onto a grassy courtyard near a classroom building. "Niall would never ignore a summons from the Gods," Maeryn says.

I nod, agreeing. "Where was he the last place you saw him?"

Maeryn parts her lips to answer, but just as she does, I spot a familiar figure, racing down an outer corridor. I frown as Laria's hair flies behind her head, her dark gray uniform skirt catching at her thighs as she ignores everything around her and sprints towards the end.

Maeryn's head lifts and turns, following my gaze. Her eyes narrow. "Is that one of the Terra who has been harassing Niall?" Her voice is cold as she asks the question.

"Yes, but—"

She doesn't wait for me to finish. As soon as she has her answer, she takes off running. This time, I let a curse slip free as I grind my teeth and follow after her.

CHAPTER 43

KIERA

Maeryn surprises me. I expect her to catch up to Laria in no time, but she slows her speed as I race behind her—casting careful looks around so that I can keep my speed human and so that we're not drawing unwanted attention. I'm sure the Darkhavens are furious with me—certainly Ruen will be.

Maeryn waits until Laria turns down a side corridor, slowing her own steps as we make it further away from anyone still lingering near the arena. As if she senses something, Maeryn doesn't make her move until Rodney comes into view. The larger, bulky, dull-witted man lifts his head, and a hand to wave at his sister, pausing when he spots Maeryn at her back and then me.

Before he can shout or call out in warning, Maeryn is on him. Her body flies past Laria's and her hand clamps around his throat in an instant. I follow suit, grabbing Laria and covering her mouth with my palm as Maeryn drives the larger of the two into a nearby classroom— empty save for the abandoned seats and the four of us.

The wall shudders as Maeryn slams Rodney against

it. She turns to look back at me. "Him too?" she confirms, fury twisting her normally so placid features.

I nod. "Maeryn, you can't kill him."

She turns back to Rodney as Laria begins to struggle in my grip. It takes no real effort for me to pinch her nose shut as my palm remains over her lips. I lean down close to her ear. "I suggest you don't make a sound, Laria," I warn her. "I'm not exactly in a forgiving mood today and neither is Niall's Mistress."

Laria's eyes widen as she glances from me to the Mortal God currently pinning her laughably much larger brother into the wall with little more than a small hand on his throat. Even if Maeryn's natural Divinity is geared towards healing, she still has the same added benefits of her Godly blood. Extra speed, strength, and agility.

"I'm only going to ask this once," Maeryn sneers into the man's face. "Where. Is. Niall?"

Rodney wheezes, his face darkening into a bluish-purple as his air supply is cut off. She grips him tighter, not realizing that his lack of response isn't intended. "He can't answer you if he can't draw breath," I remind her.

Maeryn blinks and releases his throat immediately. Rodney crashes to the floor at her feet, coughing as he sucks down air. I release Laria's nose and mouth and she, too, gasps down large lungfuls.

"Where is Niall?" I ask her, holding her still against me, her back to my chest. Maeryn turns glittering green eyes on the Terra in my grip.

Laria freezes and the noisy gulping breaths she was previously taking stop altogether as a hiccupping squeak of fear comes out of her. I tighten my hands on her arms until I know they're bruising.

"Answer the question," I snap. "Where is Niall?"

"W-why would you th-think we—"

Maeryn abandons Rodney's shaking body and is in front of Laria and me in a split second. Her hair flies forward with the speed, whipping into the side of her cheek as she comes to a halt. She doesn't seem to notice.

"*Where is he?*" she demands.

Laria whimpers. "W-we tied him up in D-Dolos' office," she says shakily. "T-to teach him a l-lesson."

A lesson? I close my eyes, begging for peace and tranquility. It doesn't come willingly. Tying Niall up in the Dean's office isn't a mere punishment from his peers. It's a death sentence unless we get to him first. Dolos wouldn't necessarily care why Niall was there or that he wasn't there of his own free will. Sneaking into a God's office without permission is tantamount to treason and he'd just gotten through telling everyone that he would no longer be providing mercy to those who broke the rules as he had supposedly done with me.

When my eyes reopen, it's to find Maeryn's face bearing down into Laria's trembling frame. "Why?"

Laria starts to cry. Tears leaking from her eyes and rolling down her cheeks as she shakes against me. "I-it's her fault," she blubbers, nodding back to me. "She shouldn't be here. She's a disgrace to the Mortal Gods and Divine Beings. He's been going around telling everyone that she was forgiven by the Gods and thus she shouldn't be punished, but because of her, we all—"

Maeryn's palm snaps out and grabs hold of Laria's face, tightening until I know there will be lines of purple fingerprints engraved in the Terra's cheeks for days following this. I don't even feel sorry for her.

"If you ever come near my Terra again," Maeryn says, her tone quiet and lethal. Her nails dig into Laria's skin, drawing blood. I blink, but don't say a word to deter her as she continues. "If you harass him, speak to him in anything but a polite tone, no—if you fucking look at him ever again..." The wild mossy green eyes of hers darken. "I will find you and him," she nods back to Rodney as he holds his throat, staring up at us where I'm holding his sister hostage before one of the Mortal Gods they worship so devoutly. "And I will slit your fucking throats and watch you choke on your own blood."

"B-but you h-have healing a-abilities—"

Maeryn laughs, the sound anything but amused. "I choose to heal," she tells Laria. "If you come for what is mine, I will choose to kill. Do you understand?"

Laria nods quickly. "Y-yes, Ma'am."

Maeryn looks back at Rodney, who lowers his eyes immediately, wide shoulders trembling. "Y-yes," he answers her.

Maeryn steps back, eyes falling to me. I reach back and jerk my tunic out of my waistband, grabbing my dagger and lifting its blade until the sharp end of one side is directly against the artery in Laria's throat.

"Say a word of this to anyone and you won't have to worry about her coming to find you," I say.

Laria quickly shakes her head. "N-no," she blurts. "No, of course not. We won't say a word."

I run the wicked length of my blade over her neck, letting her feel the prick of its stinging edge and she squeaks out a fearful plea to stop, one that I ignore. A small line appears against her skin, not deep enough to kill, but just enough to let her know that this is no play we're putting on. Unlike the Gods, every move I make is not meant for entertainment, but for survival and protection.

In the next instant, I release Laria. Her legs wobble and she steps forward as if surprised that we're letting them go so easily. A line of blood dribbles down her neck towards her collarbone. She reaches up and touches it lightly, and when her fingers come away with the red liquid, she bolts for her brother. Grabbing ahold of him and the two quickly leave the classroom.

"We have to get to him before Dolos returns to his office," I say, looking at Maeryn.

She nods, and together, the two of us slip out into the quiet, empty hallway. Neither of us says another word as we move. She doesn't ask about the dagger I put back in my tunic beneath my jacket and I don't comment on the obvious affection she's showing towards Niall—certainly more so than any Master or Mistress I've ever seen reveal to a Terra servant.

THE LAST TIME I traversed the corridors of the Gods' building, I'd been led by the Academy guards and sure that my doom was waiting at the end. The long hall-ways—with one side decorated in stained glass windows that throw shades of red, gold, and blue onto the floor and walls—feel somehow longer now than they had before as Maeryn and I sprint down them.

She doesn't seem to notice just how easily I keep up with her pace. Still, I fake a few heaving breaths every once in a while when she bothers to glance back, giving her a strained smile when unease is crawling up my throat. Her eyes had flashed with red and black back there. I suspect, had I not been with her, she would have ripped Rodney and Laria to shreds for putting Niall in danger.

The wider corridors of the Gods' section of the Academy echo with our footsteps, rising higher and higher above our heads to the arched ceilings. Concern laces each heart beat as I note that, despite the time of day, there are no other Gods here. Perhaps they're all still at the arena as I'd still seen plenty of them, unconcerned with the rush to leave as I'd slipped free from the Darkhavens and rushed to find Maeryn—and now Niall.

Maeryn slows and I take the lead. "This way," I tell her, diving to the right. She follows easily, but as we're about to round another corner, she snakes her hand out. Her fingers curl into the back of my uniform jacket and the neckline chokes me as she pulls me to a sudden halt.

"What—"

Soft murmuring voices reach my ears and Maeryn wastes no time in whipping both of us into a darkened alcove where a standing pedestal rests with a stone bust atop it. The bust trembles as we dive behind the pedestal and I reach out, steadying it and ducking back down as the two voices get louder.

Sweat coats my palms and I reach back, fingering the hilt of my dagger now replaced at my back holster as the footsteps get nearer. Two figures dressed in long black robes pass by, neither of them glancing in our direction.

"—will be most displeased if he learns of this," says one of the figures—Pachis, a Lower God I recognize as one of the instructors of Mathematics. Despite his Divinity, unlike most Gods, he's a rather bulbous male with a round countenance that causes him to waddle as he walks. He appears as more of a God of Gluttony than one of study that I know him to be.

"That will be up to Dolos to deal with; it has nothing to do with us." The thin, reed-like man who replies has a sharp voice and even sharper features. Peeking out from the other side of the pedestal, I frown. I had seen Hatzi, the God of Travel, around campus many times before, and as always, his continued stay within the walls of the Academy confuses me. If Gods gained power from what their powers concerned, why would the God of Travel choose to stay in one place?

Their words, however, sink into my mind a moment later and a whole new question takes the place of the last. What exactly is Dolos having to deal with? Does it have to do with the Council of the Gods?

"Come on." Maeryn's grip locks on my wrist as she drags me out of the alcove as soon as the Gods turn a corner and disappear from sight.

Dolos' office is nearby. So close I can practically taste the triumph of getting there and freeing Niall without any of those Divine fools being the wiser. I stifle the victory singing in my blood though. Too often, I've witnessed opponents in sparring rings celebrate before a battle was truly over and it never ended well for them.

I lead Maeryn the rest of the way, our footsteps speeding up and then slowing as we hit the next corridor and I stop before the red-painted door that I'd been in front of weeks ago—right before I'd been dragged to the dungeons and imprisoned and starved for three days. The gold filigree etched into the corners and backing the plaque at the center glimmers in the light.

I try the knob and grit my teeth when I find it locked. It must have been unlocked previously for Laria and her brother to have gotten in and no doubt, they locked it from the inside before leaving Niall here. A muffled sound emerges from inside. Maeryn nudges me out of the way and tries the handle as well. She jerks and slams down on it once before I can stop her. Despite her strength, it doesn't budge.

"Don't," I say quickly. "We can't leave any trace we were here or else Dolos will think someone broke in to steal something."

She shoots her green eyes back at me, brows furrowing. "Then what do you suggest we do?" she demands.

I glance at her hair and reach for the black pins I see keeping several strands tight to her scalp. "Let me borrow these," I say, plucking two from her head. A few wayward curls, too short to reach her ponytail, fall forward.

Maeryn doesn't jerk back or deny me the pins as I get to my knees and brush her hand aside. Her eyes linger heavy on my back as the hard floor digs past my trousers. Wiping sweat away from my palms, I bend both pins and twist them until I have a makeshift lock pick. It would have been easier to use my spiders, I suspect, but I'd rather not do so in front of Maeryn.

I've never been more thankful to Ophelia for teaching me all the ways a human would perform these tasks instead of relying solely on my abilities than I am right now. Sticking first one end of the pin into the lock, I feel for the cylinders inside and once I have them positioned down, I stick the second hair pin into the hole and breathe out. A quick deft twist of my wrists and a fucking prayer, the door unlocks with a *snick*.

Quickly yanking the pins free, I stuff them into my pockets and race inside, Maeryn following after me. As Maeryn scans the room and spots a figure huddled on the floor near the fireplace, I close and relock the door behind us. It won't stop the God from entering should

Dolos come back while we're untying Niall, but it would give us some warning and a few precious extra seconds.

Niall lies upon the floor, half of his face a molted purple as if someone had bashed him good. Blood crusts the split skin that mars his upper cheek and a makeshift gag keeps him from speaking as he struggles against the ropes binding him to a metal frame bolted near the fireplace, usually meant for pokers and such.

Maeryn curses as she goes to her knees before him and rips off the gag. "Are you alright?" she asks, voice tight with concern.

I glance from Niall to the door to the desk. Something feels ... odd about all this. Niall breathes heavily, the sound rough and struggling as he answers. "I-I'm so sorry, Miss Mae—"

"Don't apologize, Niall," Maeryn interrupts him. "Don't you dare. Let's just get you out of here and then I'll heal you."

My eyes settle on the desk as the sound of Maeryn and Niall's quiet conversation flows in the background. Papers are strewn about as well as quills. Left haphazardly out for anyone inside to see. *Why?*

I glance away from the desk to the rest of the office. Nothing else is out of place. It is just as ornate and clean as it had been when I'd last been here. I take a step towards the desk, eyes moving over the words written on those pages. A few strides carry me around the back end of the wooden frame and I bend, scanning the contents.

They're letters, I realize. I shouldn't realize it though. Because the language written in careful script on the pages isn't the one I've grown up with. It is not the common language, but that of the ancient tongue. The one Theos often uses to call me *Dea*—*treasure*. I lift the first one and read.

Dolos,

Tryphone is growing weary of his daughter's refusal and Caedmon's lack of reply to his summons. A Council will be called. Ensure that Caedmon is there or else I worry that his ire will erupt upon us all. I expect he will want a list of the most powerful children ready to be taken after the Council ends. Have them ready for removal and you shall be given your reward.

Your sister,
Danai

Confusion wars with interest. The King of the Gods has a daughter? How had I or any of the others never heard of her? Surely, I would have been forced to listen to this information from Niall back when he'd lectured me on the great God King's benevolence before.

My eyes land on the sender of this letter. Danai. That's the same name of the Queen of the Gods, isn't it? Danai is Dolos' sister? That, too, was not something I knew. Certainly, it couldn't be common knowledge if I'd never heard anyone mention it. Why, too, is she telling Dolos to have a list of powerful God children ready? Where are they to be taken?

So focused on the paper in my hand, I hardly notice the turn of the knob until Maeryn's sharp gasp reaches me. Snapping my head up, I gape in shock as an elder Mortal God appears in what most certainly should have been a locked door. The key in his hand, however, is merely an afterthought of realization as his eyes widen when he spies the three of us in the room—two Terra and a Mortal God, all of whom are trespassing.

I drop the letter and hurtle over the desk in an instant as he parts his lips. The key falls from his hand as he reaches for the hilt of the sword on his heavy belt. My dagger is out of its holster and embedded in his throat before a single sound can escape.

Blood bubbles up, oozing out of the wound on his neck as I find myself crouched over him, my body practically sitting on his chest as the light in his eyes dims and then goes completely cold.

Numbness sinks into my fingertips and crawls up my hands and then my arms. I look back as Maeryn gets to shaking feet, pulling Niall up to stand next to her. Both of their gazes land on the Mortal God lying beneath me.

"You killed him." Niall is pale and trembling as he staggers a step and Maeryn catches him before he goes down. "You—" Niall's eyes lift to meet mine, soft brown like that of a trusting animal. He blanches at whatever expression he sees on my face. I don't know what I must look like, I can't hardly feel my own skin much less know the twist of my own appearance.

"That's not possible." Maeryn shakes her head. "You can't kill him. You're human."

A hissing noise grabs my attention and as I lift my head, twin black eyes meet mine from the shadow across from the open door. A snake. I close my eyes with a curse. One of Kalix's no doubt. He must have sent it to follow me after I'd slipped away from them at the arena.

As if to prove my assumption correct, seconds later the sound of pounding footsteps reach my ears and three large bodies fill the doorway. Ruen, Kalix, and Theos each take a look at the scene before them.

Me with a dead Mortal God guard under me, my dagger in his throat, to Maeryn and Niall, standing a few feet away, gaping at me in shock and horror.

I'm breaking all my rules today, it seems.

CHAPTER 44

KIERA

When I was fifteen, there'd been a particularly rough mission that required both Regis and me to work in tandem. It was a rare mission in which multiple targets were under the same contract. Regis and I had spent weeks scoping out the stronghold of a seedy brothel in Carth, a rather ordinary small city with a God Lord that didn't seem all that interested in ruling so much as holing up in his castle and drinking night and day.

The disinterest of the God Lord had led to several human men rounding up young women with no protectors and forcing them to sell themselves to anyone with enough denza. Fortunately, one of the women that had been taken and forced into sexual servitude had actually been someone with a protector—a protector that had been away hunting due to their dire straits when she'd been taken.

The man had sold all his earnings from the hunt and offered his own body up to the Guild in exchange for a contract to kill the perpetrators who stole his sister from their dilapidated home. The earnings hadn't been enough, nor had the offer of his future services and life to the Guild. The man had left one of the many taverns where Guild members reserve private rooms for client meetings with a hollow sort of look I'd seen so often in slums and in the faces of those who served time in Ophelia's dungeons.

By some miracle, the man had returned two days later with a bag of denza coin heavier than a human skull. As he'd dropped it on the table before Ophelia, not even caring that he was one of few clients to ever meet her in person—much less me, who'd been standing at her back as an extra guard that day—he'd leaned over and said a phrase that, to this day, I've never been able to forget.

Evil is not the tyranny of the Gods. It is not even the cruelty of life. Evil is the act of apathy, and madness is begging for difference only when you need it. If you don't save those women now ... there will come a time when you are the one who needs saving, and it will not be evil to see you shatter under someone else's reign of greed and madness. It will simply be indifference.

Those words had struck my heart in that moment. The truth of evil that I'd so long, by that point, assumed was clear. The Gods were evil. They were bad. They were conquerors who squashed all who did not bow before them.

Yet that man's pleading eyes, the anger in the trembling of his limbs, everything in me had told me that, in order to get that money, he'd done unspeakable things. Perhaps even things that I would never do myself—and by fifteen, I had done enough of them.

Ophelia hadn't even batted an eyelash as she'd lifted the bag of coin towards her. As ostentatious and grand as the man's gesture had been, a simple glance was all it took for me to realize that even that amount wasn't enough for a meeting with the leader of the Underworld, much less one of her top assassins in training.

Still, she had taken the man's money and she had sent not one but two assassins. When Regis and I had found the women in the brothel, seen the decayed insides of the rancid building and the rags they wore—stained with all manner of fluids that made my insides churn—we had been only too happy to cut down any of the men who'd kept them there against their wills as they'd attempted to flee for their lives.

Not a single man had made it out. We'd killed them all, and we had relished in their slaughter.

Now, as I sit in the Darkhaven chambers high within the north tower of the Mortal Gods Academy of Riviere, I think about that man's words. The last plea he'd had for his sister's salvation and I hope that my actions against those disgusting pigs will at least grant me some sort of pardon of my own.

In spite of my actions over the last ten years, the people I've killed—those who certainly deserved it and those who may have been redeemed—still weigh on my chest, a burden that will never be lifted.

"So, you're a..." Maeryn stares at me, her eyes wide as she paces across the room, her body moving with lithe grace as I sit on the center lounge before the fireplace.

"Mortal God," I say, nodding. "Yes." I grimace to think of what Ophelia will say when she finds out I've betrayed her so. Unlike the Darkhavens, Maeryn is not under any blood contract to keep my secrets. I eye her as she stops and blows out a breath.

I've performed enough evil deeds in my life that if

possible, I would truly like to keep from killing her. I've not had a female friend before and I can imagine that if things for us had been different, Maeryn would have been a very good one.

Down below, in my private room, Niall is resting, a note left on the bedside to join us if he wakes before we can retrieve him and Aranea watching to make sure he doesn't leave without alerting us. After being attacked by Rodney and Laria, it comes as no surprise that he fainted at the sight of the three Darkhavens gathered in Dolos' office doorway.

I can't even be upset that they'd followed me, not when the moment Ruen had seen the body beneath me, he'd taken charge and ordered everyone into action. Kalix had hefted the dead guard's fallen frame over his shoulder as if he was used to disposing of bodies while Maeryn had caught a fallen Niall and lowered him to the ground.

Ruen had ordered Theos to bring the three of us—Niall, Maeryn, and me—back to the Darkhaven chambers while he cleaned up the mess left behind and got rid of any traces that we'd been there.

Theos moves away from the bar cart and drops a glass into Maeryn's hand as he passes her. She takes it and looks into the amber liquid for a moment before tipping it back and draining every last drop. Once done, she slumps into a nearby chair and shakes her head.

"I can't fucking believe this," she mutters before gesturing to me. "I mean, I knew you were different—you don't act like any Terra I've ever known, but ... a Mortal God?" She sits forward, setting her now empty glass on the table as she stares at me. "Your Divinity should be noticeable," she murmurs, eyes roving over my face and down my skin as if she can delve deep and peel the layers of my flesh back to reveal my Divine blood underneath.

"Now that you mention it," Theos takes a seat with a glass of his own. "After what you told us—if you don't know who your God parent is, is it possible they weren't actually a God, but a Mortal God? Perhaps you're more removed from the bloodline than we originally thought. They only started forcing contraceptive herbs on us in the last few decades. Older Mortal Gods were free to procreate a while back."

I shake my head. "She was a Goddess," I answer them. "My memories are faded but my father knew her well."

"Then how—"

"It probably has something to do with the brimstone." I scrub a hand over my face, feeling far more exhausted by the day than I have by anything else in a long damn time.

"*Brimstone?*" Both Maeryn and Theos sit up and say the word at the same time as the door to the chambers opens and Kalix and Ruen appear.

Ruen frowns at the three of us as he strides past, stripping off his strangely wet shirt. I glance out the window, but there's no rain. How had he gotten wet?

My eyes move back to him just as the tunic is peeled off his back and my lips part in shock as the lines on his back come into view. In training, Ruen is one of the few Mortal Gods who always keeps his shirt on. Now, I can see why.

Horrific white lines up and down his back, wrapping around his sides and speckling his shoulders mar his flesh. Scars. Dozens upon dozens of them crisscross over his flesh, some longer than others and some barely perceptible even with a clear sight of them. He disappears into his room before I can say anything, but I can't speak even if I wanted to. My throat closes.

It takes a lot to scar one with Divine Blood or brimstone. Ruen hadn't just had one, but so many that they'd practically taken up his entire back. How many times had he been wounded—*punished?* I wonder distantly—for all those injuries to close over and leave their mark upon him.

"What's this about brimstone?" Kalix asks, pleasantly as if he's just returned from a quick walk that invigorated him.

Maeryn sends him a repulsed glance but returns her gaze to my face as if expecting an answer.

Shaking off the image of the absolute devastation of Ruen's back, I bend forward and gather the long rope of my braid, sliding it away from my neck. "There's a shard of brimstone embedded in my flesh," I answer, tapping over the spot that sometimes heats and hurts when I try to overuse my abilities.

Silence meets my admission and when I let my hair drop and sit back up, there's not just one pair of eyes that are staring at me in horror—there are four pairs, including a freshly dressed Ruen. Kalix doesn't necessarily look horrified so much as his brow is furrowed in confusion and irritation.

"You have a shard of brimstone in your neck?" Ruen's voice is low and dangerous.

I look at him. "Uh, yes?"

"How long have you had it?" Maeryn asks.

My attention returns to her as she continues to stare at me as if I've sprouted a second head. I've read books of creatures with such an ability, but I've never been one of them. Still, I cup the back of my neck as heat echoes down my spine as if the brimstone is aware of my words.

"About ten years or so," I answer.

"Ten *years?*" Theos' whisper is a shaky question.

I turn to him. "It doesn't hurt," I say. "Not really."

"Brimstone repels Divine blood," Ruen states, moving around the lounges until he's standing in front of me. I sit up and away, but he captures the back of my head in one wide palm. "Bend down." His order is so abrupt and he's already exerting pressure against my skull. I'm too tired to argue so I cant my head, facing the floor as his warm fingers touch the back of my neck.

A shiver chases down my spine and I curl my hands into fists as he prods at the place between my skull and shoulders while he wraps a hand around my hair and holds it out of his way. I inhale and the cold scent of salt and ocean breeze enters my nose. It's so different from his usual parchment and mint scent that I spend the next several seconds trying to figure out why his smell has changed. Could they perhaps have gone down to the cliff-side and dumped the Mortal God guard's body into the ocean?

A sharp lance of pain slices through my head and I yank back. "*Fuck!*" Tears prick at the back of my eyes as they slam shut. Fire crawls over my flesh and the urge to vomit presses up my throat.

In and out, I heave and slowly, with trembling endurance, the pain fades until it's little more than a dull throb that I know will leave me with a lasting ache. When I finally have the energy to look at the others standing around the room, Ruen's face is a mask of fury and Kalix has moved closer as he stares at me, his green eyes replaced with pure crimson.

"We have to cut it out," Kalix says.

"I can't." I shake my head and stop when the throb echoes up into my skull once more. "It's part of my contract with—" I swallow the rest of my words as a knock sounds upon the Darkhavens' chamber door.

All heads swivel as a soft, shaking voice filters through the other side. "Um, p-pardon my intrusion?"

Maeryn is out of her seat and across the room in an instant, throwing the door open and pulling Niall inside. She looks him over, hands moving to his face and down his arms. "Niall? Are you okay? Do you feel sick?"

He holds up a piece of parchment and turns shadowed eyes on the rest of us. "I-I got this note," he says by way of explanation instead of answering his Mistress' questions.

Maeryn waves her hand and plucks the note from his hand. "Yes, Kiera left it to let you know to come here when you woke."

He shakes his head. "No, I-I saw that note. I left it behind," he says before swallowing. Niall straightens his spine and reaches for the paper in Maeryn's hand. She lets him. "A bird was tapping on the window and it had this tied to its foot."

Standing, I brush past Ruen and ignore him as he growls for me to sit back down. Maeryn moves to close the door behind Niall, but before she can, Aranea skitters inside and I sigh, bending and holding my hand out for the spider queen. She hops onto my palm and then slides quickly from it to my shoulder as Niall turns widened eyes to the creature he hadn't even known was following him.

I take the note from Niall's fingers and scan it. My mouth falls open in shock.

Return to Riviere Meeting House. Your Master summons you. — C

The script that I normally see on these notes is different. The letters are sharper and angled, as if written in a hurry or in irritation at being assigned the task at all. The last letter, the signature, doesn't carry Regis' curvy R either.

Carcel. I close my eyes. He's arrived, and of course he doesn't care what kind of position it puts me in to respond to his fucking summons. Unfortunately, he can't have come at a more inopportune time.

CHAPTER 45

KALIX

9 years old...

Pitiful. *That is the word I would use to describe the woman before me. She is beautiful enough for a human. Tall and slender with that tapered waist Azai seems to appreciate. She was once even more beautiful than she appears now, her limbs swinging by the rope wrapped around her neck, stunning enough to entice the God of Strength in spite of her mortality.*

The other servants within the manor have whispered of who she had been ten years before, in the year leading up to my conception and then birth. As most other Gods keep servants—both Mortal God and human alike—Azai had chosen only the finest humans to attend to him as if beauty was something needed in order to clean a fireplace or cook a meal.

Azai is Azai though. To him, it is a requirement. For what kind of life must a God live if he must be subject to seeing ugly faces day in and day out? Yet, in spite of all the beauty and wealth surrounding him, this woman—my mother—was, at once, above them all. Enough so that he'd spilled his seed inside her and even allowed her to remain here, acting as a true lady in one of his country mansions that exist well outside of any of the God cities or smaller God Lord territories.

Yet, as the years had waned, so, too, had her youth and beauty and though Olivia Bortello had managed to ensnare Azai's attentions and affections for nearly a decade, that time was coming to a slow, crawling death.

Considering that this *was her reaction—her limp body, soiled upon itself the moment her heart had ceased beating— to Azai's lack of interest in her now, to the nights and weeks he spent frolicking with other Gods, Mortal Gods, and humans alike, I suppose that a long creeping demise was not one she could have borne.*

Pathetic, really, *I think absently as I walk across the study and take a seat in one of the wingback chairs before the cold, empty fireplace. Ruen will be quite upset by Olivia's passing. Despite the fact that she never cared for him since he repre-sents yet another infidelity, he won't like that she's died like this. The woman assumed she was owed loyalty by the God of Strength, a laughable thought, yet Ruen always tells me I'm a lucky to still have her. Lucky to live with her when there are many other Mortal Gods who are without any parents at all.*

Instead of staying within their Divine parent's homes— even hidden extras that this one is—they reside within the chambers of the facilities where those who've yet to show any sort of Divine ability stay. Those children do not always know who their God parent is, only that they have one. They are kept like animals in small, dank cells until their God parents decide to kill them or release them into the wild—the answer is usually to put them out of their misery.

I never felt that sense of gratitude though. Not to Azai and not to Olivia. And if Ruen is honest with himself, he would rather kill Azai than show any sort of thanks to our sire. Olivia, though, had been different for him. Perhaps Olivia reminded Ruen of his own mother—the human that had refused to bring him to Azai when he learned of his existence. Azai had killed her for the treason, of course, and Ruen had seen the whole thing.

He had nightmares and as annoying as it was to hear his screaming and crying in the middle of the night, it is far more frustrating when he refuses to share them with me. At least knowing how it all happened would be a good bedtime story.

I sigh as the door to my father's study opens and Brigita, one of Azai's favorite maids, comes in, startling to a halt when she sees my mother's body hanging from the chandelier, a chair tipped over beneath her feet with various crates and books scattered around. The chandelier is far too high for most to hang themselves from. If anything, I admire her tenacity to get the job done.

"Oh my Gods!" Brigita's scream echoes through the room and I flinch, clapping my palms over my ears with a sneer. Is it all human women that shriek with such a shrillness that it threatens to break my eardrums or just the ones Azai employs? I wouldn't know. Despite Ruen's claim that I'm lucky to live here and not one of the facilities as we prepare to enter one of the Mortal Gods Academies, I've never been allowed to leave this place.

All Mortal Gods need to be documented and kept track of. That is the one rule I have been forced to live by. All else … are mere suggestions in my mind.

Brigita runs from the room, her high-pitched whining echoing into the outside corridor as she calls for help. I look up as Olivia's body turns, the heavy weight of bones and flesh without a soul to inhabit it twisting against the grain of the rope. The knot she tied loosens and after a beat it snaps, breaking free, and sends the body toppling to the floor with a somewhat satisfying crunch and then thump. Had she been alive, that fall would have most assuredly broken both legs.

The sound of rushing footsteps enter the room as more of Azai's servants come careening into the space, pausing when they see Olivia's body hunched over and sprawled on the ground. The eyes of Mandrake—Azai's least favorite butler— lift to meet mine. Casually, I reach over and pick up one of the books stacked nearby. Just to show him that I actually came in here for something else and wasn't interested in sitting here, staring at a dead body until someone came to find it.

I mean—to be fair—it had been my intention to sneak into this study and procure some of the liquor Azai kept here— since these books are all merely for show. The God of Strength doesn't read. Ruen's lucky I found her before he did. He's the one who truly prefers to use this study when Azai is away for his long stretches.

"How long have you been there, Master Kalix?" Mandrake demands as he comes further into the room. A sobbing Brigita can be heard from the hallway as the doorway opens a bit more and two other servants—a gardener and a cook come inside, pausing at Olivia's body before sighing and moving forward.

"A few moments," I answer.

"Why did you not inform anyone of your mother's..." He glances at the body as the gardener, a tall buff man whose name I decline to remember, chokes out a breath as he nears the scent of urine and death. "Situation?" Mandrake finishes.

I shrug, unconcerned. "I am not a servant," I say. "It's not my job to inform you of anyone's situation unless they request me to." I gesture to the body that the gardener and cook arrange before another maid comes in—not the weeping Brigita—holding a sheet. They take the sheet and cover the body with it as the cook starts barking orders for someone to retrieve supplies to make a stretcher and carry her out of the room before Azai gets back. "She did not request it of me," I finish. Not that she could since she'd already been long-dead by the time I arrived.

Mandrake stares at me for a moment longer, silence stretching between us as the noise of the other servants clangs at my aching ears. Distantly, a familiar voice filters in from the open door. Ruen's voice.

"What's going on?" I hear him ask.

Mandrake whirls around as I hear Brigita beg Ruen not to go inside, but Ruen doesn't listen. He pushes the door wide and stops as the gardener quickly covers Olivia's face with the sheet and steps back. Now, it's truly silent. Even the annoyance of Brigita's quaking sobs have ceased. It's as if everyone is holding their breath as my brother—my older brother, Azai had told me, though it's only by a few months—takes in the scene before him.

Tilting my head to the side, I watch and wait for his reaction. Will it be yet more screaming and crying such as when he has those nightmares he refuses to tell me or anyone else about? The scar that runs down the side of his brow crinkles as his face blanches. The horror quickly descends into sorrow and then placid apathy.

"I see..." Ruen looks away from the sheet covering my mother's body to where I'm sitting by the empty fireplace with an unopened book in my hand. His eyes fall upon the book before rising to my face once more. He sighs, as if he's unsurprised by my lack of melancholy. "You should get this cleaned up before Azai returns," Ruen says to Mandrake. "He'll be upset if his study is ruined."

I bite down on my own lip to keep from chuckling. We both know Azai won't care unless he's brought back guests.

Sometimes he does, just to play house for a short while. Some of his Divine bed partners refuse to have children of their own since they'll simply be taken away eventually, so he allows them to dress both Ruen and I up and play pretend.

It is from Azai that I've learned my role. Objects can be broken and replaced, but people are like dolls. You dress them up, you own them and care for them, but in the end—the only real value they hold is what they can do for you. Olivia has been unable to do a thing for me since giving birth to me. Therefore, her death ... albeit frustrating in this uproar of the household was not unexpected nor is it truly life altering. Her death doesn't affect my life. Though I'm sure she'd meant it as a punishment to Azai, both Ruen and I know that when he learns of it, he'll care even less than we do.

Eying my brother as Mandrake seems to sag in both disappointment and a small amount of apprehension, he nods to Ruen and begins setting about the task of helping the other servants clean up the mess Olivia made in her suicide.

By the end of the half hour mark, the body has been removed to somewhere else in the house and Ruen sits across from me, staring at me somewhat blankly.

"Do you feel nothing?" he asks once the last servant has left and closed the door behind them, not a single one suggesting that the two of us should leave this place. It's just a room, after all. Who cares if it's seen death now?

"I feel a little hungry," I admit, placing the unused book back on its stack.

Ruen's eyes narrow and his brow furrows, that white scar splitting his brow in two practically glowing against his skin. Azai gave him that scar. He doesn't say as much, but I know it. What else but a Divine creature can harm another of Divine descent?

Ruen inches forward on his seat and stares at me. "Even if

you don't feel the emotions, Kalix, sometimes, you should at least pretend that you do."

I know which emotion he speaks of. My gaze leaves his and returns to the spot on the floor that's now been cleaned and the books and crates and chair removed. "You want me to act sad?" I ask, turning back to him. "Why?"

"It unnerves others that you don't seem to feel," Ruen states. "It makes them scared of you."

I shrug. "Their fear is not my problem."

Ruen makes a sound of frustration. "If too many people fear you then the Gods will take more notice of you," he bites out. "Do you want Azai to start noticing you more?"

I stiffen. Azai's interest has always been a vague sort of thing in the back of my mind. For my earlier years, before I realized the futility of my mother's schemes and desires—and how they had very little to do with me—I'd attempted to gain his favor on her behalf. The God of Strength had merely looked at me with either amusement or irritation. The caustic disinterest had left me feeling ... unwell. I didn't care for it, just as I didn't care for him.

No, I did not want Azai's interest.

"I think you and I can work together, Kalix." Ruen's words are quiet, but resonating with a deep seething sort of sound that I recognize. It is the same feeling that crept into my chest when I wanted to play with a servant but they were too busy for me or they didn't want to do the things that I wanted. It is the same sort of sound I hear in my own voice when I use my persuasion on the animals that roam the grounds. Azai had caught me once and though he'd not seemed angry, the garden cat I'd been using it on to force it to acquiesce to my demands to pet it had disappeared for several days, showing up later beneath the wheel of one of Azai's carriages.

I'd buried that cat in its favorite place in the gardens,

angrier than I'd ever been. I didn't hurt the animals. No. They were my toys. I had to take care of them. I had been careless to let Azai see my interest in the wayward creature. Cats were special. They scratched and clawed at those they found unworthy and I enjoyed bending them to my will, forcing them to see me as worthy of their affections. Azai had killed the creature to teach me a lesson and that, I did not forgive.

It had been mine. Mine. And I had failed to protect it.

Now, I don't play with the animals anymore. At least, not the ones that Azai could see. Now, only the slithering creatures that every other servant fears keep me company when I need it. Those beasts, I will not fail. Those beasts belong solely to me.

"Did you hear me, Kalix?" Ruen's question pulls me out of my thoughts and I shake my head, turning my attention back to him.

"What?"

Ruen huffs out a breath, annoyance making a muscle in his jaw pulse. "I said that I think we can work together. Azai doesn't care about us, you know that. He could have us killed in an instant if he wanted. He—and all the other Gods merely want to use us. You don't strike me as the type willing to be used."

I think about that. He's right. I dislike the idea of Azai using me for his benefit. He doesn't deserve it. "What are you suggesting then?"

Ruen leans forward, dark blue eyes glittering with intention. This is the most I think he's ever interested me. Perhaps Ruen is like that long dead cat I'd lost. Perhaps he could be another companion—a far more durable one.

"I've heard that the Academies are brutal. We're going to be shipped off there soon," he says. "We need to make sure that when we arrive, we make it clear to all the other Mortal Gods —no matter who our sire is that we have far more potential."

I tilt my head. "How do you propose we do that?"

Rifling in his pocket, Ruen withdraws a parchment. "I've been writing to a fellow Mortal God," he admits. "He's a boy our age and he doesn't live far. He didn't grow up in the facilities either, but his God parent is friends with Azai and requested that we be ... writing companions. Azai knew you would refuse. He's a good kid, lonely though. His name is Darius."

"You want to make an alliance with this Darius?" I guess.

Ruen shakes his head. "I want to find friends we can rely on," he states. "We need allies and we need friends. I think you and I can survive this world—and whatever Azai plans for us—if we stick together and start making some connections."

I am not a thinker or a planner—not in the way Ruen is. As he speaks, however, I can see the potential in his proposition. My gaze returns, once more, to the spot on the floor where Olivia's body had laid and then up to the crystal chandelier where the frayed rope that hung her frame has been removed. Olivia could not help me in this world beyond my creation, but Ruen, on the other hand...

Perhaps it's not such a bad idea to form friendships. Ruen can be my new cat. A companion with more strength and persistence. Ruen, unlike my feline friend, won't break under Azai's pressure. No, in fact, I would hazard to say that one day, Azai might break under his.

I would like to be there to see it, I decide.

∼

Present Day...

THE OLD MEMORY fades as I stare at the woman across the room. Kiera is not a cat, defiant and seeking out

433

worthy companions. She is not one of my serpents, loyal and easy to manipulate. She is a monster all her own, but she represses it, tamps down the anger roiling within her and the chaos that threatens to spill forth until her mortal bones vibrate with the need to unleash it all.

There is a monster that lies sleeping inside all of us—my brothers and me. For Theos and Ruen, it was born from the increasing resentment and hatred towards our sire. Azai. For me, however, I was born with the creature. It's a quiet, hulking beast that's usually content to slumber within my chest and mind. There are times when I go days, even months, without the monster waking.

Now, as Kiera lifts her pale face from the short scroll parchment barely the length of a finger in her fist, the monster cracks a single eye open. As if the beast can sense the words about to come from her lips—words that I know neither of us will like.

There are smudges of purple shadows beneath her normally vibrant gray eyes. The color that usually roils with storm and madness that calls to me is muted. The monster within shifts, unsettled.

"Kiera?" Theos steps forward and when he reaches for her—the sudden revelation he was introduced to just a few short hours ago seeming to have no effect on the strong pull he feels towards her—she backs up a step.

No, the beast and I will not like what she is going to say.

"I have to go."

Silence greets her announcement. The monster cracks its other eye open. Scales slither beneath my skin. My gums tingle. My gaze sharpens.

"*No.*" Her gaze falls upon my face as I deny what I know is not a request from her.

She stiffens and her lips curl downward. The displeasure and annoyance on her face flashes over her expression briefly. They're quickly pushed back though as she takes what I'm sure she thinks is a calming breath. I know the truth though. I know that beneath the surface of the facade she's been wearing, under her mask of civility, Kiera Nezerac is just like me.

There is a darkness inside her that calls to me. A deranged creature that craves chaos just as much as she craves a mate to relish in that chaos with her. She is angry, though she pretends not to be as wild and unhinged as I know her to be. Like calls to like and her rage calls to my own.

"I wasn't asking you," Kiera snaps, crumpling the remains of the scroll in her fist as she lowers her hand back to her side.

"You are not leaving the Academy," Ruen states before I can reply.

Kiera's chin juts out, defiance curling her scowl even more as her brow furrows and her gray gaze sparks with indignation. "You don't get a choice in this. I have to go. I've been summoned by my guild."

My eyes shoot to her fist. Was that what the note had contained? A summons? I look back at her face. She is not one that can be summoned, and yet ... the brimstone in her flesh tells a different story.

Ten years, she had said. That's how long it's been sitting inside her, slowly poisoning her blood, leaking away her Divinity. She has no idea. If she did, then she would not act so calm to reveal that little piece of information to us.

"You just left this morning," Ruen snarls. "Surely, it cannot be that important—"

"The man Regis and I have been waiting for is here," she interrupts him. "I *have* to go." The unspoken warning lingers in the air. She has to go or ... else whatever mortal spell—certainly a stronger blood contract than the one she holds with the three of us—will punish her.

I reject the idea of letting her go alone with my entire being. Already, I wish to bend her over the couch, brush away her hair, and rip that blasted shard from her skin. Any screams or cries of pain would fade the moment I pull it free. In fact, nothing will matter if I just remove it now. I step closer, debating on doing just that, calculating how fast I could reach her and overpower her. Blood spells are strong, though, when held with Divine blood. Even if her Master is not of Divine origin, *she* is. If it's ripped free without knowing the details of whatever deal she's made that allows that stone to stay inside her, the consequences could be dire.

Seething, I blow out a long breath. "You cannot go alone," I snap.

Ruen looks at me as if I've lost my mind. I have, but it was so long ago that I don't miss it anymore.

"You would stand out too much," Ruen replies as if he can sense my increasing need to bind this female to me, despite her lies and treachery—perhaps *because* of them.

"I will send one of my familiars," I say, just as Theos speaks.

"I will go with her."

All eyes fall on Theos, including my own. I scan him, with a cloak—dirtied, perhaps some different clothes. I glance at the skinny boy standing half behind Maeryn. Maybe if they changed their attire it could work.

Before I can say anything, however, Theos moves to Kiera and turns to face Ruen and me. "I'm not taking no for an answer," he snaps. "The two of you knew what was going on before me, you fucking owe me this."

I don't like it. Not going myself. It makes my skin prickle with irritation. Ruen and I exchange a glance. Usually, it is Theos and I against Ruen's stoicism and nettlesome fastidiousness. It is strange to find us on the same side for once. Not since the day of my mother's death have I felt this kinship with Ruen, or maybe the memory was simply percolating at the back of my mind all these years, just waiting for a moment to rear back up and remind me of the deal I'd made with my elder brother.

"Nightfall," Ruen finally says, turning away from me. "You leave after dark and you come back before dawn. Is that understood?"

Relief flashes across her face before she tempers it and reaches up, adjusting the lapels of her coat, stuffing the note inside—no doubt she'll burn the evidence later. I'd seen the remains of old notes, charred to ash in the metal tray of her candle stick holder on her nightstand.

"We should get back to our residences, too," Maeryn announces. "With classes canceled, I don't suppose I'll see any of you for a while."

My eyes flick to her and darken. "Kalix, walk them out." Ruen's command is ripe with an undertone of warning. My smile comes easily.

With pleasure, I think, knowing that ensuring these two don't reveal our little liar's secret is another reason he's saddled me with this task.

The Terra boy's wide brown eyes flick up to meet mine before a squeak sounding like that of a frightened mouse erupts from his throat and he jerks his head down once more. Maeryn scowls at me and steps closer to him as if I intended to scare the pathetic excuse for a male. Rolling my eyes, I turn away from my brothers and Kiera and head towards the door.

Leaning around Maeryn and her Terra, I open it and usher them both outside. A quick word of warning to both of them fueled with my own brand of force will likely leave the human urinating in his trousers. Maeryn, however, will likely threaten to disembowel me.

Why my little liar wishes to keep weaklings like these close to her, I will never understand.

CHAPTER 46

KIERA

A strange sort of sinister dread sits in the pit of my stomach as Theos and I make our way out of the Academy an hour after sunset. Though he had wished to wait a bit longer, my instincts are screaming at me to listen to my gut and my gut says that I have to get back to Madam Brione's. As soon as I was able, I sent a message to Regis—not Carcel—informing him of some of the changes that have taken place since the early morning. Carcel will likely run immediately to Ophelia and I'd rather try to figure out the best way to break this news to her with Regis before she finds out about the wretched disappointment I've become since she last saw me.

We use the same illusioned exit and entrance that Ruen had brought me back through earlier in the day. Theos whispers the strange spell of the ancient language, too fast and low for even me to hear—just as Ruen had—and the vines twist away from the carved opening for us to pass through. Once we're on the other side, we keep to the wall and sneak around the exterior of the Academy, avoiding the sentries' eyes.

Unlike how it had been traveling with Ruen and his easy illusion that would mask our presence, Theos keeps me closer to his side, practically covering me with his cloak as well as my own as if I'm not the one trained to move in the shadows. The moment we're out of eyeshot of the sentries, I push away from him and stride towards the open path that crests the next hill down into the city of Riviere.

Theos doesn't speak for a long time, simply following along as I hail the two of us one of the many public carriages the moment we get far enough into the city streets that they become more commonplace. Clambering inside, his face twists at the stench of body odor, but he doesn't comment and takes a seat next to me, across from a slumbering and snoring man with his fat arms crossed over a protruding stomach.

I cast my gaze to the window, spying the clouds hovering overhead, parting just enough for the moon to shine through where it's hanging in the far away distance. For several moments I debate ridding myself of my tail—Theos. As if he senses my intentions, his hand comes down and his fingers graze mine. He weaves them together and I bite down on my lip, wishing I had the nerve to jerk away from him, but he agreed to a blood contract to keep my secrets. I have no reason to hate him now.

Yet, still, an unnerving queasy sensation has taken root in my intestines, twisting and coiling them tight until they're so constricted, I swear they'll rip apart within me. I close my eyes and count the stops the carriage driver makes. At the fifth one from the time we enter, the big man across from us snorts himself awake and hollers about missing his stop, leaping from the cab with surprising, if not bumbling speed.

The sixth stop has a set of young women getting into the carriage, their small giggles and incessant fluttering lashes as they stare at Theos, despite the fact that he's changed into drab peasant clothing meant for human skin rather than a Mortal God's. The seventh, thankfully, is their stop and they get off without any further attempt to talk to either Theos or me.

"Are you going to remain silent the whole way there?" Theos finally asks.

I blow out a breath. "Do you want me to talk?"

"I think it'd be preferable to this uncomfortable awkwardness."

"What's uncomfortable or awkward about riding in a cab?" I ask. "I'm perfectly fine. I'm sorry if it offends your delicate sensibilities."

The heat of his gaze lands on the side of my face, prickling at my awareness. "Don't do that," he says.

Finally, I look at him. "Do what?"

Golden eyes lock on mine. "You know what," he says. "You're getting defensive because you're scared. We agreed to the blood contract, Kiera. We won't betray you. I'm only coming along to make sure that you're safe and that you don't try to run off."

"Why can't I?" I demand. It's become increasingly clear to me that there is no client. Everything Ophelia has done to put me in the path of the Darkhavens has been a test—one that I have miserably failed.

"Run off?" he clarifies, brow puckering in confusion.

"Yes," I snap. "You know as well as I do that it would be better for me if I were to just leave. Then there would be no chance of discovery."

Theos' brow eases and he gives me a pitiable look that makes me want to punch him in the face. I rip my hand away from his and curl my fingers into the fabric of my cloak to stop from doing just that.

"Kiera, it's too late for that; you know that as well as we do. The Gods have already noticed you. Your presence would be missed and they would track you down. Take it from someone who knows—Ruen is well aware of what will happen if you disappear. It's why he refused to let you come by yourself."

"Ruen knows, huh?" I laugh bitterly. Something cracks in my chest. Fear and something else—an emotion I can't name. I stare out the window unseeingly. "What does he fucking know but how to be a pampered son of a God?"

Theos' body goes rigid at my side. "There is a lot that you don't know about us," he murmurs. His voice is so quiet that it almost gets swallowed up by the repetitive creaking sound of the wheels of our carriage turning against the cobblestone streets. "We might all have the same father, but we've all had different upbringings. I never knew my human mother, but Ruen and Kalix … they did. Kalix lived with his until she died, and Ruen..." The hesitation in his voice causes me to finally glance back at him.

"Ruen's mother what?" I ask, cursing my own curiosity.

Theos shakes his head and frowns. "I'm sorry, I shouldn't have started that—it's not my story to tell, but you should ask him about it sometime. He might tell you. You have more in common than you think, especially now that we know you're an undocumented Mortal God."

I cross my arms over my chest and the carriage rattles

as it turns a corner, careening a bit too close, and my side slides into Theos'. He catches me and I pull away again. My attention falls away from his face, back to the window and the passing buildings and streets, lit by gas lamps.

"When we get to where we're going, I want you to stay outside," I say, changing the subject entirely. "I told my brother that one of you knew this morning and he wasn't happy about it. When I tell him about everything..." I bite down on my lower lip, worrying it between my teeth before releasing it when I taste blood. "I need to talk to him *alone*."

"Ruen said there was a device that made it difficult for him to hear you today," Theos says. "As long as you make sure that isn't a problem, I will let you go in, but make no mistake, Kiera, I will enter if I think you're trying to run away. You come back to the Academy with me after all of this—that is non-negotiable."

Everything is negotiable, I think snidely, but I don't dissuade him. It's not worth the argument. "Fine."

"Fine," he shoots back.

The two of us fall back into silence and it isn't until the carriage reaches its final stop, as close to the slums as it dares get that I haul myself out of my seat and open the door before either the driver or Theos can get to it. I jump out onto the street, my booted feet cracking against the sidewalk and cobblestones. Theos is quick to follow, the burn of his attention searing into the back of my head as if he half expects me to bolt any moment.

I won't. No doubt he and his brothers predict that I'll try to run soon. If I choose to do so, it'll be when they all least expect it.

"This way," I say, gesturing over my shoulder as I curl two fingers and urge him to follow me.

We take the long path since there's no real time limit on this trip now. Dawn is far off. Theos trails me silently, an ever-present shadow as we curve through streets and alleys. We move down long darkened roads with only one dim gas lamp to illuminate the faces of buildings and anyone who might be hiding in the shadows. The shadows grow closer, giving me hints as to which ones to avoid and which ones are safe. Some of the slum streets have no lamps at all or if they do, they're cracked and broken, untended for what seems like a long time.

"Fuck!" Theos curses and jerks back, jumping nearly three feet away from me as a woman tosses something wet from a window, nearly dumping it right on top of us. He covers his mouth with his hand, eyes widening. "Is that fucking piss?"

I shrug. "Not all of these buildings have indoor plumbing, *Master*," I reply curtly before walking away.

He curses again, quieter this time, but the sound makes my lips curve the smallest amount in amusement. Theos doesn't say another word until I raise my palm and press it back against his chest as we turn down the street of Madam Brione's shop and boarding rooms. He stops.

"What is it?" he asks, gaze flashing around our surroundings as if seeking out a threat. I roll my eyes again. If anything, *we* are the most threatening creatures on this street. Even drunk or angry, no human could truly take us—despite what Regis had said before. I'm convinced that the man he killed can't have been a Mortal God. Either that or Ophelia had given him a brimstone blade. Though, why, I wouldn't know or understand. They're expensive enough as it is and rare to attain. I shake my head, that's just one more thing that I'll have to discuss with Regis when I get inside.

"We're here," I tell Theos before I point to an alley across the street. "You can wait there. I'm going inside there."

Theos looks to the alley to the front of the shop that I gesture to and then back to me. His expression hardens. "Don't use that device, Kiera," he reminds me. "If I feel even the smallest bit of suspicion, I'm coming in."

My shoulders tense and I throw them back, turning to face him fully. "You will not," I grind out. "You will stay in that fucking alley until I come get you. This is not a game, Theos. You might be a spoiled Mortal God used to training for entertainment purposes but this isn't play-time. I won't use that damn device, but you don't get to dictate to me either."

Golden eyes flicker black and then back to gold. Theos doesn't reply for several long moments. Then, as if testing or tempting me with his actions, he takes a step away and then another and another, until he's almost swallowed up completely by the shadows of the alley I'd told him to stay in. Just before he disappears from my vision altogether, I hear his last words.

"Don't deceive us, Kiera. You won't like us when we've decided to keep something as ours and it tries to run away."

Thorns of anxiousness prick at my insides. *Us*, he had said. Not just him. I bite down on my lip again and once more, I taste blood. This time, I don't stop. I lick the blood from my mouth and turn and stride into Madam Brione's shop.

CHAPTER 47

KIERA

There are sconces on the walls of the hallway—old and dusty—lit up in a way I haven't seen before when I enter the shop. A familiar figure stands behind the dusty counter littered with trinkets and cobwebs. Madam Brione leans into the wooden platform leafing through the pages of an old book. She glances up when the door closes behind me, eyes blinking behind thick-rimmed glasses. She pulls them off and sets them to the side before smoothing a shaking hand over her usual flyaway gray curls. She nods back towards the kitchen. "Waiting for you," she says. "Back there. Door on the right."

Door on the right? I thought those were her own personal rooms. I don't comment though, and instead thank her and head down the short hallway to the kitchen I'd been in that very morning. The window facing the back is closed now and latched. I turn to the right and pause in front of the door I'd assumed Madam Brione stayed in.

I knock twice and the door jerks open a moment later,

Regis' pale and worried face standing there. He steps to the side and I enter. His anxiety doesn't help my own and I twist my fingers into my cloak before catching myself and releasing the folds.

"Where is he?" I ask. "Carcel."

Regis flinches and steps away after closing the door behind me. My eyes scan the room within. It's not a bedroom, I realize but a sitting room. The walls are covered in a rich red wallpaper, a thick rug rests in the middle of the room with chests lining one side and chairs and lounges encircling the center, various tables placed haphazardly here and there for drinks to be set upon as almost an afterthought rather than true additions to the room. There's no sign of Carcel in here though.

I spy a door on the opposite side of the room from the one I'd come in through. Light dances beneath the space where the door ends and the floor begins. No voices come from beyond it though.

Regis is unusually quiet. I face him again. "Regis?"

He doesn't look at me when he responds. "Ophelia wants to see you." His tone is solemn and I feel something evil wrap its claws around my ribcage, squeezing so tightly I'm scared it'll fracture.

"Ophelia?" She's here? "What about Carcel?"

Regis still doesn't look at me. "Ophelia decided to meet up with him and travel to Riviere," he says. "That's why it's taken him so long to get here. He was waiting on her."

"And she wants to see me?" I repeat.

He nods.

Somehow, I manage to keep my voice even when I reply. "Regis ... what's going on?"

Silence meets my question. Long, deep aching silence.

Finally, he looks at me, and when he does, his lips twist into that fatefully telling uncomfortable frown. "You know what it's about, Kiera."

The claws contract. I told him about the Darkhavens in that last message I'd sent. I'd told him that they knew... *everything*. Regis' face is haggard, even more so than he'd seemed this morning. As if the few hours we'd been apart had shaken him deeper than even the ridiculous conclusion he'd come to in assuming he'd killed a Mortal God on his own. My ribcage shatters into a million pieces. The sharp edges stab into my heart, slicing it open in a way I haven't felt since the night my father died and my whole world came crashing down.

"*You told her.*" It's not a question, but a statement. Regis is the only one outside of the Darkhavens that knows, the only one that I've ever trusted enough to tell my secrets and my failures to. I can't breathe.

"I had to, Kay."

"Don't fucking call me that." *Traitor.* I want to scream the word at him, but I can't even bear to taste it in my mouth even if that's exactly what he is. "You know I don't trust many people in this world, Regis." The words escape my quickly numbing lips. Perhaps my lacerated heart will simply stop beating before I have to face my true Master —the one who holds the reins of my fate. That would be a blessing. "I *trusted* you."

He turns to face me, his pale cheeks reddening as an unfamiliar glistening enters his eyes. "Kiera," he starts, "she had to know—you're in too far. You've gotten too close to them and you're not listening to me anymore. I told you that they don't give a shit about you. They don't care—"

"They signed a blood contract to keep my secret!" The

scream echoes out of me, startling both of us. I've never yelled at Regis. Not in the ten years we've known each other. His blue eyes widen. I feel sick to my stomach.

Releasing a harsh breath, when he reaches out for me, I step away from him. Regis freezes. *Don't.* I want to scream at him. *Don't look at me like that as if* you're *the one that's hurt.*

Lifting my palms to my face, I scrub them down against my cheeks hard, pulling the skin until my hands reach my jawline and then drop away completely. I let them hang down on either side of me as I stare at the ground, trying to find even one minuscule ounce of forgiveness in me. All I come up with is the mutilated feeling of betrayal that echoes within the chambers of my once whole heart.

It hadn't hurt nearly this much when Ruen was the one betraying me, when he'd turned me into the Gods for disrespect with some ill-conceived notion that he could get rid of me if he threatened me enough. But that was because we'd had no relationship, no truths and no understanding of who the other was. Regis, however, is the only friend—*my oldest and first friend*—who has known everything about me from the start.

The pain of his words sits like sharp, jagged rocks at the base of my stomach. Each breath causes them to swell up and stab at my insides, reopening wounds before they can close over with my incredibly fast healing. It's a fresh kind of agony, one that hurts more with the passage of time rather than getting better.

Regis tries again. "This mission has gotten too dangerous," he says, the struggle of his expressions and how he can't seem to maintain a cool facade showcasing just how hard it is for him to contain his guilt.

"Mission?" I repeat the word with a shake of my head. "You still don't get it?"

His brow creases. "Get what?"

I bare my teeth at him. "There is no fucking mission, Regis," I snap. "It's been months and the client never even gave us a target!" My breaths come heavier and faster. "Haven't you ever wondered what was taking so long? It's because there is no target. This was all a test from the beginning." It's the only thing that makes sense. "Ophelia..."

"You think Ophelia tricked us?" Regis stares at me in shock.

"Not *us*," I clarify. Never us again. "And she didn't trick—she tested. That's what she *does*. Ophelia doesn't trust anyone, not even her most prized possessions and her proteges." Maybe I should've picked that trait up from her.

"If you don't think there's a target, then what's the point of staying in the Academy anymore?"

Regis' question isn't unfounded, but at the end of the day, I don't get to choose. "Who's to say?" I shrug. "At the end of the day, I'm just a servant to Ophelia's whims."

"You don't really believe that," Regis' reply is instantaneous and it bubbles up a laugh out of me.

"Don't I?" I counter. "I'm under a blood contract, Regis, or have you forgotten that fact?"

"She's never treated you like a real servant," Regis snaps. "She's raised you like her own daughter."

"*No*." My denial is bitter and full of venom. Maybe, once, there'd been a time when I, too, believed that. When I *wanted* to believe it with every fiber of my being. The sad thing about reality and fantasy, though, is that some things can't become true with just a wish. "I am *not* her daughter. I can never be her daughter." I say the words as much for myself as I do for him.

No mother would ever turn her daughter into the monster that Ophelia has expected me to become from the beginning of our relationship.

I meet Regis' gaze, letting it all drop away. The pain. The hurt. Even the anger. None of it will help me now. It's meaningless. Just like our relationship. It always has been. He warned me in the beginning and I simply didn't listen.

"What did you say when we were kids?" I bite down on my tongue hard enough to taste blood. "Back when we were still in training and you hated me and the fact that I carry the blood of the Gods in my veins?" He flinches, knowing exactly what encounter I'm referring to.

He'd been standing over me with a sword in his hand dripping with my blood. It'd taken months in the training trials for him to see me as more than another pompous child of the Gods. Nearly two years to drop the sly insults and saving each other's asses on more than one occasion for me to feel like we'd bridged the gap between hate and friendship.

Now, I stand here, watching that bridge burn, smoke rising from the vestiges as it fills my lungs and chokes me. And there he stands, holding the match that lit it all.

I repeat his warning word for word. "'*You'll never truly be able to hide who you really are.*'" I laugh and shrug as they come free. "You were right. I wasn't able to hide it anymore. I'm not mortal. I'm not a God. I'm one of *them*." Those wicked, evil things that he hates.

"Kiera—"

I don't let Regis finish whatever he'd been about to say. I see no reason to. Instead, I turn away from him, and feeling the burn of emotion in the back of my eyes, I sink myself deep into the pit of the darkness that Ophelia had ingrained within me. I take five steps towards the door waiting for me, not stopping even when he calls my name again.

It's time to face the results of my choices.

Choosing lies. Choosing them. Choosing myself.

The knob is cold against my skin as I grip it and twist. I step into the room, smaller than I anticipated. It's only the size of an office with no windows and wallpaper that matches that of the sitting room.

It's not the wallpaper that draws me to an immediate halt though as I spy the three individuals inside. It's not Carcel, sneering at me as he always does, with a fresh smattering of cuts across his knuckles, or even Ophelia, of course, with her cool, detached gaze that stuns me the most.

The world tilts as the man between them rises to his full height, straightening away from the table the three of them stand in front of. Gone are the robes of deep jewel colors. Gone is the facade of kindness. I hadn't seen him at the arena, I remember dimly as dark earthen eyes meet mine. I'd wondered where he'd been. I don't have to wonder anymore.

The books. The words of secrecy. None of it had made sense. I'd just assumed he knew because he was ... he is...

"*Caedmon,*" I say his name. The God of Prophecy.

THANK YOU FOR READING!

If you enjoyed A Reign of Storm and Madness then don't forget to leave a review here and pre order the next book in the Mortal Gods series

About the Author

Lucinda Dark, also known as USA Today Bestselling Author, Lucy Smoke, for her contemporary novels, has a master's degree in English and is a self-proclaimed creative chihuahua. She enjoys feeding her wanderlust, cover addiction, as well as her face. When she's not on a never-ending quest to find the perfect milkshake, she lives and works in the southern United States with her beloved fur-baby, Hiro, and her family and friends.

Want to be kept up to date? Think about joining the author's group or signing up for their newsletter below.

Facebook Group (Reader Mafia)
Newsletter (www.lucysmoke.com)

.

Also by Lucinda Dark

Fantasy Series:

Mortal Gods Series

A Sword of Shadow & Deceit

A Reign of Storm & Madness

The Blood of Gods & Monsters

TBD

Awakened Fates Series (completed)

Crown of Blood and Glass

Dawn of Fate and Valor

Wings of Sunfire and Darkness

Twisted Fae Series (completed)

Court of Crimson

Court of Frost

Court of Midnight

Barbie: The Vampire Hunter Series (completed)

Rest in Pieces

Dead Girl Walking

Ashes to Ashes

Sky Cities Series (Dystopian)

Heart of Tartarus

Shadow of Deception

Sword of Damage

Dogs of War (Coming Soon)

Contemporary Series:

Gods of Hazelwood: Icarus Duet (completed)

Burn With Me

Fall With Me

Sick Boys Series (completed)

Forbidden Deviant Games (prequel)

Pretty Little Savage

Stone Cold Queen

Natural Born Killers

Wicked Dark Heathens

Bloody Cruel Psycho

Bloody Cruel Monster

Vengeful Rotten Casualties

Sinister Arrangment Duet (completed)

Wicked Angel

Cruel Master

Iris Boys Series (completed)

Now or Never

Power & Choice

Leap of Faith

Cross my Heart

Forever & Always

Iris Boys Series Boxset

The *Break* Series (completed)

Break Volume 1

Break Volume 2

Break Series Collection

Contemporary Standalones:

Poisoned Paradise

Expressionate

Wild Hearts

www.ingramcontent.com/pod-product-compliance
Ingram Content Group UK Ltd.
Pitfield, Milton Keynes, MK11 3LW, UK
UKHW030824310325
5233UKWH00027B/93